ThanQ God
for the downloads, the pathways,
and the purpose.

ThanQ
for showing me how imperative it is
to dig.

To Jason
for the vows, and for making good
on every single one, every single
day.

To Nathan
for inspiring me with your moral
compass and your profound
wisdom.

To my folks
for making every dream of mine a
possibility.

To my students of yesteryear:
May you find yourselves in this book
and in more ways than one.

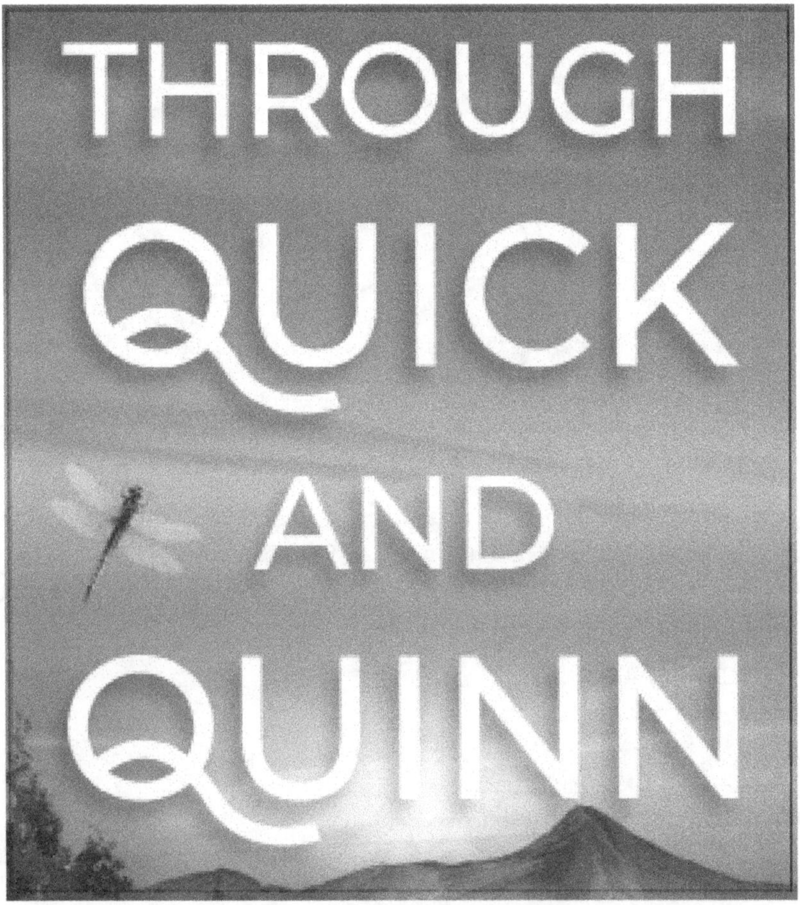

THROUGH QUICK AND QUINN

ERICA MIMRAN SHERLOCK

DEFIANCE PRESS
& PUBLISHING

Through Quick and Quinn

First Edition: 2025

Printed in the United States of America

10 9 8 7 6 5 4 3 2 1

ISBN-13: 978-1-963102-70-3 (Paperback)
ISBN-13: 978-1-963102-69-7 (ebook)
ISBN-13:978-1-963102-71-0 (Hardcover)

Published by Defiance Press & Publishing, LLC

Bulk orders of this book may be obtained by contacting Defiance Press & Publishing, LLC.
www.defiancepress.com.

Public Relations Dept. – Defiance Press & Publishing, LLC
281-581-9300
pr@defiancepress.com

Defiance Press & Publishing, LLC
281-581-9300
info@defiancepress.com

CONTENTS

I can't breathe. Air is getting caught between my sobs and my screams.

"Geoffrey! Geoffrey!" I fall to the ground, dizzy and gasping. I choke on my tears and start coughing, which finally alerts the people around me to pay attention. Had I not been screaming long enough or loud enough? Did they think it was a game?

A lady bends down next to me and asks if I need help, if I'm okay. The look of concern on her face reminds me that I have a mother of my own, and I yell for her as I sprint to where she was in line just a few minutes before. I see my dad's head above the others and I push my way to him, collapsing into his arms.

"Deck! Deck, are you ok?" Dad is fanning my face and searching for answers there, but my mom already knows.

Hysteria takes hold of my mother. "Declan, where is Geoffrey? Declan!"

I can hear the fright in her voice right before I pass out.

PART ONE:

From the Start

~~Declan:~~

A Decision of Indecision

What would a child get if he was blessed with a mother who saw meaning in every single thing and a father who just chuckled and went along with it all? A name like Declan Alexander Broderick Williams.

My mom used to say that every piece of my name had meaning, that she couldn't deny me any of them.

Declan
Origin: Irish
Meaning: full of goodness

Alexander
Origin: Greek
Meaning: defender of men

Broderick
Origin: English, Welsh, Irish
Meaning: brother

My dad chalked it up to her indecisive tendencies, that she couldn't choose a name. But she did decide. She chose all three names that came before the given one. She knew that I would be a model big brother, always protecting my future siblings with goodness. Manifestation, she called it. Not that it really mattered. No one called me by any of those names when I was growing up. Everyone called me Deck, even him. Especially him.

Until no one dared to.

~~Declan~~ Maverick:
The First Dig

It was a Saturday in June. Summer break. I wrapped up elementary school and was dreading the start of junior high in the fall. That dread, combined with the incessant, dull nightmare that I couldn't wake up from since spring break that year, just meant that I was sleeping nonstop. Or at least trying to. Or pretending to.

My folks walked into my bedroom that afternoon, probably around two o'clock. They flicked on the lights and called for a family meeting. My dad was the one to begin the chat, which came as no surprise since my mom had basically become a selective mute.

"Hey buddy, we want to have a chat. Sit up, son."

I blinked away my pseudo sleep and forced my body to oblige. My dad started talking about how much they love me, how that could never change, how they only want what's best for me, how they were worried. Easily three minutes of the usual stuff. Enough time for me to cognitively awaken.

"Declan, we—"

And that was it. I heard my dad say my name for the first time in ages, and my entire world shattered in slow motion. Again. I could hear him talking to me. I could process what he was saying. Too hard to stay here. I'll do better in a new environment with new faces. Clean slate, start from scratch, next town over, new friends, blah blah blah.

All I could really focus on, though, was the sound of my name. Declan. I hadn't heard it for as long as I could remember, so when he said it that day, it struck me differently.

Declan. But I didn't hear "Deck-lan" as I should have. I don't know if it was my fuzzy sleep brain or what, but I could have sworn he said, "De-clan." As in, undoing a clan. As in, undoing our clan. Our family.

I started sobbing hysterically, screaming about how my mom got the meaning wrong. That my name wasn't about being full of goodness. How could I be full of goodness if I'm the reason for the de-clan? I felt like I broke in half, doubled over in my dad's lap, begging to erase it all. Somehow through the uncontrollable crying and nonsensical blubbering, my parents got it. They understood. Or at least my dad did. He told me I could choose a new first name if I wanted. I had no idea what my mom was thinking and hadn't since the incident. I could have guessed though.

A new town. A new school. A new name. New, new, new. Maybe it would help.

And so was born my first dig.

I searched on the internet for hours that day. It felt cathartic almost, casting aside any names that reminded me of, well, anything. Characters from shows I used to watch with him? Those were out. Names of friends he had at school? Out. That was round one. I moved on to round two, filling pages upon pages in my notebook with potential names and their meanings. A total waste of time. Because when I saw it, I just knew.

Maverick
Origin: American (that made sense, considering I was born and raised)
Meaning: an independent man who avoids conformity; a free spirit

Maverick. I loved it. And no, not because of *Top Gun*. I didn't even see that movie until my sophomore year in high school, and I would not have named myself after a role being played by that actor. Just saying.

Ok, so, Maverick Alexander Broderick Williams.

Ugh. Seriously? That's ridiculous.

Alexander. Nope. Not a defender in the least. Not after what happened that spring break. Out.

Broderick. Brother. I thought I should keep the name, but Maverick Broderick? Nope.

Maybe Brody, I thought. Turned out Brody meant "ditch" or "muddy place." Ummmm, no thank you. That was literally the last thing I wanted to think about, especially when it came to my brother.

Maverick, it was then. Just Maverick.

At the time I didn't really understand the first meaning, but I knew that I wanted my spirit to be free. Free from the sadness and the guilt. I definitely lived up to the non-conformity thing, without trying or perhaps without even realizing it. Interestingly enough, though, the name never stuck.

~~Declan~~

~~Maverick~~

Quick:

The Name That Stuck

Seventh grade. New school, new town, all the new stuff. Well, except for friends. I didn't care enough to try to make any, but I still had some all the same. Maybe not friends. Acquaintances?

There was this one kid who I kind of hung out with that year. Aiden. No, Kayden. Hayden? Brayden. No, not Brayden. There wasn't a consonant blend at the beginning of his name. Jaden? I never remembered the name of the kid who basically named me. Not really my fault though. Everyone called each other "bro" and "dude" back then anyway.

I didn't memorize his name, but I did his goofy face, probably because he was always sticking it right in front of mine. "Hey, wanna walk to P.E. together? Hey, wanna study for the history test together? Hey, wanna sit together at lunch today?" It was constant. Constant questions, but never a space to answer. He just kept talking. It was fine with me. The more he talked, the less I had to.

He named me on a Thursday in October that year.

For two months in gym class, we'd have to start by running a mile. Coach said it was a warm-up, that we needed cardiovascular exercise, that it would wake us up and our endorphins, too. All of us went along with it, but I knew the truth. At the top of every hour, Coach got a fifteen-minute break. Not a bad gig.

That Thursday in October was a little different though. Coach incentivized us, offering a free pass for the following day's running and fitness tests to anyone who could finish the mile in under seven minutes.

Challenge accepted.

I checked my laces. I took some deep breaths. And then I knocked that mile out in five minutes, seventeen seconds.

"Dang, dude! How the heck did you run that so quick? Are those some magic shoes? Did you even know you could run that quick? What the heck?" Yep. All questions, no space to answer. Fine by me. I needed to catch my breath a bit.

We walked to history class together after that, and Aiden/Kayden/Hayden/Jaden was still reeling over the mile, that I had been keeping this superhero power a secret all this time. Not but an hour later, he considered his new assessment of me as officially confirmed, given what happened in our next class. The teachers must have had a meeting and decided on this thing together. That, or the mid-fall laziness kicked in. But our history teacher offered the same type of deal that Coach did, on that same Thursday.

Berkey started off every history class with a trivia question. It was her thing, I guess. "Just for funsies," she would say. I knew most of the answers, but I only begrudgingly muttered them when no one else would get it and it was taking too long. But that day, that Thursday, was different. If I was first to answer correctly, I wouldn't have to take the vocabulary test the next day.

Challenge accepted.

"What are the two types of lava?" Berkey smirked when she asked the question, convinced that she stumped us and that everyone would be taking the test. That debunked my laziness theory.

I knew that I knew the answer, but I didn't know it right then. I remembered seeing it in a book I had in the bathroom when I was younger, one of those kid encyclopedia books. I used to read that book for hours. I could even remember the lava types being on the left side of a left page, towards the top. There were two big photos in round frames with lots of bright oozing lava drops all over the page. I could even see the font! Ugh, it was on the tip of my tongue, but I couldn't grasp it. Probably because it wasn't English.

What was it? Hawaiian or something?

"Simone!" Berkey was shocked someone was going for it. "What's your answer?"

Simone said something stupid, like hot and cool. Of course Berkey couldn't say it was stupid, but we were all thinking it. A couple of other kids gave it a go, too, but Berkey kept saying the same thing.

"No, no, not that. Good try! Anyone else?"

And then I remembered. It clicked. Just popped into my brain, like a download.

"I got it," I uttered. "A'a and Pahoehoe." It was Hawaiian, so surely I mispronounced them.

Berkey was stunned. It was silent for a solid ten seconds, minimum, while the whole class waited to hear if I was right.

"What the what?!" Leave it to Aiden/Kayden/Hayden/Jaden to break the silence. "How the heck? First the mile, and now this? Dude, you are so *quick*!"

And that was that.

Not Maverick.

Quick.

Quick:

A Cynic Was Born

Life during junior high was a blur. I was going through the motions. I got through my classes okay, I continued to tolerate (and at times even appreciate) my eager friend, and I enjoyed my spot under the radar. Well, I didn't "enjoy" it. I just preferred being invisible to the alternative.

At home, I let my parents think I was doing better. I felt like I needed to do that for them. They were already in so much pain, I didn't want their concern for me to make it worse. So I smiled more. Slept less. It seemed to work during the seventh grade.

Around eighth grade, things started to shift a bit. Perhaps because they were less worried about me, my folks had more time to focus on themselves. My mom self-medicated, not nearly as slyly as she thought she did. And my dad worked. Worked and worked. We barely saw him, which probably didn't help my mom's situation much. As for me? I read.

Not casual reading. Not chilling in the hammock for some light reading. I binged, obsessively reading for hours upon hours on end. No breaks either. I'd fall so deep into the words that I would forget to eat, drink, pee.

I was sure my parents thought that my reading was a distraction. A way to avoid the real world. An escape. A way for me to temporarily forget the fact that I was suddenly an "only" child with an addict and an absentee for parents. And maybe that would have been a valid opinion if I was reading fiction. Or fantasy. Something like that.

But I wasn't.

I was digging. Not in dirt, although I did feel like my fingers at the computer keyboard worked together as a metaphorical shovel of sorts. Without even realizing it until it was much too late, I robbed myself of even more of my childhood by opening my eyes to the truths of the world. To the evils. I ripped off my own rose-colored glasses and became a cynic when I was barely a teenager. I researched everything from clones and aliens to fluoride and sunscreen, and almost everything in between. While kids my age were counting down the hours until their next chance to hang out at the mall where they could practice the art of flirting, I was doodling 5G towers in my notebook and brainstorming questions for my next dig.

I loved it. I came alive in front of that computer screen, typing in new search keywords, comparing information, questioning the sources. It invigorated me, and in some ways, it helped me deal with our reality. Maybe because time did that naturally and this was my favorite way to pass that time. All I knew was that I couldn't wait for my next session, and I reveled in the fact that I could do it alone. I treasured my solitude, especially since the one person I wanted to spend time with was gone. Those digs were for me and for me alone.

I never would have guessed that I would want to give up the shovel. More than once.

I never would have guessed that I would share my digs. And want to, nonetheless.

I certainly never would have guessed that I would research the one thing I swore I never would.

Biggest shock though? I definitely did not see it coming, that second shovel.

Quinn:

Hard-Pressed

My detailed memory of that pivotal day remained completely intact for many moons.

The smell of the resilient celery wafted with the breeze. It was growing in our amateur garden, determined to push through the low odds of surviving in desert heat and being grown from random food scraps that we decided to toss into the dirt on a whim. Even with its increasingly full leaves, the celery was being overshadowed by an excessive forest of long stalks of green onion, also grown from food scraps, that we always forgot to harvest. The stalks had become so long that some had fallen over, almost as if defeated, and those small cracks in the onions released their own aroma as well. For years, if I smelled hints of celery or green onion, my eyes would well up with tears instantaneously, with no warning and certainly without permission.

It was two weeks after my eighth birthday, and my dad and I were outside in our small but deliberate backyard. We called it our oasis, and there was simply no denying that it was my favorite place in the world. Next to the homemade garden boxes that housed a variety of foods ranging from dead and rotting to surprisingly green was my childhood sandbox. I would spend hours upon hours in the land of sandy imagination, playing with large blocks as a toddler all the way through to my elementary years, pretending my dolls were at the beach being rescued by princes from faraway lands. On warm days, of which there were plenty, Dad and I would splash around in the pool until I was so tired that I would practically fall asleep on the raft, floating about and already recognizing in my youth how truly happy I was. I would look across the yard to the grassy patch where the timeworn swing set and the cherished, perpetually utilized playhouse were and think about how lucky I was that *my* backyard happened to be the best place on earth.

It was a Saturday afternoon and we were covered in the dust of my new sidewalk chalk, a birthday gift that Dad somehow sensed I needed without me even knowing it. After eating lunch that day, we headed to the oasis to put the chalk to good use, creating flowers and sun rays of every shade. Before I knew it, we were tracing our hands and our feet, doubled over in giggles at the nonsense we were drawing.

"Your mom is going to have a conniption fit," he laughed. "Look at your pants."

I was covered, my white shorts a canvas of dusty colors. "Hurry! To the grass!"

We scooted and rolled, patted and shook, but we erupted in laughter when we quickly realized that our clothing would not survive unscathed, especially now that we had added grass stains to the mix. The giggles finally came to a simmer, and I just laid there on the grass with a grin that felt larger than my face. So happy, so content. The sun wrapped me in a blanket of warmth, and I closed my eyes to take in all of the senses of the oasis: the smells I had come to love, the feel of the damp grass on my skin, the sound of the pool filter creating a magical melody with the soft snores of my dad relaxing nearby.

A majestic blue dragonfly whirred by, so close to my face that it startled me. I allowed my attention to follow it, watching the way it danced about, zooming around invisible corners and unexpectedly stopping to hover. At one point, it landed on a blade of grass directly in front of me, almost as though it was greeting me. Time stood still for the dragonfly and me as though we were the only beings on the planet, simply taking each other in and—at least on my part—appreciating the presence of the other. I was afraid to move, afraid to break the connection with my new, sublime friend. I was as still as an eight-year-old could be, that is, until the link was shattered by something completely unexpected.

It was the sudden shrill of horrific screams coming from inside the house.

For some strange reason, I felt that if I ever had the courage to go back out to the oasis, my dragonfly would be there waiting for me: An impossibility that I chose to believe throughout the rest of my time in that home. I later learned that dragonflies symbolize change and the ability to adapt to it, a significance that was not at all lost on me. Over the years, I saw my majestic blue dragonfly countless times but only in my mind's eye. I somehow inherently recognized that he was with me that day, and at that exact moment for a reason, and I was hard-pressed to believe otherwise. It was a bizarre comfort I depended on from that point forward, without fully understanding it.

I was also hard-pressed to understand what happened that day. Or why.

The piercing sound of agony was coming from the fathomless depths of my mom, holding the lifeless body of my three-month-old brother.

Quinn:

Years of Tears

S udden Infant Death Syndrome took Troy from our family during his afternoon nap that July. For ages, I struggled to comprehend how SIDS was even a thing. My ill-fated parents had already lost two children to miscarriages after I was born and before Troy crossed to the other side. The devastation was incomprehensible.

For three harrowing years, my parents suffered through every possible emotion as they rehashed the most dreadful day of their lives. They repeatedly tried to bargain with God and the universe, knowing that they did everything by the book. Troy was sleeping on his back on a firm mattress, sharing the space with absolutely nothing. As much as they wanted to, my parents never snuggled up with Troy to share the bed and they never allowed toys in his crib. The room was even set to the cool temperature suggested by all the parenting resources. Making sense of what happened was an impossibility, and yet they tortured themselves as they struggled to understand.

There were times when my mom and dad clung to one another. I would see them hugging so tightly, burying their heads in each other's chest to muffle the sobs, to muffle the begging, trying to release the unimaginable pain. Some days, I felt like I was intruding when I would happen upon those moments and I would hide in my bedroom, but more often than not, the wave of despair would take me as well. I would wiggle my way to the center of their huddle and we would rock ourselves back to a calm state, chanting words of encouragement. Those were just for me though. My parents never actually felt encouraged that time would heal the wound they shared.

Unfortunately, there were other times, too. Times that their inconceivable anger would be unleashed through howls of blaming rhetoric that could be heard even above the sounds of smashing glass and overturning furniture. I made myself scarce, retreating deeper and deeper into my bedroom. Escaping through books, music and art, I sleepwalked through those few years as our family tried to heal. Some days, I would run away to Terabithia, yearning for our own oasis that was merely steps away. I longed to forget that my baby brother was gone, and I ached for the version of my parents that I so desperately missed. Those escapes may or may not have been a healthy way of dealing with my emotions, but my parents appreciated that method of mine over the music technique. Those were the days of blasting angry punk rock in my room and thrashing about while screaming lyrics that I barely knew, let alone understood. I felt relief after these therapeutic sessions of sorts, having wailed to the point of physical exhaustion. It was clear to me, though, that the times I withdrew to my bedroom to draw were the times that I truly allowed myself to mourn. Pages upon tear-stained pages of sketches, illustrating all that was absent and all that caused my heartsickness. Those were the days I skipped dinner and found myself sleeping on a pile of paper and pencils, waking up to see graphite smeared on my cheeks.

My biggest escape of all was school, although the year I was in third grade was consigned to oblivion. It was the following school year that Mandy came into my life and, to be completely honest, Mandy helped save me. I later found that to be ironic, however, since she was also the one who tried to destroy me.

Quinn:

Oasis, Abandoned

My parents somehow managed to claw their way out of those first few years without Troy. Surely time heals wounds, like they all say, and I was sure the countless hours of individual and family therapy sessions helped them along as well, but the selling of the house undoubtedly played a monumental role in the shift back towards normalcy.

I struggled with the idea of leaving my childhood home, but even as a preteen, I inherently understood that it was what my parents needed. So, the summer before sixth grade was spent packing up the only spaces I have ever known, a conflicting experience to say the least. On the one hand, I was excited to move into the new house. It was a quick walk from Mandy's house, and my soon-to-be bedroom was larger with an attached bathroom. To be expected, though, there were so many parts of me that did not want to leave. That became explicitly clear on the day I needed to pack up anything from the backyard that I wanted to keep.

With a pounding heart and eyes brimming with tears, I ventured out into the oasis for the first time since that fateful day. Guilt overwhelmed me as I took in all that I saw: an abandoned garden that was once full of experimental surprises, now full of hardened, dry soil; two ragged dolls left in the sandbox, disintegrating slowly to their demise; a neglected pool begging for attention; and dull, dead grass baking in the relentless sun.

Buckling under the shame and collapsing to my knees, I shook with the seemingly endless sobs that gushed from my body. I realized in that moment that Troy wasn't the only one who died that day. The oasis did, too, except I was the one who killed it. I abandoned it. I deserted it. I cursed it with a long, painful death. To see my paradise like that, knowing that it was the sibling that cradled and cared for me throughout my younger years, realizing that it was then too late to make it right, filled my soul with a profuse amount of guilt and regret.

I allowed myself to grieve for what seemed like hours, vacillating between sobs and apologies, both of which were instantaneously silenced by something that sounded vaguely familiar. I instantly recognized the nearby high-pitched hiss of a dragonfly's wings and looked up to see one dancing about. I nodded at the brown dragonfly, knowing it was right; things were definitely about to change, whether I had the ability to adapt to it or not.

Quinn:

Three Simple Words

My upper elementary school years were a blend of pointless spelling tests and flashy science experiments devoid of any curricular content, but my blossoming friendship with Mandy somehow dwarfed the annoyance of the routine at school and helped me to forget my sadness at home. If we weren't trying to control our maniacal laughter over our MASH results during silent reading time, we were cheering each other on at Double Dutch during recess. We were attached at the hip, with everything from planting silly notes for each other in random places in the fourth-grade classroom, to trying to hypnotize each other at sleepovers throughout all of fifth grade. We were together constantly, never tiring of one another. It was an incredible feeling to know that I had a friendship so reliable, one that I could count on for anything at any time. We didn't just wear the matching set of necklaces that read, "Best Buds" when placed side by side; we often talked about what it meant to be besties. Countless nights were spent in giggles, but also in all seriousness, as we imagined meeting our future husbands who surely would also be the best of friends, which naturally meant that it would make sense for us all to live together. We planned our lives and never doubted that we would spend them accordingly. Of course, in our innocent youth, we didn't consider all that life could throw at us and how unexpected our responses could be, but we figured that out quite quickly when my family moved into the new house.

My mourning came flooding back with a vengeance. It was one thing to lose my brother when I was eight, but that household move also created a shift in our family that I ended up struggling with off and on for quite some time. My physically present mother became completely absent during some of my most formative years. My mom was burying herself in her work, trying to push her way through the days in all the ways that society deemed appropriate, while leaving me to navigate the tricky waters of adolescence without her.

My mom went back to work my sixth-grade year, just after we moved. She was a teacher, and the best kind of one, too. She dedicated herself fully to the classroom and all of the fortunate students on her roster. Dad would smile through her constant rambling at the dinner table, whether it was regarding her research ("Did you know that there is much controversy surrounding the idea of a student's attention span? Some researchers say that children can only attend for two minutes longer than the number of years of age, but others say that students should not be expected to listen to new information for more than ten minutes at a time!"), her daily stories ("You wouldn't believe what that Maxwell did today! Imagine, coming in from recess to see my entire desk covered in Post-it Notes! Here, look, I took a picture!"), or her frustrations with administration ("How is it that some people who couldn't last five minutes in the classroom are making such important decisions about how we teachers run those very same class-rooms?"). Dad was glad to see my mom moving on and plunging forward. I wasn't. Often times I would feel jealous of her students, and even her administrators. They got the best of her—the passion, the drive, the love, the anger. When it came to our house, her emotions ran at the surface level. All we ever talked about was the schedule, the carpool, the grocery store, the weather.

I spent much of sixth grade at Mandy's house, but my resentful anger towards my mom kept creeping up and bubbling over, making our friend-ship much less enjoyable. Mandy wanted to practice putting makeup on each other's faces and stay up late watching romantic comedies, but I couldn't seem to bring myself to have fun anymore. To put it bluntly, I was ticked off. I wanted Troy back, and I wanted my mom back. And I wanted to play in the sandbox with my dad.

About halfway through that school year, I exploded. My family was sitting at the dinner table, yet again listening to another story about one of my mom's precious students, when something triggered me. It was the look on her face. It was the look of a proud mother, eyes brimming with joyous tears and a smile full of love.

Some kid named Brandon earned that look.

"What the heck, Mom? I'm sick of hearing about your stupid job and your stupid kids. Why the hell can't we talk about anything else? Something real for once? So because you somehow graduated from therapy and we moved houses, we just fake our way through life now? What about Troy? What about me?" There was so much rage behind the questions, which was quickly fueled even more by her response.

"Please do not curse. There are plenty of clean words to help you express yourself," she calmly announced as she swept up our plates and headed to the kitchen.

Dad told me later that he could see my fury about to erupt, which was why he suddenly swept me up, grabbed his keys, and carried me out the front door.

He drove in silence. I sat with my arms crossed, seething in self-pity, occasionally mumbling under my breath and more than occasionally taking it out on the car with my feet and fists. Still, he drove in silence.

When we arrived at the bookstore, I made it abundantly clear that I had zero intention of going in. Dad calmly walked around to the passenger door, opened it, and offered me his hand. His silence and his patience outlasted my refusal, and I finally, begrudgingly, flopped my hand onto his. Without a word, we walked into the bookstore and he guided me directly towards the back to an area I had never seen before. There were sections of books on self-care, spirituality, gardening, and other topics that I honestly did not even realize existed.

He turned to me, cradled my face in his hands, and locked his tear-filled eyes with mine. He said three simple words, three words which I carried with me for years and years to come: "Feel. Deal. Heal."

He walked away and left me standing there with tears streaming down my long face, my eyes blinking in a bizarre mix of confusion and comprehension. I stared at his retreating form and then watched him settle into a worn couch, getting comfortable for what he clearly thought would be a long evening. He caught my gaze and winked, and I felt a rush of warm love wash over me. Calmness spread, and along with it, a new type of curiosity. I inherently understood that I was on a mission, and I instantly became intrigued with an overwhelming intent to figure out exactly what that mission entailed.

As though a participant in some sort of bookstore marathon, I perused shelf after shelf of eclectic literature. I made a conscious effort to overcome my discomfort with sections about which I knew nothing, allowing my fingers to do the walking and all the while hearing my dad's words in my head. It was a mantra of sorts, and I was determined to find something in those shelves that was just for me, something that would help me feel and deal so I could heal. It was the most open-minded I had ever felt up to that point, and I acknowledged that I felt older, more mature. I was suddenly ready to embark upon a new journey.

I meandered into a section of books with photographs of rocks and for a moment, I thought I was in the geology section. With a closer look and the absorption of the titles, I realized that wasn't where I was at all. I was surrounded by books on crystals and energy codes, on mindfulness and chakra alignment. Enthralled, I feverishly flipped through book after book, reading chapter titles, taking in graphics, and subconsciously making a stack of books on the floor beside me. I was completely entrenched in that curious realm and when the intercom screeched the store's closing time, I was so startled I knocked over my stack.

"How many are we getting? One? Two? All of them?" My dad grinned as he took in the scene. He was hovering over me as I was sprawled out in the aisle, books all around me begging to be taken home. I simply smiled at him, and we both simultaneously ascertained that we would meet our shared goal: I was going to be okay.

He bought me every single book I wanted that night. He didn't utter one word about the literature section that ended up calling to me. Even though he didn't understand the first thing about chakras or stones, or how that could possibly help with my healing journey, his unconditional support was so strong it was palpable.

I spent the rest of that evening at home immersed in a mindfulness book. I figured that was the easiest thing to tackle, since I was an amateur. That evening turned into a week and then a month, and before I knew it sixth grade was coming to a close. My friendship with Mandy had settled into a routine within the school walls, as we stopped hanging out on weekends and such. I tried sharing my new passions with her, but she would just roll her eyes and tell me that I was "weirding her out." She sparked up some new friendships, which I was really okay with, and I continued to dive further into my studies. By seventh grade, I was meditating on a daily basis and working to align my chakras. I was journaling, I was grounding, I was smudging, I was releasing, I was growing.

I was healing.

By eighth grade, Mandy and I barely talked. She had a new best friend, Desiree, and they were constantly in one another's company. It made me happy to see her laughing and carrying on with Desiree at school. I felt like our friendship underwent a natural detachment, and since I was not harboring any resentment or ill feelings, I was surprised to discover that she did. She made her feelings towards me crystal clear a month before graduation, when she wrote about me all over the school's bathroom mirrors. Some mirrors included illustrations of cauldrons, others incorporated pointed black hats, but they all shared the same bold-faced title written in all capital letters: QUINN IS A WITCH!

Hey,

Today was exhausting. I literally have no other word for it. I'm exhausted. Exhausted by all the basic, shallow people I have to walk by in the halls and listen to in class. Exhausted by their conversations about absolute nonsense. Do they not realize how many important things there are to discuss? No, they'd rather just talk about their lattes and so-and-so's last post on whatever stupid social media platform.

Honestly, what exhausts me the most is the realization that today was only the first day of my next four years.

It's been two and a half years since I've seen you, and that's been a frickin' eternity. I can't even imagine what four years will feel like.

Think of you every minute. Love you.

-Deck

Monday, August 16, 2021

~~Dear Diary,~~
~~Dear Journal,~~

Note to self:

Well, I completed my first day of high school and I now have something like 719 days left. I figured I should probably start a new notebook here, since I will most likely be spending the next four years with… myself. Big shock.

It's okay. I'm good with it. I don't really belong in this high school scene, and I don't really care to. I don't see myself connecting with anyone at school, at least not on a deep level. I mean, really, who is going to want to talk with me about sound healing meditation anyway? Ugh, I don't know how to make conversation with people about ordinary things and I don't really have the desire to. Maybe I should work on that.

Do I wish that I could meet someone like me? Or at least someone open-minded enough to accept me? Yeah, of course I do. And maybe I will. Personally, I see that happening much later in life but hey, I could be wrong.

Let's be honest, though. I may have some trust issues. Still working on figuring out that one.

So for now, it's just me and you.

…Q

10/19/21

3:48 a.m.

We can see the line forming as soon as we round the corner. "Oh my gosh, Honey. Two hours, minimum." He is trying his hardest to put on his best happy face, but the wait for this ride just might create the crack in the facade.

"This is the reason we came, Marcus. This very ride." They lock eyes, almost as though they are telepathically communicating, before sharing a smile and a nod that was probably imperceptible to everyone else.

My dad squats down to my brother's eye level to whisper. "Hey, you wanna go ride in your favorite red sports car?" It takes the five-year-old a moment or two, but we all see the lightbulb turn on. His eyes grow wide and he sucks in a quick gasp before releasing an elated squeal and launching himself into my dad's arms.

"It's going to be a long two hours," I joke as we settle in line. I look behind me and am relieved to see that the line is already well beyond us. I hate when we are last. It gives me some strange comfort to know that at least I don't have to wait as long as the poor folks after me.

My mom spots a snack stand off to the side of the line up ahead. She hands me a twenty-dollar bill. "Here, Deck. Go take your brother to get a churro. There and back, okay?"

Hey,

I woke up from a familiar nightmare and I knew today would suck. Sure enough…

So the counselor at school called me in to talk about how my freshman year is going so far, my classes, any questions, blah blah blah. Probably some formality they have to check off their October to-do list. He starts talking about what classes I'll have going forward and I'm not gonna lie—I got triggered. Get this. They have us taking math classes like calculus and then more calculus, but nothing about financial literacy? Seriously? What's the percentage of the population that actually uses calculus versus the percentage of the population that needs to, I don't know, know how to manage their money? Ridiculous. It's total crap. The more I think about it, the more I think it's done on purpose. Like, are they trying to break us with stress and totally irrelevant and incomprehensible concepts for teenagers? Or just keep us financially stupid and dependent? Both, I bet. Needless to say, my counselor probably flagged my name in the system when I left our little chat.

Anyway. Happy 8th birthday. I miss you, bud.

-Deck

Hey,

Caught Mom sobbing her eyes out today. It's been a while since I've seen that. I think she tries to do it in secret, probably to protect me. Actually, I don't think that. I'm pretty sure she despises me and has zero interest in protecting me. Dad says she doesn't want me to be reminded of what happened, but what they don't realize is that nothing can suddenly remind me of what I think about 24/7. He has told me time and time again not to blame myself, but I do. And I always will. And as much as she'll never admit it, I bet Mom blames me, too.

I can't wait for Christmas break. I haven't had as much time to dig as I would like because I've been bogged down with busywork for school, so I'm pumped to have the extra time. I'm going to spend it looking into the months of the year. I haven't stopped thinking about it since yesterday. Smack dab in the middle of Spanish class, I realized that October/octubre comes from "eight." Right? Like octagon and all that. So then I start going through the months… Sept is "seven" and Dec is "ten"… so all our numbered months are wrong? What? Dude. It's like cracking a code and then all of a sudden realizing that I stumbled upon a big, fat secret that's staring everyone in the face. I'm dying to figure it out.

Love you.

-Deck

Friday, January 14, 2022

Note to self:

It is quite interesting to consider how much can change in a relatively short amount of time. Just two years ago, Mandy and I were inseparable. A year ago, Mandy and I were still friendly. Today at school, not so much. I happened upon her in the hallway and she squawked something about me being a "weirdo freak witch." It did not bother me, and honestly still doesn't, but what stuck with me was the look on her face. It exuded utter disdain.

Perhaps I hurt her more than I realized, and definitely without intention. I meditated on it and contemplated trying to clear the air with her, but I don't think it is the right time to do so. Nothing I say will be received well, and to be honest, her viewpoint of me isn't really my work to tackle.

I'm in a good place right now. Things with Mom are even getting better. We're going for doughnuts tomorrow at some new little shop that opened, just me and her. I'm hoping we will talk about something other than her work, but I highly doubt we will talk about my interests. They clearly make her feel uncomfortable, like I'm some spiritual energy wacko, and I know she's hoping it's a phase. Well, we'll see how it goes!

…Q

○○○

omg idk how I was ever friends with her!

Desiree / 7:47 p.m.

that Quinn chick? ikr I can't even picture it lol she seems like such a loner

7:47 p.m.

ofc she's a loner who would want to be friends with a weirdo freak witch she doesn't even hide it did you see that necklace thing she was wearing

7:48 p.m.

no what was it

7:48 p.m.

some black magic weird crystal thing

7:50 p.m.

so she doesn't have any friends? that's sad

7:50 p.m.

for real
whatever

Hey,

I hate this time of year, bud. I frickin' hate February. Well, not as much as I hate April, but still.

I don't want to celebrate my birthday, but Mom and Dad want to make everything look and feel as "normal" as possible, so much so that they try too hard and it's just way too forced. I legit hate it. And it doesn't stop there. Dad is over-the-top nice throughout March and April, and Mom plasters on this fake smile that literally makes me wince in pain. But, dude, why? Like we'll be having so much fun that one day we'll wake up and realize that it's May, and that we breezed right past April? Yeah, ok. Like that's even possible.

At least I decided on my big dig for Spring Break. I figure if I immerse myself in the mysteries of Antarctica, maybe it will feel like an actual escape. Seriously, though. What's with the government secrets surrounding that continent? There are definitely some hidden truths in that ice.

I only have one birthday wish. You know that, right?

-Deck

Saturday, April 16, 2022

Note to self:

Sometimes I fantasize how life would be different if Troy were still with us, especially around this time of year. We'd be planning a birthday party, this year being his 7th. I wonder what seven-year-olds are into these days. Pokémon maybe?

When he was three, I pictured us planning a robot-themed party. I would have spray-painted a bunch of cardboard boxes silver before the big day, and then all of the kids would decorate one. The space for their faces would already be cut out so they could wear their helmets the whole day. We'd have special robot words for the treats, and we could sing the birthday song in our best digital voices. I bet Troy would have loved that.

When he turned five, I imagined it would be a construction-themed birthday party and his friends would wear hard hats and bright orange vests. Maybe we'd even rent an actual excavator or something and let the kids ride in one! We'd put the snacks in the beds of toy trucks and there would be shovels instead of spoons. Obviously, there would be dirt cups instead of cake, and I'd totally be the silly big sister to smash his cookie-crumbed pudding into his face. He'd laugh and laugh because he loved when his silly big sister did silly things like that.

Sigh.

I visualize these things each year, but all I really want to picture is his face. I wonder what he would look like now.

...Q

Hey,

Stayed home from school again today. Been laying in my bed since I woke up. I don't even know if Mom and Dad know. They wouldn't be surprised though, since I have yet to get through an April without going dark.

The nightmares and the flashbacks get really bad this time of year. It makes me not want to sleep, but all I want to do is sleep? Sucks.

~~-Deck~~

Love you.

-Deck

04/23/22

2:51 a.m.

I can't process what I am seeing. I can't process what I am not seeing either.

Why is his perfect, untouched churro laying on the nasty concrete? Why isn't he reaching for it? I bend down to grab it. Wait. Where are his feet?

I stand up and look all around me. I turn in circles searching for him, calling out his name. I am annoyed; I am not in the mood to play games. We just wasted over five dollars on a churro and now I am going to have to get back in line to get him another one.

I keep calling his name, shouting for him to come out and bellowing that his hiding game isn't funny anymore. I am searching high and low, rooted to my spot but rotating around to get a full view.

It starts to get louder. The chatter of the people in line, the cacophony of amusement park rides, the squeals of delight coming from toddlers everywhere. My vision becomes blurry and I feel like my head is spinning as I focus on all the faces that are not of my brother.

That's when the panic sets in.

Friday, May 27, 2022

Note to self:

That's a wrap! The first year of high school went by pretty quickly, now that I'm looking back at it. It was not as bad as I thought it would be. I don't mind that I don't have friends there, although it clearly worries Mom. I enjoyed my classes for the most part, and I think I grew a lot as a person this year. I feel really at peace.

For spending a lot of time outside, it astounds me how long it's been since I've seen a dragonfly. I must not have a big change coming in my life anytime soon.

I'm good with that.

…Q

Friday, July 8, 2022

Note to self:

Happy birthday to me! Mom and Dad tried to make it extra special this year, which I totally appreciated, especially since they can't relate in the slightest to what they planned for me. They took me to the annual Gem and Mineral Show… so cool! We walked around for hours, visiting all of the different booths and tents there. I was totally blown away by the vastness of it all, and I kept thanking Mom and Dad every chance I got. They didn't rush me once, and as much as they don't understand the first thing about crystals, it was clear as day that they support my interest in them.

Ok, best find of the day? Raw shungite!! I can't wait to start pouring my drinking water over it. It's supposed to purify the water and destroy viruses and bacteria. The gentleman in the booth told me all about how in 1719, Peter the Great from Russia built a spa resort called "The Marcial Waters" for the rich to take baths in, and the water flowed over raw shungite. Apparently it has healing properties? I had no idea. I learned so much today!

Today was awesome. Honestly, it was exactly what I needed. Actually, it was what all three of us needed. This time of year is so hard for us, especially with the anniversary coming up in two weeks. And while I'm truly proud of us for coming so far in our healing journey, we still have so much left to do. There's literally a hole in each of our hearts, theirs more so than mine. The void they must suffer is unimaginable to me. It's all just so sad and heavy, but I have to believe that the universe and the heavens needed Troy to have his angel wings early for whatever reason. I don't think I'll ever learn why, but maybe that's not for me to know.

…Q

○○○

I'm so glad we're not freshmen anymore!!!!!

Desiree / 4:27 p.m.

right??? some of them are so small! like really, were we that tiny and lame last year lol
one accidentally bumped into me in the hall today and I swear I thought she was going to break in half

4:27 p.m.

omg I would have died laughing

4:27 p.m.

for sure

4:27 p.m.

actually I almost did die laughing at lunch today

4:29 p.m.

oh yeah! right?! wth is wrong with her???

4:30 p.m.

I'm telling you she's a freak
who else would sit there by herself in the grass, just sitting!?!? what was she even doing?

4:31 p.m.

I don't even think she moved for like ten minutes
maybe she was doing some weird magic ritual or something
do you think it's for attention or something

4:32 p.m.

no. she's just a weirdo

Hey,

Happy birthday, bud.

If you're looking down on us from above and you notice that we don't talk about you, you have to know it's not because you were forgotten. It's not because we don't love you. We feel your absence every single second. We just can't bring ourselves to say your name, I guess. Hell, I can't even write it to you in a letter.

If you're watching, then you can sense how awkward it still is around here. Are you old enough to understand now what you're seeing? You're seeing our mom, popping pills to help her get through each day. Numbing her pain. Devoid of all emotion, even the good ones. You're seeing blank stares and random syllables of confirmation, as if she's fooling us that she's actually a true participant in any conversation.

You're seeing Dad, but not too much of him, right? Yeah. Because he spends as much time as humanly possible at his office. Anything to not be here, to not see his shell of a wife. And to not see me. The reason that everything went so wrong in his life.

Sometimes I hope that you're not seeing me.

I feel guilty for every single thought. If you're watching us from above, that means you're dead. So of course I want you alive. But what would that life of yours look like? It torments me to even think about. So many possible scenarios, but none of them the right one.

I do wish you were looking right at me, but in person. Right here in my room. We could build a fort just like the good old days. Sneak in a bunch of junk food and play stupid games of flashlight tag. Knock knock jokes. Silly videos of cats and cucumbers. I'd give anything to hear your laugh again.

I miss everything about you. And life sucks without you. School sucks. Home sucks. The world sucks.

I'm sorry.

-Deck

Wednesday, November 9, 2022

Note to self:

I'm a few months into my sophomore year in high school, and I'm trying so hard to stay positive. I focus on gratitude, since that is what lends to joy: I appreciate that I am able to earn an education, that I am fortunate to attend a school with qualified teachers, that this opportunity will open doors for me in my future. I really am grateful. I just wish there was more of a focus on the individual student and more of a drive to inspire us. There are so many things I am curious about, but our classes are full of rigorous curriculum with little room for anything else. But not everyone is energized and motivated by language, math, history, or science. What about all of the things in between and beyond?

I was thinking today…I wouldn't dread P.E. as much if I knew there was a unit on yoga. Why is it always running and soccer and volleyball and sit-ups? Don't the powers that be know how strengthening yoga can be for the body? I understand why we can't cater to every single person's interests and desires, but I sure wish there was a way to mix it up a bit.

At the end of the day, though, my education is my own responsibility. Especially in this day and age when information is so readily available. I need to learn about my own interests in my own way. It's not like school is the only time and place to learn! So, I am starting here by making a wish list.

1) I'd love to take classes on kundalini yoga and reiki.

2) I want to take field trips to the nearby mines and see how gems, metals, and crystals are extracted.

3) Oooh, I also want to explore my creative side a bit more by making things with my hands.

Oh, that's a short list. I need to keep thinking and expand my horizons. I have no clue what I want to study in the future or what I want to be when I am older, but I do know I will figure that out with more and more experiences. I absolutely want to help people heal in some way, and for now, I will lean on that fact for inspiration. Inspiration should come from within, anyway, or at least for me. Maybe I should volunteer somewhere? Do some community service?

I feel better already.

...Q

Hey,

Merry Christmas. Not that we really do that around here anymore.

Been spending my vacation catching up on digs, you know me. I came across some stuff on hidden technologies from the past, and I'm reading about how cars used to be fueled back in the day. I remember hearing somewhere about hydro powered cars, but what is this about cars being fueled by alcohol? Apparently, according to some of what I'm reading (but who knows what is really true), the emissions from alcohol-fueled cars are basically null. Which is good. And get this, the use of alcohol as fuel was supposedly starting to trend during the 1920s, you know, during the Prohibition. Sus. Then, in 1941, Ford came out with a car that was made of hemp, wheat, and other natural materials and, get this, was fueled by hemp or other farming waste. How did these technological options just come to a screeching halt? Makes me wonder...

I think I'll be on this one for the remainder of the break. When I think about it, it is curious that we never found a cleaner way to fuel our cars. And I'm not talking about electric vehicles. I did a dig on that a while back and the amount of damage done to the earth for ONE unreliable battery is beyond my comprehension. Never mind what happens with them once the batteries die. Ridiculous.

Anyway. House feels empty. Always does.

Love you.

-Deck

Sunday, December 25, 2022

Note to self:

There are good days and bad days. It's to be expected. And while I haven't mastered it quite yet, I do work hard on appreciating the yucky days because if it weren't for them, we wouldn't really feel the weight of the good days.

Regardless, today was a bad day. And I'm trying to breathe through it. I'm trying to acknowledge, respect, and value what comes with days like these. I'm trying to embrace whatever lessons I should glean, to remind myself that for as much pain and loss, we are still so very blessed. But it's hard. Today was just a rough day.

It's bizarre. We never got to celebrate Christmas with Troy, but we so profoundly feel his absence on this day. I can see the tears behind my parents' eyes, and every gift exchanged feels like it was wrapped in a layer of guilt. I don't know for what, though. Guilt for moving on, even though we really haven't and probably never will?

We did continue our tradition of making him ornaments, which felt nice. In years past, we've created everything from pinecone angels to stars made of pipe cleaners and fabric, and this year we tried something new: stamped clay. Our concentration levels made for an unusually silent craft time, and the heaviness of the quiet weighed on me throughout the rest of the afternoon and evening.

They say that everything is temporary. Bad days are temporary. It's a bad day, not a bad life. To keep perspective, that this shall pass. But on days like today, I struggle with that. Troy's death isn't temporary. Our family dealing with a void isn't temporary. I catch myself having these thoughts, and the deep breaths don't help as much as they normally do.

But then I remind myself that living without Troy is indeed temporary.

I will see him again. I know he will be waiting for me, and in the meantime, I will try to appreciate the hard times because they make the great times feel even greater.

...Q

Hey,

It's almost April. Most people love this time of year. The weather, the flowers, the greenery. Not me. I want to climb into a hole.

Miss you, bud.

-Deck

04/02/23

2:47 a.m.

I can't breathe. Air is getting caught between my sobs and my screams.

"Geoffrey! Geoffrey!" I fall to the ground, dizzy and gasping. I choke on my tears and start coughing, which finally alerts the people around me to pay attention. Had I not been screaming long enough or loud enough? Did they think it was a game?

A lady bends down next to me and asks if I need help, if I'm okay. The look of concern on her face reminds me that I have a mother of my own, and I yell for her as I sprint to where she was in line just a few minutes before. I see my dad's head above the others and I push my way to him, collapsing into his arms.

"Deck! Deck, are you ok?" Dad is fanning my face and searching for answers there, but my mom already knows.

Hysteria takes hold of my mother. "Declan, where is Geoffrey? Declan!"

I can hear the fright in her voice right before I pass out.

Quinn:

A Triple Tradition

The weight of the air in our house that April morning felt like thousands of pounds per square inch. Normally, on weekends, my parents tried to get creative in the kitchen, using eggs to transform any leftovers from the week into a unique breakfast meal. It was a bizarre tradition, but we loved it all the same. On that particular Saturday, I didn't hear either of my parents utter a single syllable and all of the dinner meal remainders were still in the fridge, awaiting their eventual fate of the trash can.

It was not difficult to figure out why this Saturday morning felt different. For weeks there was a dread amongst us, knowing that Troy's birthday was looming around the corner. Troy would have turned eight in a few days, and this weekend probably would have been the time of birthday party hats and frosted cupcakes, of wrapped toys and pure delight. I was nervous to challenge my poor parents that day, but after hours of silence and sadness, I could not take it anymore.

"Troy is watching us from above and I bet it's tearing him apart to see us so sad. We need to do something. As much as it hurts, this isn't the way to honor him. Please, Mom. Dad. Please." I pleaded with my words in case they couldn't see the desperation in my eyes.

Several seconds passed before my mom walked over to hug me and asked, "What do you suggest we do, honey?"

I shrugged my shoulders. "What if we each decide on one thing we want to do together as a family today, and then we do all three things?" It was the best I could come up with.

My dad wanted to cast every single one of our photographs and videos of Troy's short but sweet life to the big television and eat snacks on the couch while doing so. Mom had her heart set on us baking a birthday cake from scratch and decorating it with all of the love that could possibly be expressed through sprinkles and frosting. My wish was for us to spend time together in the backyard by using natural elements to create a simple Zen garden. I thought it would be lovely to have a place that we built together, one we could visit when we needed to relax, clear our minds, or just think about our Troy.

As it turned out, we accomplished all three wishes. Kicking the late morning off with pictures and videos made Troy feel so present, and we found ourselves crying through giggles and laughing through tears as his perfect little face filled our screen and our hearts. It inspired us to bake the most beautiful eight-shaped cake, complete with all the fixings and ready for candles. It was surreal to experience traditions being born, knowing in real time that this was how we would spend every April for the rest of our years.

Working on the Zen garden with my parents made my heart swell. Even though this backyard was not my childhood oasis, it had the potential to become a sanctuary in its own right, and this first step was the perfect one. We were honoring Troy through building an everlasting area in his memory. To work with my parents on something that aligned with my core belief system was truly the most powerful spiritual practice I could imagine. That Saturday, we planned the simple design and gathered rocks from our yard. We went to the home improvement store as soon as it opened for business on Sunday to purchase wood, gravel, and sand, as well as a new rake and a few large stones. My parents and I spent the weekend before Troy's eighth birthday working and sweating, communicating and helping. Upon the Zen garden's completion, the three of us stood side by side, holding hands and gazing at the most precious space we had ever laid eyes on. It was the perfect place to sing "Happy Birthday" when we later lit the candles on our eight-cake. We each raked a row and wished him peace before heading inside and wrapping up our weekend.

As I rested in bed that evening, my parents knocked on my door. Through grateful tears and tight squeezes, they thanked me for what they both considered to be the best weekend we'd had as a family since Troy passed away. I agreed with a grin and suggested that we have dinner at the Zen garden on his actual birthday on Wednesday. They nodded, and in that moment, we all knew that the triple tradition would live on for always.

Quick:

Piqued, But Not Enough

Tenth grade was a snoozefest. How did an entire year pass by and feel completely uneventful? A total hamster wheel. There were a few chemistry demonstrations mixed in with some gothic literature. Some graphing calculator work jumbled up with ancient dynasties. Oh, and of course, smelly P.E. clothes.

I went to school, came home, ate, did my required busywork, ate, snuck in an hour or two of digs if I was lucky, and then showered. Rinse. Repeat. Over and over again.

I didn't have a social life, but that was my choice. My Aiden/Kayden/Hayden/Jaden chihuahua friend had finally moved on and found a new bulldog to idolize. Honestly, I missed him a little bit, but not enough.

There were plenty of people at school, and some of them even seemed interested in sparking a friendship. It was me who would always shoot them down. My chem partner invited me to three parties before he stopped asking. I started jog-walking in P.E. to kinda make the slow, lonesome kid less obvious, but once he figured it out, thanked me profusely, and wanted to go to the arcade together after school, I was out.

Tons of girls, too. Typical flirty ones who for some reason only thought they were pretty or worthy or whatever if a guy was interested in her. This one emo girl in English class told me she thought my "mysterious nature" made me "sexy as hell," and I literally laughed in her face. No surprise that she never spoke to me again. I figured she took my laugh the wrong way and I felt bad, but not enough.

There was this one girl, though, who caught my eye. She was so different. She was a complete loner, not at all a part of the high school drama. I noticed her one day at lunch, sitting on the grass with her legs crossed and her eyes closed, her face lifted towards the sun. Just sitting there. I did a double take as I walked by, not necessarily because of her looks or anything like that, but because it was such an unexpected sight. Turned out she did that pretty much every single day. While other people rolled their eyes at her or ignored her completely, I found myself making sure that she was there. It was almost as though it had become a constant in my life. It was bizarre. What was even more strange was that when she wasn't there, I found myself wondering if she was okay. Almost like worry.

Then I found myself wondering about all sorts of things. What was she was doing? What was she was thinking about? Was she meditating? I wondered if she was ever distracted by the noise all around her, or bothered by the itch of the grass on her legs during warm months. I wondered how she knew when to come back to reality and gather her stuff for fifth period. I wondered when she ate. I wondered what she ate. I wondered if she worried about sun exposure. (Did a major dig on that. Found out that as long as you weren't wearing sunglasses, your eyes would signal to your body to release the right chemicals to process the sun's rays and naturally protect you from skin cancer. In moderation, of course.)

Anyway, that isolated and eccentric girl really piqued my interest that year.

But not enough.

Friday, May 26, 2023

Note to self:

Things had been going so well at home. Mom and I have kept up our weekly dates—sometimes doughnuts, other times the movies. We even started trying to make new foods together, despite our epic fail at homemade tamales. Dinner conversations with the three of us have become normal by anyone's standards. We can even mention Troy's name and honor his place in our lives without having an unhealthy chaos storm afterwards.

I guess I should have known that the other shoe would drop.

Apparently, as a way to congratulate me on successfully completing yet another year of high school, my mother decided to pick a huge battle with me. On the first afternoon of summer break! As if I don't already know that my junior year is going to be more academically involved, she had to drill it home about how important my eleventh-grade year will be when considering my future. My grades are fine, and she even admitted that, but of course, nothing is good enough for her. She laid into me about extra-curricular activities and clubs and friends and Prom and, and, and. It felt endless. Evidently, I have all of summer to wrap my brain around what is coming and to mentally prepare myself for the pressures? What does that even mean?

I am so ticked. She is forcing me, *forcing* me, to "build my resume" next school year. She's requiring me to join at least one club at school and—get this—make at least one friend that I see outside of class. What the heck? What kind of parent requires that?

It's not like I don't want a friend. I just don't want friends from there. Who wants to spend all day talking about clothes and makeup and boys and booze and all that crap anyway? Not me.

Maybe I'll start my own club. The Meditation Club or the Chakra Crew or something like that. Ha ha!

Ugh, I'm annoyed. I need to sage the house and rid us of the negative energies.

…Q

Friday, May 26, 2023 - continued

Note to self:

Whoa…. So I smudged the house, which I love doing because not only does it clear the air, but it smells so good afterwards! Anyway, I went outside when I was done to breathe the fresh air and release my thoughts, and guess what I saw. Or rather, guess who visited? Yep, a dragonfly friend. An orange-ish one this time. I guess Mom's right. Change is coming.

…Q

Saturday, July 22, 2023

Note to self:

Needless to say, much time was spent in Troy's Zen garden today. When I woke up this morning and opened the shades, I noticed Mom methodically raking the sand with two hands, allowing the tears to roll down her cheeks and fall right into the grooves she was carving. I'm not sure when Dad visited the sacred space, but I did notice patches of sand in and around his backyard slippers when I headed out there after lunch.

With the intention of merely sitting in the garden to meditate, I took my rose quartz with me to amplify the feelings of love and peace that I held in my heart. In my cross-legged pose, I closed my eyes and thought of my brother. I pictured his baby face, and I imagined a white light pulsating out from my heart and headed up to him in the heavens. A few tears trickled from my eyes, but they met my slight smile on the way down. It brought me joy to be in that space with thoughts of Troy, even though it was on the anniversary of the saddest day of our lives. In the Zen garden, I finally felt that I could access him at any time and that he really was immortal for me now. I felt peace.

After meditating, I decided to do some labors of love in the Zen garden. Without having a fully formed goal, I just allowed my body to do the work. I collected the different rocks from around the garden, and without an end-vision in mind, I placed the stones end to end in different patterns and directions. It started to take shape when suddenly, I could see it. I could see what I was creating. Now with less contemplation and more excitement, I utilized several smaller rocks to fill in the gaps and add subtle structure. Before long, it was complete. I took several steps back to take in the full image and it literally took my breath away.

I had constructed a dragonfly.

…Q

PART TWO:
Quick & Quinn

Quinn:

Live Inspired

As I walked towards the door of my new history classroom, I could see a plain poster displayed right above the door's window. Nearly at eye level and bold in its black background with white text, it was simply screaming to be read. "Live inspired." I was taken aback by it, not because of its profound message that resonated so deeply with me, but because it was so unexpected. I even questioned if I was entering the correct class-room, sincerely doubting that this could be the resounding message that the teacher of AP United States History was clearly prioritizing.

I entered with dubious hesitation and read the confirmation on the white-board that I was indeed in the correct room with the correct teacher, Mr. Jason Erickson. I took a seat in the back of the room and spent the entire transition time in observation mode. His classroom walls were nearly bare and without adornment, and his minimalistic decor immediately helped to slow my breathing and heart rate. Mr. Erickson chose to have a clutter-free desk and bookshelf, ones that weren't covered in glass apples and bizarre bobbleheads that for some odd reason most teachers tended to collect. It was clear that every particular thing in his classroom was intentionally selected, making each one of those items that much more meaningful and significant. Aside from the typical classroom inclusions such as textbooks and pencil sharpeners, from where I was seated, I could only see two pieces of decor: one figurine of an eagle holding an American flag and one poster on the wall.

"Live inspired" was not Mr. Erickson's only message of choice. To the left of the whiteboard at the front of the room was another poster, which by all appearances was handmade. It was not a printed or laminated sign, but rather the type of thick chart paper one could purchase at a local general store. The penmanship that scripted "Mr. Jason Erickson - AP U.S. History" on the white board was clearly the same one that was used to craft the sign.

I tried to picture this grown man creating the decoration, utilizing a ruler to best center and level the words, slowly and carefully tracing pencil marks with a wide, red marker.

"Don't be burdened with conformity."

I couldn't help but stare at the simple, yet profound quote on the hand-drawn poster, my unblinking eyes brimming with liquid appreciation. The statement struck me to my core like a bolt of lightning, electrifying something within. I felt deeply legitimized in that moment, instinctively recognizing that this poster hollered the perfect combination of words to summarize my entire existence. Words of affirmation, words that yielded a deluge of validation, words that I didn't even realize I needed to internalize.

That is, until I did.

This teacher was different. We had yet to make eye contact, let alone have a conversation, but I already felt so understood by him.

Mr. Erickson was of tall stature with thin, graying hair and large, tired eyes behind his glasses. He wore an untucked plaid shirt with dark blue jeans and lace-less sneakers, which in my mind sent a message of either being casual or being fatigued. I figured I would be able to discern soon enough.

The bell rang and I looked around to see all of the seats filled. Mr. Erickson cleared his throat to begin, and I inherently understood and instantaneously appreciated that this was truly the first day of my education. Certainly, I had successfully completed over a decade of schooling and of course had learned a multitude of facts, but this class was going to be *educational*. I was on the brink of learning huge things, I could just feel it, and I could not wait to dive in. As he was taking attendance by calling out our last names, I was praying I was right about him, that his class would be unlike the others and that we would be encouraged to think outside of the box for once.

I was not wrong.

"Welcome to APUSH. I'm Mr. Erickson but you can call me Mr. E. We've got quite the full class, huh? I'm glad. The more of you there are, the better the discussions we will have!" Mr. Erickson finished his introduction with an awkward giggle that ended in a small snort. I saw some of my peers roll their eyes and one girl mouth the word "cringe" to her friend across the aisle, but I felt the polar opposite. I was thrilled. I already knew that Mr. Erickson was going to be the best part of my junior year, if not my entire high school career.

"Allow me to start with a question. What do you believe my job is as a teacher? I would like for you to ponder the question for a moment before I ask you to discuss it with the people around you. Please consider the question deeply. Don't just respond with the first thing that comes to your head. Deal?" He posed the task with such enthusiasm, I could feel his infectious energy from the back of the room. After a couple seconds of silence and then a minute or so of mumbles and sounds of agreement amongst us, Mr. Erickson brought our attention to the whiteboard. He tossed markers to eight random students, six of whom caught them, one of whom let it land on the desk in front of him, and one girl who screamed and put her hands in front of her face. He then invited them to the whiteboard to write down what they believed to be the best answer to the question.

The energy in the room was starting to buzz, and I noticed that more and more students were engaging in the activity. We watched as the eight students wrote their responses in random spots on the whiteboard, and by the time they were done, we were all quietly attending to Mr. Erickson's first lesson of the year.

"Who wrote this one?" he inquired, as he pointed to the response written in blue. A timid girl in the back of the room raised her hand reluctantly, and he shot her a smile. "Nailed it." he declared. "My job as a teacher is to help you master the skill of learning *how* to think. Not *what* to think, but *how*. That is my personal philosophy regarding teaching. I hope you're up for the challenge." Heads nodded in agreement, and I even heard one student near me mutter, "This dude seems based." I grinned from ear to ear, partially in response to the comment but mostly because I knew in my bones that my first impression of this teacher was spot on.

Mr. Erickson spent the majority of that first day talking about his basic philosophies behind not just teaching, but teaching history in particular. He jumped right into the deep end and stunned us with his forward nature, ripping off the outer layers of idealism and setting the tone for a class that he avowed would quickly become controversial.

He began by talking about how all nations, including ours, have stained pasts full of shameful mistakes, but that many have tried to redeem themselves over the years. He suggested that perhaps we should not be so quick to judge such nations by their mistakes, given that the vast majority of decisions were made by an elite few rather than the masses. Unabashedly, he also admitted that morning that he periodically struggled with his decision to teach history because he was not certain how much of it was the actual truth. "History is simply the story of the victor, agreed upon by the relevant parties. Surely the truest stories have been corrupted along the way." His words were lined with sadness when he vocalized this, something that each and every one of us noticed. He paused, took a deep breath, and summoned his enthusiasm once again.

Class continued with conversation about history repeating itself, and Mr. Erickson shared with us his belief that it does so because people fail to notice patterns, and that people fail to notice patterns because we as a society are losing our ability to think. His unmistakable passion for helping youth to hone their critical thinking skills was quite admirable, and as we were about to discover, it was the inspiration for our initial assignment.

"Ready to jump into our first project? Don't worry. You'll love it!" he exclaimed. "So, tell me, what are no-no topics?"

An uncomfortable silence permeated the room. I had a strong feeling that Mr. Erickson was fully expecting that to occur, as evidenced by his choice to take a seat and wait patiently until someone broke the ice about three minutes later.

"Politics." The student who couldn't care to even attempt to catch the green marker earlier was now the bravest to be first to participate.

"Religion," a peppy girl in the front row chimed in.

"Sex," a deep voice from the back corner muttered. Laughter ensued, of course, but even over the high-pitched giggles and the macho chuckles, we could all hear the next utterance that came from the boy sitting next to the window.

"You know, it doesn't make any sense to me. We were all raised to avoid conversations about politics and religion. We are literally told not to discuss either topic during holiday dinners and stuff. I don't get that. Now we don't know the first thing about either topic, and even less about how to have hard conversations. It's stupid. Wouldn't it be better to learn, practice, and master the art of discourse? Shouldn't we be able to have respectful conversations about hard things?"

Mr. Erickson was clearly dumbfounded, and his facial expression demonstrated a mixture of disbelief, glee, and pride. "What is your name, son?" he asked, with wide eyes and a curious tone.

"Williams."

Mr. Erickson then requested the boy's first name, but he didn't seem to want to share. I assumed at the time that he thought he was about to get in trouble, but I later learned that was not at all the case.

"He goes by 'Quick' I think," the peppy girl announced, a little too eagerly.

"Well, who here agrees with Quick? I, for one, could not have said it better myself! As a matter of fact, I want to write it down." He rushed over to a writing pad on his desk. "Learn, practice, and master the art of discourse. Genius. Absolutely genius," he murmured to himself.

I wanted to tell him he could make a poster of the quote, but it sounded too facetious in my head, and the last thing I wanted was for this new icon in my life to have a poor first impression of me.

"Wow, Quick. Thank you for that sentiment." Mr. Erickson genuinely appreciated the comment and in doing so, I felt like he proved to the entire class how safe a space his room really was.

I took a moment to glance over at the boy. I was almost certain that I had caught him watching me meditate on more than one occasion. I sensed that he was watching out of curiosity, rather than judgment, so I chose to smile at him once. He quickly turned away, but I could have sworn I saw a reciprocation as he did. The tables had turned, though, as I became the curious one. Who was this profound Quick character?

Mr. Erickson ended his first class that day with a reminder of his philosophy: He was not there to teach us *what* to think. He added on to it at that point by stating that he didn't even feel it was his job to tell us what to think *about.* With that, he gave us our first homework assignment. We were to brainstorm a list of topics that we as individuals were curious about, things we had always wanted to learn or better understand, things we wished we could learn about at school.

I left that room feeling more heartened and more emboldened than ever before. Mr. Erickson was undeniably going to push me to live inspired.

Hey,

So much for me being invisible. I don't know what came over me, but for some reason I decided to speak up on the first day of my history class yesterday. I don't even know how it happened. I just started talking. And not just talking. I dropped a majorly deep thought bomb on an entire classroom and not only did everyone hear it, the teacher made a huge deal of it afterwards. He's cool though. His class seems like it will be cool, too. Like it will make me think.

For years now, I've been cynical about school. What is the point of it all anyway? They tell us that everyone "is an individual" and "learns in their own way," but yet we all have the exact same path for the first eighteen years of our lives? And that path is one that beats us into submission, killing our intrinsic motivation and destroying our imaginations. All we do is test, test, test so you can rank, rank, rank? Bells and desks and regurgitation of facts. It's not like I don't love learning. You know I do. But I don't really know what the purpose of "schooling" is, unless of course, our educational system is designed to create meek and compliant workers who will continue to perpetuate the world as we know it. To benefit the elites. Just sayin'.

But… This history class? This teacher? He seems different. Get this. For our first assignment we had to come up with topics that we want to learn about. Anything we're curious about. Seems kinda cool, right? Like I'll actually be able to dig for homework? Sign me up.

But…then today in class he had us write down our top three so he can look at our submissions and pair us up with people who have a similar interest. Ugh. I hate group projects. All good though. I only wrote down one topic and I went with the most obscure thing I could think of. Guarantee you no one else wrote down that they were curious about the science behind vibrational frequencies killing cancer cells.

Loophole! Ha ha, I win.

Love you.

-Deck

Wednesday, August 16, 2023

Note to self:

I'm beside myself! I have never been this excited about a class, or this thrilled to have a particular teacher! Mr. Erickson is so inspiring. He's a bit quirky and awkward, but it is clear as day that he is heavily invested in our learning. In our thinking!

I believe all teachers are heavily invested, though. Or at least the great majority of them. I really do. They choose to go into this line of work because they love children, knowing all the while that it is sadly underpaid/undervalued. They care about our futures, both as individuals and as a collective. But the longer I'm in school, the more I think the teachers become burdened with state standards and testing, and before they know it, there's no time left in the classroom to do the inventive and inspiring lessons they want to do. Honestly, I think that's why Mr. Erickson strikes me as a little sad. Like he's been beaten down a bit. But then I see him muster up enthusiasm, like he's picking himself up by his bootstraps and willing himself not to give up.

Today he told us about a new program he designed that he is trying for the first time. Basically, he wants to give us the opportunity to follow our own interests and to form educated opinions based on research, and then practice having civil conversations if differences of opinion arise. This is the guinea pig year for what he named REED. It stands for Ruminate, Excavate, Educate, Deliberate. I love the acronym!

We just finished the rumination stage, where we had to really think about questions and curiosities that we have. I struggled with that one. I couldn't come up with very much, but that's okay. Mr. Erickson mentioned in class today that our imaginations may be a bit rusty and that we are going to oil the gears this year. I even got a little notebook to carry with me, so when I have a curious thought, I can write it down straight away. Maybe in the hustle and bustle of life, most of our curiosities become fleeting thoughts?

Anyway, today we started the excavation part. We were assigned a partner—I'll get to that later—and we now need to research our topic, of course citing multiple sources and such. From there, we create any sort of digital presentation to share our findings with our peers. That's the education phase, when we learn from one another. Deliberation comes when there is a REED topic that naturally lends to a discussion, if there is an organic desire to debate the research among the class.

It's brilliant! There was such a buzz in the room today, too. I think we're all kind of excited. I can't even imagine all of the things I am going to be exposed to this year, how many new thoughts and interests I may have. I heard the partner pair next to me talking about nanotechnology and I have no idea what that even is! And as I was walking out, I heard someone say something about weather weapons? What the heck is that? I guess I'll find out soon enough! I need to tell Mr. Erickson how grateful I am for this opportunity. I mean, we can all do this on our own, but what teenager would?

Ok, so back to the partner part. Apparently I have to work with this boy named Quick for the next week. I was shocked when Mr. Erickson told us that we had submitted similar interest ideas. Beyond shocked. I turned in my slip that said I was intrigued by vibrational frequencies, and apparently Quick wants to learn about the possibility of healing physical ailments with vibration. So like, curing cancer with frequency lasers or something? I don't really get it. Yet. Anyway, I thought for sure I'd be working alone, but I think I still might be. Quick doesn't seem like the "group project" type. I guess we'll see how class goes tomorrow.

Super excited. (And nervous?)

...Q

Hey,

Dude. I got paired up with the meditation girl in history class.

-Deck

Quinn:

Frequencies

The first Thursday morning of my junior year, I entered Mr. Erickson's class with the most bizarre blend of conflicting feelings: excitement and reluctance, hope and doubt, eagerness and dread. I was keenly aware that I was wading into uncharted waters. Working with a stranger on a project that had the potential to really divulge some personal aspects was honestly causing me some anxiety that seemed to keep creeping up no matter how much I meditated in the previous twenty-four hours. I had no idea how this project or how my time with Quick was going to unfold, nor did I have any control over it. All I could do was try my best on my portion of the research and focus on what I wanted to learn.

Immediately after Mr. Erickson took attendance, he had us begin our partner work. Quick sauntered over to my desk and broke the ice with his very first question. His tone was casual and ambiguous. "So do you want to work together or just kinda do our own thing?" He was shuffling about when he spoke, scooching his chair and settling into his new space, and it struck me that he needed to ask that before we had ever even spoken to one another. I sensed that he was as uncertain about the upcoming experience as I was, and for some reason, knowing that he was nervous caused my conflicting emotions to reconcile. We would work well together, I could tell. I felt myself relax, and I took a deep breath to solidify my new mood.

He stopped fidgeting and looked up at me. His eyes were dark, so much so that I could barely tell where his brown irises stopped and his black pupils began. We held our gaze for a moment before I replied, "Your call," through a friendly and genuine smile. Quick seemed to study my face, taking the time to really evaluate his impression of me and his options regarding the next week of history class.

"I purposely wrote down a weird topic the other day so I could work alone. I didn't think anyone else even knew what vibrational frequencies were," He looked down and flipped open his laptop, presumably to start researching. Alone.

"Oh, okay. No problem. I can w—" I stammered. Why was I feeling disappointed?

Quick continued speaking as though he didn't pause and as though he didn't hear me. "I didn't mean weird as in lame. I think it's a cool topic and it's awesome that you are interested in it." His fingers clacked away at the keyboard while he continued his monologue. "What do you want to learn about? The potential to heal illness? We can do something else if you want. It's up to you."

He looked up at me and made eye contact before finishing his ramble with, "Your call."

He smiled.

I stopped breathing.

It wasn't because Quick was drop dead gorgeous or anything. He was handsome, yes, with clear skin, straight white teeth, a strong jawline, and floppy hair of various dark tones. Actually, he *was* gorgeous. That was not why I stopped breathing, though. When he smiled at me, a warm feeling of friendship washed over me. It was as if there was already a connection; at least that's what I felt on my end.

That night, in the peace and quiet of my own room, I was able to sit with my thoughts and really delve into my feelings. Was I crazy for thinking that he and I would be fast friends? Shouldn't I have some reservations about this stranger? Was I overthinking all of this? Yes, yes, and yes. I decided to just enjoy the project and the present moments, without needing to label the friendship or guess what it would be like one week later.

Those five days in history class zoomed by. Quick and I were both completely enthralled with resonance frequency, and the more we discovered, the more we wanted to share with one another. At one point, when watching a video about a bridge collapsing, he whooped, "What? No way!" He had no idea how loud he shouted, partially because he was wearing earbuds and partially because he literally lost himself in his research. The class erupted in laughter, jolting him back to reality, but he just smiled at me and kept scribbling words in his notebook. I completely identified with the exuberance, and he knew I did, since I had squealed a few minutes earlier when I came across evidence of resonance frequencies killing cancer cells under a microscope.

After gathering information for two class periods, we spent the third day organizing our research and planning our digital presentation. It was so refreshing to be paired with someone who also had a strong work ethic and a common vision. By the fifth day, even though neither of us wanted to be done, we had completed something that we were both proud of. As it turned out, Mr. Erickson was quite proud as well.

"I have been watching you two all week, and I must say, I am impressed. Not only did you tackle a unique and difficult topic, but you worked together to create a phenomenal project." Mr. Erickson patted Quick on the back and nodded approvingly at me as he spoke. "I'd like for you to orally present your project to the class tomorrow. Would you be willing to do that? It would be wonderful for them to see what the gold star for REED looks like."

Quick and I looked at each other. How on earth were we already communicating through our eyes? We grinned at each other, and Mr. Erickson knew that we were agreeing to share our work with the class. "Great! Thank you both. I'll have the projector set up for you and ready to go!" he exclaimed as he headed back to his desk.

It was just about time to transition to our next period, so Quick asked if he could text me that night to go over the slides. With a new feeling of nervousness, I dialed my number from his phone with fumbling fingers, all the while praying that he couldn't feel the frequency of my heart pounding in my chest.

Quick:

Wonders

Being given class time to dig? Awesome. Learning about the potential of resonance frequencies? Fascinating. Working with Quinn? Such a trip.

Quinn was an enigma. Well, not really. She wasn't a mystery at all, actually. She was an open book and probably the most authentic person I had ever met. The enigma was how she came to be so unique. She made no apologies for being exactly as she was, which was nothing like the rest of the girls at school, and I found it to be vastly refreshing. I barely learned anything about her that week, other than the way she chewed on her lip and furrowed her brow when she was concentrating, but I spent more and more time outside of class wondering about her. I wondered what she did for fun. I wondered what led her to meditation and if she meditated at home, too. I wondered if she really was friendless and how that could even be possible.

We nailed the project, so much so that Erickson had us share with the class. I was curious to see if everyone else would think our topic was as cool as we thought it was, which it seemed they did. How could they not? The microscope video alone was enough to convince anyone that frequency is fascinating. By the end of the presentation, every single one of our peers was intrigued in some way.

Erickson used our presentation as a way to pump up the crowd, so to speak. Right after Quinn and I shared our work, Erickson announced that he was sponsoring a new club after school. Since it was the first year of The REED Club, whoever joined would be considered a founder, a distinguishing inclusion for our college applications. He was also sure to tell us that the members would be able to determine all the logistics regarding meeting days and times, and that he would bring snacks to every meeting. I found it amusing that Erickson was blatantly bribing us to join. He was trying to electrify the class and get them excited about research and discovery, but I wasn't certain that our presentation or his bribes accomplished that goal. Club attendance would answer that question.

The first meeting about the club was scheduled for Tuesday of the following week after school. I decided to go, not only because this club would provide me with scheduled times to dig but because I wanted to support Erickson. I liked the guy and I respected his passion for helping to develop critical thinkers in his students.

And I wondered if Quinn would go.

Thursday, August 24, 2023

Note to self:

My junior year is off to the best start! I love, love, love my APUSH teacher and I'm finally excited to get to school each morning. Working with Quick on the REED project turned out to be pretty dang fun and I am still shocked at how well we hit it off. Not that we're friends or anything, but it was nice to interact with someone at school. He was so easygoing and nonjudgmental that I immediately felt comfortable around him. We laughed more than I expected that we would, but throughout the whole week, I kept sensing a sadness about him. Honestly, it weighed on me a little. He's distant and guarded by choice. I saw people giving him fist bumps and trying to chat with him all week, but he is totally disinterested. I don't know why it concerns me a little and I'm aware that it's crazy to worry over this fully functional stranger, but I can't help it. I feel bad for him, and I don't even know why.

Anyway, Mom is still bugging me to join a club at school, which I have been dreading… until today! When Mr. Erickson announced his after school club, I felt like the skies opened up so the universe could present me with the most beautifully wrapped gift! Maybe my mom is right and I should participate in something at school. I enjoyed the REED process and I learned a ton, so that's a plus. And a club is formed of people with similar interests, right? Maybe I will actually make a friend or two this year. No, I don't think a lot of my classmates will join. I don't even know if Quick will, now that I think about it. It's one thing to work with someone else because it's required for a class grade, but he doesn't strike me as the type to volunteer to do it. What if it's just me? What if I'm the only one who shows up at the meeting next week?

It is what it is. I'll go to the meeting and see. Maybe it'll be just me and Mr. Erickson. Or maybe I'll be pleasantly surprised. Maybe Quick will be there.

Fingers crossed.

…Q

ooo

Desiree / 8:14 p.m.

did I tell you that I have history with that quinn girl

Mandy / 8:17 p.m.

ha ha no
lucky you

8:18 p.m.

tchr had her share her work in front of the class today

8:18 p.m.

omg how embarrassing

8:19 p.m.

lol I don't think she cared

8:20 p.m.

what was her work about
wait no let me guess
the salem witch trials

8:20 p.m.

lol hilarious

8:20 p.m.

I wouldn't be surprised

8:21 p.m.

she did a project on vibrational frequencies

8:22 p.m.

what the heck is that
some ouija board crap?

8:22 p.m.

idk it's like sound waves that can cure cancer cells or something
wanna hear the best part

8:22 p.m.

yeah I guess

8:23 p.m.

she was partners with that Quick guy

the hot guy from PE last year??

yeah
and they looked super chummy

8:24 p.m.

THERE'S NO WAY

8:24 p.m.

that's what I was thinking but it's true they were jiving for sure

Monday, August 28, 2023

Note to self:

The REED Club meeting is tomorrow after school. Mr. Erickson announced it again on Friday and today, but the interest level in class seems a bit low. The more I think about it, the more I'm willing to place a bet that I will be the sole member. I'll get to be the founder, the president, the vice president, and the treasurer. Great.

Sidenote: I was very wrong to think that Quick and I might become friends, let alone fast friends. We haven't spoken since our presentation on Thursday. We haven't even made eye contact. I guess I shouldn't be surprised that he completely retreated back into his personal bubble.

Regardless, I am going to the meeting tomorrow. My heart goes out to Mr. Erickson and getting my mom off my back is a total bonus.

Sigh.

...Q

Tuesday, August 29, 2023

Note to self:

Ummmm, I got home from the meeting four hours ago and I'm still processing... First of all, I was not the only person to show up.

Quick came.

We waited for about ten minutes before Mr. Erickson broke the awkward silence. Why was it so awkward? I worked with Quick for a week straight, and I thought we were really starting to feel comfortable around each other, but apparently not. Anyway, the three of us agreed that it was probably just us in the club, and that no one else was going to show up. Mr. Erickson gave us the out, saying that we didn't have to do the club if we didn't want to, but neither Quick nor I moved a muscle. Apparently neither one of us had any intention of leaving.

Mr. Erickson told us that the club is what we make of it, to let him know if we need him for anything. And with that he walked away, leaving Quick and me alone. He spoke first, asking if we should start by brainstorming topics, which was exactly what I was thinking. After all, rumination is the initial step, and we could figure out the logistics of meetings and all that later.

I grabbed a notebook and pen to write down our ideas. I mentioned the possibility of doing a cost-benefit analysis of eating bugs for protein, as well as the option of researching the Mandela Effect, but he seemed to be hesitant to share any of his thoughts. He validated my topic suggestions with a series of "yeahs" and "good ones" but only contributed one subject idea of his own, and it was surprisingly lame: A comparison of TikTok and YouTube Shorts statistics. Really? How does the guy who researched the healing powers of vibrational frequencies now want to learn about something so mundane? It made no sense to me. I could totally tell that he was holding back and I have no clue why. Does he not really want to join the club? Does he not really want me to?

Well, whatever. I kept going. I brought up some more ideas, like lucid dreaming, but then something super weird happened.

I mentioned milk cartons, how my parents told me once, that missing children reports used to be plastered on them, and how that's changed over the decades. Quick turned completely white. He literally froze in his seat and I swear he wasn't breathing. My heart sank to the floor when I realized that I hit a nerve. A big one. I tried to cover it up right away by shooting myself down and saying how actually, now that I think about it, I don't want to do anything like that. Nothing sad that has to do with children. He was still frozen which made me so nervous that I kept talking. Why did I do that? I think I made it worse. In fact, I totally made it worse. I tried mentioning other topics having to do with children that we could put on the no-no list, but the only one I could come up with was SIDS. And I said it as soon as I thought it. And my voice cracked. And my eyes filled up with tears. I think one even got away.

Oh my gosh, it was so bad. I mean, I guess it was good that it snapped him out of his horrifying trance, but then he was staring at me as I was trying to keep myself from crying. He did not need to see my ugly cry face. Ugh.

It was weird though. He was in no rush to push past that moment that I found to be unbearable and insufferable. It was almost as though he lost track of time, like time was going in slow motion when he was sitting there staring, just studying me. I couldn't take it. When I could finally find my voice and I trusted it enough not to crack again, I totally changed the subject. I asked him why he went by the name Quick anyway. He begrudgingly muttered that it was a long story and not a really good one, so then I started filling the space with my dang babble again, this time about why the nickname was fitting. I rambled about how he was quick to debate in class, quick to ask questions, quick to learn new things. Thank goodness Mr. Erickson walked over when I was fumbling all over my running mouth. I still can't believe I did that. What is wrong with me?

Ok, for real this time. I'm putting all my money on it. This club is not getting off the ground. It was over before it even started.

...Q

Quick:

A Bogus Vow

The initial REED meeting was a disaster. A nightmare. A horror story. It was a fiasco of epic proportions. But it was also spectacular in its own way. It started out pretty great before torpedoing straight to hell, but then it bounced back in the most unexpected way.

Quinn and I were the only two to show up. In my mind, that was the best possible scenario. I didn't want to spend any afternoons with a huge group of people, and I also knew that the sanctity of the club and its purpose would be best preserved with only a few of us who were actually serious about research. Quinn and I already worked well together, which was icing on the very small cake for two.

We started out by brainstorming research topics, and that's when the meeting hopped right into a handbasket headed straight for the underworld. In five minutes flat, not only did I completely clam up when the issue of kidnapping was mentioned, but she also showed her cards when she started crying over infant deaths. As I sat there basically gawking at her, my list of things I wondered about was growing. Exponentially.

She's the reason we climbed out of hell. She tried to change the subject to something light that lacked vulnerability by asking about my nickname. Little did she know that that subject was just as touchy as the ones we escaped a moment before. Surely she sensed my unwillingness to discuss, which led her to nervously share a series of evidential opinions regarding the appropriateness of the nickname Quick.

I left that meeting not thinking about kidnappings or SIDS. Not thinking about the club or the next session. I left thinking about how Quinn revealed something that I was almost positive she regretted. All those reasons she came up with for my nickname? All that evidence? It all pointed to one very plain fact: Quinn noticed me. What I gathered from that entire awkward debacle was quite simple.

I was not the only one wondering.

That evening, I promised myself that I would be brave enough to suggest some real topics at our next meeting. It needed to happen sooner or later, so I vowed to mention the controversial things I was actually fascinated by. If it scared her away, so be it.

Deep down, though, I didn't think Quinn would be daunted and quit the club. Otherwise, I wouldn't have made the vow.

Quinn:

Sudden Liberation

The day after our initial club meeting—which I secretly dubbed, "The Day My Nervous Mouth Betrayed Me" —was a Wednesday, and I was surprised to find Quick waiting for me outside of the classroom door that morning before first period.

"Hey." He gestured with a wave and made direct eye contact to smile at me. I was utterly shocked. Did he not think yesterday's meeting was beyond a particularly uncomfortable series of incidents? I was convinced it was a train wreck, and I went to school that morning fully prepared to accept the death of the club.

"Uh, hi?" I blinked three times as I tried to avoid his gaze and ended up looking at the "Live Inspired" poster near his head.

Quick adjusted his backpack on his right shoulder, and I noticed how nondescript it was. While everyone else in the school seemed to have a minimum of seven keychains, some of which were full-blown stuffed animals dangling from the zippers and bouncing with each step against all of the patches that adorned the backpacks, his was entirely bare. Completely featureless, his navy-blue backpack was oddly enough the most unique one on campus.

"So I was thinking we could meet on Tuesdays and Thursdays. Is that cool with you? Are you good with twice a week?" There was a new and earnest sound to his voice, and he seemed genuinely zealous about moving forward with what we had started the previous day.

"Sure, sounds great. Shall we talk with Mr. Erickson after class?" I asked, to which Quick's reply was a simple nod and a smile as he opened the door for us to enter the room. Fifty minutes later, Mr. Erickson was exceptionally thrilled to learn that we wanted to meet for The REED Club twice a week, instead of just once. We also requested that he abandon his promise regarding snacks, but his smirk revealed that he would probably bring us treats in bulk. He looked at us with such pride as his face contorted into a broad smile that seemed much too large for his head. He was unmistakably delighted that he had not only found students who did not need bribes or gimmicks to start this club, but that we seemed to value its potential as much as he did.

I arrived home that day with a bit of a bounce, I suspected from edgy and anxious butterflies who suddenly resided in my stomach. Immediately removing my labradorite crystal from its designated spot on my bedroom shelf and holding it in my left hand, I meditated with the intention of enhancing inner awareness. Why was I nervous? Why was I excited? Was it the club? The potential friendship? The potential ache that comes with the demise of a friendship? Was I worried that this friendship would rise and fall as it did with Mandy? Did my nerves have anything to do with Quick at all?

That night, as I lay in my bedroom unable to fall asleep, I stared at the stars outside my window until they became blurry and started fusing together. I tried to lose myself in the noise of waves crashing, imagining that I was relaxing on a beach in Maui rather than hearing them through the sound machine that was plugged in at my bedside in the desert. Honing in on the scent of palo santo, I breathed in deeply and accepted the simple truth that my current task on the journey of self-awareness was undoubtedly going to require more than one meditation. I was a bit befuddled by my thoughts and emotions, but I also recognized that I found amusement in it all. There was no denying that this year was going to bring much newness—new people, new experiences, new ideas—and I was ready for it.

As I meandered across the campus the next afternoon, I was keenly aware of the weather. It struck me as perfect, and as I attended to it fully, I appreciated the soft breeze mingling with the warm sun. The leaves of the trees shimmered in the light and their rustling whispers provided a flawless undertone for the birds housed within, chirping their songs of gratitude for such an impeccable day. I was so grossly captivated by blessings around me that I nearly collided with a familiar navy-blue backpack, narrowly avoiding impact.

"Hi Quick, uh, it's really nice outside so I was thinking maybe we could meet out here today? Maybe on the grass or under the tree?" My words once again came bumbling out, I assumed because our encounter was unexpected.

He flashed me a toothy grin and wholeheartedly agreed, which instantaneously resulted in the simmering of my nerves. I mindfully took a few deep breaths as I followed him to the lawn, and internally reminded myself to be authentic. I just needed to be me and the rest would fall into place.

As we settled on the grass, I decided to bravely take the first conscious step to overcoming the awkward loop in which I felt stuck. "So, Quick, where are you from? Did you move here from out of town?" I was pleased to hear my own voice, calm and even, and I noticed that it was no longer betraying me. He must have sensed the difference, too, because he did not even try to conceal his dumbfounded look.

"Uh, yeah, I guess. I moved here for high school. Why do you ask?" He picked at a blade of grass as he added, "How did you know?"

"I noticed that you don't seem particularly attached to any friends here, like ones from your childhood or whatever. I don't mean that in a bad way; I hope it isn't coming out that way."

"No, you're right. I kinda keep to myself." There was that twinge of sadness in his voice again, and I instantly felt sorry for mentioning what I thought was a casual topic but realized perhaps it was not.

I knew I needed to pivot. As my brain scrambled to change the subject somehow, he quickly followed up with, "You do, too."

"Keep to myself? Yeah. Let's just say that I put all of my eggs in one basket back in the day and it backfired. Big time. But at least you're well-liked. That's awesome." I smiled at him so he would know that I meant it genuinely, that my tone was absent of any snarkiness or judgment. He looked up at me, once again making me feel like he was studying something about me, like he was regarding me as a puzzle he needed to solve.

After several moments of silence, Quick shared through a mutter, "I'm from the next town over."

"Oh, that close? Was it hard to move schools?" There I went again, deep diving into the uncomfortable topics. It was like I couldn't help myself. I didn't know how to spend time in the shallow end.

Quick set his gaze back upon the blades he was slaughtering. "Eh, it was fine. My folks thought it was the right time, in between junior high and high school."

"Oh, so you're an only child?" I was very curious about him, and I found myself wanting to learn more about this mysterious introvert, especially if we were going to be spending so much time together.

"Yeah, kinda," he sighed. Quick then proceeded to flick off his shoes without untying the laces and tossed his bundled-up socks right next to them. Now it was I who was completely dumbfounded. I didn't know if I was more shocked, appalled, disgusted, perplexed, curious, or humored. I could not help but stare as he buried his feet in the long grass, nestling them in until they were no longer visible.

"Are you grounding right now?" I asked, probably with a little too much enthusiasm in my voice.

"What?" He looked at me quizzically, like I had spoken to him in a foreign language.

"Grounding. Earthing. Like, connecting with the earth. Never m—" My statement was abruptly halted by the eruption of maniacal laughter bursting from Quick's face. His entire body convulsed from the hysterics and he flopped backwards onto the grass, clutching his stomach with one hand and slapping the ground with the other. A smile stretched across my face as I watched the ridiculous scene unfold, and strangely, I felt a solid truth in my core: There was no contempt or disparagement to Quick's outburst, and I was not the least bit offended by it. Before I knew it, I too was overtaken by an overwhelming fit of giggles. It felt so good to let go like that, to release any tensions through that type of uncontrollable reaction. It was liberating.

I did not fully understand why I suddenly started laughing in the first place, but I absolutely knew exactly why I stopped.

Quick pointed at something over my left shoulder as his eyes seemed to dart about. "Hey, look! There's a dragonfly…"

ㅇㅇㅇ

Quick / 7:19 p.m.

hey

Quinn / 7:25 p.m.

Hello.

7:25 p.m.

sorry we didn't get anything accomplished at the meeting today
I even had some ideas for our brainstorm list

7:25 p.m.

That's okay. It was nice to sit outside if nothing else.

7:27 p.m.

yeah
I hope you know I wasn't laughing at you

7:28 p.m.

I do, but thank you for saying that.

7:34 p.m.

anyway, sorry I got weird there for a minute
guess I wasn't expecting the questions

7:35 p.m.

No, I'm sorry. I didn't mean to pry or make you uncomfortable.
I think we have something in common, by the way.

7:35 p.m.

oh yeah? what's that?
you like to ground too? ha ha

7:36 p.m.

I'm a non-only child, too.

8:12 p.m.

how did you know?

8:13 p.m.

I have the same moments of sadness that I've seen on your face,
where you suddenly remember and then feel guilty for having a minute when you forgot.

Through Quick and Quinn

yeah it sucks

8:16 p.m.

I'm so sorry, Quick.

9:43 p.m.

me too

08/31/23

3:08 a.m.

I open my eyes through a series of confused blinks and begin to take in the scene around me. I am lying on a small bed and there are two uniformed strangers in the room. Medical posters are pinned up on the wall, and I can hear a phone ringing in the background. I grunt as I try to lift my head to find something familiar, something that will help this make sense.

One of the strangers hears me shuffle and she makes her way towards me. "Hi sweetie, my name is KT. How are you feeling?" she softly asks as she sits down in a nearby chair.

"Where's my mom and dad?" I can hear my voice quivering, and a feeling of nausea washes over me.

KT offers me a cup of water but I refuse to take it. I ask the question again, this time more loudly. She tries to reassure me with shushing noises and pats on my hand. "Sweetie, your parents are okay and they know you're here. You lost consciousness, so we—"

My memory comes back to me and I suddenly feel like I am drowning in a tidal wave of terror. I scream for Geoffrey and for my parents, and the sobs only stop when I fall off the bed and my head slams against the floor.

Quick:

No Going Back

We kicked off our third club meeting with a goal: to decide upon a topic to research. Quinn said she came equipped with some ideas, and I promised myself to toss my true interests into the ring.

I let her start. I had to. She seemed to be on the verge of bursting.

"Did you know that approximately 17 percent of people who nearly die report having a near-death experience? Millions of people around the world attest to having one, and there are apparently several parallels among the accounts provided, regardless of country, culture, age, or whatever other factors. I'm totally fascinated!" She seemed to be exploding and I couldn't help but smile. Her enthusiasm was contagious.

Quinn added two more topics to the brainstorm list: the lost city of Atlantis and the mystery surrounding Amelia Earhart. I was impressed. My club partner was intrigued by topics that I deemed quite worthy of a REED project.

"Ok, your turn! What burning questions do you have? I figure we'll write them all down, and then we'll have a large pool to pull from for the rest of the year. Sound good?" Quinn beamed.

"No, I really like your ideas. All of them. Let's decide on one of those," I responded. I didn't want to offer up my ideas. What if they distracted her from her own? Or what if she felt obligated to use one of mine? Quinn struck me as the type of person who would put someone else's preferences first.

"What? No. No way! You have to share your topics. That's the deal, Quick." She tried to use her best firm voice, and it took all my effort not to chuckle at how soft her 'tough girl' act was. I didn't want to make a habit of seeming to laugh at her when she talked.

I tried to tell her that I really didn't have much to contribute, that I would keep thinking for next time, but she wasn't having it. Without saying another word, she decided to make a huge display of closing her notebook, clicking off her pen, planting it on the table, and crossing her arms.

Two minutes.

That was how long it took for her to break me.

"Fine. Ok. I will give three ideas, too. Happy?" I smiled at her, in sheepish admission that she won. New twinkles appeared in Quinn's eyes and her grin was winsome, radiant, and infectious. She flipped open her book, pen in hand and ready, and looked at me with eager wonderment.

I sighed. "Here goes nothing," I thought to myself. I looked down at my hands, cracked my knuckles, and started bouncing my right knee, all clear signs that I was a little nervous to reveal myself in this way. Other than in my letters, I had never let anyone in on my digs.

I took a deep breath and exhaled a huge mouthful of words in about four seconds flat. "I'd be interested to find out the real truth behind the Titanic sinking, who really killed JFK in '63 because I'm pretty sure it was the CIA, and what the heck is in those damn chemtrails they're spraying in our skies." There. I had done it. There was no going back at that point. I forced my eyes to focus back on her face, and what I saw made my stomach drop. She looked appalled. Horrified. Distressed. I was pretty sure I just made her blood run cold. Was she offended? Disgusted? Her countenance made my level of regret escalate, and fast.

I felt like an absolute idiot. Not only for voicing my thoughts, but for having them at all. It was the first time I ever wished that I never grabbed a shovel, never dug a rabbit hole, and never jumped in it. It was a bizarre feeling. But it was also quite fleeting, because as soon as I processed what this new sentiment was, Quinn softly broke the silence.

"You, Quick, are the most fascinating person I have ever met."

Hey,

Wow. Today was a first. If someone had told me a year ago, or even a month ago, that I would meditate on the quad at school, I would have laughed in his face. Well, here I am. The guy who did just that. Right there on the lawn in the middle of campus.

I left my hat in English class so I swung by after school to grab it, and who do I run into? None other than Quinn. I see her every day in History, I catch a glimpse of her at lunch times, and of course we see plenty of each other on Tuesdays and Thursdays, but I did a double take today when I saw her. Wasn't expecting to run into her, I guess.

We made small talk for a couple minutes, which by the way I am so glad we're getting past the awkward phase. It takes us less and less time to break the ice with each encounter, so that's good. Anyway, we chatted about my hat and history class and the fact that she was so glad we picked the REED topic that we did. She said she started researching chemtrails, which governments around the world have already admitted to using, and the reasons they've given for doing so. At first I felt bad when we ended up picking one of my suggestions, but I let it be her call and, to be fair, she really is excited about it.

So as we were leaving the building, she asked what I was doing after school. I told her that I didn't have a lot of homework and that since the weather was nice, I might go for a walk or something. She then told me that her favorite thing to do in great weather is meditate and asked me if I have ever done so before. I told her that I hadn't, and she asked me if I wanted to "give it a go" with a short fifteen-minute session. I think the words came out of her mouth before she even realized it.

I guess I hesitated a little too long because she started to retract her invitation, so I cut her off and said that I could give it a try. That was when she got quiet, probably because she was shocked. I told her not to look so surprised, and that I had done a dig on the benefits of mindfulness and meditation practice. She goes, "Oh yeah?" in this playful voice, so then I really decided to stun her.

I started mild. I rattled off some basic benefits that are pretty common sense. You know, like how mindfulness helps people to improve their social-emotional intelligence and has been shown to lessen stress, anxiety, and depression. I think I also threw in there that it helps with better sleep and concentration, too. I then took it up a notch and told her about some of the physical benefits of meditation, like how some studies show it helps to regulate the immune system, reduce inflammation, and calm the fight-or-flight response.

When I tell you that her mouth hit the floor, I'm not exaggerating. Ok, maybe a little. But she was legitimately astounded.

So we headed toward the quad where there's a big grassy area in the sunshine. When we sat down, I got kinda weird. I was uncomfortable and had no idea how this was going to go. She totally picked up on it, and she said something that was completely out of left field but was also uber profound. She goes, "You know, Quick. Your attitude entering a situation greatly affects your experience and the outcomes thereof." She let the words kinda hang there for a minute or so as I processed them, and I got where she was coming from. I took a deep breath, told myself to have an open mind, and nodded at her. And then we started.

She told me to relax in whatever way I wanted. To sit or to lie down, and to have my eyes open or closed. I chose the second option for both. She told me that like all things, meditation takes practice, and that I would probably not have a tame mind which was okay. To just try to focus on my deep breaths, counting them if I wanted to, and to let all my other thoughts float by like clouds in my mind's sky. I was nervous. Nervous that if I was still and quiet for too long, I'd be thinking about you. So I counted my breaths. I kept losing track and starting over from one, and was slightly disappointed when the highest number of breaths I could count without losing track and attention was only seven. What the heck.

After a few minutes of breathing, she told me to try to focus on the sounds I could hear, to heighten that sense. I think that was my favorite part. I've never really paid attention to birdsong before, even though I read that listening to singing birds can calm the nervous system. Birds chirp when there are no predators around, so their songs send a safety signal to our nervous system. Makes total sense now. I loved the harmonies of the birds, but I also paid attention to the oak tree leaves, the distant cars, and the nearby neighborhood's dogs barking.

Before I knew it, she was telling me to gently open my eyes and to slowly sit up when I felt ready. I couldn't believe fifteen minutes had passed and asked her if we really did go for that long. Her smile told me that it had, and weirdly expressed some sort of pride for what had just happened.

I still can't believe how relaxed I felt. I really enjoyed it. Like, a lot. And I wanted to thank her, but I didn't really know what to say.

She's such a trip.

Anyway, miss you. You're the reason I couldn't get past seven.

-Deck

○○○

Quick / 8:55 p.m.

hey

Quinn / 9:01 p.m.

Hi there.

9:01 p.m.

just wanted to tell you that you were right

9:02 p.m.

I love hearing that, lol.
But what was I right about?

9:02 p.m.

you know, your life lesson thing

9:02 p.m.

And what life lesson was that exactly?

9:02 p.m.

that whole attitude entering a situation thing

9:03 p.m.

Oh. Well, I don't know if that qualifies as a life lesson, but thank you.
Does that mean that you enjoyed the meditation today?

9:03 p.m.

I did thanks

9:04 p.m.

Oh my gosh, yey! I'm glad you did!
Thank you for trusting me to do that. I get that it can be awkward.

9:05 p.m.

yeah, but your life lesson comment was a good way to start it off.
you know, like to have an open mind. it helped.

9:05 p.m.

That makes me really happy, Quick.
Thank you.

_9:06 p.m._

thanks
see ya

_9:06 p.m._

Good night, Quick.

Tuesday, September 26, 2023

Note to self:

Okay, so I have become completely obsessed with researching chemtrails these last couple weeks, right? Quick and I have divided up the subtopics and we're both making progress at club, but I've also been digging in my spare time at home. Well, tonight it came up at dinner with Mom and Dad and while I've never thought about how it would go if I did tell them about it, I would have never expected it to go the way it did.

Until today, all they really knew about the club was that it was in its pilot phase and that because I joined at the start, I am officially a founder. That of course thrilled my mother to no end and she couldn't stop talking about how it was such an amazing thing to put on my resume. They also knew that it started with only two people, but they never really followed up to see if the club had grown or anything like that.

So tonight we're sitting there at the table and my dad brings up The REED Club by asking how it's going. I told them that I was thoroughly enjoying it and that I didn't anticipate learning as much as I did. They both commented on how that was great and then my dad asked what topic I was currently researching. As soon as I told them, my mom made zero attempt to hide the dubious reaction that was painted all over her face. I continued to tell them about the admissions already made by particular nations and all that, and my mom interrupts me with, "Oh honey, be careful. You are starting to sound like a crazy conspiracy theorist." And, per her usual, she followed her nonchalant bombshell with a sudden need to depart the table in a calm and collected manner, this time to load our cups into the dishwasher.

I took a deep breath and tried not to get defensive. I am not going to let noise from my mom taint what I'm doing or how I'm feeling about it. I excused myself from the table and did something I had never done before. I called Quick.

He picked up on the second ring and sounded completely taken aback. I can't blame him. No one actually talks on the phone these days, especially not us. Anyway, I told him that my mom called me a conspiracy theorist and he chuckled a bit before asking me how that term made me feel. I was like,

"I don't know, how does it make you feel?" I hate to admit, it came out a little snotty. Looking back, I probably should not have called him when it was all still fresh. Oh well.

I wasn't expecting him to answer my rhetorical question, and I certainly wasn't expecting the answer he gave. He said it made him feel proud. He then went on to explain what he believed the origin of the term "conspiracy theorist" was, and that it became widely used by politicians and the like to ridicule dissenters or devalue accusatory statements. He said he would be proud to be called a conspiracy theorist, or a CT as he called it, because CT could also stand for critical thinker. And if I know anything about Quick, it's that he prides himself on asking questions and finding his own answers.

I appreciated what he said and I wanted to process it a bit more, so I thanked him and ended the conversation. That boy really makes me think.

So here I am thinking.

I'm thinking so much that my mind is now a swirl of revelations, and I need to write them down to sort them out and settle my head.

Okay, let's start with this. What is research anyway? It isn't simply looking something up. Like when I dig on chemtrails, I am juxtaposing information from multiple sources, and they're all sources that I think are reliable and valid (hopefully). Research isn't just fact-finding. There's a level of discernment that goes with it. And like Quick mentioned last week with his meditation, you have to have an open mind. That is crucial with research. You can't start researching something with your mind already made up; then all you would want to find would be "facts" that confirm your bias. Bottom line then: Research is fact-finding through open-minded gathering of information from multiple valid sources, without inserting our own emotions or opinions into the process.

Okay, so why research? It shouldn't be to prove an opinion or to prove that you're right. It should be to seek truth. Honestly, isn't that the only reason? Shouldn't we all want the truth? Like with chemtrails, I want the truth. I want to know the absolute truth. And as hard as some of it is to swallow, and as disgusted as I am sometimes to unearth certain truths, isn't that still what I want? What I deserve?

I understand that not everyone is going to feel this way or want to spend their free time researching or whatever. I get that. But I shouldn't be discouraged from doing it for myself, and Quick is totally right: People use the term "conspiracy theorist" to shame others and to dissuade them from digging. Oh my gosh, that is such crap! He's totally right. It seems so obvious now!

You know what? I am proud. My mom can call me whatever she wants. It doesn't matter. It doesn't change the truth or what I know of it. Phew. I feel so much better. I think I'll go soak in a lavender bath and relax a bit before bed. My head is still swirling with thoughts, but not really about research. Honestly, I keep having the same nagging thought for the last two weeks.

Why did Quick do a dig on mindfulness and meditation?

...Q

Hey,

Had lunch with Quinn today. I joined her on the quad and brought a bunch of snacks from Mr. E's stash since we never really eat any at club. I felt kinda bad, like I was stopping her from meditating, but she kept saying it was okay and that she wanted me to sit with her. So I did.

It was cool. We chatted about lots of random stuff, like music and movies, and I realized afterwards that we didn't talk about club once.

I know you're probably thinking this is some kind of love story, but it's not. I realized lately that I have literally gone an entire day without speaking a word to anyone. More than once. That can't be good. And I have to admit that I enjoy spending time with her. She's quirky and she's different. She's easy to talk to. And she keeps it interesting because I never know what to expect with her.

Am I attracted to her? I guess I could be. She's smart and she's witty and she does have beautiful eyes. But it's not like that. I'm honestly just happy to have a friend. Someone to spend time with without any pressures or expectations. It's easy and I can see now that I was missing the element of human contact in my life.

So yeah, I guess I have a new friend. It's weird though. Sometimes I view her more as a riddle. Like something I'm trying to figure out or to solve. Like a real-life dig. There's more to her than meets the eye, I can tell. Like I said, she keeps life interesting.

She probably thinks I'm a bit of a riddle too, though. Like today, she told me she was going to try making homemade churros and asked me if I wanted her to bring me one tomorrow. I'm sure she thought my "NO!" response was way over the top. Hence, a riddle.

I feel lighter. Maybe a little happy? I don't know. I feel guilty about it, but I know you'd tell me not to.

Love you.

-Deck

○○○

Mandy / 4:17 p.m.

omg you won't believe what I just saw!!!

Desiree / 4:20 p.m.

what??

4:20 p.m.

that guy quick omg I can't

4:21 p.m.

what about him??

4:21 p.m.

HE WAS WALKING THE WITCH HOME!!!

4:22 p.m.

whaaaaaaaaaaaaaatttttttttttttttt

4:22 p.m.

ikr!!
so I totally followed them and was trying to listen to what they were talking about

4:23 p.m.

AND??

4:23 p.m.

I can't
I'm gonna throw up

4:24 p.m.

omg mandy just tell me!!!
did they kiss or what?!?!

4:24 p.m.

no ewwww gross omg do you think they do that

4:24 p.m.

MANDY

4:25 p.m.

oh right sorry
get this they made plans to go hiking this weekend

4:25 p.m.

NO WAY

4:25 p.m.

what the heck does he even see in her
so gross

4:26 p.m.

aaaw I think it's kinda cute actually

4:26 p.m.

UMMMMM NO!!!

Note to self:

I came straight upstairs after school today because I need to better understand the cluster of emotions I am currently experiencing. Since I was feeling a bit anxious, I grabbed my black tourmaline crystal to help me feel safe, calm, and grounded. Not only that, but I needed to have a good grasp on what is happening before talking to my parents about any of it.

Quick and I have been working together for about a month and a half now, and without much effort from either of us, a natural friendship has blossomed. It isn't surprising, given that we have so much in common. On the surface, we are both on the introverted side and prefer to blend into the background. Our similarities run a smidge deeper when we get into the fact that we both love "excavating" information, as Mr. Erickson would call it, but even deeper than that is our unspoken commonality of being non-only children. So, yes, it makes perfect sense that we've somewhat become friends.

It is completely normal for a fresh friendship to encounter new aspects as it develops: swapping contact information, texting each other, having lunch together, etc. While it was awkward for a bit, and sometimes still is, none of these events really rattled me.

And then today happened.

Quick was waiting for me at the gate when I was leaving school this afternoon and he asked if he could walk me home. I think I mentioned to him at one point that I live about a half mile from the school, so it didn't really weird me out. It's not like I thought he was stalking me or anything.

We ended up having a nice stroll where we mostly talked about favorite meals and foods, but when we got to my house, Quick asked me if I wanted to do something with him over the weekend. I thought about how I enjoy spending time with him, and how long and boring weekends can be sometimes, so I agreed. We decided to go for another walk tomorrow morning along the trails behind my house. Apparently they lead to some cool recreational area. How did I not know this?

Fast forward through my black tourmaline session of deep breaths to the point where I tell my parents.

I headed downstairs and noticed Mom in the kitchen, prepping dinner while listening to an audiobook. Before she would notice me, I headed towards Dad's office to chat with him instead. I knew he'd be easier for me to talk to. And if Mom got upset that I didn't go to her, I could use her noise-canceling headphones as an excuse.

Dad, as always, greeted me with a genuine smile and asked me how my day was. We chatted for a minute before I told him that I made plans with a friend to go walking tomorrow morning. I could see the surprise, but also the relief and the elation on his face. I'm sure my parents have worried about my preference for isolation over the last couple of years, so his reaction was understandable. He gestured for me to sit down on the small couch beside his desk, clearly wanting to hear every single detail I would be willing to share. The first thing he said was, "So tell me, honey, what's her name and how did you two become friends?"

I smiled at him as I tackled the second question. I mentioned history class, our first REED project, and our current bond as the only two members of the club. Dad was like a tail-wagging puppy, complete with perked ears, a nodding head, and a playful grin. I couldn't help but grin right back. Gosh, I love my dad.

Well, then I said that "he" would be swinging by at ten the next morning and we would leave from here, given the location of the trails. I saw the gears turning, I saw my dad's face fall for a split second, and then I saw his decision to play it cool. So he did. And I knew I was right to tell him first, especially when he told me that we should tell my mom together, rather than me alone.

Needless to say, Mom freaked out a bit. She kept asking things like, "Who is this boy?" and "What are his intentions with you?" and other crazy mom questions like that. I maintained my calm composure, refusing to let her energy affect mine, and I kept reassuring her that we are merely friends. After a few minutes, my dad pulled her aside and I could hear the hoarse whispers about how I was finally making a friend, how they needed to trust me, and how I've never done anything not to deserve that trust. My heart swelled with gratitude. I realized tonight how much my parents love me. As much as my mom's reaction wasn't my favorite, I know it came from a good place, just like my dad's did.

I waited patiently, rooted to my spot, for them to finish their secretive, yet obvious, conversation. They walked back over and sandwich-hugged me without saying a word. I'm not going to lie; I got choked up. It was a beautiful moment, and one we should have more often. With her face nestled in my hair, Mom kindly stated her one condition: He must come to the door tomorrow to meet them.

That condition sits perfectly fine with me. Let them see that this is purely platonic. And I don't really get embarrassed by much, so I have no problem with Quick meeting my folks.

But something is still unsettled in my stomach. The question of the day, the reason I am journaling, the last piece I am trying to figure out...

Am I a little anxious about the recent happenings because I'm wary of a new friendship? Skeptical and cautious because of my last one?

Or is it because Quick is a guy?

...Q

Quick:

Chortle and Charm

Quinn texted me the night before our little adventure on the trails. I didn't know if it was to warn me or what, but she said that I needed to come to the door to meet her parents before we left. I was already planning on knocking, but I hadn't really thought about the parent part. I figured it would be fine.

I woke up early that Saturday morning, much to my dad's surprise. I told him I was going for a hike and I needed to prepare some things, which seemed to keep his questions or curiosities at bay. I grabbed some water bottles and shoved them in my backpack, which already held a picnic blanket and a deck of cards. When I pulled out two brown lunch bags, though, and it was clear that I was packing double the sandwiches and double the snacks, he couldn't help himself. He asked who I was going with, and I replied, "Just a buddy of mine from school." And that was that. My dad stopped prying, probably because he knew that was all he was going to get out of me anyway.

I headed out around 9:45, figuring the ten-minute walk to Quinn's house would land me there at the right time. Not too early. Not late.

Knock. KnockKnock. Funny how my stomach flipped to the same rhythm of the knocks. Flip. FlipFlip. I realized I was nervous at the exact moment that the three of them answered the door together. Quinn, her mom, and her dad. Altogether, three faces shoved in front of mine simultaneously.

Her dad was first to speak, inviting me in after shaking my hand. The four of us stood awkwardly in the entryway while we exchanged handshakes and hellos.

"Hi, I'm Tate, Quinn's dad. I hear you go by the name Quick, is that right?" Again, her dad was the one to initiate a friendly exchange, while his wife stood there and glared at me. To her credit, she was at least trying to mask the scowl with a smile, though it was crystal clear that it was literally pain-ing her facial muscles to do so.

Then she spoke up. "What kind of name is Quick? What is your real name anyway?"

Quinn gasped, probably taken aback by the uncouth nature and tone of her mother's questions. I tried to soften the moment with a little chortle. I agreed that it was a silly nickname and explained that the name was given to me in junior high and, against my wishes, it stuck. Apparently my charm worked, because I was able to avoid the second question and before I knew it, Quinn's dad was telling us to have a nice time, to be safe, and to please be home before dark.

Before the front door closed behind us, Quinn was already apologizing. I told her not to worry about it, and that her parents have every right to show concern for their daughter. The corners of her mouth made their way north, and she silently nodded at me to signal that she would release what hap-pened and let it go. I'm glad she did, because I wanted to have a carefree, chill day with my new friend. And that's exactly what I got. For the most part.

Quinn:

Seen and Certain

My alarm sounded at eight o'clock that Saturday morning, but I didn't need the typical chirping of crickets to wake me. I had already watched the sun peek over the horizon nearly two hours before, allowing the fresh light through my bedroom window to awaken my mind, body, and soul the way God intended. Sprawled out on my bed and in the comfort of my myriad cozy pillows, I welcomed the day with utter relaxation and total tranquility. While I had no idea what the day would bring, I understood that serenity came with surrender. By the time I floated out of bed, I was mentally prepared for whatever the universe had in store for me that day.

I chose to listen to the Solfeggio frequency of 639 hertz as I readied myself for the upcoming escapade. I thought carefully about what clothing would best suit a day of mild hiking, packed extra water and electrolyte packets for hydration purposes, and even threw some gloves and trash bags into my backpack in case the universe wanted us to encounter an area in need of garbage removal.

My parents and I greeted Quick at the door and upon seeing his face, I realized how much I was looking forward to our day. After a bizarre exchange with my mother, which Quick masterfully handled with grace and courtesy, we walked out of the house and towards a new level of friendship.

Just a two-minute walk from my home was the start of a trail that I hated to admit I never noticed. A clear path of decomposed granite was lined with a variety of desert rocks, meandering through the landscape of cacti, yucca, succulents, and acacia. The beauty of the desert was never lost on me, and that day was no different. If anything, I appreciated the scenery against the backdrop of our mountains more than ever.

With the curves of the trail came an assortment of questions and answers, stories and factoids. Quick and I found ourselves in effortless conversation, sharing with natural ease and pausing only to drink a bit of water or to remove a pebble from a shoe.

As we neared the recreational area, we simultaneously noticed a huge uptick in litter on the ground. Quick was obviously irritated and commented about how he would never be able to understand the selfish laziness of someone who leaves trash behind. I voiced my agreement but my grin was sending a different message, one that must have really confused him.

"What's with the sneaky smile, then, huh? If it bugs you so much, why do you look so thrilled?" He laughed as he posed the questions.

I reached into my backpack and grabbed two trash bags. "Tada!" I sang. I used the bags as props in an impromptu ribbon dance and frolicked about in some sort of odd figure eight.

"You brought trash bags?!"

"And gloves, too!" I giggled as I tossed him a set. I could see a wave of disappointment flash across his face as he admitted that he wished he thought of it himself.

We expected to pick up such things like used napkins and straw wrappers, but we simply could not wrap our heads around finding one pant leg and a tennis racket with all of the strings removed. Consequently, we made a game of it, noting the strangest items we found and weaving them together to create a murder mystery story. Laughter ensued, and before we knew it, we each filled two bags, effectively using up our supplies. We tied them up and placed them by the park's large cans. The sheer satisfaction that came with that check mark was undeniable.

I took a deep breath and was about to ask what was next on our agenda when I heard a distant waterfall. Quick tuned in as well, and through an unspoken agreement, we followed our ears to a simple but stunning scene tucked under low-hanging canopies of leaves.

"Wow," he reflected, as he took in the sight of the water glimmering from the sun's rays that snuck past the trees. "It's like an oasis." The word made my heart skip, and I felt a warmth in my soul that I had been missing for far too long. It was nothing like my oasis; there wasn't a garden or a swimming pool, a sandbox or a grassy patch. But it was spectacular in its own right, and my ability to think about this without breaking down into tears really illustrated the growth and healing I had accomplished over the years.

Both in awe of our surroundings and knowing we had discovered a hidden gem, we spent no time deliberating where we wanted to spend the remainder of our afternoon. Quick retrieved a picnic blanket from his bag, flipped it open with a large wave, and placed it gently under the acacia tree. He hopped to a seat, patted the space next to his with his open palm, and asked, "So, are you hungry yet or do you want to play some cards?"

"Cards? As in, like, Go Fish, War, and Poker?" I suddenly found the scene absolutely hilarious and erupted in a fit of giggles. "We really thought of everything, huh? Between the trash bags and the cards… We are recreational area experts!" I plopped down next to him as my laughter subsided and grabbed the deck of cards. After impressing him with my shuffling skills, he beat me in three consecutive games of War.

Teasingly, Quick asserted that I had taken enough of a beating and that it was time to eat lunch. He had mentioned the day before that he would bring food, but I was astonished to see how thoughtful and thorough he was. Not only did he bring homemade sandwiches, a variety of snacks, and cubed watermelon, he even remembered to pack napkins and utensils. The gracious consideration he put into our lunch was humbling and I felt truly honored. I told him as such, and he merely smiled.

We ate in comfortable silence, relishing in the majestic space and the flawless weather. Upon chewing the last bite of my delectable sandwich, and without even really pondering the words I was about to release, I simply stated a very apparent truth aloud: "Today was the most fun I've had in an extremely long time, Quick. Thank you." And with that, a raw conversation began, one that became a defining moment in the evolution of our friendship.

I admitted to him that he was the first friend I had made in years, to which he surprised me with his response. "Yeah, I heard about the witch thing. That sucks, Quinn. I'm sorry. Where did that even come from?" Shrugging my shoulders, I divulged that it probably came from my crystals collection and my inner work with chakras, but that I didn't really know exactly what triggered the rumor about me being a witch. I mentioned Mandy and that she was probably hurt by the sudden change in our friendship, not to mention that she thought my avocation was beyond strange.

"Human nature is to fear what we do not understand, so I get why she was uncomfortable. Maybe it was the perfect storm, you know? I was having, uh, a hard time of things which I think caused the slow dissolution of our friendship, and then there was the hurt or anger she was feeling, and the uneasiness she felt about my new interests… It makes sense that she lashed out."

"Did it bother you?" Quick's eyes were set on mine, concentrating on my disclosure with his full attention.

"At first, yeah. It was a rough summer that year, but I pushed through it. I dedicated myself to reflection, meditation, and healing. It took me a long time to realize that other people's truths are not my responsibility. I can't control what they are going to think, and at the end of the day, I just need to be good with who I am. I don't need to be liked by everyone. Just the right ones. I don't need to collect a bunch of empty and shallow friendships. Just the right ones. Does that make sense?" The words poured from my mouth so effortlessly, and I had no qualms about allowing myself to be vulnerable with Quick. "I will be understood by the right people at the right times throughout my journey. I trust in that, and it gives me comfort, you know?"

Quick let my words simmer in the atmosphere for a moment. He never seemed to be in a rush, especially when it came to conversation. I appreciated that when he spoke, he did so with contemplation and intention. "You are understood, Quinn. I understand you."

The sentiment was so sincere that it pierced straight through to my heart. I gave him the most grateful of smiles but amicably countered, "I'm not sure you do quite yet, kind sir, but perhaps one day. You still have much to learn of me."

"Ok, well then, I see you. How's that? Better?" he winked.

I blushed. That was the physical response he was able to see. Luckily, the heart-stopping sensation was one I could keep to myself.

Perhaps because so much was communicated, both verbally and non, we quietly immersed ourselves in the nibbling of watermelon and the munching of crackers. I found it amazing how quickly the two of us passed the stage of awkward presence around one another, not to mention how swiftly we arrived at the stage of comfortable stillness. It was refreshing that neither of us felt the need to fill the space with unnecessary statements.

After quite some time and probably some inner deliberation, Quick cleared his throat. "Quinn, may I ask you something else?" I nodded, signaling him to continue. "The hard time you mentioned earlier... Was that somehow related to you being a non-only?"

My eyes instantly answered for me as they wistfully filled with tears. I didn't blink, for fear that the tears would fall.

"I'm sorry, Quinn," he said softly. As I looked at Quick, I could easily recognize that my eyes weren't the only ones struggling to remain dry.

I took a deep breath and steadied myself. "Yeah, my brother Troy died when he was three months old. I was eight." I dropped my gaze and let my head hang. We both silently understood that I was done sharing for the day. I closed my eyes and tried to redirect my focus to the present moment: the trickling water, the sun-kissed patches of warmth on my skin, the awareness of a profound leap in friendship. Respecting the moment, Quick quietly busied himself with packing up the food. When I could sense that he was nearly finished, I opened my eyes only to find him staring directly at me. His face looked different. It looked pained. And panicked.

"I gotta get back," he stated matter-of-factly, gesturing for me to give him access to the picnic blanket below me. I watched him as he rushed to bundle up the blanket in a messy heap, a far cry from the way it was folded an hour before. He was fidgety and seemed so unsettled; it was actually quite difficult to watch.

I did not push him to talk on the walk back home. He had respected my space, and I wanted to do the same. In no way was I worried that I upset him, nor was I taking his sudden mood shift personally. I already trusted our friendship enough to know that what was bothering him had nothing to do with me. Figuring that the topic of being a non-only was a trigger for him, I felt his pain in my bones. I knew he was hurting, and during that wordless walk home I noted that if I was lucky, I just might be able to witness his growth through that pain. He was definitely *feeling*, but I wasn't sure if he was *dealing*.

He had yet to heal. Of that I was certain.

Hey,

My friendship with Quinn leveled up today. No, not like that.

What started out as a friendly stroll and a picnic turned into a soul-baring session of trust and vulnerability. It's strange... I didn't see it coming, but now that it's happened, it seems so obvious that it would. I think that's called a "black swan event." Anyway, I had this weird epiphany on the walk back today. So many girls try too hard to be different, to be noticed, and to be envied by others in this bizarre, unspoken competition that is the high school scene. What they don't see, though, is that none of them stand out because they all end up looking the same, sounding the same, behaving the same.

But not Quinn. She is literally the textbook definition of authentic. She's so real and after spending the day with her, I can see that she doesn't have a superficial cell in her body. I don't think she is capable of shallow conversation, even when talking about nonsense like movies or whatever, and I definitely don't think she's capable of shallow friendships. Everything about her exudes that attitude of, "Here I am as I am. Take it or leave it." It's admirable and, at times, exhilarating.

I know what makes her different. I know what rocked her entire world and shaped her into who she is today. It was her brother, Troy. She lost her little brother when she was eight. She barely told me anything about him or what happened, but I could feel the suffering when she shared with me. The pain was pounding throughout my body like Taiko drums, and it took everything I had not to crack.

I almost broke down in tears.

I almost told her about you.

I should tell her.

But how? Just writing to you now, I'm sobbing hysterically. God, I would give anything to have you back, even for only one more day. I miss you so damn much.

Maybe telling her will help somehow?

I'll think about it.

Love you.

-Deck

○○○

Quick / 11:25 a.m.

hey

Quinn / 12:01 p.m.

Hi Quick, how are you?

12:01 p.m.

good
I had fun yesterday

12:02 p.m.

I did, too! Thank you for inviting me.

12:07 p.m.

yeah of course
sorry if it got a little too deep for you there, didn't mean to pry

12:08 p.m.

No, not at all. I chose to share.

12:09 p.m.

cool
so I've got a business idea for you

12:10 p.m.

Oh really? And what would that be?
This should be interesting...

12:10 p.m.

you publish some pamphlets or something
call it Quinn's Life Lessons

12:11 p.m.

LOL! What?!

12:11 p.m.

I'm serious, you say wise things
like profound things

12:12 p.m.

Are you still talking about the entering attitude comment?

yeah and then yesterday's too
something about how other people's opinions are not your concern

12:13 p.m.

Ahhh. Other people's truths are not my responsibility.

12:14 p.m.

exactly
Quinn's Life Lessons

12:15 p.m.

Ha ha.
They aren't even my words though.
I just hold onto things that I read that resonate with me.
Maybe you're just meant to receive the "lessons" right now?

12:17 p.m.

yeah maybe
I thought about that
you definitely get in my head

12:18 p.m.

Uh-oh. Sorry, lol.

12:18 p.m.

all good
anyway thanks for yesterday it was fun

12:20 p.m.

Thank you! It was truly a beautiful day.

12:20 p.m.

it was
see you in class tomorrow

ooo

Quick / 6:58 p.m.

his name was Geoffrey

Quinn / 7:02 p.m.

I'm so sorry.
I'm sure he was perfect, Quick.
Do you want to talk?

7:38 p.m.

no

7:42 p.m.

but thanks

7:44 p.m.

Offer does not expire.
I see you, Quick.

Hey Geoffrey,

I think I kinda figured out some things since last week. I was thinking about how Quinn still mourns for her brother but she's not in mourning all the time. There's like an air of acceptance about her. I can't quite put my finger on it, but I can tell you that I envy it a bit. Our situations are different, obviously. Not to belittle her family's loss or the indescribable grief that I'm sure they all carry with them, but Quinn isn't to blame for Troy's death. Quinn doesn't carry the guilt. I don't know if I will ever get to a place of acceptance, and I'm not sure I even deserve to. But what is deserved is for your name to be spoken. I try to honor you through my thoughts and my letters, but that's not enough. Your name, while sacred to me, shouldn't be laid to rest.

I shared your name with Quinn. That's all I shared, and to be honest, I don't know if I will ever be strong enough or brave enough to divulge any more than that. But I do know that if I've ever met anyone safe enough to confide in, it's her.

There are no earthly words to express how much I miss you.

I can't believe you'd be double digits today, bud. Happy birthday, Geoffrey.

-Deck

Tuesday, December 5, 2023

Note to self:

This first semester of our junior year is coming to a close, and when I reflect on all that has happened, I am quite stunned. My love for Mr. Erickson, his philosophy, and our club fills my heart with inspiration, which is something I was missing not so long ago. Not only that, I am learning more and more each day about the things of my choosing. This chemtrail work has opened my eyes to possibilities I never considered and has somehow, oddly enough, given me a huge confidence boost. I'm proud of myself for being a CT (either acronym is fine). Mr. Erickson was proud of us, too. He apparently shared our finished chemtrail infographic and presentation with all five of his classes.

But all of that aside, the biggest growth comes from the interpersonal. I made a friend. And not just a casual friend to talk to about nonsense, but an actual confidant. Quick and I have spent so much time together in club working on things of depth and value, that it makes perfect sense for the friendship to have spilled over and beyond the school walls. There's a trust there, and a mutual respect. There's no way I would have shared about Troy or he would have shared about Geoffrey if there wasn't a profundity of friendship.

With that being said, I am starting to feel strange about our upcoming holiday break. Will I not see Quick for two weeks? I didn't realize how much I rely on spending time with him, and now I have no idea what it will feel like to go without. I think what I am feeling is the dread of loneliness. I miss him already. How weird and pathetic is that?

Well, as always, I am pretty self-aware. And right now, I can sense that I'm being ridiculous. It's only two weeks, and I'm sure we'll text. Right?

...Q

Hey Geoffrey,

I am starting to feel a little sick to my stomach. We go on break tomorrow and I probably won't see Quinn for two weeks. Dude, I am going to miss her. I swear it's not like that, she really is just a friend. But she's so much more than that. Our friendship seems atypical because it's so deep for a couple of teenagers. Maybe that's what happens when two high schoolers bond over research questions and possible answers, not to mention their lost brothers. I mean, really. How many friends our age out there share that in common?

This was the best semester of high school. Of all of school, ever. There isn't even a distant second, and I know it's going to keep getting better and better. Because that's what she does. She is the best and she never ceases to get better. She's brilliant and she's focused, she's real but she stays positive, she's caring and she's generous. I'm so happy and so at ease when I'm around her, and I'm always looking forward to the next time I get to see her. Dude, I am really going to miss her over break.

Oh crap. Maybe it is like that.

Oh. Crap.

Monday, December 18, 2023

Note to self:

Mom asked me to head to the supermarket to pick up a few things today, and along my way, I walked right past the beginning of the trail Quick and I had ventured on just a couple of months before. As I recollected my thoughts of that day, I recalled how I was a bit nervous. I had told myself that morning, though, that there was a deep serenity in surrendering to what would be. That day worked out tremendously for us and our budding friendship, and I strongly believe that was in part due to the surrender. There was no need to control the events of the day, nor was there a need to stress about it. I knew to have peace in simply letting things unfold as they would.

Sitting here on my bed this first day of our two-week vacation, I can objectively see that I am now in a similar situation of the unknowns. Will we text at all over these two weeks? Will we see each other? Will our friendship fizzle out, grow stronger, or remain the same? There is only one way to know, and that is to let things play out. What will be will be, and accepting that will bring me the same sense of tranquility that I had on our day at the waterfall in October.

These two weeks will undoubtedly open my eyes to certain things, if I allow it. It is good to be still and quiet, to gain some sort of clarity.

…Q

Tuesday, December 26, 2023

Note to self:

In the last week, I have become practically obsessed with the art of lettering. I had no idea there was an entire subculture of people who not only can create beautiful layers of word art, but who also post the most mesmerizing videos on the internet. Upon discovering this, I swear I spent way too long watching video after video of brush tips being masterfully utilized to produce hand-drawn fonts. The videos were so captivating, it was almost as though I was in a trance.

After a dozen hours or so of watching the techniques applied by these experts, I decided I was ready to give it a whirl. Dad took me to the craft store and with my Christmas money, I purchased one set of brush-tip markers and an art notebook of thick cardstock. As soon as we arrived back home, I cleared off my desk and jumped right in. I started with the alphabet, and with reference videos nearby, I practiced each letter over and over again. Listening to frequency music of 396 hertz, I worked to push through any blockages and unlock my creativity.

I filled page after page of my new notebook, so much so that Dad noticed and bought me another one just before I ran out of paper. Like with anything, improvement was inevitable with more and more practice. I gained confidence, relied on the videos less, and even began embellishing the letters through flair and shadowing. Once I felt comfortable with that as well, I decided that my second notebook should have a purpose beyond alphabet practice.

That's when it hit me: Quick's idea about Life Lessons. On the first page of the pristine notebook and over the course of about two hours, I deliberately and delicately penned, "Your attitude entering a situation greatly affects your experience and the outcome thereof." I used two shades of blue and one of gray, and the varying sizes of letters really made the significant words pop. I loved it so much that I dove right into the next one. I thoughtfully decorated the second page with the phrase, "Other people's truths are not my responsibility." Upon completion, I was proud of the earth-toned block letters I created and the blending of shades that I accomplished. There's something to be said for using style to emphasize the meaning of the words.

Not only do I like the way both turned out, but there was so much joy in the process for me. It was relaxing and satisfying, and I am thrilled that I found yet another new avenue to achieve a meditative state! Gotta love the flow.

Feeling happy.

...Q

Wednesday, December 27, 2023

Note to self:

When I was at the craft store the other day, I noticed a huge section of items for fairy gardens. There were tiny supplies for gnomes, a fraction of the size they would be for the dollhouses I grew up with. From tables and chairs to wheelbarrows and bicycles, the store stocked it all, and everything in between. The miniature items were absolutely adorable, and as much as I wanted them, I had no need for them. Until now.

Wouldn't it be the funniest gag gift to give Quick a quote page with a relevant tiny item? So let's say, for the first lesson about his attitude entering a situation, what if I gave him a tiny door to represent entering? And for the truths lesson, I could give him a miniature plate maybe, like it's an empty plate because other people's truths aren't on it? It's a stretch, sure, and it's cheesy, but I think it's hilarious. I think he would totally get it! I guess I'll sit on the idea for now, but just thinking about it is making me giggle.

At the end of the day, I enjoy having Quick as a friend. I think the whole reason I am overthinking this two-week vacation thing is because he's a guy. Who cares? If my new friend was a girl, I wouldn't have given it a second thought. Why should I now?

I'm going to text him tomorrow.

…Q

○○○

Quinn / 11:17 a.m.

Hi Quick! How are you?

Quick / 11:21 a.m.

good, how are you

11:22 a.m.

I'm doing well!
What have you been up to?

11:22 a.m.

not much
doing a little digging on the significance of hair in native american cultures

11:23 a.m.

Oh, wow, that's interesting!
What's the neatest thing you've discovered about it?

11:23 a.m.

idk, maybe the reasons they cut it and then how they dispose of it
what about you, up to anything fun?

11:25 a.m.

I've actually been pretty creative this past week.

11:27 a.m.

like artsy fartsy stuff?

11:27 a.m.

Yes, lol.

11:27 a.m.

right on

11:28 a.m.

How was your Christmas?

11:33 a.m.

we don't really do that anymore

124

Oh, I'm sorry. I didn't realize.
My family was like that, too, but then we started some new traditions and it really helped.

11:35 a.m.

that's cool but we're not like that

11:35 a.m.

Every family is different.

11:36 a.m.

yeah, it's the way we deal I guess

11:39 a.m.

You deal by not dealing?

11:51 a.m.

pretty much

11:52 a.m.

Well, I hope you have a great rest of your day!

11:53 a.m.

you too

Quick:

That Simple

Winter break of my junior year was a confusing one. Typically, I craved time alone. Time for me to use my finger shovels, time for me to write to Geoffrey, time for me to sleep in. Whether I craved it or not, though, I was destined to spend that break alone. Christmas time was especially difficult for my parents, so it was no surprise that my mom was drugged up to the point of being practically comatose, and my dad spent more time at the office than at our house. I was on my own for meals, which explained why I was basically eating only once per day. Instant ramen. Yeah, real nutritious.

Even though my days were quiet and I encountered zero distractions, I still had a very hard time concentrating. I settled on researching the light topic of Native American braids and while I did indeed learn some fascinating things, I knew I was avoiding the more involved topics that typically swallow my attention whole. I had a list of controversial subject matters to explore, with CERN and its symbolism at the top of that list, but I could not seem to focus. It became quite apparent that the only thing I was trying to figure out was my friendship with Quinn. I thought about her much too often and found myself wishing I was with her, but I wasn't sure if it was because I enjoyed companionship or it was something more.

She texted me out of the blue halfway through vacation, I assumed because she was missing me the same way I was missing her. Probably as confused, too. We didn't text too much, just a few niceties. Later that night, while lying in bed with my eyes wide open, I suddenly realized how ridiculous all of it was. How overcomplicated I was making it. How much I was overthinking it.

I wanted to see her. Period. It was that simple.

I jumped out of bed and texted Quinn right there and then. All I wrote was, "Downtown tomorrow?" Within the same minute, she texted back, "Yes!"

Her enthusiasm always made me smile, like I could hear her chipper voice through her exclamation points. I had a feeling she was thinking of me, too. She must have been. It was after two o'clock in the morning when we texted.

Quinn mentioned she had to run to the store the next morning, so we decided to meet for lunch and then check out the shops for a couple of hours. She suggested a Mexican restaurant, and we ended up eating so many chips with salsa that the only thing we had to pay for was our fancy strawberry lemonades. We tipped our server well and joked about how it was a good thing we had plans to meander downtown since we needed to walk off the insane amount of free food we consumed.

While we skipped entering the boutiques of overpriced clothing, the art galleries of desert landscaping, and the bizarre pop-up shop of water massage tables, Quinn and I did spend quite a bit of time in a family-owned bookstore we came across. It was one of those quaint shops with a huge array of gently used books, where no two bookshelves were the same, where the genre signs were handmade, and where the prices were written by hand on little stickers. Quinn got lost in a book on Kundalini yoga for a solid half hour while I perused the section of antiquated publications. I ended up purchasing an old reader on our nation's history, curious to see if its contents would line up with what we were learning in class, and Quinn bought the Kundalini book like I knew she would the second she picked it up.

Towards the end of our afternoon, we stopped by a little coffee shop and ordered some hot chocolate with extra whipped cream. While we were sitting in the corner, Quinn announced that she had something for me. I cracked a joke about how my birthday wasn't for a couple months and I hated it anyway, but my comment seemed to fly right over her head. She reached into her bag and pulled out a book of sorts, but by looking at it, I had no idea what it was. "It's a scrapbook," she smiled, "but it's a work in progress." She handed me the scrapbook and I noticed that she was beaming. Glowing. Twinkling. As she bounced in her seat and clapped her hands together, I could see how happy it made her to give me a gift. She was literally giddy.

It was a small brown book, maybe eight inches on each side and about an inch thick, with empty sheet protector pages within. Except for the first two.

I opened it to read, "Your attitude entering a situation greatly affects your experience and the outcome thereof." I took in the colors, the lettering, the swirly things. It looked like a work of art. I was so confused; I couldn't figure out how she found that exact quote somewhere. Was it a magazine clipping? I glanced up to see the pride in her face and immediately understood. "You made this?" Surely the incredulous look on my face was easy to read, since my eyes were probably the size of half dollar coins. "You made me the pamphlet?"

"Yes!" There was that exclamation point again. I could feel the smile slowly erupting on my face as I started to piece it all together. It must have taken her hours to make this, and she made it just for me.

"Look!" She pointed back to the page where I noticed a tiny plastic door taped to the outside of the clear page cover. "There's a reminder trinket, too, so if you ever need a little something in your pocket, you can take it with you!"

I tried to thank her, but I couldn't find my voice. I was staring at the page, astounded by her thoughtfulness and fully aware that it was hands down the coolest gift I ever received.

I slowly turned the page to find what I already knew was there. The next Life Lesson. It took me a second to figure out how a plate represented the idea that we aren't responsible for other people's realities, but when it clicked, a laugh escaped my lips.

"I knew you'd get it! Oh my gosh, Quick, do you like it?" Quinn looked like she was coming out of her skin, she was so excited. Our eyes met and I slowly nodded. She settled down, released a giant sigh, and gave me a calm, sweet smile. "I'm so glad," she purred.

And in that moment, I knew.

I loved her.

It was that simple.

Hey Geoffrey,

How is this not more simple? How can I be nearly seventeen years old and still have no idea what friendship is? What love is? What I'm feeling?

Quinn is the first person I have connected with in years. Since you. Actually, she is the first person I have connected with outside of our family. Ever. She is my first real friend, the only person I feel safe around, the only person I feel brave around. I know that I love spending time with her. I know that I love her companionship. I know that I love how I feel when I am around her.

And that is where my knowing stops. Perhaps this feeling is just that, a companion's love. A friendship. How am I supposed to know?

I'm terrified that I am going to mess this up.

You know what? At the end of the day, I like things how they are. I don't need to label any of it. I just need to go with it. Go with the flow, as Quinn would say.

You know what else? I miss you.

-Deck

Quinn:

Sucker Punch

Second semester came in a flash, and everything seemed to get bumped up a notch in terms of intensity. The teachers returned from winter break with an urgency, already discussing AP exams, college entrance exams, and final exams. The workload increased, and the student stress level among the junior class became practically visible. Even at home things were escalating. My mom was constantly lecturing me about how I needed to research colleges, their majors, and their pros and cons. I did not want to get swept up in the pressures of the pointless rat race, and it was taking more and more meditation to maintain my high vibration.

Meditation, whether it be through sound healing, crystals, art, or simply grounding, was not the only thing I implemented to help me maintain perspective and balance, though. I derived so much joy from The REED Club. Tuesdays and Thursdays were the highlights of my weeks, but in all honesty, Quick and I found time to dig on a daily basis. The research became addicting, and it seemed as though each possibility we unearthed led to more and more questions. If we weren't bouncing ideas back and forth in Mr. Erickson's room, we had each other on speaker phone while we were on our laptops at home. No matter how much schoolwork we had, we managed to find the time. It was almost as if we made an unspoken promise to one another to keep our club high on our priority lists.

In January of that year, Quick and I decided to take on two different topics simultaneously. I was eager to read about the possible dangers of using microwave ovens in the home, while he was set on discovering more about the health benefits of dandelion root. Ever since he learned that a pharmaceutical company that made huge profits off heart medicine was the same company that owned a popular herbicide to kill dandelions, he was on a mission to see if there was a motive. By tackling both subjects, we covered double the ground, and because we incessantly shared our findings with each other during the process, we were learning twice as much as we did in the fall.

As luck would have it, we both began to wrap up our research in the later part of the month. One Thursday afternoon, as he and I sat side by side to create our respective slideshows, I had an epiphany. I broke both our concentration and the silence with a gasp that startled Quick so much so that he jumped back in his chair.

"Sorry, but I just thought of something! You know what we should do, Quick? We should totally start a new tradition. Every time we finish a REED, we should celebrate in some way! Right? Wouldn't that be fun?" I was speaking a mile a minute, like I always did when I was excited.

A wave of relief spread across his face. "You scared the crap out of me, Quinn."

"I know, I'm sorry. You were totally in a zone. Sorry. But it's a good idea, right? I think we'll be done by next week. What should we do?" The idea delighted me, and I wanted his take on it.

"It's a brilliant idea. Let's do it." Quick flashed me his best smile. I was starting to see it so often that even with my eyes closed, I could picture it perfectly.

"We could make downtown hot chocolate our tradition," I offered, but even as I said it, I knew it was a weak suggestion.

He shook his head. "Nah, we deserve something bigger and better for all of our groundbreaking hard work." He chuckled at his sarcasm. "Let's keep thinking."

"Bigger and better? Like what, go to an amusement park?" Now I was the one laughing at my sarcasm, but it took me much too long to realize that I was the only one who thought the comment was funny. Suddenly, I realized that something was very wrong. Quick was physically present, but he was no longer mentally with me in that room. His face had completely fallen, and his eyes were empty and hollow. He was frozen in space and in time, and even when I gently called his name, he did not give one iota of a signal that he even heard me.

Seconds turned into a minute, and I contemplated him in absolute silence. I watched as his unblinking eyes began to find their way back to the present moment, just before filling with tears. I could sense that the tears were of emotions that reached far beyond sadness. Whatever this was, it was complicated.

I waited patiently, mirroring his stillness. I instinctively knew that it was not my place to rush him or to disturb him in any way. Another minute passed. Eventually he blinked. A tear fell. The tear that rolled right down his beautiful cheek and splashed onto his keyboard. The tear that awakened him and zapped him back to reality. The tear that made him pack up his things and shuffle out of the room without saying a word.

Stunned and bewildered, I tried to make sense of what had transpired. Nausea took hold, and even though I couldn't quite yet articulate it, my stomach could feel the truth. I replayed the conversation in my head, but all that was doing was muddying the waters and confusing me even more. Mournfully, regretfully, I gathered my belongings and began my walk home. Alone.

Maybe it was the fresh air. Maybe it was the deep breaths. Maybe it was the emptying of the mind. Whatever it was, it did the trick. The truth swooped in and sucker punched me so hard that I dropped to the sidewalk and sobbed.

ooo

Quinn / 7:08 p.m.

Hi.

Quick / 9:54 p.m.

hey

9:57 p.m.

Are you ok?

9:58 p.m.

yeah see you tomorrow

○○○

Quinn / 5:12 p.m.

I didn't see you today. Were you at school?

Quick / 7:42 p.m.

no

7:43 p.m.

Oh, ok. Should I be worried about you?

7:59 p.m.

up to you
I'm fine, see you monday

8:10 p.m.

Does this have something to do with what happened at club yester-day?

9:42 p.m.

Ok, I'll give you space. I'm here if you need me.
I see you.

Friday, January 19, 2024

Note to self:

I think I lost Quick. While I fully recognize that I am not to blame for what happened because there was no way for me to know his triggers, it is breaking my heart that he is in so much pain. I'm worried he will retreat back into his hole of isolation and push me away, not because he is upset with me but because he doesn't want the possibility of any reminders of what happened.

Here is what I have pieced together:

- He had a brother named Geoffrey.

- He had a visceral reaction to the mention of milk cartons and missing children.

- He had an even more visceral reaction to the mention of an amusement park.

I am sad because I miss my friend, but even more so his sorrow is weighing on my heart. I wish I could help him feel, deal, and heal. I know that I am not fully healed from losing Troy and the family trauma that followed, and to be honest, I don't think I ever will be. It's not that I think I've figured it all out and I could teach him anything. I am just starting to think that the universe brought us together because we are supposed to help each other. I'm praying Quick can get to a point where he allows us to.

Troy's Zen garden is calling me. Maybe I'll ask Mom and Dad if they want to watch a movie or something tonight. I could go for some snuggles.

...Q

○○○

I'm a jerk

Quinn / 11:13 a.m.

I don't even think that's possible, Quick.

11:15 a.m.

I'm sorry I walked out and I'm sorry about those last texts

11:15 a.m.

It's ok. I'm sorry, too.

11:17 a.m.

you have nothing to be sorry for
I was rude and I feel really bad

11:18 a.m.

Please don't. I understand.

11:20 a.m.

ok well thanks for understanding

11:21 a.m.

Do you want to talk about it?

11:23 a.m.

no
not yet

11:24 a.m.

Okay,
Hey, so if I remember correctly, your birthday is coming up?
When is it?

11:24 a.m.

feb 8

I hate my birthday
part of the reason I was a jerk, I hate this time of year

11:24 a.m.

Well I'm thinking maybe we can change that!

no, I'd rather just skip it

Why? You deserve your day.
It's a Monday this year. What if we did something little?

like what

It's up to you! It's your birthday!
What if we had a picnic after school, for old times' sake?

old times? ha ha that was like three months ago

What do you say?

ugh fine
on one condition

Name it.

no gifts

Deal.

I'm serious, quinn

I don't want, need, or deserve a gift

I disagree. You absolutely deserve gifts and joy and everything else
life has to offer.
But I will respect your condition.

good

Ok, yey! See you tomorrow?

yeah, I'll be at school

Double yey!

Quinn:

My Favorite Question Mark

O ver the last week of January and into the first week of February, buried between an exam on trigonometric form of complex numbers in Precalculus and a test on impulse and momentum in Physics class, Quick and I found ourselves submitting both of our REED slideshows to Mr. Erickson and already discussing possibilities for the next round. We wanted to work together on this one, but we were grappling to find the right topic. Quick was leaning more towards what he called the "scams" of fossil fuels and charity organizations, but I wanted to venture more into the world of sacred geometry and the supposed magic of 3-6-9. Not only were we struggling to align our research interests at the time, but our attitudes towards his upcoming birthday were also very much askew. He was dreading it, while I was trying to play it cool and mentally counting down the days.

Finally, February 8th arrived and to say that I was prepared was an absolute understatement. I had planned the picnic of all picnics, and the anticipation made the school day tick by in a painstakingly slow manner. Carrying around a heavy insulated lunchbox all day did not help either. At long last, school let out for the day. Quick knew to meet me on the quad, so I scampered off from my last class to get there before him.

As he drifted over to where I was, he saw me placing paper plates onto the lawn. Using nine plates, I created a large question mark on the grass. After stepping back to assess the shape and situating the final plate just right, I glanced over to see a completely perplexed expression on Quick's face.

"Happy birthday, Quick! Ok, come sit with me," I commanded as I plopped down near the curve of the punctuation mark. He was clearly having a clash of sentiments: On one hand, he was perturbed by the whole idea of celebrating his birthday, and on the other, curious as to what I had up my sleeve.

He conceded and took a seat. "What on earth?"

"It's a question mark!" I blurted out, much more loudly than I meant to.

"Yes, I see that." There was an edge to Quick's voice that was unfamiliar to me.

I brought the small cooler out from behind me and opened it. From it, I removed multiple sealed bags, some with cheese, others with cured meats, and the rest with fruits and nuts. "Don't worry, I washed my hands," I announced as I began arranging the charcuterie. Once again, I noted in real time how comfortable the two of us were with the quiet. Neither one of us spoke until I was finished. Upon completion, my eyes found his, and I could see that whatever angst he was harboring moments ago had dissipated.

"Wow, thank you, Quinn. This is quite the picnic. You really didn't need to—" I cut him off. I told him that I knew I didn't need to. I wanted to. I confessed that I had looked forward to this for weeks and that I couldn't wait to celebrate him. Bashfully, he thanked me again through blushed cheeks. I could tell he was touched.

"So? Do you get it?" I asked. "Do you understand why the question mark shape?" I was too delighted to wait for his answer. "Because you love the mysteries of life! You're always asking questions, Quick, and I love that about you." This time I was the one who flushed crimson. Words always seemed to bolt out of my mouth without permission.

Disrupting a poignant pause, Quick's stomach growled loudly enough for us both to hear. We belly laughed, allowing the moment to pass. We grabbed toothpicks and started devouring our afternoon snack. While shoveling gouda, salami, and crackers, Quick and I chatted about the pets we always wanted but never had, the great American pastime of garage sales, and how neither one of us ever had the need or the desire to learn to ride a bike. Before we knew it, the charcuterie plates were bare. We ate every last morsel.

"I'm stuffed," Quick moaned as he clutched his stomach. "That was so good, Quinn. Thank you." He turned to see me bringing out one last clean plate. "What's that for? Please tell me there isn't more food," he joked.

"I don't know if you can call this food," I laughed as I took the can of whipped cream from the cooler. I shook it as hard as I could and then unloaded the entire can in a dome-shaped mound on the plate. He stared at it in disbelief, aware of the task before him.

"There's no way." Quick matter-of-factly stated. "I will literally barf, I'm so full."

I plopped a candle right in the middle of the daunting dollops of dairy. "Suck it up, buttercup. You'll be fine. But first, I have something…" I reached over to grab an item from my bag and was startled by Quick's eruptive response.

"You promised no gifts!" Quick's words were laced with anger.

I slowly brought out the box of tin foil and calmly placed it on the grass in front of me. "Relax, Quick. I kept my word. This isn't a gift." His eyes searched mine for forgiveness, and I gave it to him with ease. "This is just your birthday hat. You can't make a wish without one." I tore a large segment for each of us and began shaping mine.

Per his usual, it took him a moment to process what I meant, but sure enough, he started chuckling the second he understood. We both got such a kick out of making our tin foil hats, placing them on our heads, and then adjusting one another's until our conspiracy caps were just right. Ready to sing the birthday song, I sadly realized that I forgot a lighter for the candle. I wanted to kick myself for the mistake, but Quick pointed out that it was probably best I did not bring one onto campus anyway.

Unabashedly, I stood up to sing the entire "Happy Birthday" song to Quick at the top of my lungs, even though there really wasn't anyone around to hear it except for maybe a couple of teachers who were still on campus grading in their nearby classrooms. "Make a wish!" I exclaimed, realizing in that moment that I knew exactly what Quick's wish would be. It was the same one he's been making for the last five or so years.

I plopped back down next to him with two spoons, ready to take on the challenge of whipped cream consumption. He looked at me with puppy dog eyes that seemed to plead, "Do I have to?" Seeing his face of desperation with his eyebrows pathetically slanted and his slow blink of begging was too much for me. I completely lost it and, once again, we found ourselves laughing hysterically together over yet another ridiculous situation.

"Okay, okay, you don't have to eat it!" I cried, once we found our breath again. "But on one condition."

"I'm the only one who can put conditions on my birthday, Quinn. No deal," he winked. My heart skipped a beat, like it was right on cue. He took the candle out of the whipped cream and licked the residue off. "Okay, what do you want?"

"I want to know your real name. Maybe just think about it. You don't have to tell me right now. Actually, you don't have to tell me ever if you don't want to. But maybe just think about it?" I asked gingerly.

Quick looked down at the grass, and I wondered if he would leave another bare patch in the lawn like he had done a few months back. He took a deep, deliberate breath before replying, "It's complicated. I have a few names and it's changed over time. Well, I wanted to change it. I was going to change it. To Maverick. I was going to change my name to Maverick but it never stuck, and I wanted to drop my middle names, but I never did anything official or anything. It's, ugh, it's just so heavy. There's so much meaning to all of it. But, but my real name is—" he paused, and not for dramatic effect. The rushed and erratic stammer made it unmistakable that this was painful for him to share. "Declan. Deck. It's Declan. My real name is Declan."

"That's a beautiful name, Quick. Thank you for sharing that with me." I longed to reach out to him, to express my support and my gratitude through a gentle squeeze of his hand, but I didn't dare. We cleaned up in that comfortable quiet that we had come to appreciate, and soon enough he had walked me home and thanked me again for the thoughtfulness I displayed on his birthday.

That same evening, after completing my nighttime hygiene routine and settling into my cozy corner of pillows, I opened my laptop with a clear intention. I wanted to do an internet search on Declan Williams, the biggest question mark in my life. I wanted answers to my favorite mystery. I wanted to better understand my best friend. I got as far as the letter 'm,' but never finished typing the name or pressing enter. I stopped myself, knowing that this action was one of betrayal and one that could never be undone. I needed to respect his boundaries.

I slowly and delicately closed my computer, knowing in my core that he would tell me everything when he was ready. My selfish curiosity was not worth endangering this friendship, his trust, or our parallel journeys. I placed my laptop on my bedside table, closed my eyes, and silently wished Quick a happy birthday one last time before drifting off to sleep, smiling as I pondered my favorite question mark.

02/09/24

2:28 a.m.

I hear muffled whispers that slowly rouse me from a deep sleep. Before I even open my eyes, I can feel the enormous weight of my head and the pounding of my brain that feels too large for my skull. The murmurs seem to be coming from very far away, and I struggle to recognize the voices. I feel a cool, damp cloth being placed on my forehead and I slowly begin to blink light into my eyes. My vision is blurred and it takes a conscious effort for me to hone in on my caretaker's face. In the exact moment that I realize I do not recognize her, I am snapped back to reality and I remember where I am. And why.

She must see the look of horror on my face and immediately tells me that my parents are here. She calls over to my mom. Tear-stricken, my mom's face comes to hover over mine. I cry out her name and I ask where my brother is, but she remains silent. Her eyes are vacant and her expression is devoid of emotion.

I continue to wail, wrapping my arms around her neck and trying to crawl into her lap, but her body doesn't respond. Her arms hang at her sides and her body sways from my tugs and pulls, but she makes no effort to embrace me. I am physically exhausted, and as I lie back down, I see her stoic face and unblinking eyes.

I rest my head back on the pillow and drop my hands back down to whatever bed I am lying on. Without acknowledging me once, she robotically stands up, turns, and walks away.

Quick:

A No-Brainer

I startled myself awake the night after my annual and unwavering birthday wish. I found myself in a cold sweat, but I was not at all surprised. Flashbacks and nightmares riddled my childhood years and beyond, especially during the late winter and early spring. I always kept a bottle of water at my bedside for that very reason. I sat up, took a swig, and reconciled with the fact that it was going to be a long, sleepless night. Again. As expected.

When I was younger, I would wonder how long I would suffer from these episodes and the insomnia that followed, but at some point during my adolescence, I had accepted my fate. Besides, I deserved it. I deserved to be haunted. It was a small price to pay. Too small.

That night, however, was different. There was a little voice inside of me whose hushed tones became more audible. It told me that maybe, just maybe, I didn't deserve to suffer endlessly. It told me that maybe, just maybe, I did deserve to be loved. It told me that maybe, just maybe, I wasn't to blame for what happened to my kid brother. And it told me that maybe, just maybe, my parents didn't blame me. But if they did, that was their belief and maybe, just maybe, that wasn't my truth.

It was not difficult to recognize that the little voice sounded a lot like Quinn. It probably was Quinn. Who was I kidding? It was Quinn. And it made me feel a bit better and even inspired me enough to try something different this sleepless time around.

I reached over to grab my phone and I brought up the podcast app. I searched "guided meditations" and perused dozens and dozens of them before landing on one entitled, "Sound Bath for healing and self-forgiveness."

Um, that was a no-brainer.

I set it to a low volume, settled into a comfortable zone, and closed my eyes. Deep breaths, I told myself. Deep breaths.

I woke up to my alarm four hours later.

000

guess what I did last night

Quinn / 5:21 p.m.

Ummm, you ate tacos.

5:21 p.m.

how'd you know lol
no really guess again

5:22 p.m.

Ok, you finished your research on the truths and lies behind fossil fuels.

5:22 p.m.

nope

5:22 p.m.

I'm going to need some sort of hint or this is going to take me five-ever to figure out!

5:23 p.m.

want me to just tell you?

5:24 p.m.

Yes, please.

5:25 p.m.

I did a guided meditation

5:25 p.m.

What?! Yessssssss! That's amazing!
Did you find one online? What prompted you to do it? Did you like it?
Omg tell me everything!

5:27 p.m.

take it easy lol
I couldn't really sleep so I found a podcast
it was a sound bath? whatever that means
but yes I liked it
totally fell back asleep which NEVER happens so yeah

Quick, that is spectacular! Good for you.
I'm so glad you found a tool that worked for you, but I'm sorry you couldn't sleep.
Does that happen to you a lot?

5:29 p.m.

yeah especially during certain times
I know my triggers now
like always after my birthday

5:30 p.m.

Oh wow. That sounds rough.

5:31 p.m.

I have nightmares but most of the time they're like flashbacks

5:32 p.m.

I don't know what to say. I just hope that it gets easier with time and with healing.

5:32 p.m.

yeah me too

5:32 p.m.

Hey, Quick?

5:33 p.m.

yeah

5:33 p.m.

I see you.

5:33 p.m.

I see you too

Hey Geoffrey,

I can't believe I'm seventeen. In a year I'll officially be an adult and starting to think about leaving our folks' house. Starting my life. It's crazy to think about. Honestly, I can't really grasp that reality yet.

I'll be glad to leave home. I think Mom will get better when she doesn't have to see me every single day. Maybe that will alleviate some of my guilt. I don't know. And maybe I'll start feeling a little better, too. We're all constant reminders of pain. Of guilt. And of you.

Yesterday was a first. They forgot my birthday. Or maybe they think I'm getting too old for that kind of thing. But to not even wish me a happy birthday? It stung. I guess I'm not surprised though. How could she possibly remember it when she probably doesn't even know what year it is, let alone the month and day? I don't know what Dad's excuse is. Probably just wants to forget.

It's alright. I wasn't too bothered by it. I don't deserve a happy birthday anyway, so it's fine. Kinda weird, though, since I actually did have moments of a happy birthday yesterday. Quinn made me feel like the only person in the universe. She makes me feel like I do deserve joy.

Maybe I do. Who knows. But no matter how much joy I allow myself to feel, it will always be coupled with an emptiness. There is a hole in me that will never be filled. Plain and simple.

Love you.

And as always, I am so frickin' sorry. I'd do anything for a do-over.

-Deck

Quinn:

Creases

It was a frigid and dreary Friday in February, and even with the hint of the afternoon sun hiding behind the ominous gray clouds, my teeth were chattering as Quick and I ambled home after school. I was wearing my beanie under my fuzzy jacket hood, but my ears still felt frozen. Goosebumps speckled my legs and instinct urged me to continue rubbing my hands together as we walked. No matter how cold I was though, I felt a warmth radiating from within. There were very few things in my life that made me feel as content as my time spent with Quick. Our friendship was effortless, and I was consciously aware of and grateful for finding a companionship as accepting and authentic as ours.

The wintry weather robbed the neighborhoods of the sounds we typically enjoyed, those of dogs barking and birds chirping. We did, however, delight in our own conversation which happened to go from light to quite serious within a street block's time.

Naturally, we exchanged our most current findings and resulting opinions regarding our latest research topics. It was no surprise that discourse ensued, given that the both of us loved to play the role of a dissenter in order to challenge the other. This pattern had become a favorite pastime over the course of our six-month friendship, and that day was no different.

After a bit of banter, we walked in comfortable silence for a minute or two. A young mother passed by us on the slim sidewalk. She was pushing her toddler in a pink and brown polka-dotted stroller, a tattered doll being waved about by the girl's chubby hand. The image of my childhood dolls flashed in my mind's eye, and a sigh escaped my lips without deliberation.

"Whoa, what was that about?" Quick asked with conspicuous curiosity, surely referring to the unexpected sigh.

I shamelessly shared a piece of my soul with Quick that afternoon. My descriptions of each detail painted a picture of my childhood oasis for him, of everything from the dolls in the sandbox to the garden of food scraps. I continued with my confessions of oasis neglect and avoidance after Troy's passing. Before I knew it, I had divulged a lifetime of events to him. He didn't utter a sound or interrupt me even once, not as we walked and I talked, or as we arrived at my house and sat on the curb for another hour while I rambled on. He listened as I spoke of the specifics surrounding the day of Troy's death, along with that fateful trip to the bookstore, the birth of our triple tradition, and my rollercoaster relationship with my mom. Through all of it, Quick hung on to my every word.

It felt so good to process it out loud, and it felt even better to know it was landing on his ears. I was again reminded of how far my family and I had come, and I relished the warmth of that pride.

Quick understood that I had concluded my oral autobiography but was so busy trying to process it all that he was stunned silent. He even said as much. I thanked him for genuinely listening, and after a moment, he pensively asked a cryptic question. "Can I say it now?" The vagueness of the query made me cock my head to the side. I asked him what he meant as a wide and gentle smile lifted his cheeks to the sky.

"I understand you, Quinn."

I nodded. He was right. We locked eyes, and I knew we were both filled with conscious gratitude for our connection. "Yes, you do. Thank you, Quick." I started to ask him about his childhood, but thought better of it. I stopped myself mid-sentence, but it was too late. Half of the question was already dangling in the frosty air between us.

He took a moment, and then astonished me when he started to answer the unfinished query. "My mom can't look at me. I don't know if she hates me, blames me, feels sorry for me, I don't know what. But I can't remember the last time we made eye contact, and she can't even remember my birth—" His voice cracked. This new pain was too fresh and too raw; Quick literally couldn't get the words out. It was heart-wrenching.

I didn't trust myself to speak. Without thinking, I reached out and grabbed his hand. I squeezed it between both of mine, willing myself to send him every ounce of love and support I could through our touch. Through our very first touch.

He stared at our intertwined hands, surely aware that this act was unprecedented. Neither one of us moved a muscle. We just sat there, frozen in the moment, until he finally brought his despondent eyes to meet mine. "Do you know?" he softly asked.

"I think so," I answered with a heavy, sorrowful heart. I affectionately clutched his hand a little tighter. He squeezed back.

"Yeah, I suspected you figured it out." His eyes darted back down to our hands. I mentioned that it was getting dark, and he quickly agreed that he should head home. "Thanks again, Quinn, for everything." He gave me a sad smile, a common piece of evidence of the constant conflict he battles with, and he stood up to begin his walk home.

I contemplated his retreating form as he crossed the street and turned the corner. Everything about his demeanor hinted to his heavy heart. The sagging shoulders and the downward gaze. The mop of hair that often covered his despairing eyes. The downward creases by the corners of his mouth. My heart absolutely ached for him, and all I could wish for in that moment of time was for him to exchange those creases for the ones that accentuated the outer corners of smiling eyes.

More than anything, I longed for Quick to have happy creases.

Hey Geoffrey,

Quinn knows about you. I didn't even have to tell her anything. I guess she figured it out over the last few months by my reaction to certain things. I figured she did. It doesn't take a genius to deduce what happened, and I'm pretty sure Quinn is a genius.

Anyway, we were walking home yesterday and she opened up to me about every single possible mystery I could have ever wondered about her. I'm in awe of how open and vulnerable she can be, and how fearless she must be in order to do that. Not only fearless, but also how comfortable with herself she must be. She accepts herself and tries to deal with the hand she was dealt in the best way possible. It's admirable.

Admirable enough that she inspired me to share some things with her. But since I am not open or vulnerable or fearless or comfortable or accepting or anything like her, I couldn't get through it. I couldn't even bring myself to say words out loud. But she got it. She totally gets me. I can see it in her eyes, and yesterday I could feel it as we held our hands together.

What the heck. She makes me feel like the cheesiest, cringiest dude on the planet. I guess I don't mind, though.

Well, Quinn texted me later on last night. She asked me where I lived and told me that she wanted to swing by today to drop something off. I texted her, "No thank you," but she wasn't having it. She said her dad was going to drive her, that I could wait for her outside, that she wouldn't even get out of the car. Fine.

I didn't know what she had to give me. I was thinking maybe the third page of the Lessons book, but I couldn't figure out what that third one would be. We didn't talk about another one. I racked my brain for a bit, and then gave up and decided to let myself be surprised.

It was indeed the third page. Her beautiful lettering read, "Stretch into the uncomfortable in order to grow," and a rubber band was attached. When she gave it to me, she thanked me for trusting her enough to stretch like that in her presence. Of the three Life Lessons so far, I'm not sure which one is my favorite.

Probably this one. And probably because of the hand holding thing. Not gonna lie.

I was thinking about how much I wish you two could meet. You'd love her. And I know she would love you.

-Deck

○○○

Mandy / 6:29 p.m.

not gonna lie I'm pretty curious about that witch and her boo

Desiree / 6:30 p.m.

like if they're dating or whatever

6:32 p.m.

idk they're always together
lunch every day and he's always walking her home

6:32 p.m.

so?

6:33 p.m.

he's too cute for a witch
I need to save him from her dark magic lol

6:34 p.m.

what do you mean he's too cute
are you interested

6:35 p.m.

no I see him as damaged goods now
but I will be doing a good deed
it'll be like my version of community service

6:43 p.m.

what do you have in mind

6:43 p.m.

idk maybe I'll make nice with her again
get the scoop on the two of them

6:44 p.m.

ok whatever
seems like a total waste of time

6:45 p.m.

no this will be a fun little game

6:54 p.m.

k

Quinn:

March Madness

Throughout my childhood and adolescence, not once did I watch even one second of a sports event. Growing up in America, however, I had heard of March Madness and had a vague understanding of what it was: a college basketball tournament.

During my junior year in high school, I ascertained that perhaps the people of the basketball realm were onto something. All around me, I sensed stress, instability, and quick-tempered fuses. Our own version of March Madness.

At school, we were studying for tests and writing papers, all the while the end-of-school-year exams were looming over us. There was a readiness for Spring Break that was palpable, for both students and faculty alike. An uptick in hallway arguments over minor things, like accidental collisions, had taken hold, as well as an increase in students being ejected to the office for disciplinary action. Student stress was high, teacher tolerance was low, and school was a pasta pot ready to boil over.

Our house was not any calmer. Mom was on a daily rampage. I tried to determine the cause of her irritability so as to gain compassion and understanding. I settled on a mixture of the stress of her upcoming parent-teacher conferences, her hormonal imbalance due to her premenopausal state, and of course the tough time of year ahead regarding our Troy.

I mustered as much compassion as I could, and yet it was still difficult to navigate through our conversations that month. If she wasn't berating me about college readiness, applications, and resume inclusions, she was demanding that I do more research regarding potential university choices. It didn't matter if I tried to voice my opinions or if I complied; every instance was a lose-lose situation. She was simply foul.

Midway through this variety of March Madness, it registered with me that perhaps a fourth issue was generating this upheaval. My mom was most likely dealing with the struggle to accept my aging out of our family home.

I stopped trying to tell my mom that I wasn't sure I wanted to go to college, or at least not right away. I wanted to tell her that most of the things I'm interested in aren't offered areas of study at typical colleges, and that there are plenty of career opportunities that don't require me to accrue tens upon tens of thousands of dollars' worth of debt before I even graduate from college. Alas, she wasn't hearing me or having it anyway. While I understood that she was under an immense amount of stress, I wanted to tell her that I was, too. She wasn't the only one who was feeling overwhelmed by responsibilities, emotions, and upcoming changes. I was, too.

I tried talking to Dad, but as close as we were, he was not the type to engage in deep conversations. Besides, there were some things I wanted to talk about with my mom, woman to woman. There was a plethora of things: my different interests, my career desire to help people heal in unconventional ways, the feelings about Quick that I didn't understand, and the fact that Mandy said hello to me at school. But I knew that trying to have rational conversations with her that month would have been exercises in futility, so I grinned, bore it, and hoped the April showers would wash the madness away.

ooo

Mandy / 7:19 p.m.
hi it's mandy

Quinn / 7:32 p.m.
Hi.

7:33 p.m.
how are you

7:33 p.m.
I'm good. You?

7:34 p.m.
good, just thought I would say hi

7:35 p.m.
I'm glad you did.

7:35 p.m.
crazy that we're almost seniors huh

7:36 p.m.
Yes, it's definitely hard to wrap my brain around.

7:37 p.m.
are ur parents freaking out about college and stuff too

7:37 p.m.
Yes! Oh my gosh, it's good to know it's not just me!

7:38 p.m.
yeah
plus I'm sure its extra hard for them with troy and all

7:40 p.m.
I'm sure it is.

7:41 p.m.
hey remember that time I sat in the grocery store kid car cart thing

7:43 p.m.
And you got stuck! How could I forget?
I laughed so hard I peed my pants in the aisle. So embarrassing.

yeah but so worth it
that was like the hardest I've ever laughed and cried at the same time

7:43 p.m.

It really was hysterical.
We should have learned our lesson after the baby swing incident at the park!

7:45 p.m.

omg for sure
gtg nice chatting though
see you around

7:46 p.m.

That sounds good.

Wednesday, March 13, 2024

Note to self:

I'm really not sure what to make of this whole Mandy thing. We haven't talked in years, she's made it very clear that she despises me, and then out of nowhere, she wants to reconnect? I'm fine with it, but it just strikes me as so bizarre.

I was reading on the bench by the library yesterday when she walked over to say hello. Of course I was utterly shocked when I looked up to find her face, so naturally I stuttered a reciprocal greeting. She asked how I was, if the book I was reading was for English class, and how my family was doing. With each question, she listened intently to my responses as though she was sincerely interested. I then asked her how she was doing, but the bell rang. She suggested we catch up by text sometime, so I gave her my number before we parted ways.

Off and on all day, I thought about the exchange. I couldn't make heads or tails of it, and to be honest, I still can't. On one hand, we're juniors in high school. I'd be glad to know that we've outgrown issues from when we were immature tweenagers. I know I've grown a ton. I'm a totally different person. Surely she's grown, too. But then on the other hand, she called me a "weirdo freak witch" not that long ago… So suddenly, I'm not one?

Then, she texted me tonight. She was kind enough to make simple conversation, and then we laughed a bit over a funny memory that happened in the peak of our friendship. Maybe she's feeling nostalgic? Maybe she needs a friend of sorts?

I don't know. I want to give her the benefit of the doubt, that she has released whatever she needed to and that she's ready to bury the hatchet. I forgave her long ago and maybe she's ready to do that now. I mean, what does she have to gain by being disingenuous and pretending to let bygones be bygones? That doesn't really make any sense to me. But for some reason, I am hesitant to trust her. I am reluctant and skeptical.

I am struggling right now without a female confidant. I've been craving to connect with my mom, but that hasn't been working out lately. Maybe the universe is sending me Mandy instead?

I don't know.

As always, there's serenity in the surrender. I'll have to see how this plays out, but I have a feeling I'll be keeping my guard up. Who knows? This might not even go anywhere. She'll probably never text again anyway.

All good.

…Q

Quick:

Forward Motion

Typically, as the flowers began to bloom and the critters awakened from hibernation to revel in the warmer temperatures, my self-loathing tendency to isolate intensified.

But not that year.

I felt lighter that year. Happier. And less guilty for being happy, too. Connecting with someone was part of it, sure, but it was also Quinn. It was the essence of her. Her attitude towards life, her acceptance, her forgiveness, her authenticity, her goodness. I envied all of it, and as the season of spring kicked off, I realized that somewhere along the line, subconsciously, I was emulating her. Not only that, but I was better off for it.

I decided to switch to the conscious, and by the end of March, I committed myself to taking the difficult month of April head on. When I shared this pledge with Quinn, she reacted exactly as I knew she would. Every single thing she said was a statement of support, emphasized by that adorable exclamation point.

After all her bursts of encouragement, she finally settled down enough to hit me with the one simple yet profound question that I hadn't even considered. "So how are you going to accomplish this goal?" She giggled as she witnessed my expression change, gleaning that the actionable details had not quite been determined yet. She patted my hand and told me that not only did she know I would figure it out, but that I would be successful, too. I couldn't help but grin. She really did have a way of making me feel strong and deserving.

I contemplated the question over the course of a couple days and created a short list. As brief as it was, though, I recognized that it was a tall order, given my track record over the last five years, as well as my family's.

1. I will not miss a day of school in April.
2. I will talk to Dad about Mom's self-medicating habit.
3. I will ask Dad if he could spend more time at home.

I tried to start that spring with the idea that I deserve happiness, that I needed to forgive myself, that maybe I don't need to be punished forever. Perhaps it was because I was approaching adulthood that I realized I couldn't live like this forever. Geoffrey wouldn't have wanted me to. He would have wanted me to make something of myself and to be happy, and the patterns I had been existing in for a half-decade did not lend to a fulfilling life.

My friendship with Quinn made me feel like I had the strength to move forward, but even more so, like I had a reason to.

Quinn:

A Break

The knowledge that Quick's brother, Geoffrey, was kidnapped at an amusement park haunted me. Endless questions relentlessly invaded my mind at the most unexpected times and often paralyzed me. I figured the only way to release myself from this plague was to satiate my questions with answers. I was desperate to understand, mainly because I was desperate to help. Nonetheless, I should have known better than to insert myself into a healing journey without being invited to do so.

Out of respect for my friend, I never once did an internet search on his family. I never looked for a newspaper article, a missing person's report, or anything of the sort. That was how I justified my research; I told myself that I was simply investigating the facts regarding kidnapping, like I would any other topic. I conveniently ignored the truth of our original no-no list, and before I knew it, I leapt into a rabbit hole larger than any hole I had ever happened upon before. It was impossible to crawl out of, and once it had taken hold, it completely consumed me.

Spring Break came a bit early that year, and I spent it almost entirely online. I searched in secret, a largely considerable clue that I was venturing into the land of betrayal. Quick had no idea I was learning about the millions of children who go missing every single year, almost a million in our country alone. Granted, different sources reported varying statistics, but no matter where I looked, the numbers were appalling. What was even more horrifying, and beyond comprehension, was what I was unearthing regarding the evils of child trafficking. It was impossible to "unknow" things, and I found myself wishing I could, especially when restful sleep evaded me night after night.

My tried-and-true techniques for settling my mind became ineffective. No amount of crystal healing or guided meditations, kundalini mantras or chakra work helped me to release the toxic energy I absorbed when I was forced to acknowledge that such reprehensible evil existed. Additionally, I was being deceitful by neglecting to inform Quick of my dig. My body was physically unable to handle my choice to live unauthentically.

I knew it was only a matter of time before it all came to the surface.

Quick and I were alone in Mr. Erickson's classroom on a Thursday afternoon, snacking on celery and peanut butter while simultaneously working on our latest REED project. We chose to delve into the world of symbolism, from the intricate design on famous cookies to well-known app logos, and a host of things in between.

Grabbing another slathered stalk of celery, Quick had a moment of contemplation before devouring what was apparently one of his favorite foods on the planet. "I feel so bad for people who are allergic to peanut butter. Seriously, it's delicious," he uttered with his mouth full. "What percentage of people do you think are missing out on this delectable source of pure joy?"

"Delectable source of pure joy, huh?" I snickered. "I'll look it up. What's your guess?" I asked as my fingers clicked the keyboard on their way to the answers.

He guessed five percent at the exact time that I reacted to what I was seeing on the screen. "Woah, that's it? At first glance, it looks like only one or two percent of Americans. Hold on, let me—" I was so engrossed in the statistics on my screen that I didn't even notice Quick walked over and was standing right next to me.

"What in the hell is that?" The edge to Quick's voice sent chills all the way down my spine. What occurred next seemingly happened in slow motion. I looked up at his livid expression, saw his pointer finger, and tracked it back to my screen. Back to the tabs in the background. Back to the phrase, "child trafficking." I dropped my head in shame, speechless and remorseful.

"Have you been researching kidnapping, Quinn?" His tone was accusatory and impatient. "Quinn! What's with all the trafficking tabs? I thought we agreed to—Quinn, it was your idea not to! You were the one who—I can't believe this!" He was unmistakably livid, and rightfully so.

"I was thinking if I understood it better, maybe I could help. Maybe it would help if—"

"Why are you always imposing? This is my business, not yours. I am not your problem to solve, Quinn! I can't believe you. I really can't." The anger was subsiding, but something much worse was replacing it.

"I'm so sorry, Quick. I didn't mean to hurt you." My eyes welled up with tears and I buried my face in my hands.

"Well, you did."

A painstakingly long series of silent moments occupied the space as he collected his belongings. It was not the first time Quick suddenly prepared to depart a location, but we both inherently understood that this time, it was different.

And what he articulated on his way out the door confirmed it.

With his gaze towards his feet and his body halfway out the door, he calmly stated, "I think I'll take a break from club for a while." But we both knew what he was really taking a break from.

Hey Geoffrey,

I'm so frickin' pissed. And irritated. And disappointed. And hurt. But mostly frickin' pissed.

We agreed from the beginning not to do any digs on kid stuff, like SIDS and missing children. It was her frickin' idea. Come to find out that she's not only doing a dig on missing children but on child trafficking?

I walked out and couldn't even make it to the school gate before I threw up. Thinking of you being taken from us is bad enough, but to think that you were ~~traff~~ abused in some way, in any way, makes my stomach violently turn. I can't even go there.

I've been crying for hours. I have successfully shoved that possibility out of my mind for years now, but to have it slap me in the face out of nowhere like that, and by the one person I trust? I'm so pissed. I feel betrayed. That's how I feel. Betrayed. I should have known better than to let someone in. I should have never trusted her or opened myself up to her. Or opened myself up to anyone in any way.

Just in time for April. I'll deal with this month by myself, as it should be. It's what is warranted, what I have earned, and I hate myself for ever thinking otherwise.

Please forgive me, Geoffrey. For the millionth time, I wish it was me instead of you.

I love you, brother.

-Deck

○○○

hey des what's the deal with the witch and her boyf

Desiree / 6:25 p.m.

what do you mean

6:25 p.m.

are they still super tight in that one class you have with them

6:26 p.m.

idk I don't really pay attention. why

6:27 p.m.

I think they broke up

6:28 p.m.

whaaaaaaaaaaattttttttt why

6:29 p.m.

they haven't been together at lunch for like a week
and she's been walking home alone

6:30 p.m.

what are you like stalking them

6:31 p.m.

shut up no but seriously I think they broke up

6:35 p.m.

aaaw that's kinda sad

6:35 p.m.

sad?! why is that sad??
now I really need to know what happened
he probably figured out that she's the wicked witch of the west

6:36 p.m.

why do you care so much

6:37 p.m.

idk

6:38 p.m.

you're putting way too much energy into all of this

6:39 p.m.

whatever

Friday, April 19, 2024

Note to self:

It's been almost three weeks since Quick left our club. There has not been one peep, not even a glance in my direction. He doesn't acknowledge my existence, not in the hallway, not in the classroom, not on the lawn, not by text. I am completely dead to him, and my heart is shattered. My inability to release my curiosity, to honor his wishes, to let his healing journey organically unfold… It all cost me my one and only friend.

Mom, Dad, and I smiled and sobbed our way through our triple tradition today as we celebrated the life of our Troy. As much as I dread the reason for it, I am also keenly aware of my appreciation for what the day brought. It was as though Mom and I pressed a reset button, and I felt closer to her than I have in a really long while. Troy's birthday gives us a sense of perspective, a reminder not to get swept up in the nonsense of the daily grind and to focus on what really matters. A family afternoon centered around love was exactly what I needed, and it helped my heart feel better.

But now, sitting here in my room, all I can think about is Quick and how much I miss him. I could apologize a million times, but I don't think it will ever be enough. I hurt him in a way that I'm not even sure I understand, and I have absolutely no idea how to make it right.

Maybe that's my lesson, though. Maybe it's not up to me to "make it right." I need to stop trying to fix everything all the time. That's what got me into this mess in the first place. All I can do is work on me. I can control my thoughts, my emotions, and my actions, but I cannot control anyone else's. I have to continue to grow as a human being and work on radiating my light, and hope that it brings him back to me. When he's ready.

Hopefully it's "when" he's ready, and not "if ever."

…Q

ooo

Mandy / 8:38 p.m.

hey

Quinn / 8:42 p.m.

Hi, Mandy. How are you?

8:43 p.m.

good thanks
how are you

8:43 p.m.

I'm okay.

8:44 p.m.

stressed with all the end of year stuff

8:45 p.m.

Ha ha, yes, a little bit. Finals are never fun.

8:45 p.m.

right??
looking forward to summer break

8:46 p.m.

I am, too. Although I have to admit, sometimes I get a little bored.

8:47 p.m.

yeah I get that
maybe we can hang out sometime

8:51 p.m.

Sure, that sounds nice.

8:52 p.m.

cool see you around

8:53 p.m.

Ok, have a good rest of your night.

8:53 p.m.

you too

Quick:

The Revelation

To say that I isolated myself that spring would be an understatement of epic proportions. I completely alienated myself from everyone. I couldn't bring myself to look in Quinn's direction at school, and I went days at a time without even talking to my parents at home. Old habits die hard.

It was during this time of total solitude that I had a revelation of sorts. But not about Quinn, not about my folks, and not about Geoffrey. About my digs. This sudden revelation was quite simple but struck me as very profound: Being aware of the lies that were woven into our society was a double-edged sword.

A total paradox.

A cursed blessing.

On one hand, knowing the variety of truths and mistruths around me was freeing, like I was being emancipated. Conversely, to be totally detached from others because they were not seeing the world in the same way I did was like shackling myself instead to seclusion and loneliness. While I often felt liberated when doing my research, the lack of connection with others brought about feelings that were agonizing in their own way. There was an incessant battle within me that I could never reconcile.

The revelation didn't stop there.

The awareness of the hidden truths, even though I had only scratched the surface on a small amount of what I assumed was an endless number of topics, gave rise to a special kind of anguish. The sorrow and frustration that came with questioning everything around me was exhausting. It was nearly insufferable to have reservations about every belief I ever had, to be dubious of fundamental concepts, and to shatter the narratives of our lives.

I recognized that allowing myself to invite Quinn to share this process with me made it more bearable. Enjoyable even. I was able to experience a reprieve from a world of superficial dialogue. I could shovel in and dig deep but then still be able to navigate my days with an authentic friendship. I no longer needed to wonder if there were others out there like me, and to have that reciprocated support system was a remarkable addition to my life. I didn't realize how much I was relying on it until I abruptly rejected it.

The demise of our friendship caused a level of destruction that I did not see coming. It set me back further than I was before our bond was created, and not only did I find myself disengaging with the world around me even more, but I also found myself putting down the shovel entirely. I never imagined wishing for that "blissful ignorance" that everyone talked about, but sure enough, there I was ending my junior year of high school doing just that. I decided that I was done digging, but never for a moment did I believe that ignorant bliss would actually follow.

Hey Geoffrey,

I need someone to do this with me and you're all I've got. So here goes nothing.

> Ok, Google.
> You too, Bing.
> Brave.
> Duck Duck Go.
> All of you. Here we go.
>
> Clear browsing history.
> Clear cache.
> Clear tabs.
>
> Ok, that's it.
>
> No more rabbit holes.
> No more digging.
> I'm done.
>
> For real this time.

Ugh. I'm already bored. I guess I should have done an internet search on hobbies before I made my grand exit.

Miss you.

-Deck

Note to self:

It's been almost two months now since Quick has spoken to me. We're about to go on summer break for eleven weeks or something like that, and I can just feel it in my gut… If we go through vacation without mending this, it will be over for sure. I am missing him terribly, to the point where my stomach hurts, and I can barely think about anything else.

I've been trying to give him the space he needs, but lately I've been worried that he will perceive the space as a lack of effort due to my acceptance of our ending. But I do not accept it! And the last thing I want is for him to think I do. So, two nights ago I texted him and apologized yet again. I explained that by not reaching out I was trying to be respectful, not aloof, and that I was wrong for attempting to control his process. Honestly, I over-texted. I wanted to tell him every single possible thing, just in case it was my last opportunity to do so. So yes, I told him I missed him, that I would do anything to make it right, and I pleaded for him to forgive me. I held back nothing, and I'm okay with that.

I'm not okay with the fact that he didn't respond. It's torture.

To center myself, I spent hours last night making him his fourth page. I immersed myself in 639 hertz and surrounded myself with my rose quartz, aventurine, and amazonite crystals in an effort to summon as much heart chakra energy as I could. I poured my heart into designing the page that read, "While one cannot erase mistakes, one can and should learn from them." I utilized every shade of red that I had, and attached a small heart eraser to what I thought was my best lettering work yet.

I enclosed it in a manilla envelope and placed it on his desk as I walked by him in history class today. Quick did not demonstrate acknowledgment of my presence in the slightest, not even a blink. As I sat down, I looked toward the front of the room and caught Mr. Erickson's gaze. With a look of blended sympathy and compassion, he smiled at me. It never once crossed my mind in all this time that Mr. Erickson knew of our club's dissolution. Of course he gathered that something was amiss, and by the looks of it, it was breaking his heart, too.

I can only hope that when Quick opens that envelope, he can sense how deeply remorseful I am.

...Q

Hey Geoffrey,

This summer is going to suck.

-Deck

Friday, May 24, 2024

Note to self:

This summer is going to suck.

…Q

Quick:

Astonished

My summer vacation started off as I wanted it to. In solitary seclusion. Just the way I liked it. My bedroom was the perfect hermitage, with its dark window coverings and its close proximity to the kitchen. I was back to sleeping all the time, as much as fourteen or sixteen hours a day, and when I was awake, I was using my energy to eradicate thoughts of Quinn and the terrifying nightmare she put in my head.

For a while, my parents didn't even notice that I was a recluse. Either that or they didn't care. They didn't knock on my door once. A few times, my dad and I happened upon each other as I was throwing together some food, but the conversation never went beyond an exchange of three or four niceties, most of which were monosyllabic responses. Yeah. Good. Cool. Bye. As for my mom, she was basically a zombie. How could she possibly notice what was going on with me?

My life in this quiet, lonesome darkness only lasted about two weeks. In mid-June, my folks informed me that now that I was seventeen, I needed to get a job. Almost as though they wanted a prize or a pat on the back, they gloated that they gave me two weeks to unwind from the school year, but enough was enough. Well, my dad informed me. My dad gloated. My dad put his foot down. My mom was just physically present for it. I didn't argue or protest; I had already been considering a place of employment for a few days prior anyway.

The grocery store.

I was getting tired of eating the same crap. Instant ramen and plain sandwiches and potato chips. I figured if I worked at the grocery store, I could not only learn of the different options out there, but I could grab them after a shift. Maybe even for a discount.

After showering the next morning, I put on my least wrinkled T-shirt and my nicest pair of jeans. They were a little loose and it occurred to me that I was so tired of eating what was in the kitchen that I kinda stopped consuming food. That wasn't good. Just thinking about the grocery store, my stomach alerted me that it, too, was ready for this change.

I walked to the store that was closest to my home, which was about a mile and a half away, hoping that my first try would be a hit. Nope. The manager basically laughed at me. But I took something away from the experience and went home to create a resume. It was a pretty pathetic one, and it stung to list REED under the section, "Experience," but I printed it out anyway.

On Day 2, resume in hand, I headed in the opposite direction for about two miles. Again, I asked to speak with the manager and again, it was a miss. They weren't hiring. Try again in a month or so. I tucked that possibility into my brain's pocket and hoped I would find a gig before then.

I woke up on Day 3, and as I sat up to turn off my alarm, I took in a deep breath. As I sighed my air out, I said to myself, "I got this." I didn't plan to do that. And I didn't realize I did it until after I did it. "That damn Quinn got into my head so deep," I muttered to myself as I trotted to the bathroom.

I guess the third time really is a charm. When I arrived after the three-mile walk to the supermarket, I encountered my future first boss: a seething and stressed-out middle-aged man. Apparently, one of the guys who worked in the produce section decided to hit the road with his band and he had informed the manager that very morning. Hastily, he grabbed my resume, took one cursory glance at it, tossed it on his desk, and asked, "Can you start today?"

He asked if I knew anything about produce, and I confidently told him that I'm a quick learner. Before long, I was unloading trucks, organizing fruits and vegetables, removing expired produce, and cleaning floors and shelves. Occasionally a customer would ask me a question, but the engagements tended to be short and sweet. Not too painful. All in all, I really liked the job and ended up taking every shift that was offered. Sure, it was nice to earn money, and yes, I was enjoying the new eats I was discovering, but it also felt good to accomplish things. To be noticed somewhere. To be needed somewhere.

One afternoon, about ten days into my life as an employee, I noticed something in the produce department. Well, no. I noticed it during my very first shift. But I didn't think about it until that moment. Maybe I was no longer so entrenched in learning my duties that my brain allowed itself to do what it always did. Asked questions. Was curious. Sent me down rabbit holes.

Again.

I guess it was only a matter of time.

After that shift, I ran home at a pace that would have made my junior high buddy proud. I couldn't get to my computer quickly enough. I had a very strong feeling that there was a story behind the codes on produce stickers. Some were four digits, others five. Some started with a three or a four, others with an eight or a nine. As I sifted through the data and details provided on the much-later listed search hits, I found more than I intended. Not only were some of the codes concerning, but I came across information on preservation coatings on produce whose listed ingredients were fungicides, pesticides, and herbicides, another set of words for poison. Even worse, the great majority of the coating's ingredients were mysteriously unnamed.

I was worried I would be appalled by what I would find when I started my dig. I wanted to be wrong, but I wasn't. I was horrified.

Again.

I was shocked by how much deception existed right under our noses. I was shocked by how motivating greed must be for some. I was shocked that people would intentionally put others at risk. I was shocked that they would be able to sleep at night. So shocked that I barely slept myself that evening. But all that shock combined paled in comparison to how astonished I was when I woke up the next morning.

A brand-new bike was parked in the kitchen, with a card that read, "We're proud of you, son." It broke me. I literally fell to the tile floor and sobbed. My parents loved me, they really did. We were just all so messed up, so guilt-ridden, so awful at communication. I cried and I cried, all by myself in a ball at the foot of the refrigerator until I realized that I was going to be late to work. Not because I had a morning meltdown. Because I didn't know how to ride the bike.

And that realization made me laugh out loud.

000

Mandy / 7:18 p.m.

hey quinnie what's up

Quinn / 7:31 p.m.

Hi, Mandy. Oh my gosh, I haven't heard that name in ages.
How's your summer going?

7:33 p.m.

pretty chill not much going on

7:33 p.m.

Yeah, same here.
Are you doing anything fun for the holiday tomorrow?

7:35 p.m.

my aunt and cousins are coming over for swimming and fireworks
what about you

7:37 p.m.

Not much. I think my dad is going to barbecue.

7:38 p.m.

wanna come hang here?

7:38 p.m.

That's really nice of you to ask, thank you.
I should really spend it with my parents though.
But thank you, Mandy.

7:39 p.m.

yea no problem
remember that one fourth of july

7:39 p.m.

With the night flower?! How could I forget?

7:41 p.m.

right?! I literally thought we were going to blow up the neighborhood

7:43 p.m.

That was the reason we got smart and had a bucket of water and a
hose on hand from then on, LOL

7:45 p.m.

for sure

7:57 p.m.

Ok, well, have a good time tomorrow.
Happy Fourth of July!

7:58 p.m.

same

Wednesday, July 3, 2024

Note to self:

The last five weeks have been utterly bizarre. The minutes ticked by in an excruciatingly slow manner, and yet now that the month has passed, it has become a blur of meditations in Troy's Zen garden, tense conversations with Mom, quiet walks to the waterfall, and bookstore visits with Dad.

Being in the Zen garden still brings me so much peace, and as I do body scan meditations while lying still on the sand, I can sense my baby brother's presence through the stillness. I found myself needing to visit there quite a bit recently, as it seems like Mom and I are frequently butting heads now. I know this is her first time with a child so close to high school graduation, and surely that fills her with a plethora of emotions that she's not sure how to handle, but apparently the only way she knows how to deal with those feelings right now is to jump down my throat. If she isn't snapping at me about college applications, she is berating me with a barrage of questions regarding my future to which I do not have any answers yet.

The quiet walks to the waterfall were the hopeful moments, the ones where I imagined I'd bump into Quick along the way or arrive only to find him already there, enjoying the sounds and the scenery. But each hopeful hike ended in disappointment, as I walked back home after an hour or so with my head hanging low in shame, wishing I could earn Quick's forgiveness and trust again. Dad must have sensed something in the earlier part of the month, because he started offering to take me to the bookstore after my waterfall visits. Books are so good for my soul, and I am continually astounded by how much information is out there, waiting to be discovered. Not only did I add a few new feel-deal-heal techniques to my repertoire, but I also ventured into the gardening section and discovered the vast world of herbs. As a matter of fact, I am drinking a cup of holy basil tea right now, since it is shown to alleviate physical and emotional stress.

I miss Quick, but I'm trying to move forward in a positive way. I really am. I've dealt with loss before, a much deeper one than this, and at a much younger, less mature age. But here I am again, finding myself with an undeniable chasm. I really don't know how else to explain it. I feel like part of me is missing.

I've reached out a few times, probably once a week or so, just to say hi. He hasn't responded to any of my texts. It stings, but it makes me realize how much I hurt him. I worry that I made things worse for him, because each time I think about it, I am more convinced that he never considered the possibility of trafficking when it came to Geoffrey until I slammed it in his face. If I know Quick at all, the idea probably haunts him 24/7 now. So I get why he's done with me. I messed up pretty badly. I have to accept his choice and move on as best as I can.

Interestingly enough, Mandy has been reaching out and even suggesting we spend time together. I felt nostalgic tonight as we texted about our childhood Independence Day celebrations, but in all honesty, I'd rather make new memories with Quick than relive old ones with her. Poor Quick. His family doesn't celebrate Christmas, so surely they don't commemorate Old Glory with fireworks and popsicles. That's sad. He should. He deserves to have sparklers in his life.

Sigh.

...Q

Hey Geoffrey,

Tomorrow's your favorite. You used to call it "Boom Boom Day," which always cracked us up but you never understood why. And when you were extra little, like around three, you'd get so excited for the festivities that you'd squeal, "bed, right, and boo firecwackers!" Everything made you so frickin' excited, Geoffrey. You were truly the coolest kid.

So yeah, tomorrow's the Fourth of July. I'm going to go out on a limb here and say that, yet again, we won't be lighting any Piccolo Petes on the street and we won't be picnicking at the park to watch the big firework show either. We'll skip it, like we have all the other holidays since you've been gone.

Maybe we shouldn't be skipping the holiday, or any of them for that matter. I know why we do, because we would feel guilty to experience any of it without you. But maybe we're looking at it all wrong. Maybe it's about experiencing it FOR you, like to honor you. That's all I want to do. Honor you.

I should talk to our folks about it. I should, but I won't. Now that I think about it, this holiday is probably why Mom seems extra doped up.

I love you so much.

Happy Boom Boom Day, brother.

-Deck

07/04/24

3:03 a.m.

My heavy eyes follow the retreating form of my mother and I strain to see other details in the strange room. There is little furniture: three other empty beds against the side walls, an old wooden desk with a tucked chair and a wired telephone, and a few scattered office chairs. I notice my dad kneeling near the back of the room, his elbows on the seat of a chair with his hands clasped together and his eyes closed. "He looks so small," I think to myself, but my thought is interrupted by a deep voice resonating from across the room.

Dressed in uniform, the man is massive in stature. He approaches my father and introduces himself kindly, but his tone commands attention and respect. He begins to converse with my father and I can see the anguish on my dad's face. He is silently wiping the tears as they drip down his cheeks, not really participating in the conversation. The tears begin to slow, and I notice that his skin is turning a deeper and darker shade of red as the man continues to talk to him.

"Mr. Williams, if you could just walk me through this one more time, I'd—"

And with that, my dad snaps.

"I've already told you people everything I know! Where we were, what he was wearing, all of it! Now why don't you tell me your plan as to how in the hell you're going to find my son!"

Quinn:

Better Than a Movie

He deserves to have sparklers in his life.

That assertion, penned by my own hand, kept me up most of the night that bridged July third to July fourth. The more I considered the proclamation, the more strongly it took hold of my heart. Yes, darn it, Quick deserved sparklers. He was worthy of frolicking in the middle of the street, unabashedly releasing all reservation while waving a stick of popping, crackling bursts of firelight and giggling with the silliness that I knew he craved deep down. But even more so, Quick deserved the sparklers of life: Love for himself. Love for others. Love from others. As I had done most nights, I wished and prayed that Quick would someday see that he was worthy of the joys of life.

At some point during my somnolent phase of the evening, I crafted a scenario in my mind where I celebrated the holiday with Quick. Half-asleep, I played out an entire feature film, starting with the initial scene of purchasing sparklers and fireworks at the nearby pop-up stand and continuing on to the moment I surprised him at his house, arms full of red, white, and blue entertainment. He was so thrilled to see me that all was forgiven and forgotten, and we spent hours upon hours setting off fireworks, hooting and hollering as if each one we lit was the most exciting of them all.

Perhaps it was because of my dozy state, but I really started to believe that my mind's movie could become reality. I contemplated the pros and the cons of my choice to knock on Quick's door unannounced and uninvited, and the list of pros weighed so much more than its rival. "What's the worst that can happen?" I asked myself out loud, knowing in that moment that I was indubitably going to the pop-up stand first thing in the morning.

Aware that I would spend the afternoon and early evening with my parents, I decided to time the trek to Quick's house to put me there around six o'clock. I figured that was good timing. As the time drew nearer and nearer, I could feel the nerves rising up and the bravery simmering down, but I refused to concede to the worries that came with the "what if" questions. Most of those never happened anyway. I remembered reading once that only 8 percent of what people worry about actually occurs. I took that to mean that there was a 92 percent chance Quick would talk to me that night.

As I approached his front door, a thick wooden one behind a locked wrought iron entry, I rubbed my pink opal stone in my left hand. I closed my eyes to take three deep breaths, manifesting forgiveness and calming my heart center before mustering up all of my courage to ring the doorbell. My quivering pointer finger reached out to connect with the brass-trimmed button and I realized that my knees were wobbly from their tremors as well. One more deep breath, I told myself, and then I'll push it. Deep breath in. Big sigh out. Ding dong.

There was no turning back.

I looked around as I waited. Their porch was bare. There was not one potted plant. No wreath. No lantern. No rocking chair. Nothing. Not one sign that anyone lived there. I turned to take in the details of their front lawn, and it looked just as barren. Desert rocks. No bushes. No cacti. No trees. Not even one boulder to break up the flat sea of one-inch tan rocks. I shifted again and faced the house to see the paint chipping away, along with massive piles of wind-blown leaves and dry brush building up at the base of the wall corners. My heart sank as reality sunk in: This house looked completely abandoned. Totally unloved. It reminded me of my lost oasis, and as a frown began to form on my face, I was alerted to the fact that I must have been standing at the front door for at least three minutes. I mustered up the bravery once again.

Ding dong.

This time, I heard shuffling within the house and someone fumbling with the lock inside. The heavy door finally creaked opened to reveal who was once a stunning woman, tall and slender with lovely facial features and long locks of black hair. Now with hollow and bloodshot eyes, the middle-aged woman pushed her matted hair away from her face with her trembling hand to stare vacantly at the stranger on her doorstep. "Who the hell are you?" her raspy voice muttered, almost as though she was voicing her thought aloud, not really intending it for me at all.

"Hi, I—" I began, but my stammering was abruptly suspended as Quick pushed past his mother, swung open the iron door, grabbed me under my upper arm, and forcefully led me off his porch, around the front of his house, and onto his driveway out of sight from his mom. It all happened so quickly. There he was, standing right in front of me. Our eyes locked, and I found myself completely frozen with a thousand questions and even more realizations. Quick's mother was an unavailable addict. Oh. My. Gosh. It made so much sense.

Quick released his grip on my arm and then slowly lowered his hand to his side, maintaining eye contact the entire time. After what seemed like an eternity, he cleared his throat and softly whispered, "I'm sorry if I hurt your arm." I shook my head to signal that he hadn't. "And I'm sorry that you had to see that," he gestured toward the front door as his sad eyes glanced downward. He noticed the basket I had dropped along the way and started to apologize again. "And I'm sorry that I made you drop—"

"No, I'm sorry, Quick." I reached my hands towards his face and cradled his cheeks in my palms. "I'm so, so sorry," I whispered. I gazed into his eyes, trying to fill them with all the love I had to give while simultaneously searching for answers within them. He slowly blinked as he covered my hands with his and lowered his forehead to mine. No more words were spoken. We stood there, swaying softly together, both of us with tears streaming down our faces. Tears of sadness and regret, friendship and gratitude. Tears of love.

It was I who finally drew the moment to a close as I turned my palms to grasp his hands and then guided us to a seated position on the driveway, facing one another. Although we remained silent, still with hands held and eyes locked, the communication between us was monumental.

Never in my life had I ever been more certain of the timing of things. As painful as the time without Quick was for me, it was necessary. For both of us. I could sense that he had grown over the course of those few months, and an eager feeling of excitement welled up within me as I anticipated learning of it. I was already proud of him and I didn't even know why yet.

Never had I ever been more certain of our friendship, that it was authentically raw, perfectly imperfect, and wholly unconditional. No matter what was to come, we would experience it together. The good, the bad, the happy, the sad. We would do it all together.

And as I gazed at my best friend that early evening, never had I ever been more certain that I loved him. While I didn't understand the nuances and variations of love, whether it was that of friendship or more or both, the magnitude of love that radiated from me that night was undeniable.

While the neighborhood of squealing children around us celebrated with firecracker after firecracker, we simply sat. I squeezed his hands and he gently stroked my finger with his thumb, and as I smiled my messages to him, I could feel his thoughts, too. Nothing really needed to be spoken. We were surrounded by our bubble of friendship and forgiveness, of appreciation and adoration.

Quick released my left hand to retrieve something from his pocket. He opened his palm to reveal the small heart-shaped eraser and my own heart swelled to what felt like double its size. Without a second's hesitation, I embraced him, my arms wrapped tightly around his neck before his arms slid slowly and gingerly into a loose hold around my seated waist. "I missed you, Quick."

"Not as much as I missed you, Quinn." He unraveled our hug to look at me. "I'm sorry I haven't texted. I didn't know what to say or how to say it, but seeing you now—"

"It's like we don't have to say anything at all." I smiled. He nodded, and a chunk of his shaggy hair fell in front of his eyes. I tucked it back behind his ear and made sure we shared our gaze before I confidently whispered, "I understand you."

In that moment, Quick let go.

I watched it in real time. I could see him release it all, to the universe and to me. His broad shoulders left that place of tension by his ears and finally dropped down to where they belonged, a place I wasn't sure I had ever seen them before. With his chin held high, his eyes looked to the heavens, and he exhaled with his entire being. As difficult as it was and as much as I could hear the whimpers and pain in his voice, he pushed through. He told me every single detail he could remember from that awfully fateful day in April all those years ago, from the dropped churro and the panic to the yelling and the vomit. And it did not stop there. Quick proceeded to tell me about how long the search for his brother felt and how the investigators finally suggested for them to accept that Geoffrey was gone; about his mother's addiction, how she could never look at him, how he was convinced she blamed and hated him for what happened; about his father's continual absence and how hard it must be for him to see the shell of his wife; about his letters to Geoffrey along with the nightmares and flashbacks; about the guilt-ridden dysfunctionality that overshadowed the love he thought his father felt for him and wished his mother still did; about how he never allowed himself to think about what happened to Geoffrey after he was kidnapped; and about how easy it was to forgive me because he knew I only had the best of intentions for him.

Quick held back nothing. For nearly two hours, he spoke and he cried, he whispered and he sobbed, he yelled and he sniveled. Never moving from our initial spot on his exposed driveway, we were barely aware of the world around us. The neighbors had all retreated to their homes, their supplies of fireworks and fun depleted, and as Quick's session subsided, we noticed the silence that surrounded us.

I disturbed the stillness as I reached to grab his hand. "Thank you for trusting me, Quick."

"Quinn, I should be the one thanking you. It was ridiculous of me to ever think I could go it alone." His eyes were filled with gratitude.

"It sounds like you have your own Life Lessons to share there, Quick," I kidded. "But in all seriousness, please know this." I paused to gather my thoughts, knowing that Quick would never rush me to speak. "You don't ever have to go it alone. I will always be here with you and for you. But you should also know that you *did* do it. You have grown so much on this journey, Quick, and you *did* do all of that hard work on your own. You're brave and you're strong, and I hope you can see what I see. I see you, over the worst part of the healing journey, and as corny as it sounds and I never mean to sound condescending, but Quick, I am so, so proud of you."

Comfortable in the silence, I waited patiently for the response I knew he was formulating. In the meantime, I took in the gentle breeze and the scent of sulfur it carried with it. I let my mind wander to the memories triggered by the odor, celebrations of the past that were filled with glee, knowing full well there would never be an Independence Day that would top the one I was experiencing right then.

"You're right. I did do that. But I couldn't have done it without your support and your inspiration." He paused before he asked, "Fair?" He winked at me, and my stomach did a triple back flip like it was in the Emotional Olympics.

"Fair."

My phone dinged, and I knew immediately that it was my dad. I had completely forgotten to update him on my plans. I was about to text him to come pick me up, but Quick stopped me. "I can take you home," he announced.

"Whhaaaaaatttt?! Are you driving now?" My astonished reaction was thunderously loud and may as well have been the sparklers that were still waiting in my basket.

He chuckled as he stood up and helped me to do the same. "Here, you hold your basket and I'll hold you, how's that?"

"Quick, you cannot carry me home. That's absurd." He scoffed at me before turning on his heel and going around the back side of the house. He returned moments later pushing a bike toward me, his beautiful face brandishing the most ridiculous grin. He hopped on his bike and patted his handlebars, an invitation I simply could not refuse. It took us a couple of minutes to get going, partially because I couldn't get situated but more so because of the laughter fits.

We finally arrived at my house, surprisingly uninjured, and although it was the most physically uncomfortable traveling mode I had ever experienced, I couldn't remember a time in my life that I felt happier. I felt guilty for a snap second, and then I let it go. He was probably feeling similarly, so I decided to voice it.

I chose my words carefully. "Quick, I've never been as happy as I am right now, and I am not going to allow myself to feel guilty for it."

"Fair. Same." He squeezed my hand and I realized how much of that we had done that night, and how natural it felt to do so. "Sorry we never lit your sparklers. We'll do them next year, I promise."

I looked down at the basket quizzically. "Do you think they'll still be good in a year?" I was honestly curious about the answer and made a mental note to search for information regarding the shelf life of sparklers.

"You're so dense sometimes, Quinn," Quick chuckled. "That was the piece of my statement you picked up on?" His dark brown eyes sparkled under the streetlight, but I swore the twinkles were just for me. I blushed when I realized what he was alluding to.

"You think we'll be spending this holiday together again next year?" I quietly asked, suddenly and unexpectedly bashful.

Without an ounce of reservation, he enveloped me in his arms and murmured in my ear, "Yeah. Of course we will. We're Quick and Quinn."

I disentangled from the hug and brought my forehead to his. Our eyes locked, only inches apart from each other, and I smiled. "Quick and Quinn. Through thick and thin."

"I love that." he smiled back. And with that, I practically skipped to my front door, exuberant that the evening I experienced was better than any movie I could have ever concocted.

ooo

Quick / 11:17 p.m.

good night

Quinn / 11:17 p.m.

Good night!

11:17 p.m.

best night ever

11:17 p.m.

Best. Night. Ever.

11:17 p.m.

so far

11:18 p.m.

I like that.
I'm so happy right now. Thank you for forgiving me.

11:18 p.m.

there was nothing to forgive
thanks for not giving up on me

11:19 p.m.

Never ever never.

Hey Geoffrey,

Aside from my times with you, this is the happiest I have ever felt. You know I'd give anything to go back to the days of our childhood together, and it's taken me a long time to accept that I can't. Now I know that you'd want me to be happy, and Geoffrey, Quinn makes me so happy. But it's not like I need her to be happy. I was getting there on my own. It's just that everything is better when I share it with her. I don't know how else to explain it. She makes me feel free. It's the best feeling in the world, to feel totally free. We have no secrets and we are totally ourselves around each other. And everything is so fun with her, and even when we're not having fun, even when we're in the middle of deep and sad conversations, it still feels right to share them with her. Whether the conversation is about you, our family's pseudo-dissolution, Troy, or her dynamic with her mom... whatever the topic and no matter how heavy, our talks are honest and unconstrained.

Looking back, I can't believe how long she and I went without talking. We both agree that it was kinda good, though. If nothing else, we appreciate each other more.

We've certainly been making up for lost time. I've seen Quinn daily since Boom Boom Day. It's only been like three days, but I swear we've crammed a month into those three days. I'm still working plenty, and I love it when she surprises me at work pretending to need lettuce, but I also don't intend to grab every available shift anymore. We've gone back to our waterfall for picnics, she's taken me to her favorite bookstore, and I've taken her around on my handlebars. FaceTiming for hours is basically standard now, too.

I was telling her tonight how much I love my job and the sentiments that come with it. You know, like how it feels good to accomplish tasks and accomplish them well, to be needed and relied upon, all that stuff. She was totally fascinated the other day, too, when I told her about my latest digs on produce codes. I knew she would be. She is the most open-minded and least judgmental person I know. Well, that's not really saying much because I only know like five people, but still.

She makes me kinda more open-minded, too. Like when she talks about all her crystals and her visualization exercises, I've learned to really listen. She swears that she owes her entire healing process (since Troy) to mindfulness and meditation and all that, and I have to give her credit because she really is good. I mean like, healthy good. She's positive and always talking about how grateful she is for this and for that. Even the little stuff, like seeing a hummingbird or whatever. Quinn takes life head on and powers through hard things without ignoring them or dealing with them in unhealthy ways. More power to her. So yeah, I'm pretty open-minded about her "woo woo" stuff. It works for her. What's to say it won't work for me? I'm not saying I'm going to have crystals in my room or start trying to "align my chakras" or however she says it, but I can see myself doing some of it. Like meditation. I think people get weirded out by the word, "meditation," but really, it's just quiet time. And we can all use some of that.

As a matter of fact, I am going to try something right now. I am going to visualize you, right now, smiling down on me. Being happy for me. You'd probably be teasing, "Deck's got a girlfriend, Deck's got a girlfriend!" I can hear you singing it right now. Makes me smile.

She's not my girlfriend. But holy smokes do I adore her. I do. I frickin' adore her.

And I love you.

-Deck

Sunday, July 7, 2024

Note to self:

Oh my gosh, today was such a good day. Honestly, every day is a good day when I get to share part of it with Quick.

We rode over to the park to feed the ducks some rice and frozen peas, which they gobbled up in less time than it took for him to bike us there. I should learn how to ride a bike, too. I mean, seriously. How ridiculous is it that I don't know how to? Ooooh, I am adding that to the list of things I want to learn. Anyway, we ended up copping a squat on the grass and playing tic-tac-toe with rocks and pieces of bark. Even doing that is super fun, so long as I'm with him. He makes me smile from the inside out.

Well, he ended up talking about how he wishes his family would talk more about his brother at home, but he knows how sad his parents get with thoughts of Geoffrey. He's torn, because on the one hand he doesn't want to push his parents, but on the other hand, he's afraid pieces of his brother will be forgotten. I told him that he could always talk to me about Geoffrey, and that I would love to hear every little thing about him. So Quick told me all about this one time he took his brother to play at the park. He took a whole bunch of stuff to do, like a soccer ball and a bug-catcher set, but all Geoffrey wanted to do was play in this splotch of mud that pooled up next to a broken sprinkler head. Quick laughed throughout the entire anecdote, especially when he recalled how the mud ended up everywhere: in his hair, in his ear, in his underwear. It was beautiful to watch him recollect, to see the smiles overtake the sadness.

I think he's starting to get it. It seems like he's getting closer to accepting the truth of it, that what happened was not his fault. That he doesn't need to be punished for life because of what happened. Evil was done by evil, not by him.

And Quick is the furthest thing from evil.

...Q

ooo

Mandy / 6:41 p.m.

hey

Quinn / 6:42 p.m.

Hi, Mandy. How are you?

6:42 p.m.

good
just wanted to wish you a happy birthday tomorrow

6:42 p.m.

Oh my goodness, thank you, Mandy!

6:42 p.m.

let me know if you wanna do something

6:42 p.m.

I already have plans with a friend, but thank you.
Maybe we can hang out next week or something?

6:44 p.m.

sounds good
have a good one

6:45 p.m.

Thank you!

Sunday, July 7, 2024

Note to self:

I'm starting to think Mandy really might have turned over a new leaf. She's been texting off and on for a few months now, and it was thoughtful of her to wish me a happy birthday. I mean, really, what would be in it for her to mess with me? What would she have to gain? It seems like that would be a lot of effort to put in—all the texting, the invitations, the nostalgic reminders—just to mess with me. Let's say it's a scam. Okay, what is she going to do? Vandalize the bathrooms again? I highly doubt it. Is it so far-fetched to think that she's forgiven me? That since we're almost adults, she's liberated herself from elementary school drama? That seems more likely to me than her toying with me.

Maybe I *will* make plans with her then.

I don't know. I reread this note, and I sound super defensive. What the heck? Why is that?

Okay, clearly, I'm conflicted. I'm not making a decision until I know what decision to make. I wish I could talk to Mom about it but she's been so uptight lately, I'm not really enjoying her vibe. And Dad is a good listener, but this kind of stuff is not his forte. Ugh, I'll figure it out.

…Q

Quick:

At Least for Me

I was determined to make Quinn's birthday a day to remember, just as she did for me. Between the Fourth of July and her birthday on the eighth, I had very little time to plan, but I wanted to get it right. By the time her big day rolled around, I was feeling fairly confident in the loose plan I formulated and even more so about the gift I picked out for her. I told her to be ready by ten o'clock, and when I rode up to her house at 9:53, she was already waiting outside. She did a little dance when she saw me turn the corner, and my face broke out into a huge grin. "She's literally a living exclamation point," I laughed to myself as I rolled up next to the sidewalk.

Having mastered the handlebar-riding technique, Quinn hopped right on and we took off for downtown. We had already learned that trying to have a conversation while riding was futile, so I focused on safely delivering my precious cargo while having to lean to the left to avoid her wind-blown hair smacking me in the face.

When we came to a stop sign under the entrance arch of downtown, she thought she had the whole day figured out. "Ooooh, are we headed back to the bookstore? Getting hot chocolate?"

"Please, girl. Give me some credit."

She laughed at my response. "What? I wouldn't mind a do-over of that day. It was so much fun!"

"Yeah, but this will be more fun. Let's go." I helped her off the bike and we walked a block to our first destination. I purposefully watched her so I could see the lightbulb turn on in real time, and it thrilled me to no end when I did indeed catch a glimpse of it. She read the sign, "Rent-a-Ride," and then slowly looked around at the small lot loaded with scooters, bikes, and even a few golf carts. It took her a second, but sure enough, her eyes became the size of saucers and they twinkled like disco balls.

"Am I going to learn how to ride a bike today?" Her face practically exploded with excitement. "I was thinking about how I need to learn how to ride a bike because it's totally absurd that I don't know how, and then I could ride with you places and you wouldn't have to carry me around. But I don't mind the handlebars so we could still do that, too!"

I smiled at her. But not so much at her or for her, but more so because smiling was something that automatically happened when I looked at her. Quinn's enthusiasm was contagious. Her zest for life was infectious. And I was consciously aware that I wanted to spend as much time as I could drawing from that enthusiasm and sharing in that zest.

Helping her learn how to ride a bicycle was a cross between an epic disaster and a successful adventure, not to mention a total ten on a comical scale. As expected, since Quinn tended to voice whatever thought popped into her head at any given moment, there was an ongoing first-person narration of her experience. "So do I sit first or put my feet first? Does it matter which foot is on the lower pedal? Do I have to start with one pedal up and one pedal down, or is it okay if the pedals start at the front and back, like parallel to the ground? What is this lever for? Oh, is it the brake? I thought pushing back on the pedal made it stop. Wait, do bikes reverse? No, oh my gosh, I can't believe I just said that. I would just turn around, never mind." And all of that was before she even moved the bike an inch.

After a couple of hours, she got the hang of it. She would wobble a bit and have to slam her foot down on the ground, but she was getting from Point A to Point B. She did run into a mailbox at one point. She was so focused on not hitting it that she ended up staring at it until it basically smacked her in the face. Like I said, comical. And the way she would slough it off, laugh at herself, get right back up, and keep going? Downright admirable. And it made it okay to laugh with her when she would bail, which was a relief, because watching her learn to ride a bike was funny as hell.

When we passed by an old-fashioned mom-and-pop diner, I asked her if she wanted to take a break and have some lunch. As we parked our bikes and headed inside, my stomach did a little flip. I was slightly nervous to give her the birthday gift, even though I knew she would love it. We ordered our food and grabbed a seat by the window while we waited to eat. She was people-watching and didn't notice that I placed a small box with a bow in front of her.

"Happy birthday, Quinn," I said. She turned her attention to me and immediately noticed the box.

"What is this? I thought we said no gifts!"

"We never said that. I said no gifts for me. We never specified any rules about gifts for you." I winked. That always seemed to affect her, and I loved knowing that. "I hope you like it."

"I will love it, Quick. Thank you." She meant it. She really would love anything. I could have given her a cracked, empty snail shell and she would have thanked me for shell-ebrating her and being her favorite partner-in-slime.

She carefully removed the bow from the box, surely because she intended to keep it. She opened the box to see a stone peeking out from under an informational tag. Silently and intently, Quinn read the particulars about the Super Seven crystal, which I learned was composed of amethyst, clear quartz, rutile, lepidocrocite, cacoxenite, goethite, and smoky quartz. I couldn't even pronounce half of them but she seemed to recognize each name. The lady at the crystals store told me that the Super Seven was supposed to soothe one's energy when overwhelmed by feelings, and I felt like that was a good thing to get for Quinn. She was an empath so surely she was often "overwhelmed by feelings."

Quinn reached over to grab my hand from across the table. "I've read about these, Quick. Supposedly they are super helpful with charging and balancing the chakras system. And they can be channels for manifestation, too. How did you know of such a thing? Where did you find this?" The way her eyes glistened showed me how much the gift meant to her, which in turn made me feel like I was on top of the world.

"There's a cool crystals shop on Second Street. I poked around until the woman who worked there asked me if I needed help. So I told her all about you, and that's what she suggested." I pointed at the stone, which was clearly her new most prized possession given the way she was gazing at it and holding it to her heart.

"You told her all about me? Like what?" she asked.

I felt my cheeks go warm. I stammered some inaudible response and she thankfully let me off the hook.

"This is the most thoughtful gift, Quick. Thank you." She smiled a grateful grin. To know that I was the reason behind her smile was honestly one of the best feelings in the world. Maybe even the best.

"You're welcome. I was thinking we could go over to that shop today if you'd like. I'd love to get you something else, something you'd pick out."

"Oh, Quick, this is *exactly* what I would pick out." And with that, she winked at me. Or at least tried to. She failed, and ended up twitching her face into some bizarre contortion, which of course brought about another one of our classic fits of laughter. It must have been contagious because when the waitress brought over our food, even she started to giggle.

Over lunch, Quinn brought up the fact that Mandy had been reaching out to her via text for a few months, and how at first Quinn was skeptical, but she was starting to think Mandy really did want to reignite the friendship. She must have seen the dubious look on my face because she asked, "Do you not think she's being authentic?"

I carefully responded, "Do you think she's an authentic person?"

I could see her wheels spinning. Without a doubt, she was questioning if it was even possible for an unauthentic person to be authentic. And where Mandy fell on the spectrum of authenticity.

"Hmmmm…I'll have to get back to you on that one. But what I can tell you right now, Quick, is that I am super impressed with the lunch you ordered! Grilled chicken? A fruit bowl? Nice!" She reached over to grab a piece of pineapple. It was a perfect segue for me to tell her all about my latest deep dive into the secrets behind foods, more than just sticker codes and poisonous coatings, and how my job at the produce department opened my eyes to rabbit holes I did not even think twice about before. When I told her that there were dozens and dozens of foods in America that were banned in other countries, she was visibly surprised. We chatted about the possible reasons behind it, and the surprise quickly transformed into disgust. I knew the exact feeling she had in that moment, so I turned the conversation in a new direction.

"So I'm thinking I'll do the Perimeter Challenge. Wanna do it with me?" I asked. She hadn't heard of it before, so I explained that it meant to only eat foods found at the perimeter of the grocery store. Produce. Proteins. Dairy.

It wasn't fail-proof, but avoiding the processed crap in the center aisles had to be a massive improvement.

"I'm in!" she exclaimed as she grabbed another pineapple cube.

Sure enough, we both took the Perimeter Challenge that summer. It became a habit pretty quickly, and it didn't stop there. We had to go all in, of course, and before we knew it, we were starting our own miniature garden in pots under the patio shade on her front porch. She got a little emotional at first, especially when we planted the food scrap green onions, but she pushed through. Even though the green onions turned out to be the ones she attended to the most, the radishes from seeds were the most successful. We had romaine lettuce, cherry tomatoes, celery, and white onions growing a bit, too.

We kept our garden going all summer long and into the fall. We watered the plants and pruned them when needed, and Quinn sang them songs because she was convinced that it helped them grow. I suggested we do an experiment and only sing to some of them, but she thought that was "super mean" to purposefully cripple certain plants like that. Besides, she knew there was plenty of research to support her claim, so she serenaded our crops daily.

To say we ate from our garden would be a bit of an overstatement. We'd nibble on radishes and such, but really, not much grows in the heat of the desert. The whole thing was more about spending time together. Every single day, sometimes for ten minutes and sometimes for two hours, we hung out on the porch. It was always the highlight of the day.

Well, at least for me anyway.

Monday, July 22, 2024

Note to self:

I can't believe it's been nine years since Troy passed away. Wow. It really is hard to wrap my brain around.

I sat outside by the Zen garden for hours today, raking the sand and enjoying the peaceful privacy. I've become so comfortable talking aloud to Troy when I'm out there. I tell him about my days or I process my thoughts as though he's physically there with me, kinda like how Quick writes to Geoffrey, I guess.

At first, I chatted with him about the situation with Mandy, and it felt like he helped me make a decision: I'll take her up on the next invitation if she asks again, because how could it hurt? It's like Mandela says, "May your choices reflect your hopes, not your fears." I hope she has good intentions, so I'm going to go with that.

I then unloaded all of my feelings regarding our mother. Through my monologue, I told Troy about how much I miss talking to her but how hard it's been lately because of her overbearing pressure to study harder for placement exams, apply for schools, decide on a major, et cetera et cetera. It has dominated every conversation for months now, which is so sad. I hate that my final years of childhood and possibly the last years of living with her are clouded with arguments. It really sucks. But I did feel better after processing it in the Zen garden, and again, I felt like he helped me to decide on my next step: to talk to Dad.

So that's what I did. I waited until Mom was in the shower and then I plopped myself down next to him on the couch. He immediately paused the television and wholeheartedly listened to my every word. I explained to him how hard it is to keep butting heads with Mom, but that I'm not entirely sure I want to take the typical path that she has laid out for me. I don't know if I want to do the whole four-year university thing, and I'm definitely not ready to commit to a major. I understand that she is coming from a place of love, that she just wants to make sure I'm successful and happy, but I don't know how to make her understand where I am coming from.

Dad told me that success is defined by the individual, and that they support whatever I decide to do, so long as I am making forward progress. Everything he said made a lot of sense, especially when he explained that the reason Mom is so intent on this plan is because I haven't presented an alternative. He said that if she knew what I wanted to do instead, she would then support me in that way. I told him that I don't really know what that alternative is yet, but I guess I have my senior year to figure that out.

I feel so much better now. I know I'll find my way. And it's okay if the path changes as I go, so long as I'm growing as a person and my choices reflect my hope to help others.

Senior year, here I come!

...Q

PART THREE:

Seek & Speak

○○○

Quinn / 6:26 p.m.

Hey, how was your first day?
I still cannot believe it's our last year!

Quick / 6:27 p.m.

pretty good
I feel like I have a bunch of cake classes this year
you?

6:27 p.m.

I'm looking forward to Government class.
I agree, I think the workload will go way down this year.

6:28 p.m.

good

6:28 p.m.

I already miss Mr. Erickson though!

6:28 p.m.

I know
sucks that REED is only for juniors

6:29 p.m.

I'm hoping it takes off this year.
Fingers crossed that he has an interested group.

6:31 p.m.

wanna go visit him tomorrow?

6:32 p.m.

After school? Yes! Let's do that.

6:32 p.m.

ok

Hey Geoffrey,

Mom was a frickin' disaster today. And she looks like hell. It's been, what, five years or so now that she's been "self-medicating"? Let's just call it what it is. She's high. All the time. Some days worse than others. And for some reason today, I could see what a toll it's physically taken on her.

I was planning on talking to Dad about it a few months back, but then I was in my self-pity stage and completely dropped it. I need to do it. I need to talk to him. Pretty soon I'll be moving out, and honestly, I don't really see myself coming around for visits and stuff. Not if it's like this. What for? There's no conversation. No connections. I have a year left to help us get this right. Right?

It's going to be uncomfortable, but honestly, what have I got to lose? The healthiest ways of dealing with things happen to be the hardest ways, so I just gotta do it.

Speaking of dealing with crap, I was thinking about something the other day. Looking back, I'm surprised I didn't end up drinking or smoking pot during those first couple of years of high school. I was so miserable and couldn't really deal with life, but I guess watching Mom deteriorate kinda kept me from messing with that stuff. But I see it all around me. I feel like everyone at school is smoking pot and a lot of them are doing way worse stuff. Part of it's pressure and image, which is all so frickin' stupid, but I think a lot of it is them not knowing how to deal with life, so they escape through drugs or whatever. Like Mom. It's the easier way of dealing with crap, but only in the very short term. It's not really dealing. It's avoiding and postponing. All that crap they're not dealing with is just going to haunt them until they do. Life is hard. Way hard. Especially these days with the world being as messed up as it is. I get it, I honestly don't blame them. I'm just glad I figured out that the best way through it is to go through it. There's no escape. There are no shortcuts. At some point, we have to deal with our crap head-on or we don't move on. Period.

Ok, so then, I need to deal with Mom. And Dad. They both chose unhealthy ways of "dealing" with their grief, but enough is enough. Maybe I feel strong enough now to force the conversation? To face it with them? It's definitely time.

I love you, brother.

-Deck

○○○

Quinn / 7:31 p.m.

Quick.

Quick / 7:35 p.m.

Quinn.

7:35 p.m.

Quick, I think I have a super cool idea...

7:36 p.m.

ok hit me

7:36 p.m.

You know how we aren't doing club this year?

7:36 p.m.

yeah
but I'll still dig on my own

7:37 p.m.

Exactly! Well, what if we took it a step further?
What if we invited others to dig with us?

7:37 p.m.

ummmmm that's not really my jam, Quinn

7:37 p.m.

I know, I know! Hear me out...

7:37 p.m.

ok

7:38 p.m.

What if we started some sort of anonymous forum, like an online
message board?
We'll make flyers with a QR code, and when people go on,
they can put whatever username they want.

7:39 p.m.

ok...

7:40 p.m.

So then twice a month or whatever, we post a question...

and then they post their thoughts or findings or whatever?

7:40 p.m.

Yes! So it's like REED but in real time!

7:41 p.m.

and it would be anonymous?

7:41 p.m.

I think so! I have to do some research and figure it out, but I think that's possible.

7:41 p.m.

you think people would want to do it?

7:42 p.m.

I think so! People love chat rooms and all that.
Who knows?!

7:42 p.m.

I guess there's only one way to find out

7:42 p.m.

So... Are you in?

7:42 p.m.

only if its anonymous

7:42 p.m.

Oh my gosh, yey!!
I may or may not have already thought of a name...

7:43 p.m.

big shock lol
what is it

7:43 p.m.

What do you think of Seek & Speak?

7:43 p.m.

ha ha I like it

You do?

yes
it reminds me of "quick and quinn"

Totally.

Wednesday, August 21, 2024

Note to self:

Quick and I went to go see Mr. Erickson today to tell him about our Seek & Speak idea and to get some feedback, and I wish I took a video of his response! He was so excited, probably even more so than I am. He literally hooted and sprung from his chair to hug us. He told us how proud he was, and to leave it to students to come up with an even better idea than the teacher's. Ha ha!

Mr. Erickson knew all about message boards and volunteered to be the behind-the-scenes moderator. That way he will be the only one who can see the email addresses that are connected with usernames, so we won't be in an awkward situation of having access to that. That made me feel so much better, because I know how important it is to Quick for all aspects of this to be anonymous. Score!

Quick and I are FaceTiming tonight to plan out the first semester. I think we are going to post a new topic every two weeks, so there's time to dig but not so much time that it gets stale. We're also going to brainstorm "mild" topics, as Quick likes to call them, because if we start off by dropping some major truth bombs that make people uncomfortable, no one will join in. I haven't even started thinking of ideas yet, but it's all good. I know we'll figure it out. I'm so excited!

Okay, I'm off to make flyers, which Mr. Erickson said he will print and photocopy. He also said he would post them around the school so no one would see Quick and I doing it. I didn't even think about that!

Oh! And right when we were leaving Mr. Erickson's classroom, right when we walked outside, guess what we saw? A dragonfly! I freaked out, and Quick had no idea why. He looked at me like I had five heads. I couldn't believe I had never told him about my connection with dragonflies or what they represented. How is that even possible? Anyway, heck yeah, that dragonfly's right! Change is coming! Seek & Speak is going to be awesome!

…Q

Quick:

Here Goes Nothing

Throughout the early phases of planning Seek & Speak, the great majority of my conversations with Quinn were focused on just that. Once we decided to do it and had Mr. E's support, we realized there was much more to getting it off the ground than merely flyers and a chat room. On that Friday of the second week of our senior year, we hammered out the bulk of the details at lunchtime.

Quinn surprised me by bringing in what she could harvest from our porch garden, which was meager but still felt satisfying to eat. Like an accomplishment. It was a good thing we still had regular lunches, though, because the green onions, three tiny radishes, and the four cherry tomatoes were not going to cut it. We munched away while Quinn spoke a mile a minute about all the agenda items she had written in her notebook.

She thought it was hugely important that we defined the mission of our project. She wanted to make sure we were both on the same page, and although no one else would really see the mission, we could always look back on it if we needed to. We discussed different ways of wording it, but it did not take very long for us to realize that we were just rephrasing it over and over. The mission was simple: To get our peers to dig. We fancied up the language a bit before she wrote it down, using words like "entice" and "evaluate" or something like that.

At first, we considered having a goal in terms of the number of people who would participate in Seek & Speak, but we decided to hold off on that. We agreed that we could revisit the idea once it got off the ground and we saw how it was going. I liked the idea of a growth goal, rather than a random number goal. So long as it was making progress, even if from just one person to five, that was a step in the right direction.

The topic of anonymity came up again. Not really about the participants, but more so about her and I remaining anonymous. Quinn mentioned that a major battle in life, for all humans, is the ego versus the spirit, and that the intentions behind work are just as important as the work itself. When she said that, it struck me as so profound that I made her say it again.

The intentions behind work are just as important as the work itself.

The purpose of Seek & Speak was not for our names to be spoken. There was a possibility that Seek & Speak would gain traction, and having our names tied to it would lend to the ego. The last thing either one of us wanted was to be in the spotlight, and it was our hope that Seek & Speak would be. Our intention was based in spirit, and we agreed that if it were to become about us, it would muddy the waters.

Granted, we knew there would be criticism of some sort. There were always haters. We were as mentally prepared for it as we could be. The only thing we could do was work through it together. We didn't even know what the criticism would look like, anyway. Would it be rude comments? Would it be mocking flyers posted in jest or in retaliation? We had no clue. We made a point of acknowledging that the criticism to come was not the reason for our anonymity, but it probably was. At least for me.

Right before lunch ended, we tested the QR code and Quinn squealed when she saw that it worked perfectly. It led to the chat board and the user could create any username he or she wanted. The bimonthly question would be posted at the top, and that would be that. The only thing left to do was to decide on that first topic. We wanted it to be a controversial topic, but something mainstream. Something that was already a part of the common narrative. It couldn't be too shocking. It almost felt like it needed to be so light that it was almost funny. Something that would appeal to high schoolers.

Turned out that was tougher than we thought. We must have texted about it a dozen different times that weekend. By Sunday night, though, we had to bite the bullet. We were scheduled to post first thing that Monday morning. So, we narrowed it down to three, rolled the dice, and the last thing I texted her was, "Here goes nothing."

Of course her response was something that ended in three exclamation points.

SEEK & SPEAK!

What's the Truth Anyway?
Dig to Decide!

Do you ever wonder about the unknowns?
About truths? About lies?

Do you ever hear something and instinctively
agree with it? Disagree with it?

Do you ever defend the narrative?
Question the narrative?

Do you like to share your opinions?
Hear the opinions of others?

If so, then this is the place for you!

Below is our inaugural question. Let's have a conversation!

We only ask one thing of you:
Please be respectful of others' opinions.

Thank you, and welcome to Seek & Speak!

QUESTION #1

Professional sports games: Are the outcomes legitimate or predetermined?

j&kpitassist: there's no way games are scripted. athletes are competitive and would have a really hard time throwing a game on purpose like that. plus there are so many elements to a sports game that cannot be controlled, like an accidental fumble or a ricochet or whatever.

bolly>holly: yeah but maybe it's not scripted through the players but through the coaches and refs?

allnetbaby: oh this goes way back you can read it **on this website** that the ref in charge in the 2002 nba champs actually admitted that the game was fixed

rureddy4dis: There's money to be had, so yes they rig it.

anime4life: idk much about sports but **this guy** gives seven specific examples about manipulated tournament brackets, unhealed injuries, etc.

qwerty1234: what a stupid topic. this is a total waste of time.

rubecuber9: @qwerty1234 then go away. here's my big question with all of this… thousands of professional athletes across all sports over decades and decades, and they're all able to keep this big secret? i highly doubt it.

sofi-sof: Yeah, it's probably somewhere in the middle. Semi-controlled, semi-rigged. They can't control the player but they could totally influence the system.

○○○

Quinn / 8:39 p.m.

Have you been on the site yet??

Quick / 8:43 p.m.

I was just about to go on
is it good or bad

8:43 p.m.

I think it's good!

8:51 p.m.

8 posts
7 if you don't count the jerk

8:52 p.m.

That's a good start, right?
Mr. Erickson told me we got 71 hits and it's only the first day!

8:53 p.m.

so 10% posted
not counting the jerk

8:54 p.m.

There's always going to be a jerk, Quick. We knew that going in.
So let's choose to focus on the other seven posts. Right?

8:55 p.m.

yeah I guess

8:55 p.m.

I think it's a good start.
Maybe we picked a topic that was too specific.
Not everyone finds sports to be relatable, you know?

8:55 p.m.

true

9:00 p.m.

We can't expect to hit it out of the park on day one.
"Slow progress is still progress."
(I just spent 4 minutes looking for someone to credit for that quote
and I couldn't find it, LOL!)

you're right
idk why I'm feeling weird

9:02 p.m.

It's okay, Quick. There's nothing to lose here.
Let's just see how it goes.

9:03 p.m.

yep

08/30/2024

11:52 a.m.

Hallway in Building C

Kellen: Hey, wanna go check out that new movie tomorrow?

Connor: Oh, bro, I can't. I'm watching the Notre Dame game. You can come hang though if you want.

Kellen: Right on. Hey, you think those games are rigged?

Connor: What?

Kellen: Do you think they rig the games? Like, script the winners and stuff?

Connor: No, bro. I don't. Where did you even hear that?

Kellen: Through Seek & Speak.

Connor: What the hell is Seek & Speak?

Kellen: Bro, you haven't seen all those flyers around?

Connor: Oh yeah, I guess I have. What is it? Is it cool?

Kellen: It's alright. So yeah, what time should I come by tomorrow?

Hey Geoffrey,

Quinn gave me another quote for the scrapbook today, and to be honest, it was kind of a smack in the face. But I needed it. I've had a crappy attitude about Seek & Speak and she was totally right to call me out on it.

"Slow progress is still progress." And she attached a little silver snail charm thing.

She's right. Our site's been up for almost two weeks now, and there is a little bit of chatter on there. I'm not sure what I was expecting or if I'm disappointed or something, but Quinn and the snail are right. There are 13 people on campus who thought about something new and maybe even did a little digging that they wouldn't have done otherwise, so yeah. Seek & Speak is off to a start. "Slow" is a relative term. 13 out of 2000? Yeah. That's a slow start. But 13 more than zero? That's pretty good.

Mr. E put up more flyers today and we're getting ready to post our second topic in a couple of days. So as long as there's more than 13, we're headed in the right direction. I get nervous when I think about it, but I honestly don't know why. Especially since it's anonymous, and we could drop the whole thing anytime we wanted to anyway. Is it because I don't know where it's going? Is it because I don't want to disappoint Quinn if it's a flop?

I miss her. It's weird. I see her more than ever and we talk nonstop, but it's mostly about Seek. I think tomorrow I'll make a point of steering the conversation elsewhere. Or even telling her straight up. Honestly, I don't think we hold back anything anymore. Well, other than farts maybe.

You know what? I miss holding her hand. I'm gonna do that tomorrow, too.

Later, bro. Love you.

-Deck

Friday, September 6, 2024

Note to self:

Well, today was… interesting. We sat down for lunch on the quad, per usual, but Quick made a point of sitting next to me instead of across from me. I didn't think much of it until about fifteen minutes later. We were both pretty much done eating, and out of nowhere, he reached over and grabbed my hand. He just held it. We kept talking like nothing happened, and I think I nonchalantly recovered from my heart stopping in my chest, but I could barely focus on what we were chatting about. He said he wanted to talk about things other than Seek & Speak, which is totally fine. I can't ever imagine him and I running out of things to talk about. But I honestly can't remember the second half of lunch.

I can't stop thinking about it. What does this mean? Does he like me? Is our friendship changing? Do I want it to?

I think I'll go do a body scan, but I already know it's going to take much longer than usual for me to settle. I feel like a swirling ball of girly emotions right now. "Giddy" is the one that keeps coming to mind though, just saying.

…Q

SEEK & SPEAK!

What's the Truth Anyway?
Dig to Decide!

Do you ever wonder about the unknowns? About truths?
About lies?

Do you ever hear something and instinctively agree with it?
Disagree with it?

Do you ever defend the narrative? Question the narrative?

Do you like to share your opinions? Hear the opinions of others?

If so, then this is the place for you!

Below is our second question. Let's have a conversation!

We only ask one thing of you:
Please be respectful of others' opinions.

Thank you, and welcome (back) to Seek & Speak!

QUESTION #2

The Moon Landing: Was it real or fake?

hum&strum: Interesting topic. I've done some reading on this one before, and according to **IOP**, every claim behind fake moon landing theory has been debunked.

savvysav: Before anyone asks what IOP is, click on the link and see for yourself ;)

gallagals: so many videos of green screen mess-ups, **like this one**, but it's hard to tell what's real, what's deep fake, what's AI. very frustrating.

wannaDB8?:   I just have one question... If Neil Armstrong was the first man on the moon, who took the photo of his first step? And how were they able to publish photos in newspapers here on Earth the very next day? They had that kind of tech back then?

mega_hugs: that's three questions, ha. but, yeah, I have all the same questions. glad I'm not the only one.

rosyring: @wannaDB8? the first step photo was actually taken by a camera placed in the stowage area (**link**). but i totally see your point about the next two questions. i guess the pictures were taken from the live feed (**link**), but still. how could they distribute photos that quickly in 1969?

legomylegos: Neil A. = Alien what are the chances of that lol

scizor: a simple internet search can put this nonsense to rest. did you guys even look at the first link @hum&strum gave?

codycrew<3:   @scizor Whether you care to admit it or not, there's a lot of censorship on the internet. Take the time to scroll past the first five or ten pages of search results, bro.

volleyqueen: I think the moon landing was totally faked. But why? I don't get why they would do all that just to lie to us? What's the point?

---

chempion: this topic is so much easier for us to talk about and wrap our heads around than the generations before us. they swear by it because they lived through the event, but when you look at all of it objectively, it really doesn't add up.

247gamer: you guys ever seen the videos out there of that buzz aldrin dude? guy's pretty defensive. idk what but he's def lying about something. <u>look</u>

atlas: what the heck how do **<u>these footprints</u>** match his space boots??

born2cre8: There's a lot out there about moon landing scenes being filmed in the Nevada desert. <u>link</u> <u>link</u> <u>link</u> So hard to wrap my brain around. I totally get what you mean @ volleyqueen. If the moon landing was fake and they went through all that to fake it, why? It doesn't make sense.

madeUlaff: apparently NASA lost 14000 reels of science data from the moon landing?

watchurtung: Here's the big question: Why haven't we been back??

river_sunsets: Yeah, that movie that came out this past summer didn't sit with me right. Did you guys see *Fly Me to the Moon*?

mar<3lee: I saw it. You know what really bugs me? It our families' taxes that pay for it, so we deserve total truth. There should be so much transparency that things like this shouldn't even be a question!

rauhrauh4golf: truth.

Quinn:

A Heartened Hypocrite

Watching the first month of Seek & Speak unfold in real time was categorically thrilling. I became obsessed with the participation statistics, and the consistent upward trend of clicks and posts only reinforced the compulsion to check the numbers. There was a buzz about the school with chatter among our fellow students in the hallways, along with the endorsement of it by several teachers on campus. Seek & Speak, to put it simply, took off like a rocket.

The second topic of the moon landing was much better received than the first, partially due to its relatability to a greater number of students than the sports question, but also because Seek & Speak needed to gain a bit of momentum in its infancy. By the second week of the second round, we not only had hundreds of clicks, but dozens upon dozens of participants and more usernames being registered each day. Our peers even began to respond back and forth to one another, tagging each other in comments to either refute or further support the statements given. As with true discourse, both sides of the argument were being presented and discussed, and when we saw that hyperlinks to research were being included, Quick and I were over the moon. Surely, Mr. Erickson was elated as well. I imagined it was akin to a dream come true for him.

The swift growth of Seek & Speak made an easily discernible impact on Quick. His grumpy, negative outlook was proven to be temporary, thank goodness, and he approached me on that Friday afternoon in an absolute frenzy. For once it was him who was speaking a mile a minute and it was me who was trying to decipher his exuberant speech. He was rattling on about wanting to celebrate the initial success of our "first pet project" and asking what I had planned for the weekend, to which I responded as soon as I could squeeze a word in.

"Actually, Quick, this is not our first pet project. How do you think the garden would feel if it heard that?" I smirked, and the question made him slow down enough to catch his breath. He smiled, and to see the look of pure fulfillment on his face filled my entire heart with joy.

"I'm so proud of you, Quinn. You had a brilliant idea, you fearlessly jumped in with both feet, and look at it. It's amazing! I mean, I don't know how long it will last. Maybe it goes the whole year, maybe it's a quick little trend, but whatever. Who cares? Right now, it's awesome." He swooped in and wrapped his arms all the way around me. The hug seemed to stop time, and I did not mind one bit. He released me and placed his forehead against mine, just like we had done in July. He softly whispered, "Thank you, Quinn. Thank you for asking me to do this with you."

"I could never imagine doing it without you." He grabbed my hand as we walked off campus for the weekend. He held it the entire way to the bike rack, and once again, I was taken aback by how natural it felt. We tossed around ideas for our celebratory activity and we landed on something that would be a first for both of us: Attempting the escape room that had recently opened downtown.

By the time Sunday afternoon rolled around and Quick texted that he was on his way to my house, I did a last-minute statistics check and saw that the number of participants had reached sixty-four. I smiled to myself, acknowledging that the celebration we planned was definitely in order. Quick swung by to pick me up, I hopped on the handlebars, and we headed towards our latest adventure.

Once we made our way into the escape room and the door locked behind us, he looked at me and broke the silence by announcing in his best Sherlock Holmes impersonation, "Now we shall really see what kind of a team we make, Ms. Watson."

Put bluntly, we were not Sherlock and Watson. We spent the entire hour speaking as though we were, using our best British accents and tipping our invisible hats to one another, but in the end, our fits of laughter did not help us solve the mystery. Not even a little bit. We honored our failure with some ice cream sundaes from the shop next door, a cute little parlor that had board games available for customer enjoyment. After at least fifteen games of Connect Four, most of which he won, we decided to call it a night and head back home.

Climbing back onto the bike's handlebars and being keenly aware of the pure and simple happiness that was consuming me, I resolved to tune into my senses and mentally record every aspect of the ride home that I could. I closed my eyes and lifted my head to the dusky sky, trusting Quick with my entire being as I always did. I breathed in the cool night air, allowing it to fill my lungs just as gratitude filled my heart. The breeze flowed through my hair, and I smiled as I pictured Quick behind me, leaning to the left to allow my hair to whip in the wind. The swooshing hums of bushes as we rode by intermingled with the rhythmic sound of Quick's pedaling feet, and when I focused all of my attention, I could pick up on traces of Quick's scent. I wasn't sure if it was the smell of his hair, that of his clothes, or a blend of them, but I did know that I could distinguish that scent from any other: the scent of my Quick.

I fell asleep that night with a grin plastered on my face. My best friend and I were closer than ever, and our shared mission added a new layer of satisfying purpose to our senior year. We had so many big decisions to make regarding life beyond high school, so many big changes in the coming year, but I knew I didn't have to worry about any of it quite yet. I wasn't ready to consider the possibility of daily life sans Quick, so in the meantime, I was making a concerted effort to cherish every moment of our final year, whether it be ones of silly accents or quiet bike rides. The next morning, I could feel my smile before I even opened my eyes, but that smile quickly faded when I logged on to Seek & Speak. A few comments had been added since the afternoon prior, but the latest one really struck a chord that I knew was going to create a problem. The user presented a good point, but I knew that it was nonetheless a moot one:

3sistas4theW: Isn't it hypocritical for Seek & Speak to encourage us to share our truths, and yet the people behind it remain anonymous?

ooo

Quinn / 7:52 a.m.

Good morning, Quick. Have you checked S&S recently?

Quick / 7:53 a.m.

I checked yesterday I think

7:53 a.m.

Okay. When you get a chance, please do.
The last post warrants a conversation, I believe.

7:54 a.m.

?

7:55 a.m.

It's not bad, and I don't think it's anything we have to address.
We should just check in with each other about it.

8:02 a.m.

ok I read it
their anonymity is voluntary
they can make whatever username they want

8:03 a.m.

Yes, that's true. They can sign in with their first and last name if they
want to.
I don't think that's the issue.

8:03 a.m.

so what's the issue

8:05 a.m.

I believe they are talking about us. Our hypocrisy.

8:06 a.m.

ugh you're right

8:06 a.m.

Quick, please know that I am not pushing you. I know where you
stand on this.
I'm happy with how it's going!

yeah me too

Remember our mission? To get people to dig? We're totally accomplishing it!

8:08 a.m.

yeah

9:03 a.m.

Hallway in Building G

Tristan:	Hey, what do you guys have now, English?
Logan:	Yeah, you?
Tristan:	Math class. Hey, did you guys check out that Seek & Speak thing?
Parker:	Is that the QR code I'm seeing all over the place?
Tristan:	Yeah.
Logan:	Dude, one of my teachers offered extra credit to go on there. It's pretty cool. I've been on a couple times now.
Parker:	You been on?
Logan:	Yeah, it's kinda interesting. There's, like, a question at the top and then everyone just sorta comments and stuff.
Tristan:	I liked both topics so far, but the moon landing one got way more traction. It's actually still going and people are still adding their two cents. Kinda cool.
Parker:	Moon landing? So, like, what, it's a conspiracy thing?
Logan:	I guess? I didn't see it that way. The last two topics have been things that there's already chatter about. It's not like they're putting things out there that we haven't already heard about or whatever.
Parker:	What was the first one?
Tristan:	If sports are rigged.
Parker:	They are. A hundred percent.
Tristan:	Uh-oh, dude, careful. You'll sound like a conspiracy theorist.

Parker:	For sure. So do people just go on and give their opinions? What's the point?
Logan:	No, people are legit doing research and posting links and stuff. It's cool. I gotta be honest, I'm curious about the next topic.
Tristan:	So you think you'll go back on?
Logan:	Yeah. Might even post.
Tristan:	Right on.
Parker:	I'm gonna check it out. Y'all have me curious.

○○○

so I've been thinking about that post off and on all week

Quinn / 10:12 p.m.

Which one? The hypocrisy one?

10:12 p.m.

yeah
it's pretty valid

10:13 p.m.

It's okay, though, Quick. We don't have to respond or acquiesce.

10:14 p.m.

I know but don't you think they all know it's us anyway
I mean, seriously, who else would it be

10:15 p.m.

I never considered that.
What are you saying?

10:16 p.m.

that we should be honest and speak our truth
that we should set a good example for truth seekers
that I should be as fearless as you are

10:16 p.m.

Are you sure?

10:16 p.m.

yeah

10:17 p.m.

Why don't we sleep on it and talk tomorrow at lunch?

10:17 p.m.

ok

10:18 p.m.

Good night, Quick.

10:18 p.m.

night

Hey Geoffrey,

Well, it's official. We talked about it ad nauseam on Friday and all weekend, too, but the decision has finally been made. Quinn and I are going public tomorrow on Seek & Speak. Honestly, it's not even that big of a deal. No one will even care, and that's if they even notice. This whole "anonymous" thing has been my issue and now I can't even remember why it was an issue in the first place. Because I don't want to bring attention to myself? Because I want to be invisible? Is that even still true?

I'm a little uncomfortable but it is what it is. I'm ready. Doesn't really matter what happens anyway. At the end of the day, it's Quick and Quinn through thick and thin, and that's what I care about. I have her back and she has mine, so it'll be fine regardless.

Like I said, though, it's not a big deal. I don't think anyone will bat an eye or even pretend to care. Hopefully they care about the topic though...

Love you, bud.

-Deck

SEEK & SPEAK!

By: Quick and Quinn

Do you ever wonder about the unknowns? About truths?
About lies?

Do you ever hear something and instinctively
agree with it? Disagree with it?

Do you ever defend the narrative? Question the narrative?

Do you like to share your opinions? Hear the opinions of others?

If so, then this is the place for you!

Below is our third question. Let's have a conversation!

We only ask one thing of you:
Please be respectful of others' opinions.

Thank you, and welcome (back) to Seek & Speak!

- -

@3sistas4theW Thank you for bringing up the issue of anonymity last week. While all participants have the option to remain anonymous or name themselves through their username, you brought up a very valid point regarding us as the creators behind Seek & Speak. You are right in that we should absolutely be setting an example by owning our truths. We appreciate the challenge you brought forth! The fear of what others may think can be crippling, even imprisoning, but we hope that all of us can combat that fear. We should stand up for what we believe, even if standing alone. That level of safe integrity is something that we strive for and wish for everyone. With that being said, let's dig!

-Quick Williams and Quinn Washington

QUESTION #3

Fluoride?

StArSeEd: Hmmm… Shall I state the obvious? That's not really a question. But it is very open-ended, and I am curious to see where this one goes…

Utoober: **Here is a list** of all the nations that have banned fluoride for consumption. Notice, we're not on it.

3sistas4theW: Woot, thanks for the shout out. This is pretty cool, Quick and Quinn. Hope to put faces to the names one day.

outtathapark: What the actual what?? The post has me shook. My family just bought baby water for my new cousin and it has "added fluoride." What the heck for? Babies don't even have teeth?

outtathapark: And what the heck is baby water anyway? Like it's different than teenager water or adult water? Omg what a total scam. I didn't even think about that when we were buying it.

eyesign4u: I'll research the reason for the bans.

sweetathlete: right on, i'll look up the benefits

<3ourchicks: what on earth is the pineal gland? i've taken anatomy and i've never heard of that. apparently fluoride calcifies it?

need4speed: They don't hide the benefits. We know those…Protects our teeth from decay, stronger enamel, etc.

PriceShake4As: @need4speed Who is "they"? The more I consider the answer to that question, the more I feel that this is of supreme importance. The "they" will lead to the "why." What do you all think?

danCpranC: @<3ourchicks I have never heard of the pineal gland either. **Check this out**

StArSeEd: Holy crap. Here's what I found in ten minutes flat on why fluoride is banned in so many places. <u>link1</u> <u>2</u> <u>3</u> 4 <u>5</u> <u>6</u> <u>7</u> I'm going to buy new toothpaste TODAY. And allegedly it's linked to lowering IQ?? Greaaaaat.

Utoober: I completely agree about the "who" and the "why," but I bet that's a huge web of connected rabbit holes. I also bet that greed is fueling it. **This** sounds to me like it's over the target but I only researched for about a half hour.

live.on.stage: Ephesians 6:12, just sayin'.

swish&flick: did you guys see **this**?! "forever chemicals" including fluoride in band-aids?! what the actual what??

○○○

hey how goes it

Quinn / 7:22 p.m.

Hi, Mandy!

7:22 p.m.

sorry I haven't texted, been busy

7:23 p.m.

Oh that's alright. I understand.
Besides, I haven't texted either!

7:24 p.m.

just wanted to say congrats

7:25 p.m.

For what?

7:26 p.m.

this online thing is yours, right?

7:27 p.m.

Oh, Seek & Speak? Yes, Quick and I started it.
Thank you! We're enjoying its progress.
Have you been on?

7:28 p.m.

not yet
I actually figured it was you two behind it

7:29 p.m.

Oh yeah?

7:30 p.m.

yeah I heard about your big project with him last year

kinda reminded me of that I guess

7:32 p.m.

Ha ha, that's true.

7:32 p.m.

I heard you have huge numbers
what's it up to now

7:34 p.m.

Last I checked, we have over 100 participants who are actually engaging.
It's so exciting!

7:34 p.m.

that's awesome

7:37 p.m.

Thank you. How are you doing?

7:40 p.m.

good thanks

7:42 p.m.

Okay, well let me know if you want to hang out sometime.
We dropped the ball on that over summer.

7:42 p.m.

sounds good
maybe coffee

7:42 p.m.

Or hot chocolate with whipped cream, lol

7:42 p.m.

ok talk soon

7:43 p.m.

Okay, have a good one!

Friday, September 27, 2024

Note to self:

I feel like I have to pinch myself every morning when I wake up. I simply cannot believe how well Seek & Speak is doing! We already have over one hundred active participants, and they really seem to be invested in it! They are digging and sharing, questioning and encouraging. I'm in awe. Of course we have a few haters on there as we expected, but to be honest, the participants are the ones who are handling it. They basically tell the rude ones that if they don't like the forum, to go somewhere else… and it's working! I guess it really is like the childhood bully; if the haters don't get the response they want, they go away. Perfect.

The forum is everything we could have hoped for. We know that it will probably turn out to be short-lived, as most trends are, but in the meantime, Seek & Speak has become the talk of the school. People have mentioned it to me in classes, Quick said he hears people talking about it in the hallways pretty much every day, and today I happened upon a conversation between a teacher and some students that made me so happy I almost squealed and revealed that I was eavesdropping. These three girls who are on Student Council—I think their names are Julia, Sondra, and Talia—were talking to their advisor about the televised morning announcements. They want to bring the fluoride issue to the attention of the entire student body and suggest using fluoride-free products! The advisor, Mrs. Gillerrels, was seemingly impressed and asked them how they heard of the issue and became so passionate about it. The one named Talia answered, and I still can't believe her response.

"Through Quick and Quinn!"

I'm dead serious! That's what she said! And I didn't even put in the exclamation point. That's how she said it! "Through Quick and Quinn!" Holy crap, I am still in shock.

Through Quick and Quinn.

Through thick and thin.

Feels like fate.

…Q

Quick:

The Elephants in the Forum

In the early phase of S&S, Quinn called me out for forgetting our first scrapbook quote. She was right. My attitude sucked. But at least it didn't take long for my wariness or my negativity to transform into exuberance. I didn't care about the numbers or statistics, like she did. She needed an objective measure to validate what we were doing, but I didn't. I didn't care about the anonymity either. Once the cat was out of the bag, I realized how little it mattered. I didn't care if people knew my name or didn't, if they approved of S&S or didn't. All I knew was that other people were digging. People our age. About topics that mattered. And even though I hadn't felt "alone" in a long time, it still felt good to know that Quinn and I weren't the only ones.

Between the hallway chatter and the increased traffic on the forum, it really started to feel like S&S was a movement. When I saw that @annaboo suggested we post a new topic weekly instead of every other week, and then reading how much @tinyburger and @guchiguchigoo loved the idea, my excitement level skyrocketed. It felt like we had arrived. We did it. S&S made it. And if it fell apart the very next day, it would still go down in my book as a total success. Man, that spurred such an invigorating sense of pride.

Quinn, of course, was beside herself when she learned of the request to post weekly. Her jaw hit the floor and she was speechless. For about four seconds. Then the whirlwind of her unfiltered questions, comments, and exclamations hit like a speed round of an automatic weapon loaded with words and phrases. Barely taking any breaths, she went from, "Oh my good-ness!" and "Can you believe it?" to "I need to get my notebook!" and "Isn't this so exciting?" and a dozen others in between. Once again, her energy was infectious and I let the joy rain down on me like a faucet on full blast.

We headed to Mr. E's room to share in the moment, but as soon as we caught a glimpse of him, we knew he had already read the latest S&S comments. He was grinning from ear to ear and practically hopped over his desk to sprint our way when we walked in. It thrilled him to no end to see this evolution of REED and how many students were engaging in it. Willingly. And enjoying it.

That night, after seeing Mr. E and remembering his passion for critical thinking, a nagging feeling took hold and I couldn't shake it. Since S&S had taken off and had a pretty solid base, I thought that perhaps it was time to address the elephants in the forum. I wrestled all night with how I would word it, so much so that it completely slipped my mind to run it by Quinn. And I felt so accomplished when I finally finished it in the early morning, that I just posted it right then and there. I realized my error the moment I woke up a few hours later, but I also inherently sensed that Quinn would be cool with it. Because she was the coolest.

And she was. Because she was.

SEEK & SPEAK!

By: Quick and Quinn

Do you ever wonder about the unknowns? About truths? About lies?

Do you ever hear something and instinctively agree with it? Disagree with it?

Do you ever defend the narrative? Question the narrative?

Do you like to share your opinions? Hear the opinions of others?

If so, then this is the place for you!

THERE ARE ELEPHANTS IN THE FORUM.

Misinformation and Disinformation.

Let's address them directly and see if we are all on the same page in regard to mis- and dis- info.

* What is the difference between the two?
* How can we combat them?

Suggestions:

* Keep your own confirmation bias in check. Focus on facts.
* Check the source. Check the source's source.
* Consider the biases of the source.
* Consider what information is included, and what is not.
* Reflect on the tone and emotion of the message.
* Juxtapose the information with that of multiple sources.
* Ponder and examine alternative views and statements.

What are your thoughts?

Check back on Monday for our 4th question!

○○○

Quinn / 8:47 a.m.

You. Are. A. Genius.!!!

Quick / 9:19 a.m.

oh yeah?

9:23 a.m.

Yes! I loved your post about critical thinking tips.

9:24 a.m.

I'm sorry I didn't run it by you
it just kinda happened

10:11 a.m.

That's okay! It was brilliant.

10:12 a.m.

trying to keep up with you, lol

10:12 a.m.

We make quite the team!

11:02 a.m.

sorry didn't mean to ghost you, had a math test
we do make a good team

11:13 a.m.

I have to say, I miss you.

11:14 a.m.

I'll see you in a couple minutes at lunch
I'm kidding, I know what you mean
s&s is exciting but it kinda took over

11:15 a.m.

Yes, I agree.
Let's do something fun this weekend!

11:17 a.m.

some quick and quinn time?

11:18 a.m.

Thick and thin time.

11:19 a.m.

sounds good to me

Hey Geoffrey,

I don't know if it's because high school's nearing its end or if it's because I'm feeling a little more confident with things lately, but I've got some big goals looming around in my head that I need to tackle. Well, just two.

First, I want to talk to our folks. If I can come clean with hundreds of people, strangers nonetheless, and remove the invisibility cloak I've been wearing for so long, then surely I should be able to talk to my own parents. They deserve that more than strangers do, right? I've been putting this off for way too long. It's time. I feel like I've said that to you before, but I'm serious. It's time.

The second one is about Quinn. I have to tell her how I feel. I worry that if I don't, one day it will come spilling out like word vomit and I'll freak her out. Scare her off or something. There's just one problem. I don't know how I feel.

Yeah I do.

I love her. So much, Geoffrey.

But how do I know if it's just mad respect for her? Or just massive appreciation for her? Or if it's love love. Like the real deal love. I'm pretty sure it's the real deal love. I would do anything for her, Geoffrey. I've thought about it. I literally think I would do anything she asked of me.

But I'm terrified that I'll mess up our friendship. I think I'd be lost without her, and I'd rather have our friendship than nothing.

I'll tackle the parent goal first. Who would have guessed that talking to my folks about absenteeism and addiction would be the easier of two conversations?

Miss you. I think of you every day. I hope you know that.

-Deck

○○○

I think it's finally time

Desiree / 6:51 p.m.

ok I'll bite
time for what

6:51 p.m.

to hang out with quinn

6:52 p.m.

this again?

6:52 p.m.

it was her idea!

6:53 p.m.

yeah but you put it there
you've been scheming for months now
what's the point

6:53 p.m.

people should know the truth about her

6:55 p.m.

you keep saying that
didn't you take care of that four years ago

6:55 p.m.

it's different now

6:57 p.m.

how

6:57 p.m.

it just is

7:01 p.m.

because of her online thing?
because people know who she is now?
are you jealous??

7:01 p.m.

WHAT? NO
I just think they should know who they're dealing with

7:03 p.m.

but if you already know the truth why do you have to meet with her

7:03 p.m.

I wanna know the deal with the two of them

7:04 p.m.

like if they're a couple or whatever?
who cares

7:05 p.m.

if she's a witch and they're a thing, that makes him evil too

7:05 p.m.

that's messed up, mandy

7:05 p.m.

what is

7:11 p.m.

all of it
this whole thing is messed up

7:11 p.m.

whatever des

Quinn:
My Own Thoughts

The fifth of October was a Saturday that year, and Quick started the day off by catching me completely off-guard. With trash bags and playing cards in hand, the first words out of his mouth when he greeted me on my driveway were, "Happy anniversary, Quinn."

"Anniversary?!" I guffawed. I really did guffaw. A huge and unexpected burst of laughter forced my head to snap back. I knew in the moment that the overreaction was probably stemming from a state of nervous energy.

He waited for me to settle down. "Well, almost," he winked. There was that wink again. Skip skip. "It'll be one year on Monday since our friendship leveled up."

"I'm sorry, leveled up? How do you mean?" I glanced at the items he was brandishing and smiled at the memory. "The day of our hike? Oh my gosh, Quick, that was such a great day. How did you remember?"

He shrugged his shoulders and looked down at his bicycle wheel. "I wrote to Geoffrey that day about how our friendship leveled up. That was the day you told me about Troy, Quinn. That was the day I knew we would—"

"Become the best of friends?" I finished his sentence.

"You turned me into such a softie, Quinn. The things I say when I'm around you are so cringy." He laughed. "What other kid my age talks like that?"

"Who cares? I love it," I beamed and threw my arms around his neck. "So are we doing what I think we're doing today?" I felt another burst of energy coming on, and I started to gleefully giggle and clap as he nodded. "Yesssssss! Are we walking or riding?" He answered by parking his bike on the patio next to all of our pots and putting his things into his backpack. Our off-season garden brought a grin to his face, and he turned to me with his hand extended, an invitation that I gladly accepted.

It was not the least bit difficult to recreate the day. We both remembered it so vividly, and we shared as many moments of laughter and moments of comfortable silence as we had the year before. The trees and the waterfall were just as lovely, and I was so glad to relive the good times with him, rather than remember the times I went alone hoping to see him there. It was truly a perfect day, and we even said as much on our walk back home. It was hard to believe that we had only known each other for a year or so. It felt like I had known him for my whole life.

"It's weird," I pondered aloud. "In some ways, I can't believe it's been a year, but in other ways, I can't believe it's only been a year. Does that make sense?" I asked him while we strolled back home, hand in hand.

"Yeah. I feel like I've lov—" Quick's face turned crimson red and I could feel his clammy palm go rigid. We walked in silence for a couple of minutes, and I wanted so badly to shout, "I love you, too!" but I could not bring myself to do it. My heart was hammering in my chest and I was really struggling to keep my butterflies at bay. I was drowning in my own thoughts. Did I really love him? What was happening? Finally, I mustered up the courage to speak, squeezed his hand, and changed the subject. I asked about our next Seek & Speak topic, and that conversation led us all the way back home.

After thanking him profusely for yet another impeccable day of "Quick and Quinn time" on the books, he tossed me the pack of playing cards and suggested I practice before next time. "Ha ha, very funny," I smirked as I pretended to punch him in the gut. He took the opportunity to grab my forearms and pull me in for a hug.

"See you Monday," he squeezed, and with that, he was off. I stood there, rooted to my spot, my eyes glued to his back, and I watched until he turned the corner. He really was beautiful.

Sadly, the perfect day came to a screeching halt almost the moment I walked through the front door. It was almost as if my mother was waiting for me for hours upon hours, and each minute that passed made her more upset. She screeched about how I was gone all day, how I'm spending all my time with "this boy," how I'm not taking my senior year seriously, and how I haven't even applied to colleges. That was when I cut her off.

"I knew that's what this was about, Mom! That's what it's always about!"

I squared my shoulders towards her, displaying that I wasn't afraid to have this conversation.

"Well, what else would it be about? You have huge decisions to make, young lady, and all you're doing is frolicking about in La La Land with some boy who doesn't even have a real name!" She was so angry that she was spitting. Literally spitting. Every word she said sprayed saliva onto her chin, her shirt, and the carpet between us.

"What the hell does that even mean, Mom? What are you even saying? Quick has nothing to do with this." My hackles went up and my surging instinct to protect him made itself very clear.

"He has everything to do with this! You are not focused on your future, Quinn!"

"Yes, I am, Mom! Just because I don't want to do what you want me to do doesn't mean I am not focused!" I shouted back at her without considering my words or my tone. She went completely quiet, and I had to replay the moment to figure out why she stepped back and was now looking at me with wispy eyes of disbelief.

"I'm sorry, Mom. I shouldn't have yelled at—"

"Are you saying that you don't want to go to college? Is that what you are telling me right now?" Her whispers came out quivering, clearly illustrating the mixture of fear, disappointment, and seething fury.

I took a deep breath. And then another. I wanted to keep an even, cool tone. "I didn't say that, Mom. I just don't know yet exactly what I want to do. There are other options, you know? Other than college. There are so many things I could do that don't require that."

"Like what, Quinn? Like what?" I could tell she was trying to calm herself as well. "College will open so many doors for you. It will give you the opportunities you deserve."

"Yeah, and it will give me a crap ton of debt. And for what, Mom? So I can be indoctrinated with narratives funded by who-knows-what? I'm not interested in all that. That's not how I want to start my adult life." I didn't even realize that I felt that way until I said it out loud, but once I heard my voice, I knew that was how I felt in my core.

"Indoctrination? Funding by what? What kind of nonsense? Where did you even hear that? Through Quick?"

And that was it. I lost it. I don't know what angered me more, that she mentioned Quick in a derogatory manner again, or that my mother didn't think I was capable of having my own thoughts.

"Through Quick? No, Mom! Through Quinn!"

I turned on my heels and stormed out.

○○○

Quinn / 9:09 a.m.

Hi.

Quick / 9:11 a.m.

hey happy anniversary
don't you have an english quiz right now

9:11 a.m.

I finished.
Quick, I want to meditate at lunch today.

9:11 a.m.

ok of course
are you ok

9:17 a.m.

I'm okay, I am just super irked right now.

9:17 a.m.

about what

9:18 a.m.

My mother.

9:18 a.m.

oof I'm sorry
want company at lunch?

9:18 a.m.

Only if it's yours.

9:18 a.m.

you got it

Monday, October 7, 2024

Note to self:

I'm going to focus on the positive. I'm going to try my best to follow all of my negative thoughts with a positive phrase. Let's give it a go.

I am bothered by the fact that Mom is being so harsh about next year.

> *But at least* I have a mom who cares.

I am so pissed about her attitude towards Quick and the comments she made.

> *But at least* she isn't being ridiculous and telling me I can't see him or whatever.

~~I am offended~~

Let me rephrase that. I try not to get offended by other people's opinions that don't align with my truths.

Okay, I am annoyed that Mom thinks I can't think for myself and that Quick influences me in that way.

> *But at least* I know the truth.

I have my own thoughts. Quick makes me feel more whole, but it's not like he's my entire world. Besides, I have other friends. People are super nice at school now, now that they know who I am, and they like Seek & Speak. I'm sure some of them will turn into friends. And I have Mandy. She's a friend. As a matter of fact, I am going to see if she wants to hang out after school on Friday.

While I'm focusing on the positive... I have to bring up Quick. He's the best. He knew I was upset today, but he didn't push. He meditated with me, unabashedly in front of anyone and everyone who would have paid attention to us on the quad at lunch. And afterwards, when we were eating, he reached over to squeeze my hand a couple of times, just to communicate that he was there for me if I needed him. He didn't have to say a word; I knew that's what he was telling me. I told him about the college argument— I left out the stuff about him— and he just listened. He really is the best of the best. I couldn't ask for a better, more accepting friend.

Aaaaw, see? Just like that, I feel better. It really is about gratitude.

Wait a second. Maybe the solution is for my folks to spend time with him? So Mom can see what a great person he is?

…Q

○○○

hey turns out I don't have to work on friday
wanna do something after school?

Quinn / 1:40 p.m.

Oh, shoot, Quick! I'm so sorry.
I thought you were working so I made plans.

1:41 p.m.

right on, that's cool

1:43 p.m.

Mandy and I are going to grab some ice cream.

1:44 p.m.

whoa... ok
you good?

1:45 p.m.

Yeah, it should be interesting. We haven't hung out since we were kids.

1:47 .m.

I hope it goes well

1:48 p.m.

I'm sure it'll be fine.
Water under the bridge.

1:50 p.m.

I hope you're right
text me from the bathroom if you need me to come save you, lol

1:51 p.m.

Oh my gosh! I hope I won't have to do that!

1:53 p.m.

I'm sure it'll be fine
just be careful
maybe don't share all your deepest, darkest secrets on your first date

1:55 p.m.

Noted.

Quinn:

Like Old Times

It was bizarre to be nervous throughout an entire day at school just because I was going to grab ice cream with Mandy afterwards. I had known her for nearly a decade and we were inseparable for years. Besides, I was totally comfortable with who I was whether she liked me or not, so the nerves took me by surprise. I had to admit to myself that I was still questioning her intentions, and therefore had reservations about the rekindling, but I really did want to give her the benefit of the doubt.

Without either one of us stating it, we both inherently understood that we chose to get ice cream after school as a trial run of sorts. It was only an hour or so, not some long commitment of a day's worth of activity. Regardless, I still found myself anxious that day, looking at the clock and counting down the hours until I would be home, and it would be over. It wasn't the best way to enter the situation, to just want to get it over with, but that was the truth of the matter.

As it turned out, it wasn't that bad. As a matter of fact, it was pleasant. Even delightful. Being that we were childhood friends, we knew so much about the foundations of one another's lives that the dialogue came naturally. She updated me on her family just as I did for her, and within a few minutes, my nerves had settled. It was a harmless conversation that I was truly enjoying, even when it led into matters of more current times. By all standards, it was a typical conversation between old friends, as we bounced stories about classes, teachers, friends, hobbies, and the like.

"Are you going to Hoco next week?" Mandy asked, after popping the last of her fudge-dipped cone into her mouth.

A blank stare came across my face. "What's Hoco?"

"Homecoming, silly! It's next Friday. Are you going with your friend, um, what's his name? Quick?"

I paused to consider her tone. I replayed her question and studied her face. I did not sense anything being laced with any sort of judgment; she seemed to be asking a genuine question. However, I had become so accustomed to the acceptance of thoughtful pause in conversation with Quick that I thought nothing of my delayed response. Clearly she thought I was taking too long to respond.

"Um, hello? Earth to Quinn?" She nudged my forearm with her finger and flashed me a toothy grin to show that she was teasing.

"Uh, no. No, I'm not going to Homecoming. It's not really my thing. Are you?" I reciprocated. Mandy squealed in delight, "Yes!" and then spent the next five minutes telling me all about this cute boy she liked, how she was dropping hints for him to ask her, how he finally did, and exactly what her dress looked like. I caught myself smiling at her; it was amusing to see her share her joy. I was sincerely happy for her. For a minute there, it felt like old times.

We stood up to leave and I glanced at my phone to see that almost ninety minutes had passed. I was surprised when I saw what time it was, and I felt a little silly for being nervous about something that turned out to be so easy. She gave me a tight hug, promised to text me pictures of her in her dress, and ran off to do a little shopping before meeting her parents for dinner.

On my way home, my thoughts veered towards Quick. They usually did, especially lately. I couldn't shake a nagging question that I never considered before: Did *he* want to go to Homecoming? There had been posters and announcements about it for weeks and I hadn't even given it a first thought, let alone a second one. I assumed he hadn't either. He would have mentioned it if he wanted to go. Right? Right. There was no way he wanted to go.

Right?

Quick:

Death Grip

I made a conscious effort not to text Quinn during her time with Mandy, but I had my phone in my hand the entire time. Just in case. When she called me that late afternoon, I picked up before the first ring even completed its chime. Too eager to answer but I didn't care.

Just by hearing the sound of her voice when she said hello, I knew that the visit went okay. I was relieved for her. Actually, for me. Thinking about Mandy hurting her in some way was really doing a number on me, so I was glad to lay that to rest. As I listened to her rushed synopsis of their visit, I could tell she was itching to tell me something.

I was wrong. She wasn't sprinting through the story because she wanted to tell me something. She wanted to ask me something. All of a sudden, she blurted out, "Did you want to go to Homecoming?"

Without missing a beat, I started laughing. Hard. I slapped my knee and everything. And then as quickly as I started laughing, I stopped. "Wait, why? Did you want to go?"

"No, did you?" She was quick to respond.

"No. Are you sure you didn't? We can go if you want to, Quinn, or if you—"

"Quick, I don't want to go. I didn't even think about it until Mandy mentioned it, and once I did, I figured you didn't want to either. I just wanted to make sure."

"What if we did something instead?" I asked. We both agreed to brainstorm something new and fun to do, and before I even had the chance to make good on the agreement, she texted me the next morning that she had the perfect activity planned. Lots of exclamation points.

The next Friday, while most of our peers were getting all fancied up and taking photos before tearing it up on the dance floor, Quinn and I were set to have a Homecoming of our own. She wouldn't tell me what we were doing, but I knew we were up to something good when she greeted me on her driveway wearing overalls and holding a pair of straw hats. "To the corn maze!" she announced, holding the hats up to the sky like they were a sword. "But first, come say hi to my folks." She dropped the bomb and then turned around like nothing happened. She started walking towards the front door, but it took me a couple of seconds to process what she said. She turned around to smile at me, and of course I followed. I knew I'd follow that smile anywhere.

Quinn invited me inside and we found her parents sitting at the kitchen island. Her mom was drinking tea and her dad was vehemently trying to clean his eyeglasses. They looked up to see us, and it was immediately apparent that they were as surprised by the visit as I was. I experienced a bit of deja vu as we exchanged niceties; again, her dad was the friendly one while her mom focused on not slitting my throat with her teaspoon. Or at least that's how it felt. When I met her the year before, she asked about my real name in a tone that was dripping with cynicism, but this year, she was silent.

As Quinn and I turned to leave, I swiveled back around to address her mother. "Oh, and Mrs. Washington? To answer your question from yester-year, my real name is Declan. Thank you for asking, and I apologize that it took so long for me to respond." My comment oozed with gracious respect, and I deliberately used my softest eyes to connect with hers. I watched as her shoulders dropped and her face released tension. I quickly followed up with, "And thank you for allowing Quinn and me to go to the fall carnival. Have a nice evening."

She was stunned silent as I turned back towards Quinn. My instinct was to grab Quinn's hand, but I refrained. Her face wore a blend of surprise and utter glee, which I found to be highly satisfying.

As soon as we were out of earshot, I asked her what prompted the invitation to go inside. She confessed that her mom was struggling a bit with our friendship, basically blaming our time together as the reason for what her mom perceived as the lack of focus in terms of post-high school planning.

Quinn told me that if her mom could spend time with me, even just a little, she would undoubtedly see how wonderful and supportive I was. Her mom would change her tune and absolutely love me, she was sure of it.

And as soon as we were out of eyeshot, I took her hand in mine. I had started to notice how empty mine felt when hers wasn't in it. If I had it my way, I'd hold her hand the entire night.

Lucky for me, I was able to. Our interlocking fingers made the unexpected tough conversation about the unknowns of the upcoming year a little easier to get through, and she had a death grip on my hand when we tackled the corn maze in the dark. By the time I got home, I honestly remembered very little else from the evening. Just that death grip.

Best part of the night, hands down.

Note to self:

Woah… Big night. Time to process.

Quick and I went to the fall carnival tonight. Well, wait, let me back up. Quick came inside to chat with Mom and Dad for a couple of minutes before we went, and I'm pretty sure he left Mom pleasantly surprised. He was direct but polite, and his good nature undoubtedly shined through. So that's good. Hopefully the more she engages with him, the less she'll blame him for my "irresponsible" choices.

Anyway, from the second we left the house until the moment we hugged good-bye, Quick and I held hands. But, like, actively held hands. We've interlaced our fingers before and we've held hands plenty here and there, but this was different somehow. I don't know, I'm still trying to put my finger on it. We haven't put a label on our friendship. We haven't labeled our relationship in any way. I don't even think we feel the need to. We know we are the best of friends, and due to our circumstances and similarities, our friendship feels like it is on a deeper level than typical of teenagers. We hold hands for us, not for others and not to make some announcement.

Tonight, it felt like we held hands because they belong together, and we both know it.

We meandered around the fall carnival, chuckling at the impatient kids waiting in line and almost feeling sorry for the parents who ended up playing the games to win the prizes for their crying children. We rode the caterpillar ride, ventured into the house of mirrors, and nibbled on stale popcorn, but for the most part, we talked. Mostly about the coming year. I have been starting to process the possibility of us being separated and I wanted to hear his take on it, but he said he didn't even want to think about it. He knew we needed to, though. At first it was nervous chatter, but as we discussed the different scenarios, we noticed that we started to feel better. We admitted that it was the unknowns that were making us nervous, in terms of where each of us would be, what we would be doing, and how often we'd get to see each other, but we realized that our friendship does not fall under that category of the "unknown." In fact, it is the opposite. It is completely known that our friendship is as strong as a fortress, resilient and protected. As long as we both continue to put the effort in, it can and will withstand distance and time. We acknowledge that the minutiae of the friendship may change, but like a tree with deep roots, the core of it will remain sturdy. Maybe even more so.

A hovering burden was lifted from my shoulders once we wrapped up our conversation. Knowing that Quick and I are on the same page, we will make the best of whatever comes our way. We will support one another's choices and until then, there is nothing to stress about. Deep breaths in. Deep breaths out.

I did get a little embarrassed tonight, though. I completely freaked out in the corn maze. It wasn't even a haunted Halloween one! But it was dark, and I didn't know where we were, and there were shuffling noises in the breeze. I swear, I didn't think we'd ever find our way out. As much as I always enjoy Quick's company, I hated that corn maze! I could have done without that part, but our night was way better than it would have been if we went to Homecoming. That's for dang sure.

...Q

Hey Geoffrey,

Once I left Quinn's, I couldn't wait to get home to write to you about it. But I came home to a nightmare. Another frickin' nightmare.

I turned the corner on our street and I saw the sirens in front of our house. Turns out Dad came home from work to find Mom unresponsive on the kitchen floor. Faint heartbeat, barely breathing, the whole nine yards. Who knows how long she had been there.

I got home in time to see the paramedics load her into the ambulance before rushing her off to the hospital. I knew the second I saw her that she probably overdosed on those damn meds. And no, it's not lost on me that tomorrow's your birthday.

Dad called from the hospital a little while ago. "Mom's stable and is going to be okay." That's word for word what he said. What a load of crap. Her body may have been jolted back into working order, but there is nothing "stable" about Mom and I haven't seen her "okay" in years, so yeah. Doubtful.

Apparently, she's going to rehab. The doctor or the nurse or whoever gave Dad some recommendations and he's looking into facilities now. Probably like a 30-day thing or whatever.

I waited too damn long to talk to her. I am so wrapped up in my own self-centered life that I kept putting the most important conversation on the backburner. I'm a coward. I let things go unsaid, I watched her slowly deteriorate into a shell of a stranger, and I justified my choice to do so. For years. I shouldn't have let it fester. I'm so pissed at myself right now. And at Dad who's never frickin' home. And at her. They're the adults here, not me.

Ugh. Even that sounds like an excuse.

What if I lost my chance to apologize? What if I can never make it right? What if I never see her again? I can't deal with this, Geoffrey. I can't. I can't lose her, too.

If you're up there, watch over her. I mean, I know you already do, but just protect her, ok? I don't know what I'm trying to say. I need her to be better. I miss her. I miss her so frickin' much. It's like I lost all three of you at the exact same time. Sucks so bad.

Love you. I'm so sorry.

-Deck

10/19/24

2:41 a.m.

There is an eerie silence in the car. The only noises are those of the vehicles on the road and the constant sounds of my mom's muffled sobs. The mound of used tissues on the center console has grown to the size of a basketball, not including the ones that have fallen onto her seat and floorboard. I glance over at my dad. His glassy and unblinking eyes are staring at the road ahead, his knuckles completely white as they grip the steering wheel.

My leg is asleep. I shuffle in my seat to reposition, and the sound of my small movement brings my mother's attention to the present situation. Her sniffles stop and she holds her breath as she slowly turns her head an inch in my direction. Her head is still facing the front windshield, just towards the driver's side rather than straight ahead. Her eyes continue to look more left, though, where I am sure she catches a glimpse of me in her peripheral vision. Her mouth becomes terse and her upper lip scornfully pulses. Remembering that I am in the car causes a visceral reaction in her, and the sorrow becomes something much different. Rage. Hatred. Disgust.

I turn away, unable to look at the contempt and disdain that my mother is wearing on her face. Tears stream down my cheeks as I think of my kid brother. I am mourning both his tragic absence and the coming dissolution of our family, already aware that our family will not survive without him.

OOO

hey
sorry to text so late, just woke up from a flashback
I hadn't had one in so long damnit

3:21 a.m.

came home to quite the shocker last night
mom was unresponsive, ambulance took her to the hospital
I wanted to let you know that I need a minute
I'm not running away, I am not isolating from you
I just have to hunker down a bit

Quinn / 5:40 a.m.

Oh, Quick! I'm so sorry.
Is she okay??
What can I do?

6:21 a.m.

nothing to do but thank you
she's stable now, heading to rehab at some point
I need some time alone but I don't want to worry that I'm hurting you

6:22 a.m.

No, I completely understand. Don't worry.
Whatever you need to feel, deal, heal.
Please let me know if you need me.
I'm glad she's going to rehab, Quick.

6:24 a.m.

yeah me too
and I will deal
you taught me that it's better to slough than to stuff

6:25 a.m.

I love that, Quick.
Yes. Please don't stuff it down.

6:31 a.m.

I won't

I miss you already but it's okay. Take your time.
I see you.

I know you do, thank you
it's a source of strength for me, Quinn

You are my rock, too, Quick.
Remember I'm here if you need me.

tt+t

Hey Geoffrey,

They took Mom to rehab today. Looks like she'll be there for about a month, I guess. I am worried about her. I mean, I'm glad she's there because she needs it so badly, but I wonder what withdrawal will be like for her. Will it be akin to people who are coming off street drugs? I was going to dig a little on it, but then I thought better of it. The rehab facility will take care of her, and hopefully remnants of our mom will come back to life slowly but surely once she detoxes.

I did talk to Dad today. After he gave me the scoop on Mom, I asked him if he'd be around more now. I told him that he works too much and I don't want to be alone all the time anymore, especially not now. He just looked at me, Geoffrey. For like thirty seconds. I don't even think he blinked. And then he started crying. Like, hard. He was trying to apologize. I couldn't really make out all his words, but the pain and anguish were clear as day.

I've never really thought about things too much from his perspective. I mean, yeah, I've thought about how much it would suck to lose a son. How frickin' sad and empty that would feel for a parent. But I saw something else today, too. Like Dad's been trying to be the strong one. And like he's been trying to keep the family together by providing for us. And by pretending things are normal? I don't know. But he kept apologizing, and I heard him say the word, "fail," about twenty times. I felt so bad for him. He's trying to be a good dad, but he's showing love in all the wrong ways. Or at least not the ways I need him to.

We hugged a lot. I told him all the things—that it's ok, that he didn't do anything wrong, that he is a good dad, that I love him—you know, all the things I've been wishing they'd tell me for the last five plus years. Sigh.

It feels like a shift, though. Like things were forced to move, you know? We've been standing still for so long, but this thing with Mom pushed stuff in the spotlight. I don't think it can go back to how it was. Especially not with Dad and me after today. The conversation went so much more easily than I expected, and I can totally see me calling him out on it if he went back to being absent all the time.

I'm with Quinn. She said she was glad Mom is in rehab, and I am, too. Things will improve. They have to, right?

I told Dad I want to go see her but Dad said she's not ready yet. Makes sense. She's probably detoxing bad. I don't want to see her like that, and I bet Dad doesn't want to either. She's gotta do that on her own, and I bet she wouldn't want us to see that process either.

At least she's ok. I'll see her soon and I'll be able to say what I need to say. It's so frickin' agonizing to know that my own mom despises me, but I have to face it and talk to her. Force her to talk to me.

Quinn slipped me an envelope in class today. It had a crystal in it with an explanation card. Lepidolite. It's a cool purplish color and apparently it's a stone that helps someone to stabilize. At first I thought she meant it for my mom, but as I read more, I knew it was for me. It helps with emotional healing, especially by releasing old emotional habits. I immediately thought of my tendencies to self-blame and self-loathe. I used to be pretty good at those. I think Quinn was reminding me not to go back to them. I'll tuck it in my pocket.

I told her I needed a little time and space, but I miss her already. And I feel a little guilty for missing her. Like I should only be thinking about Mom? That's dumb.

Keep your eye on Mom, brother.

Love you,

Deck

Wednesday, October 23, 2024

Note to self:

I'm trying not to worry about Quick, but I can't help it. I'm terrified he'll fall back into old patterns of anger, isolation, and self-punishment, but I also know how much he's grown in the last year. He is open to facing his struggles and deals with things so much better than he used to. I was so impressed the other day when he texted about sloughing, not stuffing. He knows it's better to deal with something and let it shed from him, rather than stuff it down and bury it deep within. I really am trying not to worry. I know he's got this.

I guess I can just tell how sad and worried he is. He's texted a little here and there these last few days, which is good, but my heart pains for him. I can't imagine having to deal with losing a brother but feeling like you're to blame for it, and then on top of that, to feel that your parents blame you for it, too. Quick really, truly believes his mom hates him. I cannot even imagine how awful that must feel.

In the meantime, I am handling Seek & Speak on my own, which is of course okay. It is still going strong. Actually, it's booming. The statistics for the last topic, Area 51, were off the charts and to be honest, it is kind of taking on a life of its own.

I think I will focus on being artistic tonight. I read about this study that was done in the 1960s that related creativity to genius. They tested five-year-olds to see how they solved problems using creative thinking, and 98 percent qualified as geniuses. However, five years later, only about 30 percent qualified, and ten years later only 12 percent of the original children qualified at age fifteen. How sad that we stop nourishing our creativity as we age. I, for one, do not intend to let that happen. Even if I'm not the best artist or what have you, I'm still going to nurture my imagination! So tonight, I think I will work on a new quote for Quick's scrapbook. Given what he is currently dealing with, and since I'm hoping he will find the good in it, I think I'll go with Tony Robbins' quote: "Life doesn't happen to you, it happens for you."

And then I'll have to think of a trinket to go with it. That's a tough one.

...Q

Quick:

Grappled

I wasn't sure exactly when it happened, or perhaps it was over the course of the previous year, but as I sat with my father one night on the couch, I realized that I had trained my brain to find silver linings. I found myself thinking that Mom being at the rehabilitation facility was not only good for her, but it consequently allowed for Dad and me to reconnect on our own time, at our own pace, and in our own way. He cut back his work hours, admitting that his purposeful inefficiency was the reason for the late nights all those years. I liked having him home. It was still quiet, but we made a habit of eating dinner together before watching television on most nights. There were attempts at awkward conversation, and like with all things, those conversations became easier with time.

One evening, while Dad was teaching me how to barbecue, I told him that I had forgotten how much he loved to cook. We talked a little about my job in the produce section and how even though I only worked a couple shifts a week, it opened my eyes to how awful our food choices were. I thanked him for teaching me how to prepare the night's dinner, and he responded so despondently, commenting about the short amount of time he had left for the countless number of things a father should teach his son. He regretfully spoke of how I basically had to raise myself, that I even had to teach myself how to ride a bicycle at such a late age. Jokingly, I retorted that he could still teach me how to drive, and as the unplanned words were coming out of my mouth, I knew how desperately I wanted that. For both of us.

We both wanted it.

We made plans to discover the logistics behind a driver's permit and the process for earning a license, and then discussed a tentative schedule for time behind the wheel with him guiding me from the passenger seat. The more we chatted about it, the more excited we both became. It led to a brainstorming of tasks I had yet to learn from my father, and I couldn't type them up on my phone's list app fast enough. Unclog a sink. Change the filters. Add salt to the water softener. Change a tire. Earn good credit. The list kept going and going, but each thing we added widened our smiles. As we wrapped up the evening, I tacked "barbecue" onto the list, and handed my phone to him. He checked the box, and there was no denying the prideful tear in his eye or the gratitude in his grin. Thankful for the renewed relationship. Thankful for the evening's events. Thankful for the time together and all the times to come.

I headed upstairs and my thoughts about driving raced around the track in my head. This shared experience with Dad was going to be so good for both of us, and I instinctively grabbed my phone to tell Quinn the news. Mid-text, I tossed my phone on the bed. I wasn't going to tell her.

I was going to surprise her.

If I did my math right, and if Dad and I hustled in the hours like we planned, I could get my driver's license around Christmas. The thought of her face when she would see me behind the wheel for the first time… That would be enough exclamation points to last me a year.

As I thought about Quinn, my heart ached with how much I missed her. Not because I had seen her less that week, but because it never felt like enough. No matter how much time I spent with her, I always wanted more. I still struggled to identify the feelings I was having, whether it was deep admiration and appreciation for the friendship, or if it was that and more. I didn't know. I just knew that she made me happy. Ridiculously happy. She made me feel like I could be me, but I still wanted to be better. For her. And I wanted to do the same for her, to make her happy, to fill all the voids and gaps that she had. To help her grow like she did for me.

Our friendship often times felt like it was more about me. Her helping me. Was it because most of her healing was done before we even met? We did focus more on Geoffrey, to the point where sometimes I even forgot about Troy. She was so positive and seemed to have everything together, so much so that I would fail to remember her trauma. I knew that she was still working through that trauma, that she still had hard days. Days that she would get lost in their Zen garden. Days that she needed to meditate extra. She would have those days for the rest of her life. How could she not? She literally saw her brother's lifeless body.

My mind created an image of Quinn's mother holding Troy and it made me feel sick to my stomach. I couldn't think of anything worse than a baby dying. Suddenly, with no warning. Just randomly like that.

And then I remembered that nothing is random.

And then I put my shovels to work.

Two hours later, I was covered in regret, knowing that must have been exactly how Quinn felt when she dug on child trafficking. It stemmed from a place of love, of wanting to understand, wanting to empathize, wanting to help. And then the reality set in. The nausea took over. I spun out, asking myself endless, judgmental questions. What did I do? Why couldn't I bury my head in the sand? Now what? Would I tell her? Or omit the truth, which is an act of dishonesty? How could I look her in the face, but not tell her what I learned? And if I told her, wouldn't it make things worse? Open up old wounds and carve some new ones? Did I really want to do that?

I grappled with it until the morning, but I came to the conclusion I knew all along. I had to tell her. Just not yet. I'd find the right time, I told myself, but I knew full well that there was never going to be a right time. How was I going to tell Quinn that I thought SIDS was not nearly as accidental as it sounded?

Quinn:

The Perfect Thing

T hrilled to hear that Quick and his father were spending quality time together in the evenings, I tried to give him the space to focus on that relationship. We still texted and talked every day, and I could see that he was in a better place. As much as I missed him, our adventures, and our FaceTime sessions, I was happy for him. He needed this time with his dad, and would need it even more so once his mom came home.

Mandy caught up with me in the hallway one morning and asked if I wanted to hang out after school. I saw no reason not to, and when she suggested we go to her house, I had to contain my excitement. I hadn't been there in ages, and with so many fond memories of the place, I thought it would make for a fun afternoon.

After raiding her refrigerator and loading up on our own sloppy version of a deconstructed charcuterie board of lunch meats, cheese, and fruit, Mandy had the idea to look at some of the old photographs she had from elementary school. We jumped to the couch and with each picture, we remembered more and more hilarious moments of our childhood. The shared memories brought us to tears, we laughed so hard, especially when we reminisced about the time we played Truth or Dare at recess and someone had to pretend he was a dog peeing on a fire hydrant right when the principal walked by. We couldn't remember if it was Ara, Jack, or Jaden, but it didn't make the memory any less hysterical.

Once she caught her breath, Mandy exclaimed, "I got it! We should totally play right now. Oh my gosh, okay, Quinn. Truth or dare?"

"What? We are too old for this game! What kind of dares would we even do?" The idea made me laugh even harder.

"You're right. Just truth. Hmmmmm." Mandy was deep in thought while I was busy wiping my tears and trying to breathe evenly again. "Quinn. Are you and Quick an item? Truth."

"What? No. It's not like that."

"Yes, it is! Don't lie, Quinn! I totally see you guys holding hands all the time. It's super cute." She nudged my shoulder with hers and her eyebrows did a little dance. Then she took it a step further and pursed her lips together to make kissing sounds. I couldn't help but laugh. She looked absolutely ridiculous. "So, have you guys kissed? What's the story with you two?"

"I told you. It's not like that." I could feel my face turning red. I wanted to change the subject, but Mandy was not about to drop it.

"So you haven't? Well, do you want to? You should kiss him, Quinn! You two are totally into each other!"

There was no hiding the blush now. My entire body felt like it was sun-burned. "I don't know about that, Mandy. I don't think it's like that with us."

"Yes, it is. Do you not see the way he looks at you?" She was so animated, she literally stood up to use her entire body to speak to me. "He frickin' likes you, Quinn. Like, a lot!"

"I don't know, Mandy. He's hard to read, and he doesn't share much. It took him forever just to tell me his real name and about his fam—"

She might not have even picked up on it if it weren't for my reaction. It was the first time a true curse word escaped my lips. And of course Mandy jumped on it like a lion to its prey. "Oh my gosh, that's right! Quick can't be his real name! What's his story anyway?"

In slow motion, I watched her expression go from "gossip girl" to "evil vic-tor." Her eyes revealed a calculation of sorts as they darted around in their sockets, and as she reached for her laptop mumbling something about the perfect thing to take them down, I hung my head in shame. I walked slowly out the door and down the street to my house, confident that she was so absorbed in whatever plan she was concocting that she didn't even realize I left. She got what she wanted, and as much as I didn't understand what that was or what it was for, I knew it wasn't good.

Friday, November 1, 2024

Note to self:

As if the disaster that unfolded at Mandy's house was not bad enough, I came home to hear Mom and Dad arguing about my college decisions. Or rather, the lack thereof. What a greeting. Actually, they didn't even realize I walked in, so I headed right up the stairs and shut my door.

I can't believe I fell for Mandy's crap. I don't even know what the crap is, but I know that she didn't really want to reconnect. That she hadn't really grown past our childhood drama. Her drama. Not mine. Ugh. I should have listened to Quick. He didn't tell me what to do, and I know he never would, but he knew right out of the gate that Mandy was bad news. What did he ask me that one time? If she was authentic, or if I thought she could be so? Something like that. Damnit, I messed this up so badly.

Okay, let's process. I drew attention to the mystery of Quick's name. I almost mentioned something about his family, but did she pick up on that? Or did she only process the nickname part? Surely by now she has scoured the internet, but to discover his name? Or about Geoffrey? And she wants to do something with that information. What could she do with it? Okay, worst case scenario. Ummm, she says something to him and catches him off-guard at school. Oh, that would be so awful. What if she pulls the bathroom mirror crap again? I don't know what I would do if that happened.

Oh my gosh, this is so bad. He'll never forgive me. I betrayed him in the worst, worst possible way. I have to figure this out. I have to stop this. I'll beg her. I'll plead. I'll make her understand how awful it would be to bring up that pain.

Who am I kidding? She wouldn't care. And even if I get her to agree to keep it quiet, she'll still know. And she'll always have that ammunition. I'd never know when she would use it or how. No. The answer is to neutralize her ammo. To render it useless.

Shoot. I have to tell Quick.

Ugh, I long for the simplicity of my life that was. The one back at the oasis. I miss those days. But I know today was just a bad day. Not a bad life. I'm blessed in so many ways, and it's important to consciously reflect upon that. I am super blessed. I have wonderful parents who love me (even though I can still hear them arguing), I am healthy and safe, I have a bright future (that I have no clue about yet), and I have the world's greatest friendship. What else could I ask for?

Oh, I know.

Not to lose Quick. Shoot.

...Q

OOO

Quinn / 8:23 p.m.

Just saying hi!
Hope you're having a good time with your dad.
What was on the learning list for today?

Quick / 8:27 p.m.

I worked today
but tomorrow's lesson is gfi vs. gfci and circuit breakers
ha ha
how are you

8:28 p.m.

I'm okay. I miss you.
But only a little bit, lol.

8:28 p.m.

yeah me too
thanks for picking up the slack with S&S

8:29 p.m.

Easy peasy! Actually, I'm not really doing anything with it anymore.
Did you see how @i'mwalkin'ere suggested they start posting their
own topics?
It totally took off!

8:31 p.m.

I did see that
and @craftyKKay's suggestion of the mandela effect
they are all over that one, biggest topic yet I think

8:33 p.m.

For sure! She's brilliant.
So how are you doing?
How's your mom?

8:34 p.m.

I think I'm doing ok
it's been so good with dad
mom's ok I think? hopefully due home by christmas

That's so awesome, Quick.
Are you nervous about her coming home?

8:34 p.m.

a little I guess
not really, dad and I are ready I think

8:35 p.m.

That's amazing!

8:36 p.m.

how are you doing

8:37 p.m.

I'm looking forward to break, I can tell you that!

8:38 p.m.

same
let's do something fun

8:39 p.m.

Everything we do is fun.
Do you mean something new?

8:41 p.m.

ha ha yeah

8:44 p.m.

Oh, I know!
Let's go roller skating!

8:44 p.m.

consider it done
I might have a surprise for you by then
how's the night school gets out sound

8:44 p.m.

Whaaaaat...
It sounds like a perfect way to kick off vacation.
So can I have a hint? I love surprises!

yes, I know this about you
I'm gonna go before I spill the beans, lol

8:45 p.m.

Okay, have a great rest of your night.
I'm sending you a huge hug.

8:45 p.m.

wish it wasn't via text
first thing tomorrow?

8:45 p.m.

Consider it done.

Hey Geoffrey,

Things are going so well with Dad. We've gotten to a comfortable place with each other, and I look forward to our nightly dinners. And to the arbitrary lessons, too. We chat with more ease and we even go beyond the small talk sometimes. Did you know that Dad believes giants once walked the earth and that much of the mountainous terrain we see is petrified giants? Ha! You know I'm going to dig on that one. One day. Probably not anytime soon. I've been busy driving, trying to cram in all the required hours so I can surprise Quinn over break. Dad's even thinking of working from home full-time once Mom gets back, so he and I will be able to share his car. Pretty sweet deal. Anyway, Dad is going to visit mom tomorrow for the first time. We agreed that it's best that he go alone, before I do. Just in case.

Learning all these "Dad lessons" is really making me think about my future. I need to figure out what I want to do next so I can set myself up to be a catch, you know? What girl out there would want a bum who can't change the air filters? And what girl out there would want a bum with no direction in life? So Dad and I talked about some different options and I made a decision. I applied to the university in town and some of the local colleges. I don't know exactly what I want to do, but that's ok. Maybe once I start taking a couple of classes, I'll feel a pull towards something. I just know that I want to stay nearby. I missed out on a lot of time with our folks and this thing with Mom has really got me thinking about our family. In a way, they went from having two kids to none, and I need to do what I can to make up for that. I'm not saying it's entirely my fault that we've lost our way, especially since they're the adults, but the blame game is stupid. We are all a part of the dynamic, so we all contributed to the dynamic. And now I need to do my part to mend it. Me skipping town and moving far away is simply not on the table. At least not yet.

I told Quinn my decision. Well, the part of the decision that I made, that I am staying in town. She was supportive, as always, and had kind things to say about me and my choice to prioritize my family. I guess there's no more hiding from this thing with Mom. It's time to face reality because it's right around the corner.

I hope I can handle the news of Quinn's decision as gracefully as she did mine. When I think of the possibility of her moving away, every system in my body seems to shut down. But I have to be happy for her no matter what. It doesn't matter how far away she is. Our friendship will withstand it. It has to.

I guess first it has to withstand the news about my dig on SIDS. It will. She's the most forgiving person I know. Maybe she'll need some time but eventually she'll forgive me, I hope. I'll do whatever I need to do to make that happen.

Yes, Geoffrey. Because I love her. I'm convinced it's the real deal.

Miss you,

Deck

Quinn:

A Wave

Quick and I had become so aligned with one another that our connection went well beyond the milestone of finishing each other's sentences. The evening he told me about his decision to stay home the following year to attend a nearby school was the exact night that I myself committed to making a plan for my looming future. I had been putting off the inevitable, using the excuse of "waiting for a sign" to know what avenue to take, but once the arguments made their way to being between my parents, I knew I needed to take the next step.

Since that first fateful trip to the bookstore with my father and all along the journey that followed, I wanted to help heal others. I wasn't interested in the medical field, per say, but rather in alternative methods of healing. So, I started the process with the accustomed practice of a simple internet search. As I read the seemingly endless pages that were chock full of career ideas, the enthusiasm within me started to bubble over. Each time I came across another possibility that excited me, I bounced a little higher, clapped a little harder, and exclaimed, "Ooooh!" a little louder.

The list started to grow. What started out with acupuncturist and herbalist soon incorporated such prospects as energy healer, massage therapist, reiki practitioner, thermographer, yoga instructor, and dozens more. Before I knew it, I was organizing my findings into a chart of information. Running down the left side was the array of possible career choices, and along the top of the chart were such considerations as the number of years of schooling, the cost of schooling, the average salary, and the rating of my own interest. Plotting the information not only made the task feel less overwhelming but I felt that seeing the big picture would help me make the best decision for myself.

Hours sped by. The only sounds were those of my keyboard and my sudden gasps of excitement. Everything was flowing with such ease that I knew I was on the right track. I could feel the dread of the decision fading away into the darkness and being replaced by an eagerness that I could hardly contain. I had nothing but options. I was blessed with the privileged ability to get out into the world, to follow my passions, to decide what I want to study and practice, and to make my adult life happen through my own choices. Sure, there would be hiccups along the way, but nothing big enough to stop me. My childhood was nearing its end, and for the first time, I felt ready. I was even starting to welcome it.

I woke up the next morning and immediately grabbed my laptop from my nightstand to look at my chart. Pride consumed me, and I practically launched out of bed. I couldn't wait to show my parents. I still had much to research and even more to consider, but I was headed in the right direction, making forward progress.

As I expected, my parents were thrilled. My mom started talking at a pace much too quick for even a savant to calculate, throwing out suggestions and questions at record speed. My dad squeezed my shoulder as he walked past me to grab a muffin from the counter, and then he walked over to her to shove it in her mouth. We burst out in synchronous laughter, and I threw my arms around each of them to thank them for their support, their patience, and their love.

That night at the dinner table, my parents asked about the next step in my process. They knew I had a method to my madness, and I was grateful that they respected my desire to figure things out in my own way. I told them that I wanted to research the career options I found. I needed to truly understand each one of them because, to me, the most important column on the chart was my level of interest. I wanted to spend my time doing something I loved, and I never wanted to feel the dread of having to go to work. Even at seventeen, I knew that was no way to live.

The research consumed me. I added columns to the chart with everything from typical working hours to whether or not there was an opportunity to be self-employed. Becoming self-employed started looking more and more attractive to me as I read about the flexibility, the earning potential, and the independence it provided. I filled pages upon pages of my notebook, and as I did, I remained as present as possible in the moment. I worked without distraction, allowing myself to hear the whispers of my intuition as

I purposefully made my way towards my future.

Just as I suspected, the rows of the chart started to narrow down. Within a week's time that included dozens of research hours, I went from seventeen possibilities down to a top ten. Then a highlighted seven. Then a boldfaced five. And before long, I had a top three.

My parents did an amazing job of showing interest but granting me space. They were sure to ask how it was going each night and the vicarious excitement on their faces meant so very much to me. I chose not to share my top choices with them, or the process of narrowing it down as I went, mostly because I wanted to make the decision based solely on my thoughts and considerations. I didn't want the noise from others to influence my choice. Besides, I thought it would be much more fun to reveal the final decision without any hints along the way. As the choice became clearer, I became increasingly excited about telling them.

And to tell Quick.

But then I remembered that I had something else I needed to inform him of, too. And that piece always brought a wave of nausea mixed with panic. A wave that meditation and crystals did not seem to alleviate.

Quick:

Maybe, Just Maybe

The last day of the first semester seemed to take forever to reach. I wrestled with the motivation to even get out of bed that Friday morning, but I had to push through my final two exams before I could celebrate with Quinn that night. The minutes felt like hours, and I spent most of the school day looking at clocks and struggling to concentrate. Apparently Quinn was having a similar experience, since I received a series of texts from her throughout the day.

Six more hours!
Five hours and twenty-six minutes left!
Five hours and eleven minutes!
Four hours to go!

I was all set to pick her up from her house at four o'clock that afternoon. Quinn was expecting me to chauffeur her to the roller rink via the handle-bars on my bike, and while she knew I had a surprise for her, there was no way she suspected that I'd pick her up in my dad's car. I considered filming her reaction, but I knew that if I relished the moment in real time, I'd be able to remember every detail anyway.

She stopped meeting me on her driveway ever since she decided that her mom needed to know me so she'd love me, so I parked up the street from her house and made my way to her front door. When it was opened, I realized that Quinn wasn't the only one in for a surprise that night. Her mother not only answered the door, but she greeted me with a genuinely friendly hello and a hug. "Come in, come in! Please tell me. Would you like me to call you Quick? Or Declan?"

I stammered as I tried to find my bearings. The shock had not worn off yet. "Um, if you wouldn't mind, I'd prefer Quick. Thank you."

She ushered me to the kitchen with her arm tucked into mine, leading me to the island to offer me a snack and a beverage. Quinn's father said hello and shook my hand as I walked over. He tried to stifle a chuckle, probably because of the unmistakable evidence of my stunned state. His wife's welcoming kindness was completely unexpected and produced utter astonishment.

"What was that all about?" I asked her as we said our good-byes and headed out the front door.

"I'll tell you later," Quinn smiled cryptically. Then she stopped short and turned to face me. "Hey. My mom's question got me thinking. Do you think you'll ever go by your real name again?" Her face turned tender as she reached for my hand.

I released a deep breath and nodded. "I do. I just need my mom to be the first one to use it again. It won't feel right otherwise. Does that make sense?" My eyes searched hers. I couldn't help but feel like so many of my answers were behind those beautiful eyes.

"Absolutely it does, Quick. It makes perfect sense." We walked towards the driveway and my heart began pounding in my chest. I was so eager for the moment that was waiting for us. She looked about with a bewildered expression. "Ummmm, Quick? Where's your bike? Did you bring it? Or are we taking mine?" I waited for her to look in my direction, and when she did, I held her face in mine and touched my forehead to hers.

"Turn around, Quinn." I whispered.

She held her forehead to mine as she whispered back, "Why? Is your bike in the bushes?"

I laughed as I spun her around and placed a blindfold over her eyes. The scent of her hair wafted towards me and I could feel my knees get weak. The strong urge to confess my feelings was becoming increasingly difficult to ignore.

"Oooooh, is this the surprise? Did you get a new bike? Oh my gosh, did you get roller skates for tonight?" She snickered at her own joke, presumably imagining us roller skating to the rink. She continued to entertain herself with guesses and giggles as I led her up the street. When we reached the car, I stopped walking and removed her hand from mine. I reached into my pocket, retrieved the keys, and placed them gently in her right hand. I closed her fingers around them and then I just watched. Waited and watched.

It went almost exactly as I expected. It took her about three seconds to figure out what she was holding and what it meant, and once she did, she gasped for air like a fish out of water. She ripped off the blindfold, saw the car in front of us, and screamed, "Oh my gosh, Quick, did you get your license?" She didn't even wait for a response. She went right into the squealing and the jumping, the hugging and the exclamation points. "Tell me everything. Right now!" she demanded once she settled down.

"Surprise. I got my license. What is there to tell?" I chuckled. "Come on, let's go." I opened the door for her and she crawled in, smiling proudly at me.

"Oh, so chivalrous of you, my dear. Why, thank you," she said in her best British accent as she tipped her nonexistent hat towards me.

There wasn't too much chatter in the car, probably because Quinn could sense that I was a little nervous to be driving with her for the first time. She fiddled with the radio a bit at first but ended up rolling down the window and enjoying the wind. I glanced over a couple of times and saw her beaming face angled towards the sun. Such a beautiful sight. And one that made me feel so content. Almost as content as I felt when she reached over and squeezed my hand at a red light.

After scarfing down some pizza and renting our skates, we spent two solid hours awkwardly causing each other to fall on our asses. We held hands the entire time, but more so for balance rather than affection. If our hands weren't locked, one of us was gripping the other's shoulder or pulling on the other's shirt. Even once we started to get the hang of it, we still bailed plenty of times. We were so exhausted, we ended up sitting exactly where we landed, laughing about the fall and groaning over the thought of having to get back up. Bruises and all, it was a blast. We must have looked like total fools, but luckily for us, we never cared about that. There was always a liberation that came with not concerning ourselves with the possible opinions of strangers, and that night wasn't any different.

We headed back to her neighborhood and decided to go for a stroll, and that was when things shifted. Maybe because we were no longer distracted by surprises and pizza and skates, but instead alone in quiet stillness, I was distinctly aware of my SIDS secret creeping back into my consciousness. I couldn't think about anything other than the fact that I was lying to her, but I wasn't ready to tell her yet. I wanted to be very thoughtful about how to approach the conversation, and at that time, I was too focused on the conversation I had to have with my mother a few days from then.

Quinn seemed distracted as well. I figured she was tired or was sensing my uneasiness. The latter seemed more likely. Either way, feeling "off" with Quinn was torturous. I drove home that night knowing that the only way to fix it would be to get those hard conversations out of the way. Talk to my mother and see if we could reconcile as Dad and I did. Then talk to Quinn and tell her what I think happened to Troy. And then maybe, just maybe, work up the courage to confess my feelings for her.

Honestly, I did not know which of the three would be the hardest. None would be easy.

Friday, December 20, 2024

Note to self:

Tonight was amazing, until it wasn't.

The surprise of him driving? Amazing. Especially the blindfold part. It was super sweet that he put so much thought into how he would go about telling me. Oh, and we did the forehead thing, which I will never ever tire of.

The pizza we shared? Amazing. It was delicious, for starters, and I just love how comfortable we are with each other. Tomato sauce all over our faces, stringy cheese hanging from his chin, me laughing while eating and then almost choking… We're never embarrassed around each other. It's the best feeling, truly.

Roller skating together? Amazing. Well, it was definitely a disaster in terms of successfully getting from Point A to Point B, but since our goal was to have fun, we nailed it. We had the most epic, cascading twin fall ever—he says I was the first domino, but it was totally him—where we were both flailing and trying to grasp onto each other, each movement making the fall worse and worse until we ended up flattened on the rink floor. I'm looking forward to counting the bruises, scratches, and various marks on my body tomorrow. And I know I am going to wake up so sore! But it was worth it. Totally worth it.

But then, we went for a walk around my block a couple of times. It felt so weird all of a sudden, and I know it's because I have this horrible secret that I'm hiding from him. I really need to tell him about Mandy, and I need to tell him, like, yesterday, because the only thing that can make this worse is if he finds out in any way other than directly from me. Once we started walking and it was just us in the peace of the night, all I could think about was this awful untold information. I kept trying to be brave enough to tell him, but I couldn't seem to find the right words, so I kind of retreated into a strange silence.

I don't care how crazy it sounds. I am going to practice telling him. I process best out loud, and so the more I use my words, the more I'll be able to find the right ones. I want to fast forward to the time when I tell him, and then fast forward right past it to the point when we're okay again. When he's forgiven me. I need to come clean as soon as possible so we can have the rest of winter break to reconnect and get back on track.

When I close my eyes and picture what I want, I can see it so clearly. It's the same image in my mind's eye every time. He's sitting on a couch, angled in the corner, and I'm nestled up against him with my back to his chest, his arms wrapped tightly around mine. And we're just sitting. Being still. Enjoying one another's presence.

I seriously want that more than anything.

...Q

○○○

big news
we pick mom up tomorrow

Quinn / 7:11 p.m.

Wow, that is really big news!
How are you feeling about it?

7:11 p.m.

pretty good I think
maybe a little nervous

7:12 p.m.

I'm sure. That's totally to be expected.
Do you think you'll have the big talk with her tomorrow?

7:12 p.m.

idk I have to see how it goes

7:13 p.m.

You'll know when it's the right time.
I'll be thinking of you.

7:14 p.m.

thanks
can't believe it's christmas in a couple days

7:15 p.m.

Right? I just got some big news, too.
Well, not nearly as big as yours. Or as important.
Mom and Dad are taking me to Florida for Christmas.
We leave tomorrow!

7:16 p.m.

right on, that's cool
when are you due back

7:17 p.m.

I think we fly back on the 30th.

7:18 p.m.

damn that's a long time

I'll be thinking of you.
I'm so glad you have this vacation time to focus on your family.

yeah me too
and you too
have a great time

I'm sure I'll text you every day, lol

good, I would hope so
wanna hang when you get back?

That very same day.

ok countdown is on
miss you already

Me too. Super big hugs.

Quick:

Period

When my father left to bring my mom from the rehabilitation facility, he gave me an approximation as to when they would be arriving home. That was the longest three hours of my life. I tried to keep busy, but my ability to sit still long enough to concentrate on anything was temporarily inaccessible.

I paced. I did jumping jacks. I paced some more. I made a ham and cheese sandwich, took one bite, and then left it sitting on the plate. I went back to pacing and glanced at the clock. Nineteen minutes had passed. I tried closing my eyes to sleep away an hour or two, but my mind was racing and I had a headache. So many questions about my mom were running through my mind, I couldn't even keep track of them. I considered writing them down just to get them out of my head, but when I went to the junk drawer to grab a pencil, I couldn't remember what I was going to do with it. I was all over the place.

The minutes ticked by, and as her impending arrival drew near, I could feel my nerves firing on all cylinders. I had to relax. I laid down on my back, right there in the middle of the family room, and I closed my eyes. I breathed in slowly and deeply, and exhaled even more slowly. I knew that the breath controlled the heart rate, and since I could control my breath, all I needed to do was breathe. My heart settled into a healthy rhythm and since I was calm for the first time all morning, I realized that I was terribly sore. All my muscles ached, like I had been tensely contracting them without resting. I closed my eyes again and committed myself fully to completing a body scan. Focusing on my face first, I noticed that I was furrowing my eyebrows, tightly squinting my eyes, firmly clenching my jaw, and flaring my nostrils like some sort of dragon. No wonder my head was pounding.

I cleared one area at a time, and scanned from head to toe. While my face sent the most signals that I needed to relax, my fists and my butterflies were also dead giveaways. After a solid half hour, I finally felt like I had released my nervous energy. I was ready to see my mom.

I took a seat on the couch in our living room, an area that I always thought was a waste of space since we never formally entertained. I would have much preferred a library or a game room with a foosball table instead, but it remained an unused room with unused furniture since the day we moved in. Until that day. The couch was in the direct line of sight of the front door, and I didn't want to wait even an extra second to see her.

When the front door's lock unlatched, my heart skipped a beat. And much to my surprise, it did so more with excitement than anxiety. I stood up as she walked over the threshold, and without saying a word, she fled towards me with open arms. We completely enveloped one another in a hug like no other, our heads buried in the other's neck. Her long hair became matted from my nuzzle and wet from my tears. I was completely overcome with emotion. I felt like I was seeing my mother for the first time in over five years.

When I heard that my cries were reciprocated by hers, that her apologies were repeated over and over just like mine were, it hit me that all the worry I was feeling before stemmed from the fear that she wouldn't. That she wouldn't feel emotion. That she wouldn't feel the need to hug and cry and sob and squeeze. I was so wrong.

After several minutes, she finally released the hug and whimpered, "I want to get a good look at you." She held my face in her hands while her eyes searched mine. "Look how grown you are. I lost so much time." The regret on her face was unmistakable.

"I'm right here, Mom." She looked so beautiful, exactly as I remembered her from my childhood. From before. It was clear how much her time in rehab helped her, and my heart was filled to the brim with pride for her.

She smiled gratefully. "I think we're long overdue for a chat. What do you think?" I nodded. "Would you like to have it now?"

I reasoned that it was as good a time as any, and when she asked me if I wanted to say anything first, my mind went completely blank. All the things I planned to tell her, all the things I planned to ask, gone. I stared at her, opening my mouth to speak a few times before closing it with nothing said.

She waited patiently, and then I finally squeaked out the only words I heard in my head. "I love you, Mom." I threw my arms around her again, and as I caught a couple sobs in my throat, she led me back to the couch for us to sit down. I looked at her and whispered, "I'm so glad you're back."

"In more ways than one. I'm back in more ways than one." She held me for a little while longer before she started talking again. "I've thought long and hard about all the things I need to say to you, and over the last month, I've written and rewritten a letter to you. I realized it was the only way to make sure I said it all, and then you can read it as much as you need to or want to. I'd like to read it to you so I can get it right, if that's okay?"

I nodded. I took a deep breath and pressed the mental record button in my mind. I knew this would be a monumental moment in my life and I didn't want to miss one millisecond of it. I watched as she retrieved the letter from her pocket, her hands shaking. It was then she who took the deep breath before beginning to read from the piece of paper that I would carry with me for years and years to come.

My dearest Declan,

Let me begin by telling you that I love you more than anything on this planet. It tears me up from the inside out to think that you ever thought otherwise, and it is my solemn promise that I will prove my love to you each day for the rest of my time here on earth.

My sweet boy, I am so very sorry. I failed you in every possible way. I failed you as a mother—I forced you to grow up all on your own. I failed you as a role model—I forced you to watch me handle grief in a terribly unhealthy manner. I failed you as a friend, a supporter, a guide, a protector, a provider. The list is endless, as is the depth of my regret. I can only pray that one day you will forgive me, and I will never stop trying to earn back your trust.

I need you to know something. I never blamed you for Geoffrey's kidnapping. I only blamed myself, that I put you in that situation to begin with. I realize now that you mistook my lack of engagement with you as blame, hatred, and worse, but Declan, it was the very opposite. I was so ashamed of myself as a mother that I couldn't bring myself to look at you, to face you. Because of me, you lost your brother. It is so clear to me now that in my altered state I some-how convinced myself that I was protecting you, but what I really did was condemn your childhood into one where you lost your brother and your mother at the exact same time. And what's worse is that my physical presence was a constant reminder, and probably a constant trigger as well.

As an adult, I found it impossible to navigate my way through life after the tragedy. Clearly. But yet, I wrongfully expected you to be able to do it. While we should have been working through it together as a family, no matter how hard it was, I pulled away from everyone I loved and convinced myself that you would be better off without me.

I say these things not to make excuses. I was wrong. And I am so very sorry.

We lost our Geoffrey, and then I foolishly and unnecessarily lost you, too. My two deepest regrets. I didn't have to miss out on your childhood, but I did. I would give anything to get that time back. I was stuck in the past, reliving memories and begging to somehow change the past, and in being stuck I completely lost the present. I'll be damned if I lose the future, too.

My time in rehab was hard. Earned, but hard nonetheless. I am grateful, though, because I was forced to do something I hadn't done since that day. Be alone with myself and my thoughts, without numbing them away through drugs. I was forced to face my truths and face my reality, and as difficult as it was, I found my way back to my inner self.

I read somewhere that healing is a cyclic process. You face things, you realize things, you feel things, you release things, only for you to face another facet or aspect of the situation. But it is through this healing process, it is through this reflection, it is through this accountability that your pain is set free. It takes so much courage to face the pain, instead of burying it deep. It takes even more courage to approach that pain with honesty, and I am so proud that you were able to do this in your own way, in your own time, and at your own pace. I wish I was as brave as you are, and that it didn't take me a near-death experience to see it.

I now firmly believe this: Emotions are like our best friends. They only want what is best for us, and because of that, they want to make themselves known. I had to learn to allow my emotions to reside with me, and I realized that it was much easier to acknowledge them than it was to bury them. Once we see that our emotions, both the good ones and the bad ones, are here to help us navigate

*this world by telling us what we need, it becomes more of a priority
to grant them their deserved presence in our lives.*

*I'm not saying I'm healed. None of us are and I don't believe any
of us will ever fully be so. Perhaps being completely healed would
feel like we were dishonoring Geoffrey. There will be good days and
bad days ahead of us, but I promise you that I will be here for all of
them. If you'll have me.*

Please forgive me when you feel ready to.

I love you,

Mom

By the time she finished reading her letter, my face was soaked in tears. I
didn't bother brushing them away. I let them fall as they came, each one
representing a time when I wished things were different, when I missed my
brother, when I needed my parents, when I thought she hated me, when I
hated myself. Those tears allowed the emotional release that I had bottled up
for over half of a decade. As much as I had grown and as much as I was able
to find joy again in the last year, I wasn't fully healed. Just like Mom said.

She carefully folded the letter and offered it to me. I placed it in my lap and
reached over to hug her. "Thank you, Mom. That was everything I needed to
hear, and then some."

"I'm so sorry, Declan."

I shook my head. "It's okay, Mom. We're here now and we'll be closer
than ever. But Mom? It wasn't your fault either. Evil was done by evil.
Okay? Period."

With glistening eyes, my mom nodded. "I love you, son. Period."

○○○

are you home yet
wth you've been gone forever

Quinn / 8:41 p.m.

We just landed!

8:42 p.m.

damn that means I don't get to see you today

8:42 p.m.

Unfortunately not.
Tomorrow??

8:42 p.m.

it's a must
I have a lot to tell you

8:43 p.m.

I cannot wait to hear every single morsel.

8:43 p.m.

yeah I cant wait to tell you about mom
and I want to hear all about your trip

8:43 p.m.

Yes! I have so much to tell you.
But, Quick, I have some news that you won't like, too.

8:44 p.m.

that sounds ominous
but I have some of that too

8:44 p.m.

Okay. I'm a little nervous.
Are you okay?

8:45 p.m.

I'm ok
you?

8:45 p.m.

I will be so much better once I get to see you.

8:45 p.m.

same

8:47 p.m.

Well, let's get the bad news out of the way as soon as possible. Deal?

8:47 p.m.

yeah I don't want to bring any crap into the new year

8:47 p.m.

Exactly!

8:48 p.m.

wanna come over for new years eve?

8:50 p.m.

Woah. That's kind of a big deal, no?

8:50 p.m.

what part? the part about nye or the part about my house

8:52 p.m.

Both?

8:52 p.m.

it's fine, my parents really want to meet you
we can hang out here, talk, eat, watch the ball drop
only if you want to

8:53 p.m.

Let me see if my folks are okay with me going over.
And if they're okay with me being out until after midnight.

8:54 p.m.

yep
if not we can celebrate east coast time

8:54 p.m.

I cannot wait to see you, Quick.

8:54 p.m.

likewise
but more

Monday, December 30, 2024

Note to self:

We just got back from Florida and we had the best time! My parents were so amazing. I am seriously blessed to have such supportive parents. I can't wait to tell Quick all about my decision regarding next year. I mean, yes, I will miss him with every single cell in my body, but every time I think about what I'll be doing, I get so excited. I know it's the right decision, and I know my best friend will be thrilled for me.

He asked me to go over to his house for New Year's Eve tomorrow. It seems like a big deal to me. I'll be officially meeting his parents (because my run-in with her on the Fourth of July should not count), and it is so soon after his mom's return. And then what about the fact that it's New Year's Eve? Ummmm, does that mean we kiss at midnight? I can't even think about it without freaking out on the inside.

Anyway, I asked my mom if I could go, and the conversation quickly became something I was not entirely prepared for. She immediately asked me about the level of my relationship with Quick, and when I asked her what she meant, she point blank asked me if we were "intimate." I literally almost died. I gasped and choked and laughed and was horrified, all at the same time. Clearly she could see from my reaction that we were not, but she didn't miss a beat and hit me again with another question. Actually, two questions. This time, she asked if we were boyfriend-girlfriend and if we "engage in French kissing." Who even says that?

Once I settled down, I explained to her that we really are just friends. She said she believed me, but that she was surprised because we seem much closer than "friends." I told her that we are indeed closer than typical friends, that we are the best of friends and connected on a super deep level. She then asked what makes it so, and I told her that he and I shared something unique and very profound in common. I was planning on telling her, but I didn't need to. I could see it register on her face. Her eyes filled with tears and she squeezed my hand.

When she got up to walk away, she softly said with a smile, "Of course you can go. I trust you."

So, I guess I'm going. To Quick's house. To meet his parents. To tell him my good news. And the bad news. And hopefully he doesn't kick me out before midnight.

I kind of hope he does. I don't know what I'll do when the clock strikes twelve.

...Q

Quinn:

Assurances

N ot only did both of my parents drive me to Quick's house, but they both insisted on walking me to the door. They wanted to meet Mr. and Mrs. Williams before their daughter spent hours upon hours with a young man, and understandably so. As we were driving over, I had a daydream in my head where both of our moms and both of our dads also became the best of friends, and then we'd always spend all the holidays together. I caught myself having such absurd thoughts about my future with Quick that I made myself blush.

The four parents greeted one another with kindness, and after a few minutes, my mother and father felt comfortable enough to leave. Quick's parents gave mine the assurances they needed, which also settled my nerves a bit. Once my folks headed out, Mrs. Williams faced me directly. "Quinn, dear, please accept my apologies for our encounter over the summer. That was not my finest moment."

"Of course, Mrs. Williams. Thank you." I wasn't sure what else to say. I was remarkably impressed with the forward manner in which she accepted responsibility. I took it as a good sign, and it only made me more eager to hear Quick tell me all about her homecoming.

"Please, come to the kitchen. Declan and I have been preparing fun little finger foods all day. Do you have any allergies, Quinn?" I shook my head no, which was all I could muster. I was reeling from the fact that I heard her call Quick by his given name. It was a great name, and it sounded all the more beautiful coming from his mother's mouth.

After nibbling on bacon-wrapped dates and a charcuterie board that put the one I made for his birthday to absolute shame, his parents retreated to their den to watch a movie. Quick and I stayed in the living room, as promised to my parents, and I was so excited to have him all to myself again.

"Quick! Oh my gosh, tell me everything! I am so stinkin' happy for you, Quick. She seems so good!" I was trying to whisper, but my enthusiasm was hard to subdue.

"First things first," he winked, as he reached over for a hug that made up for the last eleven days without one. We untangled and he leaned back on the couch, his face suddenly wearing a distressed look. "Quinn, I thought we agreed to start with the not-so-good news first, no? I gotta get this off my chest." It hurt my heart to see him with such anguish. I didn't want him to suffer with it for even one minute more than he had to.

I squeezed his hand. "Of course, Quick. Please go ahead."

He proceeded to rattle off a stream of consciousness full of vague sentences that seemed to circle around a major central point that he was leaving unsaid. If he wasn't repeatedly apologizing and saying that he finally understood why I did the same thing last year, he was professing how much he wanted to help me and protect me. I was trying to follow what he was saying and attempting to make sense of it, when he mentioned wanting to take away all of my pain. It slowly started to click in my brain and was simultaneously confirmed when he confessed that he felt like a hypocrite. "Quick?" I disrupted him mid-sentence. "Quick, is this about SIDS?"

The terror on his face said it all. He had researched SIDS, just as I had researched trafficking, and the secrecy of it was tearing him apart. "I'm so sorry, Quinn. You've always been right to face the truths, no matter how difficult or how uncomfortable. And so I have to face you now. I completely understand if you never want to talk to me again. I cut you off for months for the same thing, which makes this even worse. And the worst part is—"

I placed my hands on his cheeks and lovingly smiled at him. "It's okay, Quick. I'm not upset."

"You're not? Seriously, you are such a better person than I am." Relief washed over him, and I had to resist the urge to crawl into his lap and wrap my arms around him as tightly as I could.

"No, I am not, Quick. Look at you. Look at how torn up you were. You are the most caring, most empathic, most thoughtful person I know. I am so lucky that I found you." He placed his forehead to mine and I gently closed my eyes, taking in the warmth that I felt being that close to him. A minute or so passed, and I realized there was more to the conversation at hand. "Besides, I guess I wasn't entirely honest with you either, now that I think about it. I suspected foul play with SIDS for a long time, and I ended up doing a shallow dig on it a while back. I learned enough to confirm my intuition, and then I closed the chapter on it. I know the truth and I'll have to make choices in the future based on that truth. And that's that."

Something I said stunned him silent. He stared at me, his mouth agape and his eyes as wide as golf balls. "You dug on SIDS? How could you stomach it?" He went on to tell me how he was in awe of me, my bravery, and my boldness. I told him that it actually helped me heal even more because I was able to put some things to rest, and that now it was his turn to put something to rest. I was not upset with him in the slightest and, if anything, I was grateful that he not only cared enough to research it, but that we got to a place in our friendship where he felt he did not need to run or hide from uncomfortable situations anymore.

"I looked up Ephesians 6:12, you know. When Seek & Speak's topic was fluoride and that username 'live on stage' mentioned it? It's super profound, Quick. I would never be upset with you. It's the bad guys at the top of the food chain that we should all be upset with. The rulers. The authorities. The powers that be. They're evil, and you are the opposite."

I squeezed his hand and glanced at the clock. Four more hours until midnight.

Quick:

Check

New Year's Eve 2024 was one for the books.

Quinn met my folks. My folks met her folks. Everyone was pleasant. Check.

I had two hard conversations left. And I planned to have both that very night.

Somehow, I got the words out and told Quinn about my dig on SIDS. Actually, that's not true. She pieced together all my random sputterings and deduced it was about SIDS. I merely confirmed that it was. Hard conversation, number one. Check.

I wasn't really surprised, but yet I was still so blown away by her reaction to my confession. She wasn't angry in the slightest. I thanked her profusely for being so understanding, accepting, and forgiving. What really blew my mind was the fact that she had already dug on SIDS on her own. I was amazed by her courage. Truly astounding.

Once that was behind us and I was done sighing with relief, I noticed that Quinn's face was now the one harboring worry lines. I remembered that she had something to share with me, too. Something I wouldn't like very much. I promised her at that moment that no matter what she had to tell me, I would be just as understanding and just as forgiving as she was with me.

"I wouldn't blame you if you weren't, Quick. It's pretty bad." A single tear raced down her left cheek.

I gently wiped her tear away with my thumb. "We can deal with whatever it is, Quinn. Get it out and we'll move on. And from now on, no more secrets. Deal?" He held out his arm for a handshake and accepted my hand as confirmation. "We got this, Quinn. Through thick and thin, remember?"

"Yes. The secrets torment us and make it worse than it needs to be, right? And I would rather you be upset with me and have to earn your forgiveness than keep lying to you." She glanced down at her fidgeting hands. She couldn't even look at me.

"Wait, you lied to me?" I asked. I tried to keep my voice steady, and I hoped I delivered my question without a sting. I promised to be understanding and I was determined to keep that promise.

She hesitated. "Well, yes. I have been purposely omitting information and keeping something from you. So that qualifies as lying to you. And you deserve better than that."

There was something in the way she said it, something about the way her damp eyelashes shimmered in the light as she blinked another tear of shame down her impeccable face, something that sent a chill of electricity through my arms as I reached for her perfect hands. The moment had arrived, and I didn't even realize it until the words came cascading out of my mouth. I didn't stutter. I didn't pause. I didn't need to search for words. Without any effort, I eloquently and confidently spoke my truth.

"That is where we disagree, Quinn. I could spend my whole life being the best version of myself, and I would still never deserve you. You are the most extraordinary person in every possible way and nothing you tell me could ever change the way I feel about you. I am absolutely crazy about you, Quinn. I've wanted to tell you for so long but I was afraid of what would happen to our friendship. But I can't deny it anymore. I am in love with you, Quinn."

Hard conversation, number two. Check.

Suddenly I realized I had another goal to check off my list.

I leaned towards her and cradled her face in my hands. I took it as a good sign that she didn't pull away from me, so I moved in closer and brought my lips near hers. We held them there, just a centimeter apart, and quietly shared our breath until I couldn't take it for a second longer. I planted my lips on hers and kissed her so tenderly, wanting her to feel how soft and pure my love for her was. I could have stayed in that moment forever.

Kiss the girl of my dreams. Check.

I reached my hands behind her head to gently pull her closer to me, my fingers entangled with the hair at the nape of her neck. The movement must have broken the spell, though, because she immediately pulled away after I did so.

Clearly bewildered, she stammered, "Are we taking this to a new level? Because if we are, I have to say my piece first. I'm not starting this, whatever this is, with a lie."

"Okay, Quinn. You're right. I'm ready. Say your piece." I tried to clear my mind from perseverating on the bliss I just experienced, but I was struggling. Bad. I was literally staring at her lips when she was talking. And even when she wasn't.

She spoke the next words so quickly that it took me a second to process what she said. "I accidentally slipped about your name, and I kinda mentioned that your family's been through a lot, but I don't know what she's figured out. I think maybe Mandy found out about your brother." She buried her entire face in her hands and started to cry. I stared at her in utter disbelief. I didn't know what I was expecting her to say, but it definitely wasn't that.

A minute ticked by. And then probably another. She was still crying and apologizing into her palms, and I was still sitting there like a statue trying to catch flies. Finally, I found my voice.

"I need a minute."

I slowly stood up from the couch, ambled to the bathroom, and closed the door behind me.

Get the wind knocked out of me. Check.

Quinn:

All Along

My eyes tracked his movement as he walked away, my vision blurred through tears. The sound of his slowly shuffling feet across the tile floor woefully crooned a hymn of defeat. His head hung low, directing his vacant eyes towards the ground and draping his shaggy hair over his face like a curtain that was sheltering him from further betrayal.

Too much happened too quickly for me to process. Quick overflowed my heart with his professed love, only for me to completely shatter his heart moments later. And the moments in between… Wow. I still felt the tingle on the back of my neck and a pulsating sensation throughout my suddenly lonely lips.

Initially, a wave of panic swept over me as I hypothesized what he was thinking, what he would do next, and how things with us would go. The wave, though, was swiftly replaced by profound insight, the enormity of which was life-altering. I was in love with Quick. While he was locked up in the bathroom, I was dumbfounded on the couch, overwhelmed by the realization and acceptance of something long overdue. I loved him. I loved his honesty and his selflessness, his brilliance and his open-mindedness, his authenticity and his moral compass. I loved the way he challenged me, the way he exposed me to a world of questions, the way he nurtured my soul. I loved the way he loved me.

I was not sure how much time had passed when Quick walked back into the family room. He casually strolled over to the couch and sat by my side, leaving less than an inch between us. Without uttering a single word, his mouth was suddenly on mine. It was even more passionate than the first one, and without a secret hanging over my head this time, I allowed myself to fully surrender to his touch. I relished every detail, knowing I would want to relive it over and over again. The plumpness of his bottom lip. The lingering taste of bacon. The faint smell of his shampoo. My fingers cradling his face. His hands on my waist.

I had never thought about it before, but this was a first for both of us. Neither one of us had any idea what we were doing, but it didn't matter. There was such an energy of emotion and mutual appreciation that it all just felt so right. Even when we bumped our front teeth on one another's, we broke the kiss for a good laugh. It was him and it was me, so it was perfect exactly as it was.

"I'm so sorry, Quick. I never m—"

"I know, Quinn. I know that you would never intentionally hurt me. Ever. We'll take the Mandy situation as it comes. Okay?" I nodded as he continued. "Besides, I would rather the whole world know than me lose someone I love over it. Geoffrey deserves to be known, anyway. His story deserves to be told. It's selfish of me to keep him to myself just so I don't have to face the truth in unexpected places. Does that make sense?" I nodded again, mesmerized by the beauty of his face, his heart, and his soul. "I meant what I said, Quinn. Nothing could change the way I feel about you." He squeezed my hands and gave me a soft peck on the lips. He placed his forehead on mine and we gazed into one another's eyes. I had never felt so seen. So understood. So loved.

I could feel a lump rising in my throat, but not because I was stifling a sob. That could not have been further from the truth, given that pure elation was pulsing through my veins. What was stuck in my throat were words that needed to be spoken. Heavy ones. Transformative ones.

"I love you, too," I whispered. A giant grin erupted across his entire face, so much so that I felt it on my own forehead before we parted to sit more comfortably on the couch. "When you were in the bathroom, all I could think about was how much I love you, and of all the reasons why."

"Same." He winked. That same wink he gave me by the waterfall when he told me he saw me for the first time. That same wink he gave me on his birthday during the whipped cream challenge. That same wink that he gave me on the Fourth of July. The one that made my knees weak and my heart skip. Every single time.

"I think I've loved you all along, Quick. Since the beginning. Since last October."

"Same. Why do you think I dubbed it our anniversary?" He could see the light bulb in my mind and he chuckled, clearly satisfied with the fact that he figured it out way before I did. He pulled me in for a cuddle as I awkwardly twisted my body to place my back against his chest. Just as I imagined it. We sat like that for quite some time, comfortably relaxing as he told me all about his mother's homecoming, her letter, and their instant reconnection. He felt like everything in his life was falling perfectly into place, and hearing the joy and the peace in his voice made my heart swell. He deserved it. All of it.

Quick:

Even If

Like I said, New Year's Eve 2024 was one for the books. After our first kiss, which was perfect, and then our second, which put the first one to shame, Quinn finally got to hear about my mom. Shy of letting her read the letter, I told Quinn every detail of the time Mom and I had spent together since her return from rehab. She was truly thrilled for me and mentioned how she could already sense how much lighter I was with that weight lifted. The conversation came to a natural close just as my stomach started growling, so we headed into the kitchen to eat more of the foods my mom and I had prepared.

At around ten thirty, once I felt satiated and had a belly full of salami, Swiss, and crackers, I told Quinn that I was still patiently waiting to hear about her vacation and whatever else she still needed to tell me. My words served as a reminder to her, and she literally anthropomorphized an exclamation point with her bouncing and clapping. She shoved her last bacon-wrapped date into her mouth, chewed it up as quickly as she could, and swigged a glass of water to wash it down. I smiled as I prepared myself for what I knew would be an energetic whirlwind of squealed words.

"Okay, I was looking into this new thing I read about called thermography. Did you know that different radiation techniques like mammograms aren't even diagnostic tools? So we just radiate people for funsies? Switzerland's even banned them! And we still use them here? What the heck! Anyway, I was reading about how cancer might be related to parasites and how easy it can be to detect issues early with noninvasive thermography and… "

I felt myself grinning, just looking at her. I didn't understand two-thirds of the words she was saying because apparently my brain couldn't process auditory information at her lightning speed, but I knew she'd clue me in at some point. It was enough for me to see her so excited, passionate, and filled with purpose. I could relate. It was a fresh feeling for me, too, feeling like I had found my purpose. Well, one of my purposes, at least. And I was looking right at it.

It was her.

"… so I'll probably end up going there!" I was so busy thinking about how happy she made me feel that I completely missed the whole bit about her plans for next year. But it didn't matter. Wherever she was, whatever she was doing, I'd be loving her through the whole thing.

"I'm happy for you, Quinn."

A look that was slightly laced with trepidation flashed across her exquisite face. "Really?" she questioned. "Even if I'm in Florida?"

Frick. Florida? That state was almost as far away as possible from home. I suddenly understood why she went there for Christmas. I felt like the wind got knocked out of me again, for the second time that night. This time, though, I recovered much more quickly. Our eyes locked and all four of them were simultaneously covered by a layer of shiny gratitude. Forehead to forehead, I kissed her on the tip of her charming little nose and whispered, "Yes, really. Even if."

01/01/25

3:09 a.m.

Quinn is browsing through the dresses on the second floor of a department store that is unfamiliar to me. I am keeping her company as she considers different styles, lengths, and colors. I watch her hold a dress up to her body, glance in the mirror, cock her head to one side and the other, and then return the dress to the rack. I smile to myself, knowing that she would look breathtaking in any of the gowns. Hell, she'd be captivating in soiled rags even.

I notice a young mother and her daughter make their way to the rack nearby. The little girl is perhaps four years old and is darling with her blonde curls that bounce as she hops from one pretty dress to another.

"Stay close," the mom utters. She is sliding one dress across the rack at a time, focusing fully on her task at hand. The little girl promises to do so as she frolics to the rack nearby, where she claims her best princess dress is waiting for her.

I am mesmerized by the child's aura of simple delight and innocent wonder. How liberating to have not a care in the world! Skipping about in her utopia of imagination, the girl makes her way to the next rack over. A couple of minutes pass and she continues on to another display.

I unexpectedly feel a peculiar sensation. My stomach, now suddenly nauseous, sinks towards my feet and all the hairs on my neck stand on edge. I look around, my eyes fully dilated, and as I scan our surroundings, I see the reason for the unforeseen warning signals that my body is communicating to me.

A man is standing near the dressing room. All the stalls are open; I deduce that he is not waiting for someone. He has his eyes fixed on the young angelic girl, who has now made it three racks away from her distracted mother. As I piece together what I believe his motive to be, I notice that his eyes dart far to the left. I follow his gaze to see a woman nod at him, just before she makes her way towards the mother.

"So many beautiful choices, am I right?" The woman strikes up a conversation with the child's mother. An exchange ensues. Laughter is shared. The distraction is locked in. The woman gives a thumbs up behind her back and

---

the man near the dressing room begins to walk towards the princess.

Hey Geoffrey,

I've had a lot of awful nightmares in my time, and too many flashbacks to count, but this one was different. I woke up in a sweat and had to run to the bathroom to throw up.

What happened to you happened in the blink of an eye. And it happens every single day to children all over the globe. I was foolish in my much younger years to think people who kidnapped children did so because they wanted a family of their own. The truth is that child trafficking is a rampant pandemic. The one that no one ever talks about. Why? Do people think that if they don't talk about something, if they don't admit its existence, that then it somehow doesn't happen? That if they don't acknowledge it, it absolves them of the guilt that comes with knowing, but doing nothing?

Well, I can no longer do that. Nightmare or not, that little girl's face will be burned into my retinas for eternity. In addition to the memories of you.

I was so inspired last night by Quinn's admission that she did a dig on SIDS. To face her demon like that, wow, she's tough as nails. I don't think it's a co-incidence that only hours after learning that, I had the nightmare that I did. For the first time, it wasn't about you. It snapped me out of the false reality that your devastating fate was unique, and it forced me to register the truth. It's happening to children and families across the globe. By the millions.

You know I don't believe in coincidences. This happened for a reason. This affected me as much as it did for a reason. I need to pull a page from Quinn's book, man up, and dive into the atrocious rabbit hole of human trafficking. And not a dive into the shallow end. I'm going deep.

I think I've always known that I would get here. Maybe now I feel strong enough to do this. Brave enough. This will torture my soul in new ways and I will miss you more than I ever have before, but I know this is what I need to do.

I love you so much, brother.

-Deck

Oh, and Quinn and I kissed last night. Real deal kinda love.

Hey Geoffrey,

As you know, I started the dig at about four this morning. It's now eight o'clock. In the evening. I only stopped because my empty stomach made me, and as I was stuffing leftovers in my mouth, I checked my texts to see that I inadvertently ghosted Quinn for the last nine hours.

I was worried she would think that it had something to do with last night, you know, and the entirely new level of our relationship, so I called her. I knew my voice would ease any worries she may or may not have had, and to be honest, I really wanted to hear hers.

I told her about the nightmare, my reality check, and the meaning I gave to the non-coincidence. I spared her the newly-learned details I unearthed today, especially the ones regarding the foster care system. There's no need for us both to have nightmares, let's just put it that way. The crap I've read and seen today is enough to leave someone in ruins. Actually, I don't even know what she discovered herself when she did the dig on trafficking.

Anyway, I'm starting to wonder, Geoffrey… Shouldn't fighting this atrocity be part of my life path? I can't remember the last time I felt this strongly about a subject matter, or this passionate about a dig. Which makes total sense, of course. But I can't get the nightmare out of my head, or the fact that I could see so clearly how the two wicked, depraved miscreants planned to snatch that little girl. Subconsciously, is my brain aware of villainous plots, and therefore ways to stop them? Is this a gift that I could hone in on, nurture, and use to help eradicate such evil?

I'm really starting to think that I should look into this.

Love you.

-Deck

Hey Geoffrey,

Check this out. Turns out there are several non-profit organizations that fight human trafficking, and I read that one of them has already rescued over 7500 and has arrested over 7000. I am so frickin' inspired by their website alone!

This is it, brother. This is the fight I'm signing up for.

Here's what I'm thinking. I start volunteering for one of the non-profits. Make some connections, learn more about the field, gain experience. In the meantime, I go to school and major in criminal justice or forensics. Something like that. A career in law enforcement, especially one with a specific focus like anti-trafficking, requires collegiate education and I can't even apply until I'm 21 anyway.

I'm pumped. I'm going to tell Quinn right now. Well, no, I'll tell Mom and Dad first.

Always with you in mind, Geoffrey.

-Deck

Sunday, January 5, 2025

Note to self:

Wow, big night for Quick! We just hung up the phone and I'm shocked at how much has unfolded for him in the last few days. He sounds so inspired and incredibly motivated to start this next leg of his journey. It's kind of perfect, actually. He'll still get to go to school here like he planned, so he can stay close to his folks and maximize his time with them. And he'll be working towards the most beautiful goal, one that will really honor his brother and help to heal his family even more.

We haven't really talked about our relationship since we've elevated it, and it doesn't really seem as though there is a need to. It's silly to need to confirm terms like "boyfriend" and "girlfriend" after we've already told each other that we love one another. We are both continuing on as though this is the natural, organic progression of our friendship, which it is.

Well, tonight we talked for over an hour, and naturally the conversation headed in the direction of "us" and what next year would bring. I will be in Florida getting certified in thermography and taking some business classes on the side, and he will be here studying some sort of criminology and volunteering to fight trafficking in whatever capacity he can. We got a little emotional on the phone, not to anyone's surprise. I mean, we can hardly go two days without missing each other's company. But he was very reassuring. He seems really positive, and as much as he will miss me, he knows everything will be okay. It's not that I am broken or scared either, but rather just aware that I'll be lonely for my best friend. But he is super excited for his path, and I am super excited for mine. And how awesome is it that we both support each other fully? So lucky!

It's neat how certain words never lose their meaning. If anything, it's the opposite with the favorite phrase we share. Each time it is said, it is with pure and relevant intention. It means more each time because whenever it is used, it's in the middle of an experience that directly provides evidence of how true it is. We really are "Quick and Quinn," two souls connected. And there's no question about the "through thick and thin" part. We've experienced so many highs and lows, and of such depths, always coming out the other side stronger than ever before. Our relationship is tried and true.

So, I don't really know where we go from here. It's not like we can put the words, or the kisses for that matter, back in the lockbox and throw away the key. Nor would either of us want to. I think we're going to make the very most of these next six or so months, and then I guess just let life happen. What else is there to do? He needs to chase his dreams, and I need to chase mine. And that's what we want for each other, too. There is no doubt in my mind that our friendship can withstand the distance and time. The other part, the one with the kissing and the proclamations of love, is so new and so fresh that I can't speak to that quite yet, but I have all the faith in the world in terms of the friendship part.

Oh, we also chatted about Seek & Speak. Quick hadn't checked in for a while and was impressed when I mentioned that after trying a new topic each week, instead of every other, the majority of the forum members voted to go back to bimonthly digs. They didn't feel that a week gave enough time to go beyond the surface level with everyone's research and the relevant tangents that followed. Anyway, he's really excited to get back into it, now that he's in a better place. He wasn't sure what the next topic would be, but I reminded him that there's an official sign-up for topics now. Username KasCQ should be posting first thing in the morning. I'm always excited to see what they come up with! I still can't believe we're up to almost 250 diggers!

With that, I'm off to sleep. Tomorrow is the first day of our last semester. Next up: Adulthood.

...Q

Monday, January 6, 2025

Note to self:

I woke up this morning with a feeling of complete dread, and I couldn't figure out why. I never have an issue with going to school; if anything, I prefer to go. Of course I cannot wait to see Quick. Or to see the new topic. So what was the dread stemming from?

As soon as I hopped in the shower and the water hit my face, it struck me.

Mandy. Ugh.

…Q

SEEK & SPEAK!

What's the Truth Anyway?
Dig to Decide!

Do you ever wonder about the unknowns? About truths? About lies?

Do you ever hear something and instinctively agree with it?
Disagree with it?

Do you ever defend the narrative? Question the narrative?

Do you like to share your opinions? Hear the opinions of others?

If so, then this is the place for you!

Below is our tenth topic. Let's have a conversation!

We only ask one thing of you:
Please be respectful of others' opinions.

Thank you, and welcome (back) to Seek & Speak!

TOPIC #10

'The Simpsons' Predictions

KasCQ:	Hey, y'all! Have you heard about these predictions? If not, **check this out** and let us know what you think!
justcallmeDoc:	Yeah, they totally nailed it with the Game of Thrones dragon. I still can't believe they ruined that show with the finale.
swim2win:	@KasCQ howwwww. how is this even possible, theres no way. theres like forty predictions?
Lexipants<3:	Dude. The Ebola episode is too much. Simpsons got it right, even down to the year. Hard to wrap the noggin around that one.
MereHuh:	Agreed, but the tiger attack one stands out the most to me. Those two Vegas guys had been doing the show forever, without incident. I know it's just a coincidence, but still… creepy.
mathπrate#ninja:	i heard they predicted a nobel peace prize winner but i guess thats not really hard to do if someone looks into who is working on upcoming breakthroughs or whatever
doubleTdoubleS:	I know people freaked out over the Lady Caca Superbowl prediction, but honestly, she could have planned the entire thing based off of the episode from five years before.
crdbrd&glooo:	@doubleTdoubleS Fair point.
short&sassy:	How are we not talking about the Curling Olympics one? Oh my gosh, such a great episode.
KTUU:	Fun topic, but honestly, there's not much here. The Simpsons have over 700 episodes so they're bound to get things right here and there. Plus, it's like @doubleTdoubleS pointed out. Some things could have come true because plans were based off previous episodes.
MakeItRayne:	I agree. And the show rarely gives a year, so the "predictions" are more open-ended.

Quinn:

Stung

While I indeed woke up with a yucky feeling due to the ticking time bomb that was Mandy, I found solace in Quick's promise that we could handle whatever came our way. By the time I arrived at school and locked up my bicycle, I was happy to be back on campus and truly shocked that it was my last "first day" there. I was all smiles, from the moment Quick greeted me with a smooch until lunchtime when we logged in to see that Seek & Speak's new topic was already a hit. How unfortunate that I went home later that afternoon only to be greeted at the door by my mother and her request to "have a discussion."

She proceeded to inform me that two of her colleagues at the elementary school, Ms. Krystal and Ms. Amya, congratulated her on my "big accomplishment." Apparently, both teachers had children who were high school students and, as it turns out, also Seek & Speak contributors. My mom reprimanded me for not informing her of my new "hobby," which caused her to be caught off-guard at school.

"And not only that, Quinn, but I highly disapprove of this Seek & Speak nonsense. Why on earth would you think that's a good idea?" she snapped at me. Her hands were waving all over the place like a flag in the wind, and I had a very strong feeling it was not a white flag of surrender. "You're basically going online and telling the entire world that you're, what? Some sort of conspiracy theorist? There's stuff on there about a "fake" moon landing? Really? Oh my goodness, what's next? You're going to tell me that you're a flat-earther? This is ridiculous. You know that once something is out there on the internet, it's there for life! You want this to be on your digital trail forever? I'm sorry, Quinn, but you need to take it down. Or take your name off it. Today." Her words went from frantic to firm in three seconds flat.

Because it was my second nature to do so, I inhaled deeply and filled my lungs before responding. My slow exhale calmed my heart and my voice before I even opened my mouth.

"Mom, this isn't the first time you've said something like this to me, and I can see how much it bothers you. But I really don't care if people think I'm a conspiracy theorist. I'm not. I'm a critical thinker. There's a difference. And I think everyone should be asking some sort of question about something. About anything. We can't just absorb whatever narratives are out there and swallow them whole. That's the nonsense, Mom."

"Quinn. There are posts on there about some pretty wild stuff. How can you say they're not conspiracy theories? By definition, that's what they are. And who knows when this will pop up in the future and slam doors in your face! You're about to start your life and future employers will—"

I nodded at her, hoping to send the message that her feelings were valid. "Mom," I tried to calm the energy in the room with my voice. "I don't mind the digital trail, Mom. It's okay. I would never want to work for someone who would make me feel like I had to be unauthentic in order to be accepted. Besides, I'm going to be my own boss, remember?" I added a bit of sweetness to the question.

"Honey, I don't even understand what you're saying." She was flustered, but at least she was calming down. I took that as a good sign.

I gave her a big hug, diffusing the situation and resetting the conversation. "Mom, it's super important to me that I live authentically. That what I do and what I say stems directly from what I believe. I am never going to renounce myself or my beliefs for anyone or anything. And since I will always believe that critical thinking and sharing ideas with others are great things to do, I am not going to shy away from Seek & Speak, nor am I going to hide it or abandon it. I appreciate your concern, Mom, but I'm really proud of it. I'd love to sit down with you and share it with you sometime if you'd like." I looked at her with hopeful eyes and searched hers for acceptance but came up empty-handed.

"No, thank you. You should have shared it from the beginning," she retorted as she turned on her heel and headed to the kitchen.

Her comment stung. Because she was right.

Quick:

Ice Broken

It was a Saturday afternoon in January when I looked up from the cucumber pile I was arranging to see my mom standing in front of me. Beaming. With a camera pointing right at my face.

"Surprise! Oh honey, you look so cute when you're working!" She squealed and pinched my cheek. My nearly-eighteen-year-old cheek. The small scene she created probably would have mortified any other teenager in my shoes, but not me. I was amused. Tickled. Delighted even. These were the words I started using when my mom's joyous presence and her old-school vocabulary made their way back into my life. I was so happy to have her around, and in a loving way nonetheless, so I could not care less what other people thought. The least of my concerns were the possible thoughts of the NPCs around me.

She claimed that she needed some things for dinner, but the mischievous smile on her face gave her away. "I was missing you, too, Mom," I said, letting her in on the fact that I knew she was full of hot air. I gave her a tight hug, transferring some produce goo from my apron to her shirt. Not that she cared.

That night, all three of us were in the kitchen preparing dinner. My dad was on burger duty, my mom was making scalloped potatoes, and I was whipping up a salad with the fresh ingredients that I picked out with my mom earlier.

"Hey, whatever happened with your garden, Deck?" my dad asked as he swiped a piece of celery and popped it into his mouth. I was about to remind him that it was winter, but my mom's hysteria filled the entire room.

"You had a garden? Where?" She immediately ran to the sliding glass door and took a full, frantic tour of the backyard. By the time she made her way back inside, my dad and I were doubled over in laughter. Her reaction was too much. I caught my breath and looked up at Dad, only to see that I got the knee-slapping thing from him, which made me crack up even more.

I finally settled down enough to tell my mom about the garden, albeit a pathetic one, that Quinn and I shared the year prior. The Porch Garden. I couldn't help the pride from oozing through my words when thinking of it with such fondness. I loved spending that quality time with Quinn, hanging out in the shade and eating not-yet-ready radishes and pale green onions, just because we could. That was the best. I smiled just thinking about it, and my heart tugged a bit. I wanted to call her real quick to tell her I loved her and hear her voice, but my mom was heavily invested in the conversation at hand.

"So what do you think?" My mom nudged me with her arm. "Good idea?"

After realizing that I must have tuned out for a second, I apologized and asked her to repeat her idea. She was hoping Quinn and I would consider having a garden in our backyard this year, in addition to the Porch Garden. She mentioned how we could grow different things: potted edibles at Quinn's place and other vegetables at our place. She made sure to repeat herself plenty about how she wasn't trying to take anything away from Quinn and that she wasn't trying to control what we do; she just really wanted to share in the experience. It was sweet.

"I will absolutely talk to Quinn, Mom. That sounds like a great idea. Honestly, we hadn't even talked about doing a garden again, but I know she'll be all over it."

"Hooray! Okay, well, talk to her soon. We only have about a month to prepare and then we'll have to start planting! It's almost the season," she said as she skipped back over towards the potatoes.

"Seriously? It's only January, Mom. Last year we didn't even start until the summer." As soon as I said it, I understood.

"Yeah, and how'd that work out for you? Super great harvests?" My mom's comment was dripping with sarcasm.

Fair point.

After dinner, I headed upstairs to FaceTime with Quinn. It was crazy how I never got tired of seeing her face. If anything, I didn't get to see it enough. I watched her drink some herbal tea concoction she made, I listened as she told me about the latest book she was reading on ascension, and I told her I was honored when she walked our video chat outside so I could see her latest rock design in Troy's Zen garden. She had created two intertwined hearts as an apology to her mom for the argument over Seek & Speak. The fact that Quinn was so full of goodness, and hands down the most fascinating person I could ever hope to meet, was a thought that was ever-present in my mind. I was in awe of her, and the feeling of fortune to be loved by her was indescribable.

As always, she was interested to know every detail about my day. At first it was hard to tell what part she appreciated the most—my mom's surprise visit at work or the fact that my folks and I all cooked dinner together. Or my dad and I cracking up over my mom running to the backyard to find an invisible garden. Quinn was enraptured with each new anecdote I shared. Once I told her about my mom's idea for a second garden, though, it was clear that that was her favorite part of my day.

"Oh my gosh, Quick, that would be amazing! I would love to have a real garden in your backyard and have your mom share in it with us! What an awesome bonding experience that would be, Quick. Plus, it sounds like she knows more than we do, not that that's hard to do because we don't really know much about planting, right? But if she is talking about prepping a garden and all that? I wouldn't even know where to begin! Oh my gosh, this is going to be so fun! Plus, it'll be better at your place anyway since I'll be leaving at the end of summer—" And with that, her gleeful monologue ended abruptly and was met with absolute silence on both ends of the conversation.

We sat there staring at each other through our tiny screens. It was a somber moment, but it was also filled with pride and excitement. Such a conflicting feeling, to want someone to go but desperately want her to stay. I knew she was thinking the same thing, but I was intent on her sensing my support for her decision to go to Florida. The last thing I wanted was for her to stay because of some sort of unnecessary obligation or feeling of guilt. So I gave her the most dazzling smile I could muster and said, "Yep, you're right. It makes sense to have the garden here. Sounds good. I'll tell my mom.

She's probably going to wake up the neighborhood with all her hooting and hollering." Ice broken. Quinn laughed and I could see the appreciation in her eyes. "I love you, Quinn. You are going to kick butt in Florida, and the garden and I will be right here when you get back. All good."

"Aw, Quick. I love you, too, but—"

"But what?" I was a little nervous she was going to end this thing, whatever we were, before it even started.

"But you don't have to promise that you'll be here waiting for me when I get back. That's a lot to ask. You're going to be living your life, too, as you should. Right?" Her comment sounded as though she was already feeling the guilt that I was hoping she wouldn't.

"Right. Listen. I gotta go." I blew her a kiss and hung up. Not my kindest moment, but it stemmed from the sudden urge to see her. I ran downstairs, shouted to my folks that I'd be back in an hour, and I drove straight to Quinn's house. I texted her when I got there and I assumed she ran downstairs to greet me because she was out of breath. She sprinted towards me as I was walking up the driveway and jumped into my arms, wrapping her legs around my waist and burying her head in my neck.

"I'm sorry I hung up like that. I just couldn't get here fast enough." I whispered. "I had to see you."

"I'm so glad you did, Quick. I love you so much. And I'm clueless about what next year will bring. I'm hoping I won't lose you, that our friendship can withstand this. I know it can, but this new stuff with us, I don't know. But we have to do this. Right? I want so much to do my thing in Florida and I am thrilled out of my mind for you and your journey, and as much as I am going to miss you, we still have to do this, right?" Her eyes searched mine, and for once, mine were the peaceful ones.

"Yes, Quinn. We have to do this. You are the one who taught me to slow down, to breathe, to have faith. It's going to be a huge change for both of us and on so many levels, but you know better than anyone that change is something we should welcome. It's when we grow, right?" I wiped her tears with my thumb and kissed the tip of her nose.

"Yeah, I know. You're right. I am excited, Quick, and I know I'll embrace the change when it comes. I just, I can't imagine doing life without you. I literally can't."

I placed my forehead to hers, a gesture that had come to symbolize our affection for one another. "I can't either, Quinn. I feel sick when I think about it. But we'll take it as it comes, right? One day at a time. One step at a time. We'll figure it out."

We let the quiet moment soothe us a bit, and then she softly asked, "Do you think absence makes the heart grow fonder? Or out of sight, out of mind?" She ran her fingers through my hair before placing her head on my chest and pulling me in for a hug.

"You will never be out of mind, Quinn. Never. You are my very best friend. And I'll support you no matter what you decide to do in life. Even if you run off to Spain and fall in love with some dude named Pepe, I'll support you. All I want is for you to be happy. And right now, you being happy means you chasing your dreams. As you should. I'm proud of you." I meant every single word I said, and she knew it.

She held my cheeks as she kissed me. "I'm proud of you, too. And I want you to be happy, too. But, for the record, I would never run off to Spain. France, maybe…"

Ice broken.

ooo

home

Quinn / 9:20 p.m.

Oh, good. Thanks for the surprise visit!

9:22 p.m.

'twas the highlight of my day, milady

9:22 p.m.

Likewise, good sir.

9:23 p.m.

I have some crazy physics homework to do tomorrow
you?

9:23 p.m.

I just have a bit for Pape's class.

9:23 p.m.

sucks I didn't get her class
quite the compliment that you said she's as cool as mr. e

9:24 p.m.

Yeah, she's pretty great.
I swear, I really think the teacher makes or breaks the class.

9:24 p.m.

yep
I thought I was going to love government class but my teacher sucks

9:25 p.m.

Ugh.
Oh, so hey, did you see who's signed up to post for Seek & Speak on
Monday?

9:25 p.m.

no who is it

9:26 p.m.

Starseed.
I can't wait to see what the topic is.

9:27 p.m.

should be interesting
starseed is pretty based

9:28 p.m.

Right?!

9:28 p.m.

k I'm gonna hang with my dad for a bit
talk tomorrow

9:28 p.m.

Sounds good.

9:29 p.m.

love you

9:29 p.m.

I love you.

SEEK & SPEAK!

What's the Truth Anyway?
Dig to Decide!

Do you ever wonder about the unknowns? About truths? About lies?

Do you ever hear something and instinctively agree with it?
Disagree with it?

Do you ever defend the narrative? Question the narrative?

Do you like to share your opinions? Hear the opinions of others?

If so, then this is the place for you!

Below is our eleventh topic. Let's have a conversation!

We only ask one thing of you:
Please be respectful of others' opinions.

Thank you, and welcome (back) to Seek & Speak!

TOPIC #11

Wireless Headphones

StArSeEd: Just a heads up here… We might not like this topic or appreciate what we find. The fluoride thing did a number on me and I ended up falling into a rabbit hole that led me to wireless headphones. Not good.

anime4life: nope, not giving up my pods, dont even wanna know

legomylegos: ha ha i feel you but i gotta look. dude what if they're frying our brains

Utoober: Surely, they're not frying our brains. I think we'd be able to tell if that were the case. However, with prolonged use over time? There definitely has to be some side effects to that. I'm in. I'll post what I find.

chempion: we already know that companies put profits above humanity. the question isn't if wireless headphones are bad for us. the question is, just how bad?

rureddy4dis: At first thought, I guessed this was about volume control and hearing damage. But no, it's much worse than that. **Look.**

PriceShake4As: @rureddy4dis Yes, that's alarming. I see **here**, however, that the levels are low enough that they aren't harmful. I'll keep searching other sites.

247gamer: you guys ever hear about how all the silicon valley dudes don't let their kids use the screens that they make millions off of? this kinda reminds me of that. like, **look** at all these peeps who make money off of them but know they're bad so they don't use them

Red-n-Real: i've been digging on this for almost an hour and for every plus i find a minus. this is so frustrating to me. it shouldn't be this hard to find the truths on things that directly affect us. it's maddening.

Note to self:

I got home from Quick's house and walked by my dad's office to inadvertently overhear my parents whisper-arguing. I've learned over the years not to stop and listen because I never felt good after doing so. I usually felt guilty for hearing something that they clearly were trying to protect me from, and besides, they deserve to have their privacy. All I heard today was my dad saying that I was going to be eighteen soon and that they needed to trust in how they've raised me. It warmed my heart to hear him say that I'm "a good kid" and that my mom should have confidence in their parenting and my character. Well said, Dad!

I am assuming Mom is still irked with me about Seek & Speak. We never really went back to the conversation about my digital choices and the subsequent effects that she seems to be really worried about. I know she's trying to let it go, and I appreciated the big hug at the Zen garden when I apologized for hurting her, but it's clear that there's still a bit of a strain there. I think I need to give it some time, though. This is one of those situations that don't need a rehashing. What's needed is an acceptance of one another's choices and feelings. For us to agree to disagree.

(Side note: Seek & Speak is still going strong! The posts have comments coming in days after the fact and it's so cool to see how people respond to one another's points. It's quite beautiful to see respectful discourse unfold such that everyone leaves the forum more informed on both sides. I feel like that's the definition of enlightenment!)

As for Quick, I am so crazy about him. It is insane how much closer we became and how quickly! Ever since that night, it's like the dam broke. I don't know how to explain it. Like we were holding back tons and tons of emotion, and once the wall came down, the feelings flooded our relationship. I couldn't be happier about it, but I also have to admit that the looming change is ubiquitous. So I'm taking it one day at a time, enjoying all the moments that I can. For right now and for the months to come, we just want to spend as much time together as possible. We talk about it off and on, I think because we both need to process it before it arrives. Quick says that it will be good for us to be apart, and commented on how much closer we became after our little time-out last year. Which is true, so there is that.

I was thinking about it earlier today, how Quick is all I've ever really known in terms of a mature friendship. And definitely all I've ever known in terms of feelings beyond friendship. And the same goes for him. He is all I know, and I am all that he knows. And we're much too young to commit to anything beyond today. It would probably be good for us to spend time apart, get to know ourselves as individuals, and maybe even date other people. I don't know. I'm pretty conflicted.

I've kind of lost my way a little bit. I think I need to meditate more. The happier and more fulfilled I've become over the last year, the more I've slacked off. But I'm really starting to feel the effect of that, almost like a little void in my gut. I'm having a harder time finding that peace, a harder time surrendering. And I know for a fact it's because I have been too relaxed and inconsistent with my practice. I remember for a while really feeling that serenity in surrender—it was almost like my mantra for a while there—where I focused on being true to myself and trusting that the universe would have my back. That acceptance and that relinquishing of control brought such peace. It was a great feeling, and now more than ever, I need to work on getting that back.

Honestly, unpacking all that just now made me feel so much better.

So back to tonight... Quick's parents invited me over for dinner, which was such a nice gesture. His mom seems to be doing really well, and their family has a new light in their eyes that I think comes from true healing. I'm thrilled for all of them. It's an honor to see it, and I can't even begin to describe the way my heart swells when she calls Quick by his real name and then I get to see his eyes sparkle.

Dinner was delicious and the conversation was wonderful, but the best part was the surprise his mom had for us after the coconut cream pie. She got us the coolest grow bag garden! It's six feet by four feet, and has a grid of two rows of three garden boxes. The material is well-draining, which Mrs. Williams said is a major key to successful farming. The other major key, she informed us, is high-quality, organic dirt, so we made plans to go to the nursery on Sunday since Quick works tomorrow. I'm super excited to start this project and see how much more successful we can be this year with better materials, especially since we'll be planting seedlings in late February or early March after the last frost instead of right in the middle of the summer's heat. Ha ha!

I know my life's not perfect, and there will always be a hole in my heart for Troy, but I'm truly happy. I have a lot to be grateful for.

...Q

Quinn:

A Buzzing Visitor

Ever since I was a young child, I loved nature. I loved the smells and the sounds, the beauty and the wonder of it all. As I grew older, I found further passions for grounding with the earth, studying the magical effects of herbs, and appreciating the uniqueness of each and every living thing on the planet. Hence, it was shocking to me to realize that I was nearly an adult before I set foot in a nursery.

In an instant, it took my breath away. The smell of dirt intermingling with that of flowers. The endless spectrum of green foliage, of all shades, heights, and shapes. The cacophony of birdsong throughout. There was even a pond full of koi fish and turtles that stole my heart. I could have sat there all day, watching the majestic animals go about their simple lives, but organic dirt was calling for us.

Quick, his mom, and I headed to the information desk to ask for suggestions regarding the right type of soil and the estimated amount we would need for our garden, as well as for additional tips for amateurs like us. Equipped with answers and eager to get started, we loaded the flatbed cart and headed for the checkout. Since we were just waiting there in line, I told Quick I'd be right back. I wanted to squeeze in one more minute at the pond, even though I knew I'd feel a pull to come back to the nursery soon enough.

I sauntered over towards the fish and the turtles, a wide grin across my face. I sat on a boulder near the edge of the pond to get a good view and to relax for my mindful minute. I caught a glimpse of a baby turtle floating about in the water, its parent nearby and waiting patiently for the little one to climb onto its back. It was the sweetest sight to behold, and I internally celebrated when the young creature overcame the struggle and finally accomplished its mission. It was such a special moment that I wanted to capture it, so I retrieved my phone from my pocket and snapped a photograph. Right as I was about to stand up and make my way back to Quick and his mom, I noticed a swift and sudden movement out of the corner of my right eye. I had a buzzing visitor. A brown one this time. And all I could think to myself was, "Everything is going so well right now. Dang it. Now what?"

I traipsed over to Quick with a sinking feeling in my stomach. The change that was coming was going to be a rough one. I could just tell.

Hey Geoffrey,

Sometimes out of nowhere, it kind of strikes me how much my life has changed in the last couple of years. I was sitting at the dinner table tonight, just kind of observing the scene, I guess. I don't know how else to explain it. Like I'm there but watching from the bleachers? Anyway, there's Mom and Dad, having a normal conversation and Mom's even laughing. Talk about things I never thought I'd see. So our family is kinda normal now, well as much as we could be, and I'm happy. I'm happy at home. I'm happy when I'm at school. I'm happy when I think about my future. I'm happy when I'm with Quinn. And I'm finally in a place where I can feel joy and admit it without feeling guilty. I know you'd be good with that, so thank you.

Lunch at school has gotten quiet. Quinn has gone back to meditating on the lawn. She still meditates at home and has all her crystals and herbs and books and all that, but we've been spending our lunchtimes talking for so long now, I can't remember the last time she meditated on the quad. She told me that she needs to focus on it a bit more right now because of all the upcoming changes. It's cool that she can sense when she's feeling anxious and then just address it without letting it spiral out of control.

I'm kinda liking the quiet lunch times, to be honest. First of all, she looks so damn beautiful. She closes her eyes and literally escapes to who knows where, and as creepy as it sounds, I could stare at her peaceful and perfect face the entire time. But I don't. I've been looking up volunteer opportunities for the non-profits, reaching out via email, and reading about different majors and classes offered at the colleges around here. Don't get me wrong, I look up from the computer pretty often to glance at her face, but for the most part, I'm researching.

It's such an awesome feeling to be that comfortable with someone. To be able to just sit, be quiet, and enjoy the company. I know I'd be that way with you, too. I wish I could be. Sometimes I am in my mind, and that's better than nothing.

Love you,

Deck

SEEK & SPEAK!

What's the Truth Anyway?
Dig to Decide!

Do you ever wonder about the unknowns? About truths? About lies?

Do you ever hear something and instinctively agree with it?
Disagree with it?

Do you ever defend the narrative? Question the narrative?

Do you like to share your opinions? Hear the opinions of others?

If so, then this is the place for you!

Below is our twelfth topic. Let's have a conversation!

We only ask one thing of you:
Please be respectful of others' opinions.

Thank you, and welcome (back) to Seek & Speak!

TOPIC #12

Fluid Definitions

wannaDB8?:   I heard that online dictionaries have changed definitions of words, especially these last couple years, but I've never looked into it. I thought this would be as good a time as any and that you guys could join in on the fun if you wanted to, ha!

meh: ummm can we skip ahead to a much more pressing issue... this whole seek & speak thing is about finding the truth, right? it literally says "whats the truth anyway" under the title. so let's find the truth out. don't you think we should, QUICK?

wannaDB8?:   @meh I'm not sure what you're referring to.

meh: i'm referring to the hypocrisy of this whole sham. doesn't anyone want to know who quick is? what kind of name is quick anyway? it's not a name. so who is he? care to explain, DECLAN? who the hell are you anyway?

Hey Geoffrey,

Quinn's been mentioning it off and on since we went to the nursery, that she's got a bad feeling about something to come. Well, it's here.

I guess we knew this was coming in one way or another, and now it seems so obvious what Mandy would do. Another black swan event. She loves to go public, and she is clearly one to hit below the belt, so yeah, we should have figured she'd use S&S to release the kraken.

She signed up as Meh (classic) and went on S&S to call out the hypocrisy (yet again). Our byline alludes to wanting to discover the truth, and yet here I am with a silly nickname and no one is asking me who I am. It's funny. I'm not at all upset about being called out. I knew the second I read her post that I would come clean. Why wouldn't I? My 18-year-old self can handle things that my 12-year-old self couldn't. I am a little upset, though, that she made the forum feel uncomfortable and awkward. What a tool.

So I went back to the site later on to respond and I was shocked to see what I saw. A bunch of S&Sers had my back. Some asked her point blank what her problem was. Some said that my personal life wasn't the purpose of the forum. Stuff like that. It kinda made me feel good to read it all, like somehow we've all become this band of buddies connected by this bizarre thread. Weird, though, because I really don't know who most of them are. The level of reciprocated respect is there, though. It's pretty awesome. Anyway, my favorite response to Mandy's crap? Someone told her that it's a good thing her username's anonymous because she should be ashamed of herself. I'd never stoop that low to rat her out. I'm sure it'll come out somehow, someday. I don't really care.

I'm going to post a response. I'm not sure exactly what it will say, but I think it's time. I think I'll feel lighter, and like I told Quinn, it's what you deserve. Not to be tucked away as a secret, which I see now was for selfish reasons, but honored and remembered.

I love you, bud.

-Deck

SEEK & SPEAK!

What's the Truth Anyway?
Dig to Decide!

Do you ever wonder about the unknowns?About truths? About lies?

Do you ever hear something and instinctively agree with it?
Disagree with it?

Do you ever defend the narrative? Question the narrative?

Do you like to share your opinions? Hear the opinions of others?

If so, then this is the place for you!

- -

@meh I can appreciate your curiosity and your desire to know the truth. After all, that's why we all log on as often as we do. While I do not agree that this forum is the place to have this conversation, I will answer your question in an effort to avoid further drama through whatever rumor mill that may have sprung to life. With that being said, I also want to respect our Seek & Speak space here, so after this post, I will not use this forum to continue this conversation any further.

My given name is Declan Williams. After my younger brother, Geoffrey, was kidnapped from an amusement park over spring break of my sixth-grade year, I struggled in every way imaginable. My parents thought it was best that I start fresh in a new town and with new people, so that's when we moved here. I took the opportunity to choose a new name, Maverick, because hearing the name my brother called me was too painful. I compartmentalized my pain and sorrow so that school could be an escape, not that it ever really was.

I stopped going by the name Declan when I was a kid. Maverick never really took, and my nickname, Quick, came about in junior high. Here we are six years later. Now that I'm almost 18 and better equipped to deal with the loss of my brother, please, feel free to call me Declan.

○○○

hi gorgeous

Quinn / 8:59 p.m.

Well, hello, handsome.
How are you? Feeling okay about your post?

9:02 p.m.

yeah it is what it is
actually feel better now that it's out there

9:02 p.m.

That's great, Quick!
Well, have you been on since? Have you seen the responses?

9:03 p.m.

no
should I

9:03 p.m.

It's up to you, but let's just say...
Mandy must really feel like an ass.

9:03 p.m.

language!
lol

9:04 p.m.

I'm just so glad you got to tell your story on your own terms.

9:04 p.m.

yeah
clearly she didn't dig too hard

9:04 p.m.

Right? I was terrified she would find out about Geoffrey and do
something awful.

9:05 p.m.

yeah it's a good thing her venom is lazy and short-sighted
karma for the win

9:05 p.m.

Well, everyone on S&S has your back, that's for sure.

9:05 p.m.

yeah it's pretty cool
like we have our own little anonymous community

9:06 p.m.

Exactly!
Actually, Quick, you may need to go on there, now that I think about it.
I think you'll enjoy reading their supportive comments.
And there is a question on there that you'll need to respond to...

9:09 p.m.

oh yeah like what

9:10 p.m.

Well, some responses are directed at her.
Some are supportive of you. Everyone really respects you and the whole S&S mission.
But some comments are really focused on the tragedy.

9:12 p.m.

like they want details about geoffrey? that's a solid no

9:12 p.m.

No, no, not like that.
They want to do a dig on kidnapping.
But I thought it was very sweet that they are holding off until you tell them if you'd be okay with it or not.

9:13 p.m.

oh wow ok
well, once you know, you can't unknow
it's up to them if they want to dig on it

9:13 p.m.

Right.

9:13 p.m.

I'll get on there and tell them that I'm okay with it of course
but they really should know that there's no climbing out of that hole

9:14 p.m.

I understand.

9:14 p.m.

alright I will go log on now
love you

9:15 p.m.

I love you, too.
I'm so glad you're feeling relieved now that your story has been shared.

9:16 p.m.

yeah same
good night
with a kiss

9:16 p.m.

Good night. Kiss!

Quick:

Only One Way

When I turned seventeen, I begrudgingly celebrated with paper plates, cheese and meat, foil hats, and whipped cream. My parents didn't even acknowledge my birthday, and I was still feeling like I didn't deserve one. Only Quinn believed I did.

Fast forward one year. Proof that struggles are temporary. Proof that huge changes can happen over a short span of time. Proof that people should always live with hope.

I picked up on the not-so-stealthy planning of Quinn and my mom that started a week or two beforehand. Anyone would have. It was almost as if their bodies physically could not contain the excitement of the surprise. The giggling. The secret texting. The ridiculous acting. But I pretended to be oblivious. I didn't want to steal their joy, and watching the two of them plot together was the best birthday gift anyway.

My eighteenth birthday was on a Saturday that year, and the way it unfolded turned out to be the only way I would have wanted it. The two schemers nailed it and planned a truly perfect night in the downtown area. Mom, Dad, Quinn, and I spent the evening devouring food by restaurant-hopping for all my favorites. First we hit up PaPa's for their bacon-wrapped dates and ended up ordering two rounds because they were that good. My mom was already full by the time we got to Grammy's Cantina for the verde oxtail enchiladas, my favorite food of all time, and an hour later we all felt like we were going to pop when we finally walked into Zippy's and ordered cherry chocolate chip concretes for dessert. Delectable.

I was so glad we were downtown because I didn't want the night to end. It was the perfect place to walk off the pain that came with overindulging, given the window-shopping and the people-watching. What made it even better was my dad telling awful jokes and my mom sharing stories of my early childhood. And ending the night with the spontaneous decision to try outdoor ice skating? That was the best. Who knew that my parents used to ice skate when they were dating back in the day? To watch my parents skillfully glide across the ice hand-in-hand like that, and to share such special moments with the girl I loved, was like a dream come true.

There was only one way it could have been any better. But I knew he was with us in spirit.

Hey Geoffrey,

Well, it's official. I'm officially an adult. Eighteen. What the heck? It's hard to wrap my head around.

We've come a long way, huh? I went from keeping you a secret, pushing people away, and self-loathing all those years to actually being happy. I miss you every second and I constantly think of how you would make every situation better, but at least I'm dealing with losing you better than I ever did before. Mom's doing so well, our family is finally starting to heal together, and I am crazy in love with Quinn. The only thing missing is you, but Geoffrey, I swear to you that I am going to spend my life honoring you and other kids like you.

If that much can change between the ages of seventeen and eighteen, imagine what next year will bring. I'll be knee-deep in law enforcement classes and volunteering with anti-trafficking organizations. I know it, deep in my gut: I am supposed to dedicate my life to this purpose. Not that I could ever right the wrong that happened the day we lost you, but to maybe save other families from the same pain? Yes. I will spend my life trying to do that. Over and over again, yes.

So, hey, did you see Mom and Dad ice skating like frickin' pros tonight? It's cool to see them together. It's almost as though they are falling in love all over again. Talk about a relationship of solid fortitude and resilience. They've literally been through hell and back, as individuals and as a couple and as parents, but they never gave up. At least not fully. I'm proud of them.

I wonder if Quinn and I will end up together. I mean, right now of course I would say that I want to, but to know that she's taking off for Florida kinda puts a damper on things. But I think the time and space apart will be good for us. As individuals and as a couple. We shall see. We're young, I get that. But it feels real. Who's to say you can't meet your person when you're sixteen?

Love you, brother. And I'll never ever forget how hard you laughed when I dropped my cherry chocolate chip onto the ground within two seconds of getting it. I can still hear your laugh. The best.

Miss you.

-Deck

Sunday, February 9, 2025

Note to self:

I had such a remarkable and relaxing time with Quick and his parents last night. It was one thing to celebrate his birthday, to honor him by planning such a special evening, to see him so peacefully and purely happy, but the best part was sensing that he no longer feels he is unworthy. Being a witness to his healing journey and seeing how far he has come has been one of the greatest joys in my life, that's for sure.

His parents are so fun to be around! They are incredibly easygoing. They don't push or pressure, ask or judge, lecture or placate. His dad embraces being a total goober with bad puns and jokes, and his mom is the humble observer type. Quick definitely gets his curious nature from her. What an honor it was to watch their family interact in such loving and beautiful ways. It warmed my soul, but simultaneously made me miss my mom. We've been a little "off" ever since the Seek & Speak argument, so I decided last night to put some more effort into making amends today.

First thing this morning, I greeted her with a hug and cheerfully asked her if we could have lunch together. She was a little surprised but of course agreed. We made quesadillas and sat on the front porch, making small talk as we sat in our rocking chairs. There was a little tension in the air, clearly stemming from the topic that neither one of us was addressing, but it was still nice to spend some time with her.

I'm not quite sure how to resolve our differences in opinion, other than with time, a hope for mutual understanding, and the serenity in the surrender. I have to give her the space and time she needs. I think she's super worried or anxious about the unknowns of my future, or maybe what her life will be like as an empty-nester, but since there's not much she can do about those, she is perseverating on this online drama. Maybe she's searching for an aspect that she can control. Perhaps that's what it is, that she feels like this part of her life—the motherhood part—is spiraling out of her control. Yeah, I'd imagine that would be pretty hard. My poor mom. I need to have more compassion for how hard all of this probably is on her.

...Q

OOO

Quinn / 6:17 a.m.

Good morning! Happy Garden Planting Day!

Quick / 8:19 a.m.

oh it has a name I see
you've been up since 6?

8:22 a.m.

I'm excited. Can you tell?

8:23 a.m.

always

8:23 a.m.

Okay, I already chatted with your mom and you guys are picking me
up at 9:00.
We're heading to the nursery to pick out our edible plants!

8:23 a.m.

k then what
when do I get to eat

8:24 a.m.

We'll eat when we get back to your place, before the planting fun
begins...

8:24 a.m.

ok sounds good

8:24 a.m.

Up and at 'em! I'll see you in a half hour!

8:25 a.m.

I'm up
ha ha my mom is knocking on my door right now telling me the exact
same thing

8:25 a.m.

Hooray!
Garden Planting Day is going to be so much fun.
We'll have to take pictures to see how much the babies all grow this
season!

good idea
and kisses between each planting

Ummm, I'll think about it.

8:26 a.m.

I read somewhere that kissing near plants makes them grow stronger

8:27 a.m.

You're so full of crap.

8:27 a.m.

I'm serious it's a thing

8:28 a.m.

No, it's not.
But it actually makes sense... Kisses are high vibe for sure, right?

8:28 a.m.

lol yeah
ok see you soon

03/19/2025

9:47 p.m.

The Jones Residence

Mandy:	Hey, Mom, do you have a minute?
Mrs. Jones:	Of course, sweetheart. What's wrong?
Mandy:	Nothing, I'm just a little down I guess.
Mrs. Jones:	About what, dear? Is everything alright with your classes? And friends?
Mandy:	Yeah, it's nothing like that. I just can't stop thinking about the children who are kidnapped every year for trafficking. It's so awful.
Mrs. Jones:	Oh, honey, why on earth are you worried about that? Did something happen?
Mandy:	No, it's this thing at school and they were talking about how millions and millions of children are trafficked. It's so scary and upsetting.
Mrs. Jones:	Yes, sweetie, it is very sad. But that doesn't need to be your concern right now. It's late, you should get some sleep before school tomorrow.
Mandy:	Yeah, maybe you're right. Oh, hey, Mom?
Mrs. Jones:	Yes, honey?
Mandy:	Did I get all my childhood vaccinations? Because I heard at school bad some stuff about the HPV vaccine.
Mrs. Jones:	Mandy, where is this coming from?
Mandy:	Nowhere. It's nothing. Forget I said anything. I'm fine.
Mrs. Jones:	No. I want to know how this type of thing is coming up at school. Right now, young lady.
Mandy:	Okay, fine. Here. I'll just show you.

Quinn:

The Calm Before the Storm

I often felt the urge to pinch myself, just to make sure that the final semester of my senior year in high school really was as perfectly joyous and joyously perfect as it seemed. We began January with a new level of closeness, and we carried that elation through to February and March. From his birthday celebration and the establishment of our garden to dinners with his parents and our own date nights, I really was happier than I had ever been before. Our mission with Seek & Speak was accomplished since the forum had truly taken on a life of its own, and our academics were a cinch, allowing us to cram in as much quality time as we could. We loved having the time to do all the things we enjoyed. If we weren't video logging the growth of our garden, Quick was having me take the car out for spins. We watched movies, played board games, went for long walks, and had deep conversations while sitting on the swings at the neighborhood park.

Although we could have, we didn't spend every possible waking moment together. I was working on expanding my knowledge of herbal teas and my practice of energy healing, while Quick and his dad were tackling what had come to be known as, "The Learning List." I was still visiting the bookstore with my dad and learning to bake with my mom, while Quick was working at the supermarket and saving up for his own vehicle. No matter what the day held, every single night ended with text messages of love and gratitude, and with each passing day, we felt less anxious about the coming year. We were actively living in present moments and rejoicing in all of them. It really was the best of times.

As it turned out, those three months of tranquility were the season of strengthening. Strengthening as individuals, strengthening as a couple, strengthening our convictions, and strengthening our confidence.

It was the calm before the storm.

On a Monday in late-March, feces hit the fan.

Quick:

Fight

Quinn and I were startled by the irregular greeting we received upon entering the school grounds that Monday morning. Three girls came running towards us, their arms waving and their voices raised, stunning us with their abrupt and incomprehensible shouts.

"Do you know these girls?" I asked Quinn, as they approached. "And are they pissed at us? What are they yelling about?"

"I have math with two of them: Sabrina and Morgan. I think the other one is Rochelle? They're super nice." Quinn directed her words towards them as soon as they caught up to us. "Are you okay? What happened?"

They all three started talking at once, and I struggled to pick up on anything more than short phrases. Unhelpful phrases. Like, "unfair," "total crap," and "they can't do that."

"Woah, woah, hold on. I can't understand you. Can one of you tell us?" I looked to the calmest one to relay the message, whose name did indeed turn out to be Rochelle.

She very calmly explained to us that they usually visit Seek & Speak when they're eating breakfast before school, but when they logged on that morning, they saw a notice that the site was being blocked by administration and was no longer accessible to students. Morgan and Sabrina were behind Rochelle providing all the agitated choreography needed to really drive home the message as to how upset they were.

Quinn thanked them for telling us and promised that we'd get to the bottom of it. I glanced at my watch and sighed when I saw that there were only five minutes before classes would begin. She knew exactly what I was thinking. She squeezed my hand and whispered, "Don't worry, we'll go see him right at the start of lunch. We'll meet there after fourth period, okay?" She gave me a quick kiss and headed off to class.

My stomach was in knots all morning and my brain was trying to gather the thoughts that were bouncing around in my skull at a mile a minute. Who shut it down? Why? The hypotheses seemed to be endless. I was eager to get some answers and found myself counting down the minutes until lunchtime. I got to Mr. Erickson's classroom as quickly as I could and was not surprised in the least when I saw that Quinn was already there. She was waiting for me outside of the room, standing underneath the poster that she had pointed out to me at the start of our friendship. "Live Inspired." I chuckled to myself as I realized that was exactly what she galvanized me to do for the last two years.

When we walked in, the expression on Mr. Erickson's face signaled that he was expecting us. We skipped the niceties and jumped right into the conversation that had been awaiting us all day. He told us that he received an email from the administrator on Friday afternoon, with a forwarded message from a concerned parent attached. Mr. Erickson showed us the message from the disgruntled parent who was clearly upset about the forum's latest few topics. It read, "It's bad enough to humor kids by promoting ridiculous theories about the Challenger space shuttle and supposed lies regarding fossil fuels, but to get into child trafficking and the generational data surrounding vaccines is going way too far." The message went on to urge the school to shut down Seek & Speak, and the administrator mentioned in the email to Mr. Erickson that something this controversial could not seem sponsored by the school itself.

"I tried to explain that the forum is completely run by the students, but they're not having it, guys. I'm so sorry." The sadness in Mr. Erickson's voice was unmistakable. He was truly disappointed.

We both piped up about how it wasn't his fault and he didn't need to apologize, and then Quinn veered straight into solutions mode. "Well, that's only one parent. Have there been any other complaints? Surely we can stand up for ourselves in some way. A petition or something. I'm sure most of the student body would sign it, even if they don't participate in the forum. And I bet if we did a survey, some teachers would admit that student engagement has gone up since Seek & Speak was born! Don't they know that shutting us down like this is only going to make us want to do it even more?"

With a long face, Mr. Erickson gently told us that we were on our own. That he wouldn't be able to fight this fight with us. That he was proud of how far it went, proud of the new subculture on campus, and proud to know us. But at the end of the day, he couldn't risk his career.

Fair. It wasn't his fight anyway.

The look on Quinn's face made it very clear whose fight it was.

03/25/2025

11:34 a.m.

Cafeteria

Luca:	Dude, did you hear this crap about the school shutting down Seek?
Matson:	Oh yeah, I did. What the heck? Can they even do that?
Luca:	I guess. I wonder what happened. Bro, at first I thought the whole thing was stupid but it turned out to be pretty frickin' cool. Like, I learned a lot from reading other people's stuff. It made me think, you know?
Matson:	Yeah, same here. Well, I heard something about the topics getting a little too dicey. Like parents were getting upset or whatever.
Luca:	Where did you hear that?
Matson:	Through Quick and Quinn.
Luca:	Shoot, I didn't hear that. I mean, I don't even think my parents knew about it but I don't think they'd care anyway. My dad would actually think it's cool.
Matson:	Dude, I showed my mom the site like a month or so ago? I don't know. Anyway, she loved it, bro. She wanted to create her own username and hop on. I was like, noooo get outta here.
Luca:	That's awesome. I'm trying to think about the recent topics. Oh, like the vax stuff? Chicken pox and all that? You think that would tick off parents?
Matson:	I don't know. Maybe the trafficking stuff, bro. That crap's intense.
Luca:	Oh, that's right. That's probably it.
Matson:	Yeah, who knows. There were some crazy topics on there

though. Like the moon landing, bro? I can't believe I'm saying it, but that crap was fake!

Luca: For sure. Dude, what about the Titanic? Bruh.

Matson: Oh snap, yeah. Ha, I'm actually surprised it took this long for Seek to get ripped down, now that I think about it.

Luca: Right?

Wednesday, March 26, 2025

Note to self:

Oh. My. Gosh.

It is insane how quickly something can turn on a dime. Three days ago, I was the calmest I've ever been, and now I'm ready for battle. I'm suiting up, putting on that armor, and I'm ready to take the fight head on.

Quick and I were sitting on the quad today at lunchtime, bouncing around various ideas for solutions to our little censorship problem, when a group of four people approached us. They looked familiar, only because I've seen their faces on campus at some point over the last four years, but they clearly knew who Quick and I were. They were avid Seekers & Speakers and were infuriated by the shutdown of our site. They introduced themselves and then got straight to the point, asking what we were going to do about the situation. Without even giving us the opportunity to respond, one of them shouted, "We should organize a protest!" and in that moment, Quick and I both knew that not only was it going to happen, but that we wouldn't be able to stop it even if we tried. This is so much bigger than us.

We ended up having a very productive impromptu meeting with them right then and there. We agreed that our protest would be on Friday after school, since that would allow us ample time to prepare and we wouldn't be dismissed as just a group of students who didn't want to attend class. Someone volunteered to make flyers with the information and to post them around school, while a few others said they would make a bunch of posters. We brainstormed what the posters would say, because it was very important to Quick and I that our protest would be deemed respectful and respectable by any given passerby. We landed on a few phrases. "Free thinkers love free speech" is my favorite, and leave it to Quick to love "What's wrong with a little research?" We came up with other phrases, like "We dig to decide" and "Serious Students Seek & Speak." I like them all, and I think they are appropriate and powerful.

I have given this a lot of thought and have deeply considered where this aggrieved parent is coming from. I understand that the topics can be intense, but it is totally voluntary. And I've read back over the comments a million times. The posts are mostly questions and links, and we've all become proficient at finding reputable sources. In my opinion, if a parent is upset about his or her child reading information from a .gov website, perhaps the feelings should be directed towards the government, rather than the reader? Never mind the fact that this parent's child is most likely an upperclassman, which means he or she is nearing adulthood, and goodness knows everyone sees much worse on social media and even plain old television in general!

I'm super amped up. I'm ready for this protest. We will be respectful, but we will make our voices heard. Oh, and I am not going to make the same mistake that I did before. I am going downstairs right now to tell my parents about the protest. Heck, I'm even going to invite them.

...Q

Hey Geoffrey,

Woah. I know Quinn's a passionate person, but wow. I've never seen her like this. This protest is almost like a momma-bear thing for her. They came after her baby, and she's not taking it lightly.

I don't think I realized her leadership capabilities until this week. Watching her in action with some of the people from S&S has been such a trip. She's always been focused and organized, but to see her running the show? She's good at it, too. She listens to everyone's ideas, validates where everyone's coming from, somehow comes up with compromises on the spot, and motivates everyone to put it all into action. She's a frickin' leadership genius. I had no idea.

I wonder how it will all go on Friday at the protest. Quinn and I are in total agreement and we've made it clear to everyone that the second it becomes disrespectful in any way, we are shutting it down. We want admin to take us seriously, and acting like entitled idiots is not the way to go.

Quinn's hopeful, of course. She thinks S&S will be up and running again by Monday. I do not. I think it's dead in the water. But we're going to see it through. I hope she's right, but if she's not, I'll be here to help her pick up the pieces.

I gotta say it again. Seeing her in this new light this week? Wow. I love her more than ever.

Wish you were here.

-Deck

Shay:	Hey, are you going to the protest thing after school tomorrow?
Nate:	Heck yeah I am. Did you hear that Mr. E is going, too? Standing in solidarity.
Shay:	Right on, that's pretty cool. I know like twenty people who are going. I think it's gonna be big, like bigger than I expected.
Nate:	Nice. I hope so. I mean, this whole shut down thing is stupid. Why did they have to go straight to the final straw, you know what I mean? Like, just tell us some folks are irked and to tone it down, you know?
Shay:	For sure. And it's not like the topics are that provocative or anything. And even if they were, I would want my kid to read about things and think about the world around us. You know what I mean?
Nate:	Yep. But people are uncomfortable with anything that challenges their narrative. Especially the older they get. So like, parents and grandparents? We can't be talking to them and convincing them that too many vaccines are just too damn many vaccines. They're like, "But polio!" Seriously, pharma and tech's not the same as it was in the fifties, bro.
Shay:	Dude, Nate. I looked into that. Our grandparents got, like, three childhood vaccines. Our folks' generation got like six or eight. And we're set to have fifty-something vaccine doses by the time we're eighteen. Like, what? Something's not right.
Nate:	Yeah. It doesn't even make sense. If anything, our gen's

sicker than ever. Even if the vaccines are good, maybe the schedule has to be reworked, you know? Maybe we don't get so many all at once? So you think that's what this is about? Parents think Seek & Speak's turning us into anti-vaxxers or something? What's their issue?

Shay: I don't know. I think it's more than that. We've had a lot of topics. Trafficking, wi-fi, fluoride, artificial intelligence. Maybe it's that we've talked about a lot of heavy stuff?

Nate: Yeah, maybe. One of my friends made her family throw away all their vegetable oil. So maybe parents are annoyed that it's hitting home or something?

Shay: Oh dang. Yeah, seed oils are no joke. And pesticides, too.

Nate: For sure. So I'll see you at the protest?

Shay: Absolutely.

ooo

Mandy / 9:24 p.m.

hey des

Desiree / 9:49 p.m.

hey what's up

9:49 p.m.

not much
so ready for this year to be overrrrrr

9:57 p.m.

yeah school's kinda lame
especially right now

9:57 p.m.

for sure
why what's right now

10:08 p.m.

nothing, forget I said anything

10:08 p.m.

ummmm no what's up

10:14 p.m.

nothing I'm just annoyed about them shutting down the site

10:15 p.m.

that freak show's site??
why would you be annoyed?!
I'm glad

10:17 p.m.

well I'm not
and I'm going to the protest tomorrow, so get over it

10:17 p.m.

what the what?!?
why are you going

10:18 p.m.

because I think the site's actually a good thing

are you frickin serious right now

yes I am
I don't know what your problem is

I don't have a problem

yes you do
you're like obsessed with taking her down
she's actually pretty cool

ARE YOU DRUNK

no
but I am done with this conversation

Quick:

The Moment

Molasses. Sloths. The line at the DMV.

Those all moved faster than time did on that Friday. The protest was scheduled for the afternoon, and anticipation was hanging in the air. The entire student body and faculty could sense it. No one knew how it was going to go down. If protesters would show up. If anti-protesters would show up. If it would get ugly. If it would get shut down. How it would end.

As the day went on, a very strong feeling settled in my gut. There would be hundreds of students there. Even if just to watch. Not a lot happened in our desert city, and this was going to create a stir.

Quinn took the day in stride. Once again, I was in awe of her. She was cool and collected, wearing a homemade shirt that read, "My brain—My shovel—My right" and was adorned with illustrations. Such confidence. It made her all the more attractive.

I chose to take the passenger seat with this whole affair, but Quinn knew that I would have her back no matter how things came to pass that afternoon. When the time finally came for the protest to begin, we walked to the quad to meet with our fellow Seekers. Whoever made the flyers that week did a bang-up job; within ten minutes we had over a hundred participants ready to go. The posters, all pre-approved by the boss, came out great and were distributed among the crowd. Quinn had the forethought to bring a megaphone, another brilliant move on her part, and when she figured the crowd was reaching its peak, she clicked that sucker on. The group heard the loud squeak and hushed right away.

Self-assured and assertive, Quinn commanded the attention of probably two hundred of her peers. This girl, the quiet witch who was ostracized for years and couldn't have cared less as she meditated barefoot for all to see, was now leading a massive student body. And they were hanging on to her every word.

Quinn started it out almost like a pep rally, reiterating the purpose of Seek & Speak and energizing the crowd. She then discussed the purpose of the protest and what they were there to accomplish. While we all respected parental concerns, we simply wanted the opportunity to have a conversation to find a compromise or common ground. Her expectations regarding courteous and well-mannered behavior were made very clear, and she then ended by thanking everyone for their support and their time on a Friday afternoon.

Every single thing she said was perfect. I wondered if she practiced it. She must have. She didn't stutter once, her word choice was impeccable, and she exuded boldness and conviction. Actually, I would not have been surprised if she winged it. She was that good. But the best part? Oh, the best part was just way too good.

Her parents saw the entire thing. From start to finish.

I noticed them walk through the front gates while the posters were being passed around. They stood off to the side of the adjacent building, tucked in by the wall, completely undetected. Quinn's mom had her arms crossed with that particular scowl I had seen before, while her dad was fidgeting a bit. He was having a hard time suppressing a smile, that was for sure.

Once Quinn powered up the megaphone, I knew I was going to be torn in half. I wanted nothing more than to gaze at her, to take it all in, to watch her every facial expression and to memorize her every word. But I also knew that once Quinn discovered her parents were there, she would want to hear about their reactions to her speech, detail by detail. I gambled that someone out there would be recording Quinn's pre-game motivational performance, so I locked in on her folks. Specifically, her mom.

The arms fell to the side. The scowl dissipated. The eyes welled up. The edges of the mouth curled. The hands clasped together. The tears fell. The smile widened. And like me, Quinn's father couldn't take his eyes off it either.

That was the moment Quinn's mother "saw" her for the first time.

And it was one of the greatest honors of my life to be able to watch it happen in real time.

Quinn:

The Strongest River

B efore it even began, I figured the protest would last about an hour. That was ample time to showcase our numbers and make our request known. I wanted us to end on a high note and on our timing, and honestly, anything over an hour would have either fizzled out or gone south. I would not have been satisfied with either of those scenarios, so by the time four o'clock rolled around, I used the megaphone to thank everyone for coming and mentioned that we looked forward to hearing from administration soon.

As we were collecting the posters and cleaning up the site, Mr. Erickson came over to tell me how proud he was of the way we handled things. He called it "a beautiful balance of respecting administration while also honoring the students," which really resonated with me. It reminded me of Quick's comment back in the first week of APUSH class: We should be able to have civilized discourse to reach levels of compromise and enlightenment. I thanked him for his support and was sure to mention yet again how much inspiration he sparked in both Quick and me over the previous two years.

Just as we wrapped up the conversation, the principal made her way over and introduced herself. While I had of course known who Leanne Karim was throughout my entire high school career, this was indeed the first time we interacted. Any other time, I may have been a bit intimidated, but I was feeling more confident than ever. The protest went so smoothly and Mr. Erickson's comments put the cherry right on top.

"Hello, Ms. Karim, it's nice to formally meet you," I extended my hand for a proper greeting.

"Hello, Quinn. First, I'd like to say thank you for organizing such a peaceful and respectable event. I can see how passionately you all feel about this forum, and how responsibly you carried yourselves. Well done." She held the handshake throughout, and I focused on maintaining eye contact. I really wanted to illustrate my confidence and strength.

"Of course. Thank you," I replied.

"I will give great consideration to your ask, talk with my team members, and see where to go from here. I am sure you will understand that, for now though, Seek & Speak will remain paused." She said it with such a matter-of-factness, albeit polite, it clearly demonstrated a non-negotiable term. The forum was paused until further notice. That was that.

She smiled, thanked me again, and headed towards the building that housed her office. As I glanced around to survey the scene and the progress made in terms of the "leave no footprint" request I made of our peers, I caught a glimpse of my favorite teacher and mentor having a wonderfully animated conversation with my grinning parents. My heart skipped a beat and I was immediately filled to the brim with thankfulness. They were too far away to hear but I was enraptured by the sight, so much so that when Quick came up to hug me from behind, I was slightly startled.

"You were so great, Quinn. I'm so proud of you," he whispered in my ear as he wrapped his arms around my waist and nuzzled his head onto my shoulder.

I whipped around to give him a huge bear hug. "Wasn't it so perfect, Quick! We totally nailed it. I'm so proud of everyone! And look, my parents are here!" I pointed in the direction of Mr. Erickson.

"Yeah, I noticed them earlier. I'll have to tell you all about it, but later. For right now," he snuck in a kiss, "let's finish cleaning up and start our week-end. Yes? I'll make sure everything's good around here. I think you, little leader lady, should go around and thank all your peeps."

I grabbed his cheeks and gave him a loud smooch. "You're so right! I have to tell everyone how awesome they are. Thank you! You are the best boyf—" I started to say. Surely my face revealed my embarrassment, but he just laughed a little, winked at me, and planted a kiss on my lips before heading back over to the quad. Overwhelmed with love for him, I watched him walk away, and for the second time in a matter of minutes, I was so focused on a faraway scene that I was jolted by an unexpected presence.

This time it was my parents.

My dad, who was not a man of many words, simply embraced me, but I could feel the pride emanating from the tight hug that lingered longer than usual. When he finally released me, I turned to face my mother who was absolutely beaming. She held my cheeks in her soft palms and regarded me in a way she never had before. It was as though she was perceiving me in a new light. Her eyes slowly passed over my facial features as she went from looking into my eyes to noting the details of my eyebrows, from observing my smile to admiring my cheek bones. She was seeing me for the first time.

"Baby, I am so damn proud of you." My mom didn't take her eyes off of me as she spoke. She ran her fingers through my hair, combing it from the top of my head down to the tips, as she continued. "You were so confident today, so driven. So mature. So passionate. And such a natural leader, Quinn. I am very proud of you and this young woman you became, right before my eyes and right under my nose. I love you, baby." She drew me in for a hug right as the first tear escaped and traveled down my cheek.

Later that night as my folks and I were sitting out back by the Zen garden, my dad finally processed the afternoon's events and what he wanted to say to me. I always loved that about him, that when he spoke it was purposeful and deliberate. Out of nowhere, as we were quietly sipping our lemon balm tea, he cleared his throat and announced, "They say that someone's true character is revealed when faced with struggles or challenges. We were impressed with your character today, Quinn. You handled yourself well and to see all of the others looking to you for guidance shows that you are highly regarded. I'm proud of you, kid. Well done."

"Aww, thanks Dad. I feel really good about it, too, but it means the world to me to hear it from both of you today. Thanks guys."

My mom placed her tea on the side table near her and turned to face me. "You know, when I was in my younger years, your dad and I went on a little adventure. Remember, honey, when we floated down the river? How old were we then?" She looked to him, only to receive a shrug in return. "Who knows, maybe I was twenty-five, twenty-seven. Something like that. Anyway, you weren't born yet. I don't even know if we were married yet, now that I think about it. Honey, were we married yet?" Again, a shrug, but this time it was accompanied with a grunt that indicated that most likely they were not. "So your dad and I decided to go floating down a river. We each had our own raft and one oar, and we hopped in our rafts and away we went."

My dad cut her off to interject, "Yeah, but we had two very different experiences on that same day in that same river."

"Yes we did. Your dad basically slept through the entire thing. He was relaxed, lying back, closing his eyes—"

"Not the whole time. I was the one who saw the fish jump out of the water, remember? You were too busy tr—"

"Let me tell Quinn the story, please and thank you." She shot him a look and all three of us knew that he wouldn't be interrupting again.

"Your dad was so relaxed, Quinn. I could see him leaning back, resting, letting the river take him wherever it was going to take him. I, on the other hand, was not. I was not relaxed, not even the slightest bit. All I could see were boulders and sharp protruding rocks. Twists and turns and sudden curves. Honestly, it was so stressful for me. I was using my oar constantly, trying to avoid this thing or that thing, pushing away from this rock and that rock. At one point, I somehow beached myself on the side of a boulder and got stuck. It was awful. Just awful. That was when I started to get really mad at your dad. I was annoyed just looking at him. And then, after about an hour, I was so physically exhausted that I literally gave up. I threw my oar down in the raft and sat there cross-legged, like a pouting child. And then, I remember this one particular moment so vividly, I was sitting in my raft, exhausted and self-pitying, when I saw a boulder and a curve up ahead. But I had quit. I had given up. As my raft got closer and closer to the boulder, I could feel myself getting nervous, but I was like, 'Oh well.' And sure enough, the river floated me right past it and the curve was just a gentle change in direction. And at that moment, it clicked. I needed to relax, to let go. The river would do the rest. And it did."

"Yeah, you really enjoyed those last three minutes of the ride," my dad chuckled.

My mom joined in on the laughter. "No, come on, it was more like five minutes. But yeah, I sure did enjoy it. And right when we got to the landing dock, I wanted to do the whole thing again, now that I had figured it out."

"Did you?" I asked.

"No, I didn't. And sadly, we never floated a river again. Life kind of happened after that. We moved here, we had you, and you know the rest." I saw a flash of sadness, but she recovered quickly. "But, Quinn, I am telling you this story for a reason." She sighed, and it seemed to convey heavy disappointment. "I had forgotten the experience, or maybe I didn't hold onto its lesson as much as I should have. But today, it hit me like a freight train."

"No, it hit you like crashing whitewater waves." Dad laughed at his own joke. Mom rolled her eyes at me, which in turn made me chuckle. His joke, not so much.

She pulled me in closer to her, squaring her shoulders towards mine and holding my hands in hers. We locked eyes and after she took another deep breath, she continued. "I learned such an important lesson that day, Quinn. That it's better to enjoy the journey, especially since so much of it is out of my control. That river was so much stronger than I could have ever been, and fighting it was futile. Trying to control it was futile. And maddening and frustrating and just plain stupid. I still wish I'd relinquished control like your dad did, right out of the gate. Anyway, I realized something today as I watched you in action. This past year or so, I've been trying to control your journey, Quinn. Trying to impose my oar as I worried about the boulders I thought were in your way. And in doing so, I lost sight of what matters. I forgot to enjoy it, Quinn. I should have known all along that you are your own force and that you know exactly how you want to flow and where you want to flow to. And honey, I have to say, you are the strongest, most powerful, most beautiful river in all of the lands, and I am honored to be your mom."

I tried to find the words. I tried to tell her how much I loved her, how I admired her, how I thought she was the epitome of strength, of resilience, of grit, of resolve. I wanted so much to, but instead, it was all I could do to fold into her lap and sob.

Hey Geoffrey,

March got pretty wild there, but I gotta say, April has been mellow. All the seniors are pretty much done, and the teachers know it. Our workload dropped to basically nothing and we're all just phoning it in. Seek's on pause until further notice, and once I reminded Quinn of what she said from the get-go and that we accomplished what we set out to do with it, she chilled out.

We're on spring break right now. She and her folks spontaneously decided to head to Oregon to float down a river. Some bucket list item for her mom. I've been relaxing at home. Spending a lot of time with our folks, doing the usual. Dad and I are chipping away at the list, and apparently we're headed up to the attic tomorrow. Should be fun. Mom and I are tending to the garden, but she's more interested in looking for a clunker for me. Some cheap, old car that I can get my hands on. Maybe even fix up a bit. I've got about $5000 put aside from working at the supermarket, but we haven't found a car that fits the bill yet. It's fun looking with her though.

Hey, Geoffrey, this is the first April without a nightmare. No flashbacks. It's been a long time, actually. After doing those digs, and I think especially after making a decision as to how I can spend my future righting the wrong that was done to you, the rough nights subsided. Almost like I'm finding peace with it maybe? I don't know. I will never have a day where I don't think of you, miss you, struggle with it all. But Mom being home and doing so well, it's helping. Seeing your pictures on the walls again. Talking about you more often. It's definitely helping.

April is tough for Quinn's family, too. She invited me to join them for Troy's triple tradition birthday celebration. I guess it was her mom's idea? I am shocked, but honored. Wouldn't miss it.

Love you, brother.

-Deck

Monday, April 21, 2025

Note to self:

Our first day back after Spring Break was more of a struggle than I expected. We had such a nice time in Oregon, and between the weather being so beautiful this time of year and school letting out in a month… I wasn't expecting to drag my feet, but it totally makes sense why it took more effort than normal to do the usual. The feeling was short-lived and has already subsided though. I am back in the groove and I'll get to go back to seeing Quick every day, so it's all good.

Ever since the protest, my mom is like an entirely new person. The a-ha moment she had must have been a serious one because she is all about making up for lost time with me. She is literally soaking up every ounce of fun that could possibly be had. Even the ridiculously long car ride to Oregon was a blast, especially when she hosted her own version of "Name that Tune." She made the hotel time fun, my favorite part being when we played hide-and-seek on the entrance floor, and Dad was super cool about taking the pull-out couch so Mom and I could watch chick flicks from bed. And when the time finally came, she floated that river like a boss. I have to admit, I totally empathized with the story she shared about her first attempt at floating. It was a conscious decision on my part to accept the boulders and put the oar down, but I'm so glad I did. It was beyond awesome to experience nature and its gentle force in that way!

The ride home was just as eventful, but in a different way. We engaged in meaningful conversations, and for the first time it started to feel like we were chatting as mutual, adult friends. She didn't lecture me. She didn't chastise me. She didn't judge me. Not once. And, no surprise here, the topic of Quick was a major one. We talked about our friendship and how it evolved over the last two years, our commonalities and our differences, our growth as individuals and as a unit of sorts, and the unknowns regarding the nearing changes in our lives. Processing with my mom, even if my dad is driving the car and quietly loving every moment, is what I've always craved. Throughout my whole adolescence, I have needed her and have missed her. She gets me, and every time we have a good talk, I feel so much lighter afterwards. And wiser.

When we were almost home from our trip, out of nowhere, she suggested we invite Quick to the Triple Tradition. Talk about utter shock! I had never even considered including him. It never crossed my mind. But it crossed hers? Once the surprise wore off, I thought about how Troy would love it if Quick was there. Besides, he is almost like family. Anyway, it turned out to be great with him there. He was the perfect balance of reverent and light-hearted, and sharing Troy with someone new made the three of us feel as though my brother was even more present. By the time we were stuffing our faces with cake, my parents officially adored Quick. As they should.

He's adorable.

...Q

Note to self:

Wowza! Today had quite the unexpected twist!

I went to jump on my bike to head to school, and I was greeted by a single red rose. It was lying on my seat with a poem attached:

Roses are red
Violets are blue
I know it's not our thing
But it's something we gotta do

So pick out a dress
No doubt you'll be breathtaking
I'd love to take you to our prom
For more memories in the making

He never ceases to surprise me. I didn't even think I wanted to go, but once I read the poem, I turned into the giddiest little girly-girl who absolutely want to go to prom with Quick! I want to experience all of life with him. All of the silly, all of the mundane, all of the exciting… All of it.

I tried to match his effort with my response, but I definitely fell short. I left a poem on his windshield so he would see it after school:

You are my Quick
And I am your Quinn
I'd love to have prom
Be part of "Thick and Thin"

I can't wait to go through this with you!

See? Lame. But he loved it. He's biased though.

Oh, and Mom is the most excited of all. When I told her, she squealed, "Dress shopping!" as though she were an opera singer on opening night.

…Q

Hey Geoffrey,

I've seen a lot of beautiful things in my life.

One time when I was bike riding home from work, I caught the sunset. Made me stop in my tracks. There were so many hues of pink, orange, and yellow, and from my vantage point, there weren't any obstacles. No telephone poles or wires in the way. No large buildings. Just the beautiful sunset.

I also remember the time we went for a long walk at the park. In the center is the man-made pond, so there are usually ducks and geese everywhere. And lots of poop too. One time, we saw two ducks, snuggled up together in the shade of a huge oak tree. The female had her head nuzzled into her partner's colorful feathers, and they seemed as content as could be. Another sight that made me stop in my tracks.

But I've never seen anything as beautiful as Quinn. Never, not in all my years.

Last night was Prom. When I arrived at her house and her parents invited me in, Quinn came walking down the stairs in this simple but elegant red gown. Her hair was done up all nice and she was wearing a little make-up. No joke, Geoffrey, she took my breath away. I always thought that was a stupid expression, but now I get it. I never thought I'd use the word "exquisite" in my life, but yo, I really don't know how to put into words how gorgeous she looked. Don't get me wrong. I always think she looks beautiful. Even when we're sweating in the garden and she has dirt on her face. But last night? Wow.

We took some photos at her house, and then headed to mine to do the same. All four of our parents were gushing over us, and I think I even saw tears in Dad's eyes. Prom is all about it being fun for us, but I didn't realize how special a night it is for the parents, too. I'm glad Quinn and I didn't rob our folks of it.

Prom itself was pretty fun. I mean, neither one of us loves crowds and all that, but we had a good time. People kept coming up to us to say hi, fist bump, and say something about Seek or the protest or whatever. It's weird that we went from invisible to some bizarre form of iconic. That sounds arrogant as hell and I don't mean it that way. I'm just saying that Seek, and the principles behind it, meant a lot to a lot of people. Anyway, we had some good conversations and later laughed about how ironic it is that we made some "friends" in the last month of school. She reminded me of what she told me once, way back when. That she didn't expect to meet "her people" in high school. She gave me a kiss and said she was so happy that she met "her person" instead.

We made it to the dance floor a few times, agreeing in advance not to care how stupid we would look, but all the fast songs turned into some crazy mosh pit thing. Like we were at a rock concert or something? It was hilarious to watch, but neither one of us had any desire to get in there. We did dance to a few slow songs, but that just ended up being a long swaying hug with a lot of kisses snuck in. I must have told her a million times last night how beautiful she is and how much I love her. I never thought I'd be such a goob but I can't help it.

When we got to her house and I walked her to the front door, we chatted about how much fun we had. She ended the night with a sweet little kiss, and then forehead to forehead she told me how happy being with me makes her.

I know exactly how she feels.

It's a little scary, though. What if I can't be happy without her? I don't even want to think about it.

Love you, bud.

-Deck

Quick:

A Misty Good-Bye

The hardest part of the last day of high school was saying good-bye to Mr. Erickson. He impacted my life in so many ways, and the closer I got to leaving, the more I realized what a force he was for me. Never mind that he was the link for Quinn and me, but his ideals and passions were inspiring. If it weren't for him and REED, my entire high school experience would have been different. And those last two years of high school shaped me. I was lifted out of a dark place in more ways than one, and when I boiled it down, I knew it all started with him.

Quinn and I didn't even discuss meeting at Mr. E's room after school that day. We instinctively knew that there was no other place to be. He was expecting us. I was never as observant as Quinn, but even I could tell that he was waiting for us to walk through that door one last time.

He updated us on Seek, mentioning that the issue became a district-wide one. As it turned out, there were as many parents fighting for the forum to stay open as there were filing complaints against it. The district was hosting administrative and parent meetings that summer, and Mr. E promised to keep us updated and to do his best to keep it alive, although he admitted that he thought the students would find a new way to share digs if Seek got pulled. "Nothing can stop it," he claimed with a smug grin. Quinn and I both agreed with him, and the three of us were all smiles when we thought of the potential that the next year could bring.

"I hope you know that you are both an inspiration to so many. You reached more people than you realize and more deeply than you think. It's amazing, Quick and Quinn. You should feel proud of yourselves," he said, his voice revealing that the statement was laced with emotion.

"Well, Mr. Erickson, we feel the exact same way about you. You are the one who inspired us and showed us the way. Thank you. Thank you for supporting us and guiding us for the last two years. We owe Seek & Speak's success to you." Quinn's voice started to quiver, and then sure enough, she burst into tears and gave him a huge bear hug. He was startled at first, but then returned the hug. There was definitely a mutual respect and regard between Mr. E and the two of us.

"Not only that, Mr. E, but we owe our friendship to you. And to be honest, I would have been lost forever without it." I glanced at Quinn, and then sure enough, I got choked up and had to fight off the tears. He sensed it, and understood. He extended a hand, but I went in for a bear hug of my own.

We had a misty good-bye and vowed to keep him updated on our lives. Quinn and I were silent as we walked out of his room and down the hall. It was when we walked by the quad on our way out that I knew there was no stopping the breakdown that was about to occur. I quietly walked to the grass, sat down where I first did two years before, and let the tears fall. Quinn didn't say a thing. She just sat next to me and rubbed my back. She got it. She knew that the quad was full of so many special memories, from fits of laughter to tin foil hats, but even more so, that quad was where I found myself. Where I pushed myself to try and to discover, to release and to love.

And I walked off that campus knowing exactly that. The quad was where I first learned how to love. And not just Quinn, but myself, too.

Quinn:

My Majestic

Quick and I were invited to a few graduation parties during that final week of school, and although the ones we attended were quite lovely, the most joyous was the celebration of our own. Of course my parents and I graciously accepted the invitation to the small gathering at the Williams' house, but I had a case of the jitters leading up to the event. It was the first time all six of us would spend an extended amount of time together, and I secretly prayed it would be the first of many.

We walked into their home to see the place completely adorned in our school colors of blue and white. Helium-filled balloons with dangling strings of curls covered the entire ceiling, two-toned twisted streamers dolloped from wall to wall, and enlargements of our senior photographs under a large sign that read, "Congratulations, Quick and Quinn!" Upon entry, I was immediately touched by the magnitude of thoughtfulness that Quick's parents clearly poured into making the evening as special as possible.

The thoughtfulness went much beyond the decorations. In addition to the delicious foods from our favorite places, Quick and his mother supplemented the spread with edibles straight from our amateur garden. My favorite was the caprese salad, mainly because both the tomatoes and the basil were grown with love in the backyard. Moreover, the display of sliced stacks of crimson tomato, fresh mozzarella cheese, and crisp, fragrant basil in the shape of a Q was such a nice touch. I drank too much hibiscus tea throughout the evening, but nothing was as stunning or delectable as the cakes. One in my honor and the other in his, the small eight-inch cakes were personalized by favorite flavors, mine being lemon and his chocolate. Our names were piped by what must have been the hand of an expert calligrapher, and the graduation caps that were artistically drawn to rest upon our initial letters were both literally and figuratively the icing on the cakes. I was astonished by the consideration given to every aspect of the beautiful buffet.

The detailed planning of the celebration was evidenced even further after the six of us devoured our slices of cake, when Mr. Williams announced that both sets of parents came prepared to share short speeches. As we sat around their dining room table, Quick and I held hands as we gratefully listened to the words of wisdom that our parents wanted to impart to us as we stepped from childhood into adulthood. My parents spoke of embracing inevitable change, of finding the growth and beauty in new and uncomfortable situations, and of stretching boundaries to avoid stagnancy and regret. My mom and dad bounced back and forth in their delivery so perfectly that I knew they practiced it, and every word spoken oozed with support of my upcoming path. Quick's parents then demonstrated their love and pride through their messages of nurturing encouragement. They mentioned the importance of self-discovery through experience and that not only was it time to discover who we were and what mattered to us, but also what we were made of. They emboldened us to remember that moments of failure are treasures from which to learn, that failures are simply attempts at things not yet mastered, but that we could never fail at being true to ourselves. I soaked in every second, honing in on each word and focused on each message, and I know Quick did as well. Tears were shed and hugs were shared by all, and mine were exacerbated by gratitude when my mom revealed that she had set up her camera and recorded the entire thing. I knew I would watch that video innumerable times in the years to come.

The night continued as the mothers headed to the backyard to check out the garden and chat in the pleasant evening air. The fathers stepped into the garage to "talk shop," whatever that meant. To see our parents effortlessly forming what seemed to be organic friendships made the evening better than either Quick or I could have imagined. We plopped ourselves on the couch with a happy sigh, both of us quieted by the pure contentment. Suddenly, Quick jumped up and shouted, "Oh! I have a gift for you!" He ran upstairs, taking the flight two at a time, and I took the opportunity to retrieve the gift I had for him from the bag I had placed by the front door. I always tried to honor his aversion to gifts, so I came up with something simple. As silly as it seemed to give someone a 9-volt battery for graduation, I knew Quick would appreciate it when he read the accompanying page I meticulously designed for his Life Lessons book: Stay Charged and Follow Your Dreams.

He hugged me so tightly when he accepted his gift and told me he cherished it like all of the others, but when I saw the small black box he then placed in my hands, I knew my gift for him paled in comparison to what I was about to see. I slowly opened the velvet case and laid eyes upon a treasure like no other. Quick carefully removed the silver necklace and nodded at me, silently messaging for me to position myself so that he could place the necklace. I corralled my hair and placed it above my head as he gingerly clasped the jewelry around my neck. "Do you like it?" he gently asked, and I looked down to see the attached pendant for the first time. It felt as though time stopped, but the tears streaming down my face proved that it had not.

Blue opals. Stones of compatibility and harmony, of opportunity and ingenuity, of peace and healing.

White sapphire. Stones of intention and clarity, of focus and enlightenment, of spirituality and inner wisdom.

Two perfectly chosen stones, delicately crafted into a majestic dragonfly. My majestic dragonfly.

Hey Geoffrey,

Summer is blowing by way too fast. Quinn's birthday is right around the corner, and then bam, a few weeks later, she leaves and I start school. No matter how much time we spend together, it never seems to be enough. Doesn't matter if it's only the two of us, if we're with our folks, hers, or both. Doesn't matter if we're on a hike or watching a movie. Doesn't matter if we get on the phone as soon as we can after saying good-bye. It's never enough time.

Whether I'm with her or not, I'm thinking about the next chapter. It's constantly on my brain. And as much as I don't want to admit it to myself, Quinn and I are going to need to take a step back when she leaves. Amidst all these huge life changes, it places way too much pressure for her to have to maintain a relationship that spans 3000 miles. She needs to be focused on her thermography program, on her business classes, on making new connections, and on discovering her adult self. If she feels like she has to get back to her place so she can FaceTime me or whatever, she will not only end up stunting herself but she'll resent me for it. And I can't have that.

My head and my heart have been on the battlefield with one another about this for weeks now, but I know this is the right call. And now it's just a matter of telling her, and hopefully getting her to see that it comes from a place of love.

Besides, who's to say she isn't thinking the exact same thing? That she's not sitting at home right now worried about breaking my heart? Chances are, we'll be on the same page. We always are.

She needs to do her thing. I need to do mine. And maybe we'll end up doing "our" thing together in the end. Or maybe not. We're eighteen. What the hell do we know anyway? We're amateurs at this thing called life and a lot can happen in a year or two. I mean, look at what happened in the last year or two. Right?

No matter what, she and I will always be connected in some way.

Like me and you.

-Deck

Tuesday, July 22, 2025

Note to self:

This day is hard every year, and I'm sure it will never be easy. This year, though, the anniversary of Troy's death was especially difficult for us. I think my parents' grief was compounded by the imminent empty nest, and my upcoming move to a distant, foreign land is definitely causing a knot in my stomach. What if I can't sense Troy there? What if I feel disconnected from him? I know it sounds silly, but does it? What if my parents struggle even more in the quietness of the home? What if my absence makes his absence even more profound?

I know I shouldn't spiral down the tunnel of hypotheticals, and I am usually pretty good about clawing my way out and redirecting my attention to the here and now of reality. In all fairness, though, this is the biggest change any of us have gone through since Troy passed away. And as much as I feel this path calling to me, and as much as I know God is waiting for me on it, I still have that dang knot in my stomach.

Well, to be completely honest, part of that knot is about Quick. For a verbose girl, I have no words for my feelings. To say that I love him seems like an understating cliche, but I really do love him. He is my best friend, but on a level deeper than I can comprehend, let alone articulate. Kissing aside, because yes, I do want to kiss him every single time I see him, my strongest feelings are those of companionship. We have experienced so many highs and lows together over the last two years. We've found ourselves as individuals, but so much so through being companions. Through conversations, through sob sessions, through laughter, through new hobbies, through surprises, through nightmares, through family woes, through school drama, through it all. And through every single one, we came out closer. Our friendship grew stronger. Every single time.

The "relationship" part made it a little messy, not that I regret it. It was bound to happen. But the timing? Ugh. Do I love him? Yes. Do I want to be with him? Yes. Right now. But I have no idea what awaits me in Florida, or what's coming after that either. And when I think about missing him, it's the friendship I think about first.

We have a hard conversation coming up, and we both know it. It's okay. Neither one of us really shies away from those, especially not with each other. And at the end of the day, I know Quick and I will always be the best of friends. The friendship may look different; we may talk less frequently and see each other even less than that. But there is not a singular doubt in my mind that no matter what life throws at us, and no matter when, he and I would drop everything to be there for each other. Zero doubt. I am not worried about our friendship in the least.

His mom, on the other hand, just might be. She reached out to me last week, concerned about how Quick is going to handle my move to Florida. Through our conversation, we came up with the idea of getting him a dog. We went online to check out the abandoned pups at the nearby shelters and the instant we saw the picture of a sweet little guy named Jack, we agreed that we had to go meet him. He is what they call a "jug," a half Jack Russell terrier, half pug. He is absolutely darling, with his apricot coat and brown stripe along his spine, his curly tail, and his dark brown floppy ears. I especially adored his huge underbite, and Mrs. Williams appreciated Jack's calm demeanor.

The decision is not for me to make, but I'm really hoping Quick's parents choose to bring Jack home for Quick. I think it would be good for him in so many ways, not to mention how great it would be for the little guy. Fingers crossed that when I leave in less than two weeks, he'll have a new buddy waiting for him at the door.

…Q

Quick:

What I Knew

Quinn and her parents planned to leave at the crack of dawn on a Monday morning, given that they had a 3000-mile road trip ahead of them. As it was, I hadn't seen too much of her in the week leading up to it. She was packing up her entire life, and while I did hang out with her for a bit, I understood that it was something she needed to do on her own. Packing's a personal thing. I wouldn't want someone in my space if I were doing it.

We planned to spend that Sunday together. Just her and I. All day. Starting at the crack of dawn. And it was such a given as to how we would spend it.

Hand in hand and walking ever so slowly, as though that would somehow prolong our time together, we meandered the trail to our favorite picnic spot. Barely a word was spoken as we ate our breakfast sandwiches. The peaceful quiet continued as we snuggled on the blanket to take in the sights and sounds of our waterfall. The cascading water was perfectly in tune with the tidal wave of memories that was gushing about in the sea of my mind.

The first time I noticed her on the quad my sophomore year. The day Mr. Erickson assigned us as partners. Her brainstorming notebook. Me being relieved that it was only us in the club. The texting. My first meditation. The waterfall. The tin foil hats. The bookstore. The arguments. The make-ups. Fourth of July. The bike rides. Our first kiss. Our second kiss. Roller skating. Driving. Seek & Speak. The protest. Prom. The list was endless.

After about an hour, she was the one to break the ice. Not that the silence was icy. It was full of warmth and all the words that didn't need to be spoken. But she was the one to speak first. And since she was the brave one, she was bold enough to direct the conversation right to the inevitable.

"Quick, we should talk about us." She sat with an upright posture and waited for me to do the same. Across from one another, we held hands as I searched her eyes and she searched mine. The connection between us was so strong, we could read each other. Our moods. Our vibes. Our body language. She was spiritually brilliant, and over our time together, I picked up a little inner intelligence, too. Within a minute, we both nodded. Her tears welled up when she realized that I understood, and as she started to apologize, I stopped her.

"Please don't apologize, Quinn. Don't ever be sorry for pursuing passions and creating your future, just like you would never want me to apologize." I leaned over and placed a kiss on the bridge of her nose.

"You're right. I wouldn't. But I want you to know that I will miss you every single second, Quick. I love you in so many ways, and… " The overpowering sobs came on suddenly and completely consumed her. I wrapped her up to my chest, squeezing her against me, and I stroked her hair until she caught her breath. Tears fell down my face as well, quiet ones that I was sure she could feel as they dropped on the crown of her head.

"I'm not worried, Quinn." I pulled away from her so I could look at her perfect face as I bared my soul to her. "I'm curious, but not worried. I love you more than I can say and I know this connection is real. And special. And unique. I'm not worried about us. I'm just curious as to how we'll end up. But do I think we'll be the best of friends even when we're old and gray? Absolutely. We'll just have to see about the other part."

She scooted closer to me so she could place her forehead to mine, my cheeks in her soft palms. "I feel the same way, Quick. And you're right. Right now, the best of friends need to support each other without placing unnecessary pressure in terms of a long-distance relationship type of thing. Let's just promise to keep communicating. I don't want us to make any assumptions about why I didn't text or why you didn't pick up or whatever. Assumptions are always negative, totally based in fear and insecurity. Right? So let's be sure to stay honest, and everything will be okay. Okay?"

I answered her with a kiss. "Yes."

"Because we don't know how it will go. And I get overwhelmed when I spiral about our future. I don't want to be so focused on how we'll end up that I miss the journey there, you know what I mean? That future will come, whatever it may be. In the meantime, we have to take one step at a time and make each step the best it can be. Does that make sense?"

I answered her with another kiss. "Yes."

She took a deep breath, the kind that she taught me to take, and then another and another. I could see her entire body start to relax. She smiled at me and whispered, "I love us."

We settled back into a quiet cuddle, savoring the moments. The silence was short-lived though, and this time it was my doing. "Are you nervous?"

"Absolutely," she sighed.

"But you know you've got this, right? You're going to kill it at that program, and as strange as it will be to live on your own, I know you'll be great. I doubt anyone's totally ready to move out. It's more like something you have to figure out as you go. At least that's what I think. But yeah, you've got this, Quinn."

"I know. Things will go right and things will go wrong, but at the end of each day, I'll be grateful that I'm out there chasing it and making it happen, you know? That I'm fortunate enough to be able to do that."

"I'm so proud of you." My voice cracked a bit as she touched my cheek.

"Don't forget to be proud of yourself, too, Quick. What you're doing, both at school and at home, is nothing short of honorable. You are going to make a huge difference and be a massive light in that evil world of darkness, I know it. And you staying home to be with your folks? You're amazing. So selfless, so loving. My gosh, Quick. Please be proud of yourself, too." She sat on my lap to envelop me in a bear hug.

"Thank you, Quinn. For saying that. And for everything. You completely changed my life, you know. You saved me. You literally saved me."

"You completely changed my life, too, Quick. You shaped me. And I love you so much for it." It was one of the dozens of times that day that she told me she loved me, and each time was matched with a heartfelt profession from me. We spent the whole day relaxing and reminiscing through laughter and through tears, before finally heading downtown for dinner and dessert. The time eventually came for me to drop her off for the long and painful good-bye, and afterwards I cried as I drove home. The sadness and the emptiness felt like it would swallow me whole.

Little did I know, Quinn prepared me for dealing with the pain from that good-bye. She made sure I would be greeted at the door when I got home that night. Not by my mom. Not by my dad. But by someone who immediately stole my heart.

Jack.

I instantly knew he would help me through the next steps. He'd get me to smile when missing Quinn would get to be too much. He'd keep my feet warm when I would study for those college exams. He'd hike with me to the waterfall and he'd ride shotgun on our adventures. In that moment, I knew that Jack would greet me every single time I would open the front door. And I knew that every time I turned that door handle, I would hope she'd be there waiting to greet me, too.

But I also knew that she wouldn't be.

PART FOUR:

The Truth

Quick:

Life After Quinn

That first year went as expected.

I started college and knew on day one of the criminal justice class that I had made the right choice. School was so much more enjoyable for me, given that I was studying what I wanted to learn. I became even more dedicated to my objectives. The achievement of those goals started to feel like they were right around the corner, which in turn fueled me even more.

I made a couple buddies, like-minded people with similar aims. I had no choice, since it felt like college was full of collaborative projects, but I was glad to expand my social circle a bit. They introduced me to the world of pool halls, and it didn't take long for throwing darts to become a serious hobby of mine. I even installed a dartboard in the garage and found myself out there often, with Jack snoring in the bed I put for him in the corner. Dad would throw darts with me sometimes, or Mom would sit out there with some tea just to chat, but mostly, it was a quiet time of concentration. It became a type of meditative activity. A time to sharpen my focus, both on the board and in life.

That was also the year I threw myself into the world of weightlifting. I had always been on the taller, leaner side, but I knew I needed to bulk up before I hit the streets to help take out child-abusing criminals. I put my research skills to good use and discovered several workout plans geared towards someone of my stature, ability level, and goals, not that it took much talent or research to find. After watching a multitude of videos and using the workout plans to create one of my own, I felt confident enough to join a gym. I enjoyed it more than I thought I would, and before long, I was hitting the gym about four or five times a week.

As for Quinn, we texted regularly at first. Things were exciting for both of us in the beginning and there was always plenty to share. But as our schedules filled up, the time difference started to take its toll, and the communication about the small details of our lives started to fade away. When we found ourselves talking less often, we only had the time to share the general happenings. I no longer heard about the little things, like how thrilled she was when she discovered that the cafe down the street put chocolate-coconut whipped cream on top of her hot cocoa. And likewise, all she heard from me was basically my agenda: I went to class, hit the gym, took Jack for a walk, gotta study for an exam.

She was happy in Florida, and I was happy for her. She loved the thermography training, was feeling challenged in her business classes, and took up yoga. Classic Quinn, too, that she fell in love with yoga and practiced it with such fervor that it became a central part of her life. Quinn didn't know how to do anything in small doses. Once she decided to take the plunge with something, she was all in. I loved that about her. That was why it didn't surprise me when she announced that she was staying in Florida that summer to work on her yoga certification.

I didn't realize that I was subconsciously living on a timeline that revolved around her return home. That became quite clear when her decision to stay in Florida felt like a punch in the gut. It demolished the quiet hope within me that everything would fall back into place once she got back. Well, she didn't come back.

That first year bled into the second. More like hemorrhaged. She was so busy that I'd be lucky to hear from her a couple of times a month. Not only was she finishing up her program and still taking classes, but she somehow landed in the world of creating an online presence. She uploaded short videos in her series, "Yogi You," which most of the time was a simple stretch of the day. Her target audiences were the beginners, the elderly, the ones with limitations. People like that. She didn't seem to care that she only had about two dozen followers, but when a classmate of hers who happened to be a social media master got wind of "Yogi You," it gained a little traction. And when Quinn saw that she could reach a mid-sized audience, she decided to throw in other tips, too. Her most popular video wasn't even about yoga. It was about the need to detoxify our bodies from the heavy metals that cause brain deterioration, and how zeolite could help with that.

I missed her so much that second year. I still kept busy with my classes, my job, and the ways I was bettering myself. I settled into my routine well enough that I felt it was time to start volunteering with different organizations, too. I never lost sight of my mission. But without knowing when I'd see her again, without the end in sight, without knowing if and when she would ever come home, I started to accept that we parted ways. There were nights I watched her channel just to hear her voice, see her facial expressions, and imagine I was still close to her.

My family sensed it. Jack somehow knew when I was low, too, and he'd snuggle in extra tight on those evenings. Or he'd chase his tail with extra enthusiasm until he got me to laugh. My parents and I still spent plenty of time together, which I loved, and at some point they encouraged me to date a little. It wasn't a bad idea, so I put myself out there. Between my classes and the gym, there were plenty of opportunities to meet people. I ended up having a couple of girlfriends that year, but they didn't work out. It wasn't their fault that their names were Not Quinn #1 and Not Quinn #2.

When Quinn wrapped up her program in the winter of her second year, she called me to tell me her latest news. She decided to create a program of her own, similar to that of traveling nurses. She wanted to spend time visiting thermography centers around the nation, to see what they were like, to glean what she felt worked and didn't work, all with the goal in mind of opening her own one day. She grabbed her metaphorical shovel, compiled a list of centers, and started making phone calls. Because she was able to live, albeit frugally, off her one-on-one video conference yoga sessions, she offered to volunteer at various independently-owned centers for two months at a time. It came as no surprise when these owners pounced on the opportunity she was offering, and before she even left for her first one in Massachusetts, she had fourteen two-month sessions lined up.

Twenty-eight months. I could barely do the math. I couldn't process what she was saying, and it took everything I had to sound supportive. I was supportive. I wanted her to chase her dream and be happy. But really, deep down, I knew I wasn't supportive. I was selfish. I wanted her to come home already. The news was the absolutely devastating nail in the coffin. My dreams of Quinn were already fading, and this news brought on the death of them.

My healthy ways of dealing became unhealthily obsessive. While on one hand, I praised myself for not turning to substances, it wasn't like working out twenty-one hours a week was the beacon of healthy emotional awareness. It was reminiscent of my early days, back when we first lost Geoffrey, except this time I was lifting weights instead of fingers on the keyboard. I went above and beyond in my classes, but only as a means to stay busy and avoid the emptiness. I stopped playing darts because the quiet was too damn loud, and Jack stopped asking to go out to the garage or even to go for walks.

I realized I was making my parents worry all over again, so to rectify that, I tried another round of dating. Much to my surprise, I met someone I really enjoyed being around. We had a lot in common and ended up being exclusive for nearly six months. But as the relationship progressed and she wanted to be more intimate, I ran for the hills. I felt bad for Not Quinn #3, but not as bad as I would have felt if we continued on and then I just dumped her later.

The days stretched into weeks, the weeks into months, and before I knew it, I was set to graduate. I was so ready. Ready to give myself completely to the life I chose, to the department, to the mission, to the children. The feeling of fulfillment crept its way back into my life and then escalated drastically when I received the news that I was hired onto the police force. I knew I'd be starting at the bottom of the totem pole and that there was much to learn, but I vowed to never lose sight of my true aim. I'd put in the time, prove myself to the higher-ups, make my mission known, and eventually, I'd end up on the right task force. It was only a matter of time, and I couldn't wait to get started.

About a year into my career, I woke up one day to realize that I was happy. Truly happy. I still missed Quinn, sure, but my heart only held fond memories of her. The pain had subsided over time, without me even really registering it. I spent my days as I felt I was called to, and recognized in real time how fortunate I was to be able to do so. And that very night, I grabbed some dinner on the way home from my shift and opened my front door with a smile, knowing my Jack would be there to greet me as he always was. With his sloppy kisses and bizarre yawn-yells. With his wagging tail and the tapping of his nails on the floor as he did his little happy dance.

But I didn't get to hear the happy dance that night. I didn't get to hear his nails tapping on the wood. Because when I walked in, Jack wasn't on the floor waiting for me.

Quinn:

Eternity

Standing on the other side of that door was nothing short of terrifying. I had no idea how it would go, how he would react to seeing me. When I reached out to his mom and she lent me his house key, she told me he'd be thrilled to know I was back, but I honestly did not know if that would be the case. And if it wasn't, I would completely understand. We were apart for years and our communication fizzled out, which was mostly my doing.

I heard him insert the key into the lock and my heart immediately pounded out of my chest. My palms became sweaty. My mouth went completely dry. My stomach churned. I started to feel dizzy and suddenly had the urge to put Jack down and run, but my feet were planted as though cemented to the floor. The knob turned, the door swung open, and the look of confusion on Quick's face slowly transformed as he understood why Jack wasn't at his feet. He was staring at another pair of feet instead. His eyes moved from my shoes up my legs, to my torso and my shoulders, and then after what felt like an eternity, there he was, staring at me. Eyes locked.

I held my breath. Another eternity passed as I waited for the indicative moment to come.

Hey Geoffrey,

This day's greatness is unmatched. Well, that's not entirely true. There's a tie for first and several close seconds, but I don't think this day will ever be topped.

Close second #1 - Opening the door to see that Quinn made her way back home. The moment I saw her face, I knew our future. We grew up together, we helped shape one another, we influenced one another's lives in such deep ways. Never codependently, but rather as the individuals that we were. Without speaking a word, we both knew that we waited for each other. And the wait was so damn worth it.

Close second #2 - Hearing her squeal the word, "Yes!" when I spontaneously proposed to her. On the night I introduced her to my buddies, she realized that everyone else called me by my real name. She asked me what I wanted her to call me, and without hesitation, I requested that she call me "husband." I wasn't even planning to propose that night, but nothing ever felt so right.

Close second #3 - Watching Jack shuffle down the aisle, stopping every eighteen inches to nibble the treat that was waiting for him as he made his way to Mr. Jason Erickson. We were thrilled that Jason accepted our invitation to officiate our wedding, because he really was the only person we could imagine doing so. He could not have spoken more poignant or personalized words, especially when he ended his speech with, "Quick and Quinn, through thick and thin."

Close second #4 - Hearing the news from my captain that I was being transferred to the Human Trafficking Task Force. As promised, my brother, I will spend my life trying to right the wrongs that you suffered. Every single day. Until we meet again.

Close second #5 - Visiting our old downtown favorites with our folks to celebrate Quinn's new business. She converted our garage into a yoga/thermography studio and it is hugely successful. To say that I'm proud of her is a tremendous understatement. She figured out exactly how to fit her goals into the life she wanted to share with our family.

Tied for first - Bringing our daughter Lola home. Adopting our little ray of sunshine and watching her grow up to be the hot pink-wearing, horse-loving bundle of laughter that she is has been a blessing beyond comprehension or articulation.

Which brings me to today. To this moment.

Lola is napping with her exhausted and exquisite mother who just spent seventeen hours doing the unimaginable. I am here with a pen in my right hand, and in my left, our newborn son. Geoffrey Troy Williams.

It cannot get any greater than this.

As I gaze at my wife and our two little dragonflies, I am overwhelmed by the size of my swelling heart. It's moments like this that I am reminded of how simple life can be. How simple joy can be. How simple peace can be. We humans tend to complicate things, often unnecessarily. But the secret to life? The truth? It's easy.

Do all things with love.

Sounds like the next page in our beloved coffee table scrapbook. And it sure sounds a lot like what God told us all along in 1 Corinthians 16:14.

Love you, brother.

-Deck